Raves for *The Heart of Valor*:

"Fast-paced . . . The intriguing and well-designed aliens and intricate plotting keep the reader guessing."
—*Publishers Weekly*

"Series fans will enjoy this fast-paced adventure, appealing to the same audience as David Weber's Honor Harrington series." —*Library Journal*

And for the *Confederation* series:

"As a heroine, Kerr shines. She is cut from the same mold as Ellen Ripley of the Aliens films: tough but humane, fiercely protective of her charges, and utterly determined to prevail. Like her heroine, Huff delivers the goods. *Valor's Choice* does not make light of war, but at the same time it is incredibly fun to read. Howlingly funny and very suspenseful. I enjoyed every word."
—*Scifi.com*

"An intriguing alien race, a likeable protagonist, a fast moving plot, and a rousing ending. What more could you ask for?" —*Science Fiction Chronicle*

"This sequel to *Valor's Choice,* featuring a gutsy, fast-thinking female space-marine protagonist, establishes veteran fantasy author Huff as an accomplished spinner of high-tech military-SF adventure." —*Library Journal*

"This book is *Rendezvous with Rama* for the rest of us: exciting, mysterious and full of action and puzzles to solve. Torin is everything you want in an action heroine (or hero, for that matter), and this book will leave readers anxious for her next adventure." —*KLIATT*

TANYA HUFF

THE HEART OF VALOR

DAW BOOKS, INC.

DONALD A. WOLLHEIM, FOUNDER

375 Hudson Street, New York, NY 10014

ELIZABETH R. WOLLHEIM

SHEILA E. GILBERT

PUBLISHERS

http://www.dawbooks.com

First Paperback Printing, June 2008

1   2   3   4   5   6   7   8   9

DAW TRADEMARK REGISTERED
U.S. PAT. AND TM. OFF. AND FOREIGN COUNTRIES
—MARCA REGISTRADA
HECHO EN U.S.A.

PRINTED IN THE U.S.A.

For Ingrid de Buda, a valorous friend.

ACKNOWLEDGMENTS

I'd like to thank Steve Perry for artillery and general military advice, Steve Stavitzky, Dave Alway, and Gary McGath for helping find the words that gave the aliens a voice, and Bill Sutton and Bill Roper for assistance with metaphors. I'd also like to thank Olympic gold medalist Xeno Mueller, who graciously explained the dynamics of rowing machines.

ONE

FROM HER POSITION ON ONE of the upper galleries, Gunnery Sergeant Torin Kerr studied the Humans, di'Taykan, and occasional Krai filling the public terminal from bulkhead to bulkhead. About half, the half who'd probably never left their home worlds before they boarded the recruiting shuttle, were gathered in clumps of their own species. The other half were showing off how much more socially evolved they were than their country cousins.

"They're surprisingly cute when they're young."

Fighting to keep her expression neutral, Torin turned, came to attention, and snapped off a perfect salute.

"As you were, Gunny."

Now she could smile. "Glad to see you up and around, Major."

Major Goran Svensson returned the smile, carefully rearranging the muscles by his mouth. "Glad to be up and around." Although his nose was as prominent as she remembered, his face had the shiny, unlived-in look of new tissue and the regrowth of silver-blond hair was as high and hard as any oldEarth drill instructor could want it. The fingernails of his left hand, the hand that rested on an old-fashioned wooden cane, were a pale greenish gray and, against the matte black of his uniform, his skin was an unfortunate corpse-white. Under his uniform, the major had been rebuilt almost from scratch.

That *almost* had wormed its way into nearly every conversation Torin had been a part of in the just under twenty-eight hours she'd been on Ventris Station. At what point did the pieces of the Marine put into the tank stop being a Marine and start being merely pieces? Had there been enough of Goran Svensson put in to get Goran Svensson out, or was this just something that looked like the major and sounded like the major but was nothing more than shaped meat?

As far as Torin was concerned, it was a no-brainer. Sh'quo Company and the Battalion's heavy weapons company had been dropped on Carlong in support of Captain Svensson's people, who were in imminent danger of being overrun. Unfortunately, imminent had proven to be a conservative estimate, and all three companies had fought a bloody withdrawal to the pickup point only to find the Others were keeping the Navy too busy to get them out. During the battle, the captain had proved himself a good officer and a fine Marine, and Torin had no intention of losing either.

It only validated her good opinion to later discover he was a M'taj, one of the forty percent of Corps officers promoted from the ranks. Until she had evidence to the contrary, the only change between the Marine who'd gone into the tank and the Marine who'd come out was that the former was a captain, and the latter a major.

"Congratulations on the promotion." Major Svensson nodded toward Torin's sleeve. "I hear you were busy while I was tanked. A few battles won, a new species courted, and an unknown alien spaceship outsmarted—I'm surprised they didn't commission you."

"It was mentioned."

The major held up his hand and grinned, this second smile more like the one Torin remembered. "I don't think I want to hear your response. Actually, I don't think I *need* to hear your response, but I promise you, I don't take it personally." He let the hand fall but not before Torin noticed the way his fingers had started to tremble. "I also heard you took some time for romance."

"Sir?" If he'd said he'd heard she'd taken some time to go exploring gas giants, she'd have been less surprised.

"With the civilian salvage operator who found said alien spaceship. Some of the medical personnel here on Ventris recently transferred off the *Berganitan*, and they're very taken by your touching love story."

Torin snorted. "Love story?"

"So no romance?"

"No, sir."

"Too bad. The fine folk in PR would be all over a touching love story." Tightening his grip on the cane, he moved to the edge of the gallery and glanced down. "How many do you think we'll keep?"

A little taken aback by the sudden change in topic, Torin frowned. "Sir?"

"Most of them will finish their contract and go home. Some of them, the lucky ones, will never see battle even in the midst of a war. But in every new group there's always a couple—like you . . ." The grin flickered again. ". . . like me—who find a home in the Corps and that means there have to be a couple down there."

Ah. Keep. Now the question made sense. Torin studied the crowd again. The recruiting shuttle dropped off seventy-two recruits at Ventris every tenday—two full training platoons. 150 days later, between sixty and seventy Marines graduated from Basic. The major was asking her to distill down those sixty or seventy to the few who'd stay.

"Her," she said after a long moment. "The di'Taykan with the lime-green hair and the orange jacket. The recruits closest to her are calmer than the rest, and she's standing so that she can see both exits. She's probably from a military family that's served for generations, and she'll stay until biology forces her out."

"What about her?" The major raised his hand just far enough off the rail to indicate a tall, fair-haired Human staring at the inner entrance to the station as if she could open it through force of will alone. "She looks like she wants to be here."

"A little too much. That attitude says *I know what's best*, and it'll be a fight to get her to listen. She's probably from one of the first families, and she thinks it means something here. I very much doubt she'll make it through Basic." The fourteen first families off oldEarth were as close as humanity came to an aristocracy these days.

"I've got ten that says she does."

"I don't want to take your money, sir."

"Commendable, but I'm more than willing to take yours."

"Ten it is, then." Torin turned slightly, not enough to draw the attention of those down below but enough to direct the major's attention where she wanted it. "See the Human standing by the outer doors, just to the right of the terminal map? Brown hair, hands shoved in his pockets?"

"Looks like he's wondering what the hell he's doing here?"

"Yes, sir, that's the one. We'll keep him."

"Put your money where your mouth is, Gunny."

"I'll give you twenty on this one, sir."

She heard the rustle of fabric as the major turned to face her. "Now why would you do that?"

Torin watched the recruit lean back against the map and jump forward again, face flushed as the map announced where he was. "He reminds me of me."

"Major Svensson!"

Torin kept her attention on the major as he pivoted

carefully around the cane, wobbling slightly. Only when she was sure he'd successfully completed the maneuver and was now scowling down the gallery, did she look up at the Navy corpsman approaching at a run. Fuchsia hair whipping back and forth in agitation, the corpsman slid to a halt, looked into the major's face, and clearly reconsidered taking his arm.

"Sir, you're not supposed to be out of bed."

For a di'Taykan, the most enthusiastically indiscriminate race in known space, to not turn that statement into a blatant innuendo, Major Svensson had to have detanked in an impressively bad mood.

"And yet here I am."

"Sir, Dr. Sloan'll kick my ass out an air lock if she finds out you've been walking around in the public areas of the station." One hand rose to fiddle nervously with his pheromone masker, and eyes the exact same fuchsia as his hair widened pleadingly. "Please come back to Med-op with me."

Major Svensson sighed. Torin suspected he was aiming for world-weary, but there was too much plain old *weary* in it. "If you put it that way, Corpsman. I'd hate for you to get into trouble on my account."

"Thank you, sir. I'll get a chair."

"No. I can manage." Before Torin could protest, or even before she could quite figure out how to phrase a protest, the major added, "But if you'd be more comfortable giving me your arm so that I don't wander off again, I could live with that."

"Yes, sir." No mistaking the relief in the corpsman's voice.

Fingers of his free hand wrapped around the corpsman's elbow, the major braced his cane and turned his upper body just enough to bring Torin back into his line of sight. "I'm glad I happened to run into you, Gunnery Sergeant," he said formally. "Seems fitting we should spend a few minutes talking to each other since everyone on this station seems to be talking about us. Nearly everyone," he amended, his tone lightening as he nodded toward the recruits. "If you get a few free minutes, I'd appreciate the company."

"I'll come by if I can, sir."

"Major . . ."

"I know, I know. Don't just stand there, Corpsman, start walking."

The corpsman wisely refused to allow Major Svensson to set the pace; they moved slowly and carefully toward the decompression doors. He glanced Torin's way as he helped the major over the lip, and just before the door closed she heard the older man snap, "Yes, it is."

Had he asked if that was really Gunnery Sergeant Kerr?

Apparently everyone on the station was talking about her—except when they were talking to her and then they were talking about the major. Beginning to think it was no coincidence Major Svensson had happened to take a walk in her direction, Torin frowned down at the new recruits, not really seeing them.

She didn't like being the center of attention; that never ended well. Once certain people started overreacting to other people doing nothing more than getting the job done, life tended to get interesting. Given that she was involved in fighting a centuries-old war with an indeterminate foe, Torin figured her life was quite interesting enough.

The sound of the inner doors opening jerked her attention back to the terminal.

"Listen up, children, because I'm only going to say this once."

Torin stared in disbelief at the familiar figure standing just inside the open doors. Hands tucked behind his back, scarlet hair moving slowly back and forth, his uniform more like a matte-black shadow than actual fabric, stood Staff Sergeant di'Allak Beyhn.

A little over ten years ago, he'd stood in exactly that position, said exactly those words and had, over the next 150 days, gone on to be one of the main reasons Torin had become a career Marine.

It couldn't be the same Marine.

It had to be another di'Taykan trained by him, another di'Taykan with the same coloring who'd picked up the same phrases and mannerisms. An imitation, not the real thing. He'd had more than a few years in back when he'd been her DI, so Staff Sergeant Beyhn had to have moved on to qui'Taykan—the breeding phase—and left the military.

"I am Staff Sergeant Beyhn."

Or not.

He swept a scarlet gaze over the recruits. "When I give the word, here's what you're going to do: you're going to pick up your gear and move in an orderly fashion through these doors. Once inside, you'll make a quick left, proceed to the end of the corridor, and arrange yourselves on the yellow lines. Anyone who can't figure out how to accomplish that should consider enlisting in the Navy."

A couple of the recruits snickered.

Staff Sergeant Beyhn's expression made it clear he wasn't kidding, and the snickering stopped. "This is your last chance to reconsider your decision to become a Marine," he continued, redirecting his attention to the room at large. "No one will think any less of you if you decide to turn around and take the next shuttle home."

Torin had never heard of anyone taking him up on the offer; the recruiters made sure that anyone who got this far would make it past the yellow lines at least, but she supposed there was always a first time.

No one moved.

She checked the brown-haired young man by the map. He was frowning thoughtfully.

"Gunnery Sergeant Kerr."

All attention snapped suddenly to her as the recruits followed Staff Sergeant Beyhn's gaze up to the gallery. She saw two or three heads dip together and was sure she heard a whispered "*Silsviss*," the sibilants making the word carry.

"When you have a moment, Gunny."

Fighting the urge to snap to attention and shout, "*Sir, yes, sir!*" Torin nodded. "I'm on my way down, Staff." If he could use the diminutive, she could use the diminutive. She'd have to keep telling herself that.

He nodded in turn, one smooth dip of the head—it was hard to tell at that distance, but she thought the *ablin gon savit* was smiling, fully aware of what her instinctive reaction would be. Stepping back out of the doorway, he snapped, "Let's move, people!"

The brown-haired young man was in the last group of recruits through the doors into Ventris Station. Torin made a note to check his name; he was going to win her an easy twenty.

The station studied her identification for a moment and then let her in through the decompression door at the end of the gallery—big open spaces in stations made people nervous, so the designers added redundancies to their fail-safes—and by the time Torin dropped down a level the recruits were moving off the lines and into the hygiene unit. Given that di'Taykan hair wasn't hair at all but a uniform length, multistrand sensory organ and the Krai had no hair to speak of, the Corps had come up with a compromise for their Human recruits that acknowledged they were part of an integrated universe and managed to satisfy tradition as well. The hygiene unit removed dead tissue from all three species, so for the 150 days of Basic, it was business as usual for the di'Taykan, a slightly shinier scalp for the Krai, and on Human heads, stubble. If nothing else, the stubble made it perfectly clear that no Humans were going to get by on their looks.

Torin maintained her own hair at di'Taykan length, but she knew Human Marines who kept their personal hygiene units locked at the dead tissue setting. She thought it made them look like they'd just been detanked, but hell—if they were into an *I nearly had my ass shot off* hair style, who was she to complain?

Staff Sergeant Beyhn stood by an inner wall, watching the last recruits cross into processing. Up close, he looked tired, like he hadn't been sleeping. di'Taykan didn't get bags under their eyes, but he was close.

"They're not mine," he said as Torin joined him. "I've got a group coming up on one twenty I should be with right now, but for the last few days this place has been jumping like the seals are blown, and assignments have therefore been late coming down." He turned to face her. "You wouldn't know why, would you, Gunnery Sergeant Kerr?"

"I hear Major Svensson has recently been detanked, Staff Sergeant."

He made a noise that from a Human would have been noncommittal but from a di'Taykan bordered on insulting. "Don't give me that crap, Gunny. The whole station knows that you single-handedly brought the Silsviss in on our side and followed it up by outsmarting a big yellow spaceship and bringing your recon team safely home."

"Not all of them." Torin closed her hand around the memory of the small, metal cylinder that held the remains of PFC August Guimond.

Beyhn stared at her for a long moment, his eyes moving from near pink to scarlet as more and more light receptors opened. Finally he nodded, his expression relaxing, and Torin realized that she'd been measured and not found wanting.

A smart person would have let it go. "You thought I might be . . ."

"Getting too big for your britches."

Torin blinked. "What?"

"Means full of yourself. Picked it up from a Marine who came through on his SLC."

There could only be one Marine that fond of old-Earth idiom. "Hollice?"

"That's the name." He headed down the corridor, and Torin fell into step beside him. "So, since it's unlikely they promoted you for just doing your job, I'm guessing you've got blackmail material on that General Morris who seems to like you so much."

As it happened, she did, but since her old DI wasn't actually digging for information, she merely said, "Ours is not to question why, Sergeant."

He snorted. "Yeah, that's what they keep telling me."

Your O930 briefing has been moved to L6S23C29.

Torin tongued an acknowledgment and checked the time.

0858

No need to hurry.

"New implant? You half winced just there," the sergeant continued when she raised an inquiring brow. "Like you were reacting to the memory of pain."

She fought the urge to cup the left side of her jaw, recently cracked by the techs back at Battalion who'd installed her new unit during the short time she'd spent with her company on the OutSector station before being ordered coreward to Ventris. The bone ached and the skin over it felt tender. "Good call."

"Not really. Automatic upgrade when you hit Gunny," he reminded her. "Been a long time since I got cracked, but I seem to remember them saying it wouldn't hurt."

"Yeah. That's what they say."

"Lying bastards. Where you heading?"

"L6S23C29."

"You remember how to find your way around?"

"I do."

An ability to negotiate Ventris Station was a hard-earned skill. The word *tesseract* had been mentioned on more than one occasion. Other, less scientific words were used more frequently, the Corps having a long history of creative profanity and two new languages to practice it in. Torin had refamiliarized herself with the more unique aspects of station navigation early that morning on her five k run.

"Well, if you find your way to the baby-sitter's club sometime when I'm not hand feeding the future of the Corps, I'll buy you a drink." Then he glanced at the half dozen chevrons surrounding the crossed KC-7s on her sleeve, looked up, and nodded; that same single dip of the head. "Good work, Marine."

He'd been the first person to call her Marine. She'd just finished two tendays on Crucible, her and the rest of Platoon 29, learning to actually use all the information they'd had crammed into their heads over the first 120 days of training. They'd been in ranks, bloody but unbeaten at the pickup point, and, as the VTA's hatch opened, Sergeant Beyhn had yelled, "Double-time, Marines. We're moving out." That had been—and remained—the proudest moment of her life.

"Don't get all choked up on me now," he grinned as he opened the door into Hygiene and the sound of seventy-two recruits being sanitized drifted into the corridor. "I bet Sergeant Hayman you'd make Gunny before I got out and Jude's just contributed a solid fifty to my offspring fund."

Torin didn't bother hiding her shudder. "That's the scariest thing I've ever heard."

"That I bet a fifty on you?"

"That you have an offspring fund."

Level 6, Section 23, Compartment 29—according to the station directory, she couldn't get there from where she was. Torin snorted and headed for the nearest vertical. All routes on Ventris Station led to the main parade square. Logically, from the main parade square, it was then possible to get to any address in the station.

They should never have let the H'san help with the design. She slowed to let an approaching captain into the shaft first, waited for the next available rising strap, and stepped across a whole lot of nothing to catch hold of it. The public terminal was on level one, but there were fourteen sublevels under that. Her stomach did a lazy loop in the zero gravity, then settled.

Even with the workday underway for almost an hour, the shaft was busy. She nodded at a descending technical sergeant, politely ignored a pair of officers sharing a strap while they discussed their latest liberty, and raised an eyebrow at a Krai recruit adjusting her uniform as she passed, one foot holding the strap, both hands attempting to straighten her collar. The Krai had no problem in zero gee—no nausea, no disorientation—but other species weren't so lucky. Human and di'Taykan recruits who'd spent their whole lives dirtside were tested in zero gee modules before they were allowed into the shafts, but even then it was pretty much a guarantee that the rest of the station would be dodging wobbly globes of vomit and the embarrassed recruit trying to clean them up at some point during the first thirty days of every Basic course. Since a new course started every ten days, it paid to pay attention in the verticals.

At Level 3, Torin grabbed the bar over the door and flipped out into the deck. The link station was right where she remembered it. By the time the link arrived, there were eight Marines waiting with her, and she had less than twenty minutes' travel time left.

Not a problem.

Like the public terminal, the main parade square had been designated as an "outside" area of the station. On her way around to the link station that would take her to Section 23, Torin snapped off three salutes and then stopped by a recruit who stood staring around at eighteen potential exits in rising panic.

"Where do you need to be?" she asked.

Pale gray eyes holding an equal mix of determination and fear locked on her face. "Sir! This . . ."

"Don't call me sir, I'm not your DI. Call me Gunnery Sergeant."

"Sir! Yes, si . . . Yes, Gunnery Sergeant! This recruit needs to be at L4S12 main administration."

She checked his collar tabs. He was still in his first fifty. "Are you cleared for verticals?"

"Yes, Gunnery Sergeant!"

"Take that shaft . . . That shaft!" She reached out and turned his head. "Take it up two levels. Turn right immediately out of the shaft. Keep moving until you get to Section 12 then take the first vertical you see back down a level."

He glanced at his watch. "I have to be there in four minutes!"

It was hard not to smile. "Then you'd better hurry."

"Yes, Gunnery Sergeant!"

She watched him double-time off, turned back toward her station, and saluted a Krai lieutenant wearing a Ventris patch who was staring at her with disapproval.

"The recruits need to learn their way around on their own, Gunny."

Stifling a sigh, she stopped walking. She really didn't have time for this. "The recruits need to learn they can depend on other Marines when the chips are down, Lieutenant."

"And what does he learn if you tell him how to get where he's going?"

"That it isn't a weakness to ask for directions."

"He didn't ask for directions, Gunny."

"Now he knows he can, sir."

The lieutenant's nose ridges flared. "You can't ask for directions in combat!"

Torin did not drop her gaze to the lieutenant's chest and an absence of ribbons but was so obvious about it, she might as well have. "You'd be surprised, sir." She snapped off another salute and was in the link and gone before he realized he'd been dismissed.

She reached L6S23C29 with three minutes and forty-two seconds to spare.

And found her reputation had preceded her.

"Congratulations on the promotion, Gunnery Sergeant Kerr."

"Thank you, Captain Stedrin. And you on yours."

The captain smiled, pale blue hair flicking back and forth. "I suspect the general thought it was easier to promote me than to break in another aide. Besides, we've got an actual staff now, and he probably believes the extra bar will make it easier for me to take command."

"I don't think you'll have any trouble, sir."

Captain Stedrin's hair sped up a little. "That's quite the compliment coming from you, Gunny."

"Yes, sir." She meant it, though. When they'd first met on the *Berganitan*, Lieutenant Stedrin had been a typical "stick-up-the-ass" young officer—not, as it happened too different from the lieutenant she'd just been talking to on the parade square although the attitude was temperamentally unusual for a di'Taykan—but he'd made the right decisions when it mattered, and while he might never be much of a line officer, she'd been in the Corps long enough to know that a good staff officer, one who cared about the Marines more than the paperwork, was worth his weight in ammo. Maybe not the impact boomers, but definitely the regular rounds.

She glanced across the front of the small lecture hall to where General Morris, still without that third star and his promotion to Tekamal and apparently destined to be her personal pain in the brass for years to come, was speaking to a di'Taykan major. The deep orange hair made it a sure bet that it was Major di'Uninat Alie, the Intelligence officer who'd debriefed Torin just after she'd arrived at the station. "The general's filling her in on what he considers the pertinent points, isn't he, sir?"

"I think that's a given."

General Morris had chosen her for the mission to Silsvah. She supposed it was a compliment that he'd believed her capable of doing what was necessary to bring the Silsviss into the Confederation before the Others could recruit them, but she'd lost thirteen Marines on what was supposed to be ceremonial duty, and while she had no trouble following orders, she disliked being manipulated. He'd also chosen her to lead the recon platoon into Big Yellow, the unidentified alien vessel found floating dead in space. *Probably* another compliment. He'd needed a senior NCO capable of riding herd on a glory-seeking officer destined for promotion to placate the Krai members of Parliament, but since Captain Travik had spent most of the mission unconscious, the official reports were slightly different than the reality of the situation.

Torin really hated politics.

Fortunately, she wasn't expected to smile as the general approached.

"Staff Sergeant Kerr. Good to see you again. I've just been telling Major Alie what she can expect."

"Sir." Captain Stedrin cleared his throat, a Human noise the di'Taykan had adopted. "It's Gunnery Sergeant now."

"Why, so it is." General Morris' florid cheeks flushed darker as his gaze flickered to her collar tabs and back. "Congratulations."

"Thank you, sir."

"I'm looking forward to hearing what you have to say."

"Sir?"

"About the Silsviss."

He was staying? Well that was just fukking wonderful. "Yes, sir."

With a final, patronizing nod, the general moved toward an empty seat in the last row. Captain Stedrin let him get most of the way there before he caught up and bent to murmur something in the general's ear. Standing by the lectern, Torin couldn't hear the captain's part of the conversation, but the general's, "What now?" came through loud and clear. After a moment, and an inspection of the captain's slate, he shook his head and stomped off out the rear door.

Captain Stedrin shot her a very di'Taykan grin as he followed.

The bastard had waited until the last minute to clear the general out just to watch her sweat. Nice one. He'd known from the beginning they'd be leaving, or he'd have left his slate with the others on the table near the lower door. Torin had been warned her slate wouldn't record—Compartments 21 to 39 were configured to prevent it—but slates were designed to be ultimately flexible, and there was only one way to be certain no one would enter the information with a stylus and that was to take them out of the hands of their owners. She suspected there were certain things about the way the Silsviss had joined the Confederation that the highest levels of the Corps preferred the general population never knew. Ultimately, there'd be no way to prevent it, but—in the here and now—the top brass was doing what they could to slow things down.

"Are you ready, Gunnery Sergeant Kerr?"

She faced Major Alie and nodded, an echo of Staff Sergeant Beyhn's single dip. "Yes, sir."

"You don't look nervous."

"Are they likely to shoot at me, sir?"

The major's eyes lightened as she smiled. "I doubt it."

"Then I'll be fine."

Torin assumed every one of the thirty officers in the room—there'd be other rooms and other ranks later—had read not only her report, but General Morris' report, Lieutenant Jarret's report and probably, depending on their clearance levels, both the diplomats' and Cri Sawyes' report. She wasn't here to go over the facts of the mission one more time lest something crucial had been left out that effected the acceptance of the Silsviss into the Confederation and their eventual integration into the Corps. She was here because later, after the facts had been presented one more time, there'd be questions and she was the only one who could answer many of them.

It was both clichéd and dangerous to believe that insight into a species could be gained by wholesale slaughter, but Torin was willing to bet that, here and now, no one knew the Silsviss quite like she did.

Slate to hand in case she needed to refer to her notes, she faced the tiers of seats and began. "During the mission in question, I was a Staff Sergeant with 7th Division, 4th Recar'ta, 1st Battalion, Sh'quo Company. My orders were to put together a platoon out of able-bodied Marines to accompany a group of diplomats and their support staff—Mictok, Dornagain, and Rakva—to Silsviss under the command of Second Lieutenant di'Ka Jarret . . ."

There'd been diplomacy for a while, but then all hell had broken loose.

When she reached the point in the story where the *Berganitan* had returned to Silsvah and sent down a VTA to lift them off—the VTA they'd landed in having been lost in a swamp—she saw a few of the officers begin to stir. Either they hadn't heard what happened after liftoff and they thought she was nearly done or, more likely, she was just getting to the part they were interested in.

"The Silsviss have a pack mentality. They know where each one fits in the pack, and the strong fight to rise. They'd just joined our pack, and they wanted to see how much they could push us around."

"They wanted you to kill General Morris."

The statement came from a Human lieutenant colonel. He might have felt safely anonymous in the dim light amid the other twenty-nine black uniforms in the room, but Torin had spent too many years pinpointing smart-ass comments from the ranks to let him get away with it. Glancing over at him, she abandoned the last 4.5 minutes of prepared speech and said, "No, sir. They wanted me to believe it was the general's fault and then use what I had learned about the Silsviss to save the treaty by killing him."

"And why didn't you?"

"Because we weren't joining them, sir. They were joining us."

"General Morris' report said he was willing to die."

"I wasn't privileged to read the general's report, sir."

"But you would have killed him if it had been necessary?" He was leaning forward now, one hand pale and obvious where it gripped the dark fabric over his right knee.

Torin lifted her chin, locked her eyes on his face, and said, "As it wasn't necessary, sir . . ." She loaded implication into the pause. ". . . we'll never know."

The lieutenant colonel looked away first and, as his gaze dropped, Major Alie stepped forward. "Since we seem to have already opened the floor to questions, Gunnery Sergeant Kerr will now address any *other* points you may want clarified."

Interesting emphasis, Torin thought as a Krai major began the official Q&A.

For the most part, the questions stayed fairly close to her observations of the Silsviss military and how well she felt they'd integrate. As they revisited the same points over and over again, Torin became increasingly grateful that she wouldn't be part of the team designing the integration protocols. Given how long it had taken before the Krai joined mixed fireteams, she figured she'd be long retired before she had to worry about maintaining discipline with di'Taykan-sized lizards in the ranks.

When the briefing finally ended, just before 1300, Torin followed the major's silent order and stepped back to let the room empty before she left. With the major acting as a barrier between her and any further questions, she kept her gaze locked on the far wall to give no one a chance to draw her into conversation.

As the last officer retrieved his slate and disappeared out the door, Major Alie turned toward her and smiled. "Thank you, Gunny. Grab some food, and I'll see you back here at fourteen hundred. The officers attending this morning have orders not to approach you out of this room, so you should be allowed to get to the SRM in peace."

"Thank you, sir."

The captain who'd asked the first question had been Intell, seeded into the group by Major Alic. It was inevitable those particular questions would be asked, so the major had arranged for them to be asked under controlled conditions. The timing, before the Q&A officially began, had allowed her to cut the questions off when the information she'd wanted released had been covered. It was a smart move.

Torin appreciated smart, but she had no intention of mentioning that to the major. Intell got a little snotty when one of their subtle plans turned out to be that obvious.

The afternoon session was a near exact copy of the morning's—minus General Morris' small part. Finished at 1800, she skipped the Senior Rank's Mess and headed to a pub she remembered fondly from her last course on station. She was expecting a call and didn't want it going through the duty officer before it reached her in the SRM. Off-duty and in a public part of the station, the message would be bounced straight to her implant.

On the OutSector stations the lowest two or three

levels of the center core were set aside for off-duty and civilian personnel. On a station the size of Ventris, certain broad concourses had been set aside for stores, bars, and cantinas. The recruits were given access to the lowest concourse on their last tenday. They never saw the other four until they returned to Ventris as Marines.

Sutton's, on Concourse Two, was about half full. A group of privates and corporals were watching mixed league cricket on the big screen in the corner. Apparently it was an oldEarth sport the Elder Races had taken to the way the H'san took to cheese, but Torin couldn't see the attraction. Along the other side of the bar, eight of the small tables were full, two of them pushed close so a group of four officers and their companions could eat together. Three di'Taykan sat at the bar itself, bodies close and looking about five minutes from heading to someone's bunk for the night.

Torin took one of the small tables, where she could see both the door to the concourse and the door behind the bar leading to the kitchens, and coded her order into the tabletop. To her surprise, Elliot Westbrook, the grandson of the original owners, came out with the first part of her order.

"Gunny," he said as he set down the beer, "I hear you single-handedly got the Silsviss to join up. Any chance you can give me a scouting report on their beverage selection?"

Seemed that Major Svensson was right; everyone on the station *was* talking about her. Still, it never hurt to cooperate with the man cooking dinner and, while information about how she'd single-handedly got the Silsviss to join up was classified, what the giant lizards drank was not. What's more, if they were going to join the Corps, it was an important cultural touchstone. "The upper ranks drank fermented fruit juices, but the lower ranks usually drank beer."

"Good to hear."

"The beer was usually green."

Elliot grinned. "So they're Irish?"

When her pie arrived, he left her to it, heading back to the bar muttering notes about ales and lagers and fermentation times into his slate.

She was just mopping up the last of the gravy when the call came through.

I've docked. Section 8, slip 17.

Pushing her plate away, she tongued an acknowledgment and murmured, "On my way," just loud enough for the implant to pick up.

They were naked twenty-two minutes later.

TWO

PUSHING DAMP HAIR BACK out of her eyes, Torin rolled up on one elbow and frowned down at her companion. "I get the impression you missed me."

"Funny, because I got the impression I was right on target . . . OW!" Tugging her fingers out of his chest hair, Craig Ryder wrapped Torin's hand in his, immobilizing it. Since she wasn't planning on going anywhere for a while, she allowed him to think he could hold her. "You win," he said: "I missed you. You're just lucky I needed to register new salvage tags."

"You're talking like I'm the only one here who got lucky."

"Wouldn't dream of it." He waggled his brows suggestively. "But you are saying you got lucky, then?"

She freed her hand, moved it lower on his body, and squeezed. "A couple of times."

"Bloody cheek!"

But this time when he grabbed for her, Torin rolled off the bunk and rose to her feet out of reach. "That thing's too small for comfort."

"You'd better be talking about the bunk, mate. And you are not sitting your bare ass down on my control panel," he growled as she moved the very small distance to the other side of the cabin.

Torin snorted. "Not after what happened the last

time." Scooping his discarded shirt off the floor, she tossed it on the pilot's chair covering the majority of the duct tape and sat. One of the reasons the bunk was too narrow for them both was that Craig Ryder was a big man. Undressed, there was a little softness at his waist, but most of his bulk was muscle, his arms and shoulders so broad and heavy, they distracted from his height.

"What?"

All right. Maybe she had been staring. "Rumor has it that this is a romance."

"Really?" Craig rolled up on his side, head propped up on one huge hand. He looked amused, the bastard. "Who's been talking, then?"

She shrugged a shoulder, suddenly wishing she hadn't brought it up. "Some of the medical staff off the *Berganitan* are on station. Apparently, I'm a topic of conversation."

"Apparently?" When she shrugged again, he laughed. "Fuk, all you've done in the last year was convince a race of aggressive lizards to join up right before you outsmarted a big old alien spaceship. Can't see why they'd be talking about you. Obviously, they're talking about me."

"You?"

"Don't mean to skite, but I'm the other half of the romance, aren't I?"

Torin scratched at the drying sweat on her stomach. "There is no romance. There's sex."

"Good sex."

"Granted."

"That'll do, then." Blue eyes gleamed. "So what the hell are you doing all the way over there?"

Later, when she stepped out of his shower—which meant stepping out of his tiny hygiene unit into the main cabin—he handed her a mug of coffee and said, "You ever hear what happened to the escape pod from Big Yellow."

Torin took a drink, set the mug on the small, half-circle table folded down from one of the cabin walls, and started dressing. "It's a piece of unknown alien technology, I expect R&D has it tucked away somewhere, probably somewhere on this station—although there's always a chance that one of the Elder Races rabbited off with it. All I know is that the whole thing's been classified Top Secret, and I have orders not to talk about it during my current *the Silsviss are our friends* tour." Skimming her pants up over her hips, she reached for the mug again. "Why?"

"I rode it from Big Yellow, yeah?"

"Yeah." She knew where this was going.

"That makes it my salvage, doesn't it?"

"Technically, the *Berganitan* retrieved it."

He folded his arms, the motion causing the worn sweats he'd pulled on to fall a little farther from his waist. "I was in it. And in salvage, like life, possession is nine tenths of the law."

The vacuum jockeys from the *Berganitan* had rescued him, directing the spherical escape pod into a net in one of the ship's shuttle bays. Given the mulish expression he was wearing, Torin decided not to remind him of that. "You must have made inquiries," she said, buttoning her shirt.

"I did. No one knows anything about it."

"That's because it's classified Top Secret."

"No. They *won't* talk about Big Yellow, but they don't seem to know about the escape pod."

"You're a civilian. Neither branch of the military is likely to tell you what they know."

"Please." Fingers digging in his short beard, he snorted. "I deal with the military all the time. I know when they're fukking me around and this was more like they honestly didn't know."

Torin set the empty mug back on the table and frowned. "Maybe they didn't know. You couldn't have been talking to anyone with a very high clearance."

"That's possible."

She stared at him for a long moment. "You want me to ask someone, don't you?"

He grinned. "It is *good* sex."

"Not that good."

"Liar."

"Fine. There's an Intell major running the Silsviss briefings I'm doing. If I get a chance, I'll ask her." She slid a foot into her right boot and bent to tie the laces. "How long will you be docked?"

"Odds are good I'll be gone by 1400 tomorrow."

His tone pulled her attention back to his face. If he was off station by 1400, this was it. They'd probably see each other again when she got back to her unit. Civilian salvage operators weren't unknown at OutSector stations, but only the brass knew how long they'd keep her here. "All right, I'll ask at the morning briefing."

"Ta."

Both boots secured, she moved to the hatch and paused, left hand rising to touch her jaw. "The upgrade's got a signal strong enough to reach ships in space."

Craig's brows rose when she stopped, clearly expecting more.

She didn't have any more.

His fingers went back to his beard. "You've got the *Promise*'s codes."

"I do." Her left hand settled against the scarred surface of the hatch. The upgrade went to grades Gunny and above, so that if they had Marines dirtside, and the comm unit got hit, they could call for evac. They weren't for . . . She glanced back at Craig; from the way the corner of his mouth was twitching, he knew exactly what she was thinking. Cocky bastard. Stepping out onto the ramp, she turned again. "Be careful."

He nodded. "You, too."

"Major Alie."

The major's hair lifted. "Is there a problem, Gunny?"

"No, sir." di'Taykan didn't have the concept of personal space, so Torin stepped a little closer. They were standing, once again, at the front of Compartment 29 waiting for the morning's group of senior NCOs to finish taking their seats, and Torin figured that her odds of getting an answer were better if the major thought she couldn't be overheard. In the raw light of day, minus post-coital endorphins, this was obviously a bad idea, but she'd told Craig she'd ask—and that left her only two options. Keep her word. Or not. "The CSO who . . ."

"You're seeing." The words were tame for a di'Taykan. The innuendo was all it could be.

"Yes, sir." Torin responded to the words alone. "He was wondering what happened to the escape pod off Big Yellow."

The major's hair flattened. "The alien ship is classified, Gunny."

"Yes, sir."

"And classified means you're not to speak of it."

"No, sir."

"Not even to your *vantru*."

Given the major's expression, now was not the time to mention that *vantru*—more or less translated as primary sexual partner—was a bit strong, if only because of the di'Taykan weight the word carried and not because she was actually getting any anywhere else.

"I've got no way to keep him from mentioning it to me, sir."

"*NinLi* civilians!"

Like many sentient races, the primary Taykan religion had not only the concept of damnation but the profanity to go with it.

"Yes, sir."

But while the major had said, *"The alien ship is classified,"* her expression had added, *"What escape pod?"* It was fast, gone almost before Torin saw it. Someone watching a little less closely would have missed it entirely, but Torin had spent years learning to spot bullshit and next to some of the di'Taykan she'd commanded, for whom bullshit was a vocation, Major Alie was an amateur.

Her anger at not knowing had given her away.

Intell hated to think there were things they didn't know.

At 12:45, Torin set down her lunch tray and pinged the *Promise* from a table terminal in the SRM.

"What the bloody hell did you ask at that morning briefing?"

Torin poured creamer in her coffee, the artificial stuff significantly safer than the real cream in the other jug. There were no cows on Ventris Station. "I asked the major about your possible salvage."

"Just like that, then?"

"You wanted to know."

"I expected you to be a little more . . . I don't know, circumspect."

"I said I'd ask." She took a preliminary swallow—the coffee had probably been started by the first cook on Ventris—and added a splash more creamer. "This is not the kind of thing that I can sneak about trying to discover for you. Nor would I if I could."

"I had a visit this morning from a couple of Marines who thought I needed to be reminded of what classified meant."

That wasn't entirely unexpected. "And?"

"They pointed out that military salvage tags don't grow on fukking trees."

Neither was that. It was, after all, the only handle they had on him. "Happy ending?"

"They're letting me bail, if that's what you mean. In fact, they pretty much told me to rack off." She heard him sigh, could see him sitting back in the pilot's chair, feet resting on the spot his heels had worn shiny on the control panel. *"I'm never going to see that salvage, am I?*

Never mind. Don't answer that. Are you in the crapper for bringing it up?"

It surprised her that he'd ask. "Not so far."

"Good. Let me know when you're back at OutSector."

"I will." She cut the connection, ate her soup and her sandwich, and wasn't at all surprised to find a Marine waiting for her in the corridor outside the mess when she left.

"Come in, Gunnery Sergeant Kerr. I won't keep you long."

Torin entered as ordered and came to attention in front of the desk, staring at the gray-green plaque on the wall just over General Morris' head. It was the same color as Major Svensson's fingernails and that led down paths she'd rather not travel—although artificial fingernail was not the strangest building material she'd ever seen used. She couldn't quite make out what battle the raised letters commemorated.

"Damn it, stop doing that. You know I hate it."

"Yes, sir." She relaxed slightly into parade rest.

"What escape pod, Gunny?"

That drew her attention to his face. "Sir?"

Hands linked, he tapped joined index fingers against his chin. "You asked Major Alie this morning about an escape pod from Big Yellow."

Not a question but she answered it anyway. "Yes, sir."

"What are you up to?"

"Sir?"

"There was no escape pod, Gunny."

By the time she'd made sergeant, Torin could remain expressionless under any condition. That skill came in handy now. There had been an escape pod. She'd seen Craig Ryder get into it on Big Yellow and had seen the alien ship spit the pod out into space. One of the Jades from the *Berganitan*'s Black Star Squadron had caught it up in an energy field and maneuvered it back to the ship, tossing it into a net strung across shuttle bay one to catch it. General Morris had been there when Craig had emerged from the pod.

General Morris was a politician at heart, but he wasn't *that* good a liar.

He believed there was no escape pod.

"I spoke of the escape pod in my mission report, sir."

"No, you did not."

Yes, I damned well did. "If I could see . . ."

"No, you can't. The mission reports concerning Big Yellow are classified." He leaned back, eyes narrowed within the folds of flesh. "But I assure you, Gunnery Sergeant, there was no mention of an escape pod in your mission report. Nor in any of the others. Nor at any of the debriefings."

The recon team had been debriefed separately and then sent back to their respective units. It was possible, if unlikely, that no one else had mentioned the escape pod. But she had. She remembered it clearly.

"We'd lost the first one because we misinterpreted the controls, but the second one launched with CSO Craig Ryder inside."

The Elder Races insisted they were against violence in all forms; Torin found herself wondering how they felt about mind control. And why would they wipe General Morris' memory but not hers or Craig's?

"I understand how the kind of attention you've been under lately can go to your head, but you, of all people, should know better than to exaggerate for the sake of your audience. Not that you should have an audience," he continued as Torin blinked at him. "You know the information about Big Yellow is classified."

Okay. Firm ground here, at least. Even the patronizing tone was familiar. "Yes, sir."

"Thanks to Presit a Tur durValintrisy at Sector Central News, the greater part of the Confederation—those who were not actually on the mission—knows exactly what we want them to know. And we don't want them to know anything else." His eyes narrowed above florid cheeks. "Do I make myself clear, Gunnery Sergeant Kerr?"

"Yes, sir."

"Good. You're going to have to hurry to make your afternoon briefing."

"Yes, sir." She came back to attention, pivoted on one heel, and left the office. *Well, that was a whiskey tango foxtrot conversation.*

"Gunny."

Torin stopped at Captain Stedrin's desk.

He glanced toward the open door to the outer office, where two corporals and the Krai private who'd been sent to fetch her toiled over the general's data entry, and beckoned Torin closer.

She leaned in.

"Look, if you were anyone else, you'd have been up shit creek for that stunt this morning. I'm finding it hard to believe that the Marine I knew would make up a salvage claim even for a *vantru*. You're golden right now, Kerr, but don't let it go to your head."

"No, sir."

Lieutenant Stedrin—Captain Stedrin—had also been there when Craig came out of the escape pod.

She made it to her afternoon briefing on time, but only just. Distracted by the certainty that something hinky was going on, she dropped into the wrong vertical and had to start again from the parade square.

Major Alie met her as she entered the compartment. "Problem, Gunny?"

Torin glanced at the multi-Sector chronometer on the front wall. She had thirty-seven seconds to spare. "No, sir."

The matter-of-fact tone seemed to throw the major a bit; the movement of her hair sped up, and she frowned slightly.

Does she expect me to tell her that General Morris kept me late? Torin wondered. If Major Alie expected her to feel chastised and show it, well, the H'san would take up knitting first.

Maybe, because she was, after all, an Intelligence officer, the major was wondering *why* Gunnery Sergeant Kerr had asked about a nonexistent escape pod.

Probably not, Torin acknowledged as she stepped forward to lay out her experiences with the Silsviss for the fourth time in two days. The integration of large, aggressive lizards into the Corps was of more immediate concern than either the possible existence of escape pods or a possibly delusional NCO.

Two more days of briefings finished off the staff officers and NCOs, and she spent the day before she began at the Recruit Training Center going over her notes and making some of the changes Major Alie had suggested. She no longer ate alone; every meal in the SRM became a sort of mini-briefing. Since going out would only expose her to questions from officers and speculation by other ranks, she stayed in.

She was rapidly reaching the point where being shot at by the Silsviss would be preferable to having to talk about them. It didn't help that most of the private questions—and many of the briefing room questions for that matter—involved second-guessing the decisions that had been made in the field.

"Contamination levels were rising slowly; why didn't you stay with the VTA?"

"Why didn't you empty the armory? Why wasn't every Marine carrying two or three weapons?"

"Why didn't you put your ammo for the emmy under cover so it couldn't be hit?"

As that second-guessing was coming from Marines who'd spent most of their tour on their asses behind a desk, Torin figured it was inevitable that she'd end up in the gym late one night, pounding the snot out of some pompous desk jockey. When it finally happened, it started with a Krai technical sergeant demanding to know why she hadn't killed Cri Srah when she had him in the choke hold. Then it moved into the declaration that, if it had been his people sent into ambush, he'd have made the Silsviss pay. Finally, it ended with him pinned to the floor, Torin's knee on his throat.

She had a bite taken out of her padding—Krai invariably bit, but the padding slowed them down a little— and a few bruises.

The incident would have broken the monotony except that it had been so appallingly predictable.

She spoke to the one fifty recruits first. On their last tenday, they were almost done with Basic and, having returned from Crucible, were considered Marines— nothing left but finishing up the appalling amount of documentation the military required before posting. There were no recruits in one thirty or one forty; they were on Crucible and probably wishing, if Torin's memory of those twenty days was anything to go by, that they were anywhere else.

It took a few years of actual combat to put Crucible in perspective.

The one twenty recruits included Staff Sergeant Beyhn's Platoon 71 as well as Platoon 72 under the command of DI Staff Sergeant Connie Dhupam.

"You haven't stopped by for that drink, Gunny."

"Only time I've had free, you were with your platoon, Staff."

"They're keeping you busy." He snickered, but not unsympathetically, at Torin's expression. "This isn't your job. You should be out there keeping the kids I'm sending you alive. Why the hell aren't they putting your second lieutenant through this crap?"

"Lieutenant Jarret was unconscious for the final battle and in Med-op for the aftermath."

"And you're General Morris' golden Gunny."

Torin snorted. "For my sins."

By day one hundred and twenty, recruits had survived long hours of training both physical and mental and were showing the arrogance that was a natural result of that survival. Two tendays on Crucible would temper that arrogance, but nothing would ever completely remove it. As Major Alie instructed the two platoons in the discretion expected of a Marine given sensitive information, every single recruit leaned slightly forward to show they were listening.

It was the *appearance* of rapt attention, at least.

Most of them looked intrigued, a few looked amused, all di'Taykan hair was in movement, and the half dozen Krai were showing teeth. One or two of the recruits were showing no expression at all, and Torin decided they were in Staff Sergeant Beyhn's platoon only because that was where she'd begun.

They hadn't read the diplomatic reports, but they'd studied every word written by Marines about the battle and the political aftermath. It was possible, Torin realized, that this group of recruits could represent the first Marines to integrate with the Silsviss. They were only on a three-year contract, so it was unlikely, given the speed of politics, but it was possible. As she talked, it became obvious there were going to be a lot more questions than usual; at least a dozen recruits looked as if they wouldn't make it to the end of the briefing without interrupting.

They did, but Torin would have bet her pension that a couple of them managed to wait only because of the DIs standing behind and to either side of her.

The sergeants handled the Q&A, motioning recruits up onto their feet.

"Gunnery Sergeant Kerr . . ."

The standing recruit was a tall, medium-dark Human, her nose given remarkable prominence by the dead-head hair.

". . . is it true you have the Silsviss skull the pack leader gave you in your quarters back on OutSector?"

"Essentially. I put it in storage when I got my orders to head here."

"This recruit wonders why you kept it."

"Seemed rude to throw it out."

"Then this recruit wonders why you didn't give it back to the Silsviss for proper burial."

"Because that would have been dangerous. The skull is more than a battle trophy. When the new leaders of the pack handed it over, it symbolized them showing their throats to the victor. Giving it back would have meant we planned on killing each and every one of them."

"But giving it back now . . ."

Torin raised an eyebrow and cut her off. When she figured the pause had continued long enough, she said, "What would giving it back now mean, Recruit?"

Her brows drew in. "Disrespect?"

"Are you asking?"

She jumped at the tone. "No, Gunnery Sergeant Kerr!"

"All right, disrespect and . . . ?"

"A challenge."

The short sharp crack was the sound of a Krai in the second row beginning to snap his teeth together, suddenly realizing where he was, and trying to stop just a little too late. He managed to look sheepish and apologetic simultaneously.

"And what would a challenge mean, Recruit?"

"A fight."

"A fight," Torin agreed. She found herself wanting to remind them that every species has their own way of treating the dead but knew their DIs wouldn't appreciate her inference that they hadn't already learned that lesson. Insofar as it didn't interfere with the functioning of the Corps, the Corps respected those differences.

"A fight with who, Gunnery Sergeant Kerr?" This recruit was male, Human again, with the heavy muscle that came from working a physical job before he'd signed up.

"Depends on who received the skull."

"So if it went back to the representative of the Silsvah World Council, would we find ourselves fighting the entire planet?"

"It's possible." And that would certainly interfere with the functioning of the Corps. Which was why she had the skull in her storage locker. Well, that and because a couple of the more politically correct NCOs at Battalion didn't want the skull of a sentient species hanging in the SRM. They'd just have to choke it down when the Silsviss arrived because it was definitely going back up then.

"Gunnery Sergeant Kerr." Even at parade rest, the di'Taykan recruit's inherent grace was evident. Torin could see a long list of aristocratic forebears in his posture—no one got that self-assured in a single generation. He reminded her of Lieutenant Jarret and she would have been willing to bet his family name had no more than three letters in it. His cobalt-blue hair swept slowly back and forth as he asked, "Is there a chance we can see the skull, Gunnery Sergeant?"

Torin could feel Major Alie getting ready to step in.

"That is," the recruit added, "if you don't think the Silsviss would mind."

There was no way the major could answer that. If she knew what the Silsviss would or wouldn't mind, Torin wouldn't be there.

With no doubt that the recruit had phrased the second half of the question so that the major would not have the deciding voice, Torin kept both expression and tone neutral. "The Silsviss would understand showing battle honors to the young. They'd also understand using the skull to explain Silsviss strengths."

"What strengths can you learn from a skull, Gunnery Sergeant Kerr?" Krai, male; his voice on the edge of insolence.

"Why don't we wait until you get a look at their jaws and you can ask me that again."

"Gunnery Sergeant Kerr?" Another di'Taykan. Emerald-green hair this time. "When you were facing those hundreds of Silsviss and your platoon was surrounded and almost out of ammo, were you afraid?"

"Gunnery Sergeants don't feel fear, recruit. We eat overgrown lizards for breakfast and wash them down with a side of H'san. However, since I was only a staff sergeant at the time, I can tell you that the moisture controls on a pair of Marine Corps Class As work to design specifications."

That got a laugh.

"Gunnery Sergeant Kerr, is it true you knew Major Svensson before he was tanked?"

Motivated only by guilt for having not yet gone to see him, Torin let the major move in on that one and remind the recruits that they were here to discuss the Silsviss and only the Silsviss.

"Kichar's in love."

Miransha Kichar ignored him and continued polishing her boots.

The pink-haired di'Taykan lounged against the wall beside her bunk and grinned. "I saw the way you were looking at the Gunnery Sergeant when she snapped at you this afternoon during your little question and answer riff. You're in love."

"Is that a bad thing, Sakur?"

Sakur turned enough to direct his grin at the Krai on the next bunk. "Love is never a bad thing, Hisht. But the Gunny will never return Kichar's affection, and that's sad."

Hisht's nose ridges flared as he considered the

di'Taykan's words. His *jernine* lived deep in the forests, and until the day he'd climbed to the crown of the prayer tree and seen the airship go by, he had thought he would spend all his life surrounded by his extended family. Staring up at the silver ship, a deep curiosity had grabbed him, and he had left all he knew and followed its path and, eventually, when he finally became aware of just how much there was outside his small bit of forest, he had ended up here surrounded by people who were not people as he had known them and who did not always think the way people thought. It was exciting and confusing, and he did not always have the right words in his head to understand. "To love without love in return *is* sad," he said at last, even though he knew that wasn't the point being made.

"Even Hisht gets it." Sakur laughed. Laughed harder when Kichar glared up at him.

In the forest, Sakur's behavior would be that of a young male trying to get a female's attention. In the Marine Corps, he was merely acting like a pain in the ass. That was a concept Hisht had no trouble understanding.

Staff Sergeant Beyhn took a long swallow of his beer and set it back down on the bar of the RT/SRM. "You run a good briefing," he said. "Everyone seems to think so."

Torin dropped her head into her hands. "God, help me. I'll never see my unit again."

It was beginning to look that way.

After she finished speaking to the remainder of the recruits, right down to the latest group to step off the recruiting shuttle, the Corps wanted her to look at a few simulations of the battle and finally review the official documentation that came out of her briefings. After that, Ambassador Krik'vir, the Mictok who'd been one of the diplomats on Silsvah, wanted her to address a Parliamentary committee.

"Parliamentary committee," General Morris snorted, staring down at the request. "Half a dozen species rummaging around trying to reach a consensus on what beverage they should have on morning break. Ridiculous waste of time."

Torin had never been so much in agreement with the general.

"Unfortunately," he added, "we have no good reason to refuse them. I will, of course, accompany you to the Core."

And her prospects went from bad to worse.

On the first day of her three/ten, Torin went for her run, took care of her kit, spent two hours at the range blowing away a target she mentally painted with General Morris' face, and finally headed over to see Major Svensson. The station allowed her into Med-op, but there was a door, a desk, and a delay before she could get to the convalescent compartments.

"I'm afraid the major's physical therapy's running a bit late, Gunny." The yeoman on duty at the desk peered down at her screens. "Ah. He's with Elusoy . . ."

"Di'Taykan?" Torin asked as though that explained everything. Which, considering the circumstances, it pretty much did.

The young petty officer nodded and colored faintly. "You can wait."

"Thank you." Hands clasped behind her back, Torin wandered slowly around the small waiting room. The half dozen uncomfortable chairs were empty, but she had no desire to sit. She read the charts on the wall, checked the display of biscuits for her slate, discovered they were all at least three years out of date, and found herself back at the desk. "You were on the *Berganitan*, Yeoman?"

She looked up, startled.

Torin hid a smile. Major Svensson had mentioned there were personnel in Med-op whose last posting had been the *Berganitan*; that was why she'd looked. "You're wearing the ship's ribbon."

"Oh. Right." A quick glance down at the single ribbon on the left side of her chest. "Yes, I was there when you ... When we transported you to ... you know. And back."

"Right."

"I put together some of the data for your medical files."

"Thank you."

She shrugged narrow shoulders, a quick up and down motion, and smiled shyly. "It's okay. It's what I do. I did Craig Ryder, too. We scanned him—just a quick scan just in case—before he went back out for you."

Her tone, her expression, pretty much everything about her explained the rumor of romance the major had heard. Rubbing one finger along the inert trim of her desk, she stared up at Torin like Torin was the heroine in a H'san opera.

"That's right, I got my people out of Big Yellow, and I got the guy."

"Gunny?"

"Never mind." It was easier to be amused by the whole thing. Considering some of the other rumors she'd heard about how she'd taken out a squad of Bugs in hand-to-claw combat, this was mild. There'd only been one Bug. And she'd shot it before it had a chance to grapple. "You wouldn't have any idea what happened to the escape pod Mr. Ryder got back to the *Berganitan* in, would you?"

"Escape pod?"

"It was in shuttle bay one."

Brows, shaped to within a nanometer of regulation, drew in. "I don't remember an escape pod."

"How did he get back to the ship, then?"

"Oh, that." She smiled in relief at having the answer. "A Jade brought him in." Her desk chimed. "Ah. Major

Svensson's back in his room, Gunny, and . . ." Her fingers danced over a screen. "And he's approved your visit." The door beside the desk slid silently open. "Go right ahead. He's in M20."

"Thank you again."

"It's nothing. Gunny?"

Torin paused, halfway through the door.

"Are you, you know, still seeing him?"

Why not? It wasn't like she was ashamed of it. And it was a relief not to answer yet another question about the damned Silsviss. "Occasionally."

"Gosh."

"Gosh?" Torin repeated to herself as the door slid closed. "Gosh?" It seemed the Navy was not only enlisting preteens but then promoting them to petty officer, third class. Under other circumstances, she wouldn't have been at all surprised to find the yeoman had forgotten about the escape pod, dismissed it as unimportant next to the love story playing out in her clearly overactive imagination. However, given that her lack of memory matched Captain Stedrin's and the general's . . .

There was something wrong, but the whole station was so focused on the ultimate integration of the Silsviss that she was the only one who could see it. Or, less egotistically, the yeoman had never known there was an escape pod and, hell, it wasn't like General Morris had never lied to her before. She only had his word for it that no one else had mentioned it at their debriefings. Captain Stedrin would follow the general's orders.

Except ten years at war had given her good instincts for when things were heading from screwed up as usual toward totally fukked and right now her instincts were yelling the equivalent of fire in the hole.

The Elder Races had to be involved.

M20 was a private room, larger than Torin had expected and obviously intended for long-term convalescence. Although the bed dominated the space, there was also a pair of comfortable looking chairs and a fully loaded desk. The vid screen on the wall had been set at window, and the major, clearly aiming for realism, had chosen the station's docking yards as his view.

Post-therapy, Major Svensson looked a lot better than he had up on the terminal gallery.

He still looked newly made but significantly less shaky. If the huge smile he welcomed her with was any indication, he was also in a much better mood.

Station rumor had him so badly injured his body hadn't been able to completely rebuild and he'd been patched together with nonstandard parts. Although the fingernails of his left hand were still greenish gray and he was painfully thin, all the parts Torin could see looked standard.

"Gunnery Sergeant Kerr." Still smiling, he shrugged into a robe. "I'm glad you're here. You look bored."

"Sir?"

"What would you do if I said I could get you two weeks off station with a KC-7 in your hands?"

Two weeks away from briefings and speculation. Two weeks to actually work as a Marine. What would she do for that? "Something entirely inappropriate, sir. Something that would probably lead to you having to be retanked while you recover."

"Well try to contain your enthusiasm; you're going with me to Crucible."

THREE

"**D**R. SLOAN WOULD LIKE TO FIELD TEST some of my new parts and given that combat zones are generally considered iffy prospects for research, she's decided to send me to Crucible with one of the next one twenty platoons going in."

Torin said nothing as Major Svensson crossed the room and sat down. He seemed fit enough, but crossing three meters of level floor was one hell of a lot easier than surviving twenty days on Crucible. She added a few things to what she wasn't saying as the major fought to gain control of a chair that seemed determined to recline and massage.

"Don't let this worry you, Gunny," he muttered, catching sight of her expression as the chair finally accepted his commands. "I was technically inept with everything but a KC-7 going into the tank. The point is . . ." One corner of his mouth curved up in a self-mocking smile. ". . . I can only go if I have a babysitter. Command called it an aide, of course, but, between you and me, I'd prefer to call a spade a fukking shovel. I don't anticipate the job consisting of much more than picking me up if I fall down. You interested?"

"Very, sir." The job would consist of significantly more than merely picking the major up if he fell down.

She'd be a fool to think otherwise, but anything would be better than more time spent dealing with further inane speculation about the Silsviss. "I've still got briefings scheduled, sir."

"That's been taken into account. If you'll work through your next two days off, you can complete your briefings halfway back through the second fifty. You start again at day ninety when you get back and all our little outing will cost you is one more double briefing as you pick up the newest recruits."

"Cheap at half the price, sir. But Major Alie . . ."

A raised hand cut her off. "Right now the Corps is very motivated to keep Dr. Sloan happy and Dr. Sloan wants me field tested and I've decided I want you with me. You let Command deal with Major Alie."

"Sir, General Morris . . ."

"They'll deal with General Morris, too." Silver-blond brows drew into an exaggerated frown. He'd gained tissue flexibility since that morning on the gallery. "I'm beginning to think you don't want to go to Crucible with me, Gunnery Sergeant Kerr."

"I'm sorry you got that impression, sir. I'm looking forward to it."

"Good. I'd . . ."

Torin pivoted on one heel as the door behind her opened.

". . . like you to meet Dr. Sloan," the major continued. "Whose timing is impeccable as always. She'll be going with us."

The woman in the doorway was about a meter and a third, thin—athletic—with reddish brown hair and gray-green eyes. Impossible to tell her age; with the human life span creeping toward a century and a half, she could be anywhere from thirty to eighty. She wore no collar tabs or any other rank insignia, which was hardly surprising, Torin realized an instant later, since she wasn't wearing a uniform. Dr. Sloan—whom the Corps was so motivated to keep happy they were sending her to Crucible—was a civilian.

Command's reason for allowing Major Svensson his choice of aide suddenly became clear. Torin had gotten civilians alive off Silsvah and Big Yellow—not all the civilians she'd arrived with, granted, but there probably wasn't another senior NCO currently on Ventris with her experience in shepherding the untrained through combat situations.

"You must be Gunnery Sergeant Kerr," Dr. Sloan said, before Torin could speak. Striding across to the major, she added, "I've been hearing a lot about you lately. I imagine you'll be glad to get off the station."

"Yes, ma'am."

"Ma'am?" She rolled her eyes without actually looking up from reading the major's numbers off the top of the chair, the readout a brilliant orange against the burgundy fabric. "No. Call me Dr. Sloan or, if that's a problem, call me Kathleen. You call me ma'am, and I look around for my grandmother. How's the hand working?" The question went to Major Svensson.

"Good."

"Still aching?"

"A little."

"And the headaches?"

"They're not lasting as long."

"No more memory lapses?"

"Not that I can remember." The major tossed a grin at Torin that clearly said, *Funny, eh?*

Torin had just started to wonder if she should leave when Dr. Sloan straightened and turned to face her.

"How much do you know about Major Svensson's case, Gunnery Sergeant?"

"Sir?"

He nodded. "It's all right, Gunny. The doctor's security clearance is higher than yours and mine put together."

Given the way her career had been going lately, Torin somehow doubted that. "I know that he was severely injured on Carlong and the only thing that saved him was that the surviving corpsman attached to his company was too raw to know he should have died."

"He was a brain in a jar, Gunnery Sergeant. A brain and a spine and damned little else that hadn't been damaged."

"My teeth," said the major dryly, "are original."

"Human teeth aren't Krai teeth, but they last," the doctor acknowledged, patting him absently on the shoulder. "Gunnery Sergeant, do you know the difference between what happens in a tank and cloning?"

Easy question. She'd watched enough of her people go into tanks over the years. "The tank encourages the body to repair itself, keeping those who have been badly injured alive while this occurs. Cloning creates duplicates, and using cloning tech on any species deemed sentient is illegal."

"And the medical profession is of two minds about that."

Given the Krai's fondness for the taste of Human flesh, Torin wasn't. Tanks of Humans cloned for the dinner table was not something she wanted to contemplate.

"Had I been able to use cloning technology," Dr. Sloan continued, oblivious to Torin's culinary line of thought, "I could have finished rebuilding the major without having to resort to bioengineering. There's a limit to how long a body can stay tanked and thrive, just as there's a limit to how long a body can remain in the womb, and in order to make it possible for Major Svensson to be detanked essentially whole within that time limit I integrated polyhydroxide alcoholydes into the matrix."

"Organic plastic."

The raised eyebrow suggested polite surprise.

According to the preliminary analysis from the science team—before everything went to hell and most of the scientists had ended up bagged—Big Yellow had been made at least partially of organic plastic. Torin didn't care what the doctor's clearance might be, she was not citing the alien ship as her source. It was one thing to talk about a classified mission with someone who already had all the details because he'd been there, or she was in Intell and another thing entirely bringing it up to an outsider.

"Polyhydroxide alcoholydes are, in many respects easier to work with than Human tissue. They're less complex so they grow faster; although getting them to grow into the exact parts you need has never been easy. And you realize that when I say *grow*, I'm simplifying for the sake of brevity. I'd recently got hold of some new, more molecularly flexible polyhydroxide alcoholydes and . . ."

"Dr. Sloan convinced it—them—to become a skeletal lower arm and hand when my body was too pooped to create new bone. We need to see if this . . ." Major Svensson waved his left hand in the air. ". . . will drop off and ooze back to the safety of the lab at the first sign of trouble."

"Drop off, sir?"

"His hand is not going to drop off." Dr. Sloan's tone suggested this was not the first time she'd said those words, but she was hoping it might be her last. "It's an experimental use of a new variation of an old substance, Gunnery Sergeant, and I want to test the results under a number of different conditions. Twenty days on Crucible should give me enough data to work with. And yes," she added once again before Torin could speak, "I know what happens on Crucible. I've watched the files. In fact, I watched your file when Major Svensson requested you. Platoon 29 wasn't it? Don't worry; this trip will be nothing like that trip."

They never were. That was the problem.

The major grinned. "Still want to go, Gunny?"

An oozing, organic plastic hand still sounded preferable to spending those two tendays answering stupid questions about the Silsviss. "Yes, sir."

Major Alie was philosophical about losing her for twenty days. "I have new reports from the Marines at the embassy on Silsvah that I want to integrate into the data we already have. By the time you get back, we may only need you in a consulting position. You'll be going back to Sh'quo Company," she added when Torin showed no reaction.

That reaction she let show. "I am very glad to hear that, ma'am."

Some of these recruits might also be going to Sh'quo Company, she told herself looking out at the tiers of black uniforms and picking out individual faces as the major began the familiar opening statement. The rest would be going to units different only in that they weren't, specifically, hers. What these potential Marines were about to learn from her might keep them alive through the rocky days of integrating another aggressive species into the Corps. Thinking of the Marines, not the Silsviss, made the whole tedious process seem less tedious. After all, keeping Marines alive was what she did.

Might have been smarter to come to that five days ago. It annoyed her that she'd been as caught up in putting the Silsviss at the center of all things as everyone else. Unfortunately, there was just something about large lizards with automatic weapons that overwhelmed the mammalian hindbrain.

General Morris was slightly less philosophical about her impending absence.

"Is there a shortage of senior NCOs on this station that no one has told me about?" he snarled. "There is absolutely no reason Major Svensson has to take you rather than any one of a hundred others."

There weren't a hundred others on the station with her experience—General Morris himself had seen to that. Torin, still at attention, stared at the wall beyond the general's head and tried once again to read the raised letters on the plaque.

"We were to have addressed a Parliamentary committee . . ."

We?

". . . but suddenly a civilian doctor and a major's left arm are more important than the smooth running of the Confederation. Fine." Shoving himself back from the desk, he surged up onto his feet, eyes narrowed and nostrils flared. "Go, then. But I will have a few words to say about this to Command!"

"Yes, sir." She snapped around in a textbook about-face and headed for the door.

"Gunnery Sergeant Kerr."

"Yes, sir." And around to face him again.

"If I discover you requested this . . . mission . . ." This word dripped with disdain. ". . . I will not be pleased."

"Yes, sir."

She left while he was still working out what that meant.

"Well, Gunny, think you can handle one convalescent officer and a civilian, or should I stand ready to help out?"

"I think you'll have your own hands full." Torin's gaze flicked past Staff Sergeant Beyhn and over the two platoons of 120s lined up in the shuttle terminal, packs at their feet. "Half of that lot looks like they're ready to shit themselves, and the other half looks like they already have."

"New combats always go baggy assed," the staff sergeant snorted dismissively. "These recruits are as ready as any 120s. They know what they're getting into. They've heard the stories."

His voice deliberately carried. Torin saw more than one set of shoulders hunch forward and a rainbow of di'Taykan hair begin jerking back and forth. At thirteen tendays in, they'd overheard twelve sets of stories from the recruits who'd returned from Crucible while they were training. The stories—overheard because 150s didn't lower themselves to speak directly to lesser mortals— were invariably exaggerated enough to be dismissed and vague enough to be believed. It was one thing to know intellectually that they were probably being bullshitted and another thing entirely to prevent a visceral, emotional reaction.

Torin remembered what it felt like standing in their place. Heart pounding, palms sweating, dying to finally prove herself, and refusing to even consider the faintest possibility that she couldn't cut it.

"Boarding will commence in three minutes."

"You heard the station," Beyhn barked, turning. "Get your thumbs out of your butts and your gear up off the deck, Kichar!"

The recruit who'd asked Torin the first question after the briefing about the Silsviss skull snapped to attention. "Sir, yes, sir!"

"What in the *sanLi* do you have in your pack?"

"Sir! Everything on the list, sir!"

"Everything?"

"Sir, yes, sir!"

"You remember you're going to be humping that pack up one side of Crucible and down the other?"

"Sir, this recruit also remembers the drill instructor saying that we'll only have what we bring in and that there is always a chance we may not be able to access all of the supply caches, sir!"

"Do you also remember, Kichar, that I told you that the last thirty items on the list were suggestions only?"

"Sir, this recruit took your suggestion, sir!"

Torin hid a smile as the di'Taykan recruit with the

light pink hair rolled his eyes. Since di'Taykan eyes had no whites, it was a subtle expression and easy to hide from those who'd had little interaction with other species.

"I saw that, Sakur."

"Sir, yes, sir!"

Harder to hide from one's own species, however.

"Give me twenty," Beyhn snapped. "With the pack on," he added as Sakur started to shrug out of it. "She's keen, and he's a fuk-up," the DI sighed for Torin's ears alone as Kichar's knees threatened to buckle under the weight of her pack and Sakur dropped. "I'm not sure which one is the bigger pain in the ass."

Given the way Sakur was moving through the push-ups, Torin would have been willing to bet he had nothing in his pack that had merely been *suggested* and that he'd dumped as much of the *required* as he'd thought he could get away with. She also had no doubt that he'd manage to survive everything Crucible threw at him. His kind always did, working the angle that Crucible was intended to test potential Marines, not actually kill them.

At least not on purpose.

"Begin boarding."

With a hiss of equalizing atmospheres, the inner air lock doors opened.

Beyhn nodded at Staff Sergeant Dhupam who began moving Platoon 72 onto the shuttle. "I'll see you on board," he told Torin. "Look at the bright side. At least, working with Svensson, you know you've got yourself an officer who certifiably has a brain. Once we hit Crucible, all you'll have to do is keep your major on a close rein and impress upon your doctor that . . ."

The pause continued just a little too long.

"Staff Sergeant Beyhn?"

"Right." He blinked and nodded, his eyes shifting shades as the light receptors opened and closed. "I'll see you on board."

Torin watched him cross to join his platoon's two junior DIs, became conscious of someone watching her, and shifted her gaze just in time to catch the di'Taykan with cobalt-blue hair looking away. Looking worried. He'd asked about the skull during the Q&A after the briefing—di'Arl Jonin. She'd been right about his family name.

"Problem, Gunny?"

Major Svensson and Dr. Sloan were standing just to the left of the air lock, waiting for the recruits to fill the rear compartment before they took their seats up front.

"I don't know yet, sir. I'll keep you informed." The major looked significantly less fragile in combats, Torin noted as she crossed to his side. Although, she admitted silently, that could have had more to do with her perception of that particular uniform rather than the officer wearing it. *And speaking of wearing . . .* She stared in some fascination at the doctor's jacket. A patchwork of pockets, it covered her from chin to mid-thigh and was such a brilliant blue that Jorin's head would have disappeared up against it. "You didn't get that on station, did you, Dr. Sloan?"

"No, I did not." Dr. Sloan patted a sequence of bulging pockets, pulled out her slate, and checked the screen. "I ordered it from an outfitter's catalog," she continued without looking up. "It's guaranteed windproof, waterproof, insect-proof, and has been sprayed with a substance that makes it unappetizing to the Krai. I had a friend in med school who kept eating the sleeves off my lab coats. He thought it was very funny, but I'm not going through that again."

"Marines don't eat each other's clothing, Doctor."

"No, I don't imagine they do, but since I'm a civilian, I prefer to be prepared." She slipped the slate back into her pocket. "Are you married, Gunny?"

"Uh, no, ma'am."

"Doctor."

"Right." According the doctor's records, she'd been married for twenty-two years and, obviously, to an understanding partner given the length of time they were about to spend apart.

"Probably smart to stay single, given your job. My husband just sent me a list of all injuries suffered on Crucible over the last twenty years. There've been rather a lot of them."

"Good thing we have a doctor with us this time, then."

Dr. Sloan grinned, the corners of her eyes crinkling. "I think I'll mention that to John."

She had an earbud in, Torin realized; that was how she'd known her husband had pinged her. A much smaller version of the personal communication units used in the Corps, the pickup filament was almost invisible against her cheek. There'd been talk of outfitting Marines with a similar PCU—removing it from the helmet entirely—but in the end it was decided that in combat situations it was preferable to have Marines able to use both ears without technological interference, and as the current PCUs were small enough to be worn in the ear if necessary, there was no need to change them. Torin personally felt that the last thing the di'Taykan needed was an excuse to remove their helmets.

You can bring your lot on board any time, Gunny.

Torin tongued an acknowledgment to the shuttle's air crew. "Sir, they're ready for us."

"Our gear?"

"Already loaded, sir."

"Then let's not keep them waiting. Dr. Sloan . . ."

The doctor flicked the microphone back into the bud. "Ready. I'd like to do some tests in zero gee." she said as she watched the major step carefully over the lip of the air lock. "Do you think they'd be willing to cut the gravity on the shuttle?"

He turned just enough to flash a grin back over his shoulder. "I doubt they'll be running the gravity."

"Good thing I got the optional mag soles, then."

Torin and the major glanced down at the doctor's boots—mid-calf and the same blue as the jacket—and then up at each other. They were very nice looking boots.

"Same outfitter's catalog, Doc?"

"I'm not sure, actually. I ordered from a number of them, and it's easy to lose track when the packages start to arrive. But these boots . . ." She flashed a fond smile at her toes. "They've got environmental controls that go from one hundred down to forty below."

This meant the doctor's feet would survive conditions the rest of her wouldn't. As Torin followed her charges onto the shuttle, she wondered just what that outfitter's catalog thought they were outfitting people for.

As the only nonrecruits heading out to the Confederation Ship *NirWentry*, they had the shuttle's forward compartment to themselves. Dr. Sloan took readings while the major allowed his left arm to float freely. Torin, sitting far enough away to give them the illusion of privacy, went over the information on the *NirWentry*'s Marine packet so that, when they arrived, she could settle Major Svensson and the doctor immediately into their quarters.

Marine packets were infinitely adaptable to the needs of the Corps and as adaptable to the needs of the Navy as the Corps would allow. Attached to the transporting ship, the packets always had a small power plant for life support and at least one vacuum-to-atmosphere vehicle. If detached in battle, they could be towed to safety—although the term *safety* came with variable definitions. This trip, the configuration included two sets of platoon compartments with a shared common room, a compartment for the DIs, an upper compartment for the officers and aircrew of the VTA, and quarters with private hygiene units for her, the doctor, and Major Svensson.

The equations for Ventris to Crucible had long been

worked out and refined so they'd be spending only fifty-five hours, just under two days, in Susumi space. For a trip that short, there was only the one mess. Torin had no idea how Dr. Sloan felt about eating with a crowd of not-quite-trained Marines, but if she objected it, would be easy enough to get her a place at the table with *Nir-Wentry*'s medical staff.

In Torin's experience, the Navy ate well. With any luck, Major Svensson would be invited to dine in one of the wardrooms, leaving her to seek out old friends—or make new ones—among the chiefs and petty officers.

At fifty-eight minutes out, the shuttle's docking bell chimed.

"So soon?" Dr. Sloan looked up from her slate, brow furrowed as the major slipped his hand under the strap on his seat's arm, securing it for docking. "I could use another ten or fifteen minutes."

"Gunny?"

Was there a problem? "Sir."

"What do you think the odds are that they'd move the *NirWentry* to a berth farther from the station?"

No, not a problem; just the major playing silly buggers. "Not good, sir."

"Sorry, Doc. Gunnery Sergeant Kerr says the odds aren't good."

"Uh-huh. Gunny, how long will we be on board ship?"

"Just under two days, Ma'am. Doctor."

"Two days." Dr. Sloan smiled up at the major. "Try to remember that while I have access to the ship's medical facilities; I could order an enema for you every hour on the hour."

In Torin's professional opinion, that skirmish definitely went to the doctor.

Recruits were known to spend a lot of time thinking about Crucible—it loomed on the horizon of their first one hundred and twenty days and, after their return, they carried it triumphantly through their last ten. By the time they joined a unit or began their specialist training, they had so many other things to think about that Crucible became relegated to memory and was rarely dragged out for reexamination.

The last few days aside, Torin hadn't thought specifically about Crucible for over ten years. Fortunately, the desk in her quarters contained a full set of files on every possible training scenario as well as the nuts and bolts behind them. As the major still hadn't told her which of the two platoons they'd be accompanying, she uploaded both assigned scenarios into her slate. And then, taking advantage of the opportunity, she uploaded the last dozen scenarios run. When she finally got back to Sh'quo Company, it would help to know just what exactly their newest Marines had been through, and it wouldn't hurt to reinforce her rumored omniscience.

Individual sectors within each scenario were run from a Combat Processing Node—a hidden computer that controlled the drones and other armaments thrown at the recruits while they were inside its area of influence. Mixing and matching sectors allowed for an impressive variety of scenarios and links to a fleet of observational satellites that kept each scenario under constant observation, which meant that CPN programming could be updated and adjusted to fit realities on the ground. Marines in the Orbital Platform in orbit around Crucible were plugged into both the ObSats and the CPNs and could stop a scenario if things got out of hand or do an emergency Dustoff in the case of serious injury. As well, the CPNs could also be overruled from the ground at the discretion of the senior drill instructor.

While Torin's desk would mark the position of the CPNs within the scenario, it wouldn't extend her clearance to a release of the control codes—leaving her unable to change or even access the programming should something go wrong. That seemed a lot like tempting fate to her.

"Call me paranoid," she muttered slaving her slate to the desk and trying again. Torin didn't actually mind being called paranoid—any state of mind that got her people home in one piece was a good thing in her book.

The first three times she tried to access the codes, she was informed that they were issued to the senior DI only. *If you are the senior DI for this scenario, input your identification number now.*

The fourth time she got a security flag and her desk went dead. Her ID was enough to get it to reboot, but her next attempt at the codes pulled up a screen informing her that any further attempts would result in her desk being cut off from the system.

"I can't get them either," Major Svensson admitted when she pinged him to let him know. "And the system's locked down tight. We should have dealt with this before we left the station."

She appreciated the *we*. It was a safety backup that should have occurred to her.

"Don't worry about it, Gunny," he continued. "If anything happens to the senior DI that sets off his med-alert, his slate will automatically squirt the codes to any slate held by a corporal or above. We're covered."

"You should at least have the codes for the Orbital Platform, sir." And when she said *you*, she meant *we*.

"I agree with you, Gunny. Unfortunately, the Corps doesn't, and every point I've made in favor of one or both of us having them has been answered with a variation on *codes are issued to the senior DI only*. I suspect they want to make sure you and I don't interfere in the running of the scenario." He rubbed his regrown left hand over his brand-new face. "This is training, not combat—they may be afraid we'll forget."

They had never been in combat if that was what they thought.

*   *   *

"What the fuk is the matter with you?" John Stone reached past Kichar and grabbed the salt. "I asked for this twice."

"Sorry, I was thinking of something else."

"She's distracted by the presence of her one true love," Sakur snorted, on the other side of the table. "The gunny," he added when Stone frowned. "She can't look away."

The big Human half turned and peered toward the far end of the mess where the gunny, the major, and the doctor shared a table with the officers and crew off the VTA. "Weird eating in the same room with officers," he grunted. "Weird suddenly realizing there are gods higher than the DIs."

As everyone in earshot looked unsettled, Kichar rolled her eyes. "The highest ranking DIs are staff sergeants, so we were bound to be spending time with higher ranks eventually."

Stone shook his head. "Yeah, but the DIs are . . ."

"Training specialists. A Marine Corps career choice. That's all."

"That's all?" Sakur muttered. "They just spent 120 days teaching us to be in awe of their every utterance. Stone's right. They are the gods of our small world."

"Our world is about to get bigger."

"Yeah, but they're still the gods of Crucible," Stone pointed out, forkful of mashed potatoes halfway to his mouth.

"That's ridiculous," Kichar snorted. "We respect them because of what they know, because of what they can teach us, but they're not gods, they're Marines. Marines like we'll be."

"Oh, no." Sakur peered across the mess at the group of DIs. "We will never be Marines like that. Well, *you* might," he amended. "Given the stick up your ass. Which I'd be more than willing to replace with . . ."

"Shut up."

* * *

As the major's aide, Torin accompanied Major Svensson and Dr. Sloan out of the Marine packet when the doctor insisted they needed to touch base with the medical personnel on the *NirWentry*.

"The ability to grow polyhydroxide alcoholydes into accurate replacement bone would be invaluable to both branches of the military," Dr. Sloan pointed out when the major protested and then added in a tone that suggested he stop being such a baby about it: "They just want to scan you—not do a vivisection."

Torin could understand his reluctance. If she'd just been sprung from Med-op after nearly two years, she wouldn't be happy going back in either. She couldn't see why he'd need an aide, but she understood not wanting to leave the packet without backup. If nothing else, the doctor wouldn't be able to pick him up if his legs gave out, and no Marine, given a choice, would trust a sailor to stand them right side up.

On the other side of the packet's air lock, the bulkheads changed to Navy gray.

Both implants chimed as the *NirWentry*'s sysop picked them up, but the ship's security went to full audio when the grid registered a third body without identification. *"You are now on board the* CS NirWentry. *Personnel without implants identify themselves to the ship, stating name and rank."*

Dr. Sloan rolled her eyes. "Kathleen Sloan. Doctor. Civilian." She stressed the final word.

"Destination?"

"Sick bay. Dr. Weer is expecting us."

"Dr. Sloan, you are cleared to proceed. Advance to the end of this passage. Turn right. Continue along the new passage until you reach a vertical on your left. Take this vertical to Level 9. Turn left as you exit. The medical unit is at the end of that passage. You will be able to see it from the vertical."

"I can never decide if they're being helpful or patronizing," she muttered as they walked to the end of the passage as instructed.

"Patronizing," Major Svensson declared. "Gunny?"

"It's a Navy thing, sir." She'd heard a Marine pilot once explain that it originated from the Navy's vacuum jockeys not being able to find their asses without both hands and a homing beacon, but that wasn't something she could repeat in her current company.

From the hatch to vertical was the longest distance she'd seen the major walk; he seemed to be having no visible difficulties, but surrounded by Navy, it was unlikely he'd let any show.

He stumbled but made a quick recovery as they left the vertical on level nine.

Not quick enough for Dr. Sloan to miss. "You should have brought your cane."

"You said I didn't need it anymore."

"You convinced me you didn't need it anymore. Not quite the same thing."

Once in sick bay, an officious medical yeoman told Torin to take a chair while Dr. Weer—who'd clearly been restraining himself from meeting them at the air lock—escorted Major Svensson and Dr. Sloan to the exam room where he'd do the scans.

The major glared Dr. Weer's hand off his elbow. "Gunnery Sergeant Kerr goes where I go."

"Gunnery Sergeant Kerr will be in the way," Dr. Sloan pointed out before Dr. Weer or the yeoman could respond. She wrapped her fingers around the major's arm and gave it a little shake, as though daring him to protest her touch. "You'll be in and out faster if Dr. Weer doesn't have to maneuver around her."

"Faster, eh?" He clearly liked the sound of that. "How long should this take, Doc?"

NirWentry's CMO shrugged, nose ridges flaring. "An hour. No more."

"Fine." Major Svensson locked his eyes on Torin's face. "If I'm not out in an hour, Gunny, I want you riding to the rescue."

"Yes, sir."

He meant it. So did she.

"Staff Sergeant Kerr?" When she looked up from her slate, the petty officer, who'd just walked into the compartment, grinned. "Sorry, *Gunnery* Sergeant Kerr."

It took Torin only a moment to place her; she'd been one of the *Berganitan*'s riggers on the trip out to Big Yellow. "Petty Officer Tristir. What are you doing off the *Berganitan*?"

Tristir shrugged and, when Torin nodded, sat—in the same ugly, uncomfortable orange chairs they had back in Ventris Med-op. "Well, after our last little adventure with impact and the conservation of energy," the rigger snorted, "the *Berg*'s in for some extensive repairs. While she's in dock, the most recent crew in got moved out to other ships. I'm rigging for Dark Matter Squadron now—it's a great crew, but I miss Chief Graham and all, so I'm in for going back as soon the *Berg* needs me."

"What happened to your foot?"

The petty officer stretched out her leg and gingerly flexed long, opposable toes, the series of blisters across her instep sliding up and down with the motion. "Pilot error. Rookie L.T. brought his Jade in a little hot."

"As in burning?"

"As in melt a piece of the docking mech and spray hot metal across the bay."

"Ouch."

"Yeah, tell me about it." She leaned back with a sigh. "So, what are you doing here, Gunny? I thought we had a load of recruits for Crucible. You're not DI-ing now?"

"No." Torin could truthfully say that becoming a drill instructor had never occurred to her. "I'm a temporary aide to Major Svensson."

"The brain that got tanked?"

"That's the one."

"Well, at least you're working with an officer you *know* has a brain."

"I take comfort in the thought." She was starting to think that if she got a credit for every time she heard a variation on that theme, she'd be able to take an early retirement. "Have you heard how Lieutenant Shylin is?" The lieutenant had been ejected by her pilot, Commander Lance Sibley, just before he flew his Jade down the throat of an enemy ship, his death saving the lives of those Marines who'd survived Big Yellow. Tristir had been one of the riggers for the lieutenant's squadron.

"I heard pysch's still watching her really closely. She's still talking kind of crazy." The Krai rigger stared down at her feet. "di'Taykan don't react well to that kind of isolation."

Torin couldn't see anyone reacting well to floating in hard vacuum surrounded by half a Jade with minimum air and no control over position, but vacuum jockeys were a breed apart and, as far as she could see, a whole, working Jade provided only a difference in degree. At least ejected compartments came with a BFFM beacon.

They sat silently for a few moments, then Tristir said quietly, "That was quite the trip, wasn't it, Gunny?"

"It was."

"You, uh . . ." She dropped her voice even though the yeoman at the desk had been pointedly ignoring them both. ". . . you ever wonder where that *serley* thing was from?"

"I've done a bit of wondering." Torin spent half a second weighing her options and then figured what the hell; when the universe dropped an opportunity in a person's lap, that person was a fool if they didn't pick it up. "These days," she continued, stretching out her legs and looking a lot more relaxed than she felt, "I've mostly been wondering what happened to the escape pod. Commander Sibley did some fancy flying to drop it into that shuttle bay."

"Escape pod? What . . ."

"You didn't hear about it?" She didn't know about it. Torin recognized the expression—she should, she'd been seeing it enough. Crossing her feet at the ankles, Torin pushed *no big deal* with her posture; the last thing she wanted now was for the petty officer to mention to one of her officers that Gunnery Sergeant Kerr was asking about nonexistent, highly classified escape pods. "No surprise. You were up to your ass in repairs trying to keep your squadron flying."

They talked in general terms about the fight; Torin'd had a closer look at the Black Star Squadron in action than she ever wanted to have again. When Tristir was finally called in to have her foot tended, Torin pulled out her slate.

There was no way in hell Petty Officer Tristir wouldn't have known about the escape pod, not when one of her Jades had been responsible for bouncing it into the shuttle bay. Granted, she might have been too busy to have thought much about it when it arrived, but after the fight, on the way home in the boredom of Susumi space, the whole ship would have been talking about carrying one of Big Yellow's escape pods, and survivors of Black Star Squadron would have been distinctly proprietary about it, especially given the way Commander Sibley had died.

Therefore, logically, Petty Officer Tristir had to have known about it. And now she didn't.

Torin remembered.

Craig Ryder remembered.

Why?

What did they have in common that everyone else involved in the mission didn't?

What else besides the obvious?

Was there anything else besides the obvious?

Sex as a defense against mind control?

All the mission reports, including hers, had been classified. Had she been able to find a taker, Torin was willing to bet that, were she back on Ventris and able to get into the main data banks, she'd find all references to the escape pod had been removed from those reports.

But by whom?

There had been none of the Elder Races on the *Berganitan,* although there had been three of what the histories referred to as the Mid Races; those who'd joined the Confederation after it had been established but before Parliament had gone searching for aggressive species to protect them against the Others. There'd been a Ciptran, a few Niln, and too many Katrien given the sudden arrival of Presit a Tur durValintrisy and her news crew. Torin hadn't liked the reporter when she met her and didn't like her much better after . . .

She stared down at her slate, not actually seeing it.

After.

There was something she and Craig *and* Presit a Tur durValintrisy had in common.

After the explosion that trapped them on Big Yellow, the three of them—and Captain Travik, Torin's injured CO—had been sucked down through a meter of floor slowly enough for the alien ship to scan them. Eventually, all the survivors had passed through seemingly solid parts of the ship, but all other incidents had happened in real time. Was it possible that whatever the ship had done to them during the extended scan had somehow protected them from having the Elder Races wipe their memories of the escape pod?

There was only one way to find out.

Captain Travik had died of his injuries, his body lost to space, but, as far as Torin knew, Presit was still very much alive. Sitting forward in the chair, the slate down between her knees where her body blocked the screen from any possibility of prying eyes, Torin put together a message.

Craig: Talk to the reporter. Find out if she remembers the EP. We three may be the only ones who do.

She'd send the message the moment the *NirWentry* left Susumi space. Going out on a personal burst, it would be legally private. Most of Parliament hadn't much liked the idea of a Confederation Military at all and had done everything they could to limit their autocracy. Anything that might give away the position of ships or troops got automatically flagged and the message pulled to be dealt with by the lowest levels of Intell, but everything else from bitching about the food to describing the particulars of a battle was fair game. Given that the Corps encouraged their recruits to write home regularly, her message would probably be buried in with sixty others and not even noticed. Still, if memories were being erased, then mail might be read, so there was no point in being obvious about things. Best to give Craig just enough information and no more.

Once Presit realized something was going on, she'd . . .

She'd what?

Raise high holy hell probably.

Torin straightened and stared across the waiting room, fingers tightening around her slate.

Maybe the Elder Races had a good reason for erasing the memory of the escape pod; one Torin had no need to know. *Need to know* had been the operating credo of her entire career. Officers made the decisions, she saw to it they were carried out with as little loss of Marine Corps life as possible. She didn't deal with the big picture, she took care of the details. This whole thing could easily be part of a big picture she wasn't even aware of. By stirring things up—and having Craig prod Presit would definitely stir things up—she could be placing the entire Confederation at risk.

She could be placing Marines at risk.

Thumb sweeping over the screen to delete the mes-

sage, she got to her feet as the inner hatch swung open
and Major Svensson emerged.

"Fifty-six minutes, Gunny. Your looming presence
seems to have kept them honest."

"I wasn't aware I was looming, sir."

"Metaphorically, Gunny."

"Yes, sir. Where's Dr. Sloan?"

"Dr. Sloan and Dr. Weer are having my head
examined."

"Sir?"

"They're looking at the scans of my head to see if
they can figure out what's causing my headaches."

Torin stood aside as he exited into the corridor and
then fell into step beside him. "If they're debilitating,
sir . . ."

"You're about to suggest that we don't need to go to
Crucible, aren't you, Gunny? Don't bother answering,"
he continued before she could speak, "I know how you
think. They are not debilitating and we are going to
Crucible although, should they figure out what bits of
my brain are hurting and why, I won't turn down a
magic pill."

"Glad to hear that, sir."

"And you've got to look at the bright side, Gunny. At
least there's medical evidence that you're serving under
an officer *with* a brain."

"Yes, sir." A very early retirement indeed.

FOUR

"**WE'LL BE GOING NORTH WITH PLATOON 71**, Gunny, dropping into NHS19." Major Svensson tapped the position on the map displayed on his desk. "It's midwinter there: cold but dry. Platoon 72's going to the tropics, just over three thousand k south, but I've had enough of being warm and wet for the time being. The scenario involves us attempting to get an important civilian out of a combat zone to the pickup point; the platoon will be supporting us. Neither my orders nor yours will supersede the senior DI's."

"And the junior DI's?"

The major grinned. "I expect that'll depend on their orders."

"Yes, sir."

"You look doubtful, Gunny." He waved his left hand. "Afraid this is likely to drop off?"

"Not actually my problem, sir. I'm concerned about Dr. Sloan."

"You don't think thirty-seven Marines can keep one not particularly large civilian alive? Even if thirty-two of them aren't quite Marines? Don't worry about it," he continued before Torin could answer, "she'll be wearing an observer's chit. The system will be unable to fire directly at her."

That would have been reassuring, except experience

had taught her that direct fire was usually a lot less dangerous than random fire; soft target rounds tended toward the impersonal. It was also significantly less dangerous than artillery fire, which often resulted in large, indiscriminate explosions collapsing buildings and/or landscapes, and entirely less dangerous than friendly fire, which was unfortunately likely when thirty-two recruits were given live ammo and tossed into a simulated combat situation. Since experience had taught Major Svensson the same thing, Torin stuck with a neutral, "Yes, sir."

His expression suggested he'd clearly heard the subtext. "She'll be in full combats under that jacket of hers, Gunny, with all the built-in safeties the squints in R&D can devise and let's not forget that the system would have to get through you and me to take her down."

"That's not my concern either, sir; since Crucible is designed to challenge one twenty recruits, we should be able to kick its ass. I'm concerned about whether or not Dr. Sloan will be willing to put in the full twenty days once she gets a taste of what it'll be like. Since the point of the exercise is to get to the pickup point and the OP won't send down transport without a serious injury registering, does she know she's in for the duration? Escorting a willing civilian is a whole different ballgame than escorting one who's kicking and screaming and wanting to go home."

"I don't think Dr. Sloan's the kicking and screaming type, Gunny, and—more importantly—I think she'll stick it out. She maintains an amazing focus on the tiniest details of what she's working on—which would be, currently, me or rather . . ." He waved the hand again. ". . . *this*, but that kind of focus blurs out the bigger picture, so if we can keep her and her slate undamaged, we'll be laughing. Besides . . ." One finger tapped the map, and NHS19 expanded to fill the desktop, multicolored lights flashing throughout the section. ". . . you've already uploaded the scenario, so I'm betting that by the time we're dropped you'll be able to run it with your eyes closed."

"Yes, sir." It was good to work with an officer who knew what to expect.

Jonin was in the corridor, lingering by the hatch to her quarters when Torin left the major a few minutes later. The di'Taykan recruit looked conflicted.

"Gunnery Sergeant Kerr?"

Since Taykan in the di phase would have sex with anything that fell into their uniquely broad definition of compatible, it didn't take a genius to figure out why he was there. "No, thank you, Jonin. Not interested."

"It's not that, Gunnery Sergeant. Although . . ." He looked momentarily intrigued, remembered she'd already said no, and started again. "If I may ask you a question?"

She should have known; di'Taykans never looked *conflicted* about sex. "Go ahead."

"As I understand it, you outrank Staff Sergeant Beyhn? And the other DIs?"

That wasn't among the questions she'd expected. "Glad to see you were paying attention when they were teaching you the command structure of the Corps, Recruit."

"No, it's not that, it's . . ." His hair drooped. "If it happened that there was a problem with Staff Sergeant Beyhn, would I go to you?"

"Is there a problem?"

He looked conflicted a moment longer, then said simply, "I don't know."

About to tell him to come back when he did know, Torin reconsidered. Whatever the problem he suspected, it had visibly upset him and while he wasn't specifically her responsibility, in a general way they all were—where *they* meant not just these two platoons of recruits but the NCOs she outranked as well. "Can you tell me what kind of a problem it may or may not be?"

"I apologize, but I can't. It's personal."

His eyes were so pale, so many of the light receptors closed, she'd be amazed if he could see her at all. "Personal about you or . . ."

"Jonin!"

He snapped to attention at the sound of the staff sergeant's voice and just for a second, Torin could have sworn he looked terrified. Staff Sergeant Beyhn's sudden arrival had wound him so tight he practically twanged when he moved. "Sir, yes, sir!"

"Gunnery Sergeant Kerr is not interested in your 120 *kayti*. Ask her again when—make that if—you survive Crucible."

"Sir, yes, sir!"

"Now get back into the common room. Staff Sergeant Dhupam is about to review ways to take out a drone."

The recruits were encouraged to do as much damage to the systems on Crucible as they could. This always turned out to be more difficult than they expected.

Jonin didn't look at her again before he moved, but he half turned as he passed the sergeant and Torin, watching closely, saw his nostrils flare. The di'Taykan had an extremely sensitive sense of smell and the pheromones they produced were the secret of their success in interspecies intimacy. Since most other species found constant sexual arousal to be at the very least distracting, di'Taykan wore pheromone maskers when in mixed groups.

Was Jonin trying to tell her that Staff Sergeant Beyhn's masker was malfunctioning? If it was, it was happening at a level Torin couldn't detect. As the sergeant moved closer, she felt no desire to do her old DI up against the bulkhead—and was, in point of fact, profoundly relieved by the total absence of those feelings.

"So, I hear your major decided to come dirtside with 71. I don't suppose you influenced his decision in any way?"

"Me, influence an officer's decision? Never happen." When Beyhn snorted, she grinned. "And in this case it didn't happen; the major just preferred to spend twenty days cold instead of overheated."

"I'm happy he's happy, and I'd have to say I'm fairly happy about it myself. Sergeant Jiir, now, he's unhappy. You know how Krai hate the cold."

"I expect he'll have enough to do to keep warm."

"You've gone over the scenario?"

"I have."

"Good. It never hurts to have backup."

"Speaking of backup . . ."

"You're not getting the codes," he told her flatly. "Not you or your major. You're observers only, and I know you; given half a chance you'll think you've come up with a better way to do things, so I'm not putting the power to make changes into your hands. Now . . ." His hair flipped in the general direction of the recruits' common room. ". . . I'd better get back in there; Connie's alone with the horde. Gunny."

"Staff." Since she had no reason to watch him walk to the common room hatch, Torin entered her own quarters, crossed the room, and frowned down at the matte black surface of the desk. She'd never had a conversation with a di'Taykan so devoid of innuendo. Staff Sergeant Beyhn hadn't reacted with as much as a raised brow to either the major being overheated or the prospect of Sergeant Jiir having enough to do to keep warm. And, as disturbing as it might be when it concerned her old drill instructor, Humans always felt a low level of attraction to the di'Taykan, even with the maskers. Since the di'Taykan were doing everything they could to neutralize this, susceptible members of the Confederation learned to ignore it.

There had been nothing to ignore with Staff Sergeant Beyhn. There was nothing there.

Dropping into the chair, she called up all available

medical files on the di"Taykan. If the staff sergeant was coming down with something, it would be best to catch it before he was dropped into a Crucible winter with thirty-two recruits, a convalescent major, and a civilian doctor.

She found nothing that listed lack of overt libido— hers and his—as a symptom and had to assume that his masker was just more efficient than most. If it was blocking enough of the pheromones to drop them under the levels even his own species could scent, then it was no wonder that Jonin had gotten upset. To the younger malc's senses, it would be as if his senior DI had become a walking, talking mannequin.

Although . . .

None of the other di"Taykan recruits seemed affected—or, more accurately, none of the other recruits had come to her with the problem. The best solution seemed to involve taking a closer look at the rest of the platoon before she came to a decision about approaching the sergeant. Facing down a thousand Silsviss had less potential for disaster than coming between a senior DI and his platoon right before Crucible.

There were a group of Krai working the ropes over in a corner, but, otherwise, Torin had the *NirWentry*'s larboard gym to herself. She didn't much like treadmills, but 0530 of day two in Susumi space had seen the Marine packet filled with recruits pounding along the corridors and up and down ladders over the convoluted five k course their DIs had worked out. A few moments' observation had shown no di"Taykan, including Jonin, having any obvious difficulties as they passed Staff Sergeant Beyhn and yelled out the nine-digit core of their seventeen-digit ID number, so she headed off-packet for a little peace and quiet.

Not even vacuum jockeys ran through the convoluted corridors of the big destroyers and either the starboard

gym was the more popular or not many members of the
NirWentry's crew worked out this early.

She'd just hit the three k mark and was starting to
pick up speed when Major Svensson stepped through
the hatch followed by a yawning Dr. Sloan. They both
acknowledged her. Then, to her surprise, as the major
headed for the resistance machines Dr. Sloan claimed
one of the other treadmills, docking her slate and slipping on a visor. Had she been asked, Torin would have
said that the doctor was there only to observe the
major's workout. Just as well she hadn't been asked
since she hated to be wrong.

She also hated not being able to see where she was
actually putting her feet, but, given the new contours of
her treadmill, the doctor had no such problem and preferred an environment that involved goat tracks cork-
screwing up the side of mountains.

A fast two kilometers later, dripping sweat onto the
deck, Torin crossed to see if the major needed a hand.
He'd set his weight station into an ergometer configuration. As he sweated and swore and struggled to complete his last few reps, she checked the data pad.

"Sir, these settings are little high."

"Cleared to work at 450 watts," he panted, face
flushed scarlet.

"You're at 670 right now, sir."

"No . . ."

"Your drag factor is increasing marginally with every
rep—671, sir." The veins in his temples were visibly pulsing,
the larger veins in his throat standing out like blue wire
raising the skin. His lips were nearly purple, his lungs not up
to the demand for oxygen. His hair had spiked into wet tri-
angles. If he didn't stop, she was ending the program.

He stopped, dropping the oars, and sagging back as
the seat reconfigured as a bench. Chest heaving, his
arms fell to hang limp, fingertips leaving damp circles
on the mats. "I set . . . resistance . . . with no increases."

"Then there's a glitch in the system." Almost everyone right out of the tanks tried to do too much too soon, but—for now—she'd give him the benefit of the doubt. She reached out as he tried to sit, sliding an arm behind his shoulders and removing it as soon it seemed he could manage on his own. The major's data was already in her slate. Had his med-alert gone off, she'd have had a reason to keep holding on, but as it hadn't, she'd just have to pick him up if he fell. With any luck, he'd fall straight down and hit the mats, not the deck. "I'll tag the unit out of order; the next user might be Navy and this thing could damage their more delicate physiques."

"That's what I like about you, Gunny," the major gasped. "Always considering others. I just thought . . ." He blinked down at his hand as she wrapped trembling fingers around the curve of a water bottle. "Right. Good idea. I just thought," he began again after a long, careful swallow, "that I was out of shape. Pull started to get heavier, but, fuk, everything does."

"Look at the bright side, sir." Torin snapped her slate back onto her belt. "At least you know you can break a one-thirty/five-hundred-meter split."

"Yeah, and a shorter split might have killed me."

"Also a good thing to know."

"In case the scenario on Crucible includes a rogue rowing machine?"

"It never hurts to be prepared, sir." He was still flushed, but his skin was so fair it showed every little bit of color to an extreme. A better indication was the healthy pink of his lips and the way his breathing no longer sounded quite so pained. In Torin's professional opinion, he'd live.

"Might not hurt *you*," he barked, the sound clearly intended to be a laugh but not quite making it. "But I'm sure as hell going to hurt la . . ."

"This is apparently a version of taking it easy I'm not familiar with."

Torin turned as Major Svensson stared past her at the approaching doctor. Given the apprehension on the major's face, a Marine she'd seen use his empty KC-7 as a club to hold back an advancing squad of Others until reinforcements arrived, she was almost prepared for Dr. Sloan's expression.

"I should stuff you back into a tank until you regenerate some common sense," the doctor snapped. "Electrode stimulation does not rebuild the kind of muscle strength that allows you to act like a damned fool." When he tried to stand, two fingers on his shoulder pushed him back down onto the bench. As they weren't in a situation where it mattered, Torin preferred to believe that he didn't resist the pressure, not that he couldn't. "Oh, no, you're not going anywhere until I see if you've done any damage."

"Crucible," the major began.

She cut him off, eyes locked on her slate. "We're not on Crucible now. Nor is it likely that you'll be out sculling and performing a repetitive series of multiple overexertions while on Crucible. I thought I made this perfectly clear right from the beginning that I'd only agree to this little adventure if you acted like a sentient species instead of a Marine."

Torin cleared her throat.

"Present company excepted, Gunnery Sergeant. All right . . ." Eyes narrowed, she held the major in an unbreakable stare Torin found impressive even peripherally. ". . . I am going to see Dr. Weer about putting you back under his scanner so that we can compare your condition yesterday to your condition now."

"I'm sweatier."

"We'll take that into account. Maintaining the tight hand grip required to hold on to an oar for extended periods of time puts the forearms at risk for overuse injuries, and as each stroke also involves twisting the oar parallel to the water with a wrist extension, you couldn't have possibly chosen a worse exercise."

"Or a better one to test the new arm." He waggled pale eyebrows in her general direction.

She didn't seem appeased. "You are going to sit here until your heart rate drops to under seventy-five beats per minute, and then you're going to report immediately to sick bay. Gunny, I assume you have his stats in your slate. You'll see that he stays put until seventy-five."

"I'm sorry, Doctor, but I don't take orders from you." That expectation needed to be dealt with now, before things got dangerous. Torin met the doctor's stare with one of her own.

After a long moment, Dr. Sloan sighed and nodded. "Fine. For the major's own good, would you please keep him here until his heart rate drops below seventy-five beats a minute."

"Yes, ma'am. As long as he doesn't order otherwise."

Major Svensson waved his left hand. "No, no, I'll be good." The nails looked a little darker than they had. Torin hoped he hadn't damaged himself—for a number of reasons, not the least being that she really didn't want to return to Ventris and another series of Silsviss briefings. "I did set the machine at a resistance five," he said after the doctor left. "Not too hard a pull nor too fast a stroke."

Back on Ventris, Dr. Sloan had mentioned memory lapses. Given that the doctor would no doubt mention them again when the major joined her in sick bay, Torin said only, "I've let maintenance know it needs to be looked at, sir."

For a moment, she thought he was going to ask if she believed him, but he decided to let her comment stand.

"That looks like fun." The major nodded at the Krai flipping back and forth among the ropes in the corner, changing the subject with all the finesse of heavy artillery. "Looks like one of those big cargo nets, doesn't it?"

It did. Odds were good it looked just like the net on the *Berganitan* that had caught Big Yellow's escape pod.

"Credit for your thoughts, Gunny. Seriously," he added when she turned her attention back to him. "You were looking angrier than the moment demanded."

Angry? She wasn't angry, she was . . .

Angry.

Angry about being lied to. Angry that there was nothing she could do about it.

And a little surprised about how angry she felt.

"If you want to talk about it." He waved a shaking hand. "I'm not doing anything at the moment but sweating."

She hadn't been under Major Svensson's direct command last time they'd fought together, and it was unlikely that after the next twenty days she'd ever be under his command again. They had very little personal history and, after two tendays on Crucible, likely no personal future. But for all that, they shared a remarkably similar past and looked forward to more of the same: combat and the Corps. She respected him as both a Marine and an officer. If he was willing to listen, then maybe she *should* talk.

Anger clouded judgment.

Clouded judgment got Marines killed.

There was no point in mentioning the escape pod; the major would have no reason to know about a piece of classified salvage he hadn't personally brought in. But then, it wasn't really about the escape pod anymore.

"Major, do you ever wonder if the Elder Races are screwing us over?" She was amazed by how conversational the question sounded, none of the anger leaking out.

Or maybe, given Major Svensson's expression, she was slightly delusional. "Us?"

"Human, di'Taykan, Krai." In the pause, one of the Krai in the far corner dropped about two meters from rope to rope, catching himself by his feet as his companions yelled insults. "Soon the Silsviss."

"Screwing us over how?"

"Manipulating data. Patronizing the *Younger* Races. Only telling us what they think we need to know." *Removing information they don't want us to have.* How paranoid was she to believe that making such a statement aloud was not a good idea? Rhetorical question.

"That's a bit more than a one-credit thought, Gunny."

"Yes, sir." The rote response helped her regain control of her voice.

He leaned forward, arms resting on his legs, water bottle dangling from one hand. "We, the Younger Races, have full representation in Parliament."

"Yes, sir."

"The Elder Races promised us the stars if we'd just channel our aggression at their enemies, and they've kept that promise."

"Yes, sir."

"However, it's interesting to note that not one of the diplomatic attempts to negotiate an end to this war have ever included a member of the three races actually fighting this war. Since hostilities started before we got involved—and my *we* equals your *us*—all we have is the Elder Races' word for it that they don't know why the Others are fighting."

Behind Torin's completely neutral expression, her thoughts charged this way and that, searching for a hard target. Suddenly, she felt a lot less personally paranoid.

Major Svensson smiled and stood. "At a certain point in the rebuilding process, they have to give your brain conscious control over parts of the process, so they wake you up. I had time to do a lot of thinking ... speculating. So, the answer to your question is, it's entirely possible. Unfortunately, there's no way we—where *we* still equals your *us*—can ever be sure what the Elder Races are up to, so since *we're* in it up to our eyeballs, we might as well just keep doing our jobs." Reaching a hand under his shirt, he rubbed at the sweat drying on his stomach. "Now, what's interesting to me is that you haven't been spending quality time at the chop shop with nothing to do but think and encourage cell division so something had to have prompted your question. Care to tell me what it was?"

"I'd rather not, sir. Not without proof."

"That anger's not going to distract you from doing your job?"

"No, sir."

"Because if there's a chance it may, you need to deal with it. And I mean deal, not just lock it away—that does no one any good."

He was right. Stirring things up couldn't put the Confederation any more at risk than the Elder Races already had. She straightened, not quite coming to attention. "Yes, sir."

"How's my heart rate?"

"Seventy-six, sir."

"Close enough. Let's go see if I'm still cleared to play silly buggers with the children."

"Northern Hemisphere Section 19 is temperate and currently two months into a four-to-five-month winter. The temperature will not vary much beyond five degrees below zero and five degrees above. As the environmental controls in our combat uniforms are good to five degrees lower and forty degrees higher, why are you now being issued with cold weather liners?" Staff Sergeant Beyhn scanned his platoon and sighed. "Go ahead, Kichar, before you rupture something."

"Sir, Marines must be able to fight without tech in case the *Others* take the tech out, sir!"

"You think we'll keep her," Major Svensson murmured as the sergeant began to go over the details of the cold weather gear with the recruits.

Torin finished adjusting the fit of the new liners in her boots and straightened. "Kichar? Not likely, sir. She'll do her tour, then she'll spend the rest of her life talking about how her time in the Corps was the best part of her life. She'll talk a lot about how people who didn't serve won't understand—which is true enough about some things but will have bugger all to do with most of what she'll be referencing. She'll join a veteran's organization and organize the shit out of it. Eventually, she'll run it."

The major grinned. "Seems harmless."

"Unless she's heading for officer's training, sir."

His grin broadened. "I've had second lieutenants just like her."

"Did they survive their second battle?"

He opened his mouth and closed it again while Torin piled hat and gloves on top of her folded bodyliner. Years in it had given her enough familiarity with the one-piece garment. She was able to pull gear for both herself and the major she knew would do, leaving only the bootliners to be fitted. It was one thing if a sleeve was a bit long and another thing entirely for footwear to go wrong. Marines were infantry. They used their feet.

Major Svensson stared thoughtfully into the crowd of half-dressed recruits. "Now I feel like we should hack Kichar's files and direct her away from officer training if that's where she's headed."

"She'll survive a lot longer if she's never in command," Torin agreed, glancing over at where the recruit in question—already in her combats while most of her platoon were still working out the seals in the body-liner—was reaching for her vest. Overachievers were only a pain in the ass until they became responsible for other lives. Then they became dangerous because they tended to demand those they led share their views. Sometimes, experience dulled down the shine a bit, and the Corps got its money's worth. More often, because at least they led from the front, they didn't last long.

Beyhn nodded once in approval at Kichar as he passed her—she did, after all, have the fastest gear-up time—and then continued moving among the recruits, touching a shoulder here, adjusting a seal there. He was touching a lot. That was usual for a di'Taykan, and Torin would have thought nothing of it except he seemed . . .

Fussy?

He was a lot more involved than his junior DIs, going so far as to wave Sergeant Jiir off in order to adjust a Krai bootliner himself when it would have made more sense to have Jiir do it. Torin made a mental note to make certain the Krai sergeant checked the fit later. They weren't her platoon, but they were Marines and Krai feet with their opposable toes required a specialist's touch.

Had the staff sergeant been so *involved* when she'd been training?

Actually, when she was in training, she'd been too damned intimidated to notice.

"All right." Beyhn moved back to one end of the VTA's troop compartment and touched the big screen. "The purpose of this exercise is to move from our drop point here to our pickup here." A second touch and the pickup point lit green. "We'll be covering 340 kilometers of mixed terrain—you're getting off easy because we'll be escorting a civilian. There are three villages en route; we may control them, we may not. During our stroll, systems representing the *Others* will be trying to stop us. We'll be trying to take them out. Simple really. Even you lot should be able to do it. This map is being loaded into your slates as I speak. I'd suggest you familiarize yourselves with it, but I shouldn't have to remind you of such basic survival prep by now, should I? Any questions?"

"Sir!" A short Human, so skinny he'd look like a mushroom with his helmet on, stepped out of the crowd. "Is it likely to snow while we're there, sir?"

"Do I look like a weather satellite, McGuinty? There's snow on the ground now, and it's winter; the chances are good it'll snow. You want to know more than that, check the data yourself."

"Sir! Will we be able to access the actual weather satellite from the planet, sir?"

"No, you will not be able to access any of the satellites from the planet. I will. Whether I'll bother is another question." Half a turn and he pointed at a di'Taykan near the back. "Yeah, Ayumi."

"Sir, do the di'Taykan have to wear the hats, sir?" A pale gray toque hung off one finger and her emerald-green hair drooped at the possibility of having to cram it on her head.

"No." Beyhn held up his own toque. "Because we're comfortable at lower temperatures than either the Humans or the Krai, we do not have to wear the hat; the helmet liner will be enough. However," he continued over a ragged cheer, "we do have to carry them. Just in case."

"Sir!" Pale pink hair flipped back and forth on a recruit towering over the Krai beside him. "In case of what, sir?"

"Who the hell knows; that's the point."

The staff sergeant *sounded* the way Torin remembered him.

"You will all be issued two FG3s, you're carrying the threes because they have longer det times and that lessens the chance of some idiot losing a hand. Scouts—and this position will rotate daily—will be carrying demo charges as well. And by the way . . ." His eyes narrowed and his hair, out from his head in a scarlet corona, stilled. ". . . you will be recruits moving across country in a scouting position, you will not be Scouts. If by some miracle any of you lot turn out to be among the bare sixty percent that makes it through the eighty-day Scout course, then you can call yourselves Scouts, not

before. Now . . ." His hair started moving again.
". . . since we're a little short on heavy gunners . . ."

Heavy gunners began their training after Basic. Vids
of Marines learning to use their shiny new exoskeletons
and destroying government property in a variety of
amusing ways invariably showed up in the SRM.

". . . the fourth member of every fireteam will be issued
with the KC-9." Beyhn reached behind his back and
pulled the weapon out of a locker, blind. It looked impressive, but Torin saw he'd positioned himself to make it
impossible to fail—it never hurt to give perceived om-
nipotence a hand. "You'll remember this from your time
on the range," he continued. "I know you've only fired a
few rounds, but if you're qualified on the seven, you can
fire this. Bigger and heavier than the KC-7, recruits who
carry it tend to have a shortened life expectancy in combat, so you'll be switching off daily. Some Marines like it
better than the 7; there's no accounting for taste."

"Sir, why do recruits who carry the KC-9 end up as
early casualties, sir?"

"Did you miss the part about it being bigger and
heavier, Piroj?"

"Sir, no, sir!"

"Does it come with augmentation?"

"Sir, no, sir!"

"Then you know the reason. And take your hat off."

Nose ridges flushed, Piroj reached up and pulled his
toque off.

Leaning close to her ear, Major Svensson pitched his
voice under Beyhn's. "Need to hear any more, Gunny?"

"No, sir. He's about to assign fireteams, and that
doesn't concern us."

Gathering up their gear, they left the VTA and
headed back toward their quarters. Barely six paces
from the hatch, the all clear sounded as the *NirWentry*
left Susumi space. The background mechanical hum
changed pitch slightly as the Susumi engines shut down.

"You think Staff Sergeant Beyhn decided to choose fireteams now in order to distract the children from the possibility of a Susumi equation gone wrong?"

Torin raised an eyebrow.

"Sorry, Gunny, stupid question. Dr. Sloan's gear settled?"

"Yes, sir. She's wearing Corps combats, but the rest is hers."

"More catalogs?"

"Apparently. And I wouldn't mind getting a look at a couple of them; her bodyliner is the next thing to an HE suit." According to the specs, with the plumbing connected, it would recycle waste indefinitely, maintain the wearer's body temperature at whatever was normal for any of five separate species, protect against most types of light-to-moderate radiation, play most entertainment files, and it came in fifteen colors, including two that looked gray to Human eyes. Dr. Sloan had gotten her hands on an impressive set of long underwear.

"You think someone is selling Corps tech to the general public?"

"No, sir, but I think the Corps might want to consider changing suppliers. She's got a sweet setup on."

The major made a noncommittal noise and asked. "Trainers or off the rack?"

"For the doctor, sir?"

"Well, I know I'm not wearing any goddamned trainers, Gunny and I've got a strong suspicion you're not either so, yes, for the doctor."

"Off the rack, sir, given her observer status. I was concerned the programming in the trainers might confuse the drones."

The recruits' combats—called trainers, although the official name was Extremity Targeting Garments, ETGs—contained microcircuitry that worked with the drones deployed, Crucible directing fire to where it would do the least damage. While Torin had nothing against the *less damage* part of their function, the *directing fire* bit was a deal breaker. The last thing she wanted was her own uniform directing the enemy's fire toward soft tissue damage. She'd wear her own combats and force the damned drones to aim just like everyone else who shot at her had to.

It seemed the major felt the same way.

The recruits might have as well had they been told.

"So the Doc knows we're boarding at 0630 tomorrow; that 71 got the first drop?"

"Yes, sir. She knows."

They walked a few paces farther.

"So, what's the name of the di'Taykan with the pale pink hair?"

"Di'Terada Sakur." Torin frowned up at him. Was this a recruit who'd come to the major instead of her with a problem? And was it the same problem Jonin thought he had? "Why, sir?"

Svennsson grinned. "I bet myself that the moment you knew which platoon we were dropping with, you'd learn who was who."

Not a problem; conversation. It was going to take a while to get used to that with an officer, but they were a little short of other people to talk to. "I could be wrong about the name."

"But you aren't."

"No, sir." He knew she was right because he knew the names as well as she did. "I bet myself you'd do the exact same thing."

"We really need some more people to gamble with."

Torin grinned, hearing the major voice essentially what she'd just been thinking. "No argument, sir. I owe myself fifty credits."

"Fifty? I only bet twenty on you."

"Gunnery Sergeant Kerr; there's nothing wrong with that piece of equipment in the larboard gym. Record says resistance was set to rise incrementally every rep. No upper limit."

Torin slid a few notes about Platoon 71 off the comm screen, enlarging the chief petty officer's image. "Thank you, Chief. Sorry to waste your time."

She shrugged. "Not a problem. Your major's probably in worse shape than he thought. Can't be easy coming back after being tanked so long."

"No, I don't imagine it is."

"He was the brain in the tank, wasn't he?"

"Yes, he was."

"Well, at least you know he's got one."

"I find that a great comfort, Chief."

With the comm screen dark, Torin drummed her fingers against the inert trim on the desk. Major Svensson had believed it when he told her he'd set the resistance at five, no rises. The Chief had no reason to lie to her. Therefore, the simplest explanation was that the major had set the machine incorrectly without noticing. The simplest explanation was usually the right one, but something about the situation suggested complications to Torin, the kind of complications that were likely to show up later and bite someone on the ass.

The major was right, though; rogue rowing machines weren't usually part of a Crucible scenario.

To Torin's surprise, Dr. Sloan was not only up and ready for her 0600 breakfast but unimpressed Torin had doubted her.

"Early hours are nothing in my profession, Gunnery Sergeant. People seldom need a doctor at convenient times."

"I am well aware of that, ma'am. Doctor."

"And your VTA is not significantly different, except in size, to the vehicles used by the Satellite Ambulance Corps on Derver."

"You're from Derver, Dr. Sloan?" She knew that of

course; she'd run source on the doctor before they left Ventris.

"You really suck at small talk, Gunny."

Torin swallowed the last of her coffee. "You're not the first to mention it, ma'am."

"Doctor."

"Right."

Just before she stepped onto the VTA, Torin downloaded a new, more detailed message to Craig into the packet's buffer. All messages would be streamed out as soon as the *NirWentry* exited Susumi space on her trip back to Ventris, returning with the 150s the VTA would be lifting off Crucible after dropping the 120s.

130s as of today, Torin corrected herself.

If the Elder Races were lying about the *Others*, about the .whys and wherefores of a war they'd created the Corps to fight, well, the major was right. There wasn't anything they could do about it. But if the Elder Races were wiping memories of Big Yellow's escape pod, then *that* she could do something about. In light of larger possibilities and what those might mean to the Corps, she couldn't let it lie.

They'd trained her to fight back.

The anger born of frustration left with the message. The anger born of betrayal, she locked down, ready to use when she needed it.

FIVE

MAJOR SVENSSON COULD HAVE SAT UP forward with the aircrew, but he chose to sit back in the troop compartment. Apparently oblivious to the covert attention he was attracting from the recruits, he stowed his pack, snapped his KC-7 onto the rack, and dropped down onto the seat with a grunt. Dr. Sloan shot a single, questioning glance toward the sixty-four faces all staring in her general direction, then took the seat to his right. After stowing her own gear and the doctor's, Torin took the next empty seat, approving of the major's choice.

"Strap in, people!" Staff Sergeant Beyhn's voice filled in all the empty places in the troop compartment. "Pay attention to what you're doing; if you screw up your webbing and go bouncing around during descent, not only will I be annoyed, Gunnery Sergeant Kerr will be annoyed. And you don't want her annoyed. I'm sure she'd be perfectly willing to hang your skull next to the other one she's got."

"This would be the Silsviss skull?" Dr. Sloan asked as Torin strapped her in.

"Yes, ma'am."

"I hope we have a chance to talk about the Silsviss over the next few days. It would be fascinating to discover the differences between them and the other reptilian species already a part of the Confederation."

"The biggest difference seems to be that the Silsviss shoot back." Out of the doctor's line of sight, Major Svensson grinned at Torin, well aware of how much she didn't want to talk about the big lizards.

With any luck, Crucible would give the doctor enough to think about. With the edge of her boot, Torin shuffled the other woman's left foot slightly to one side and slid the toe of the bright blue boot under the floor strap.

"Is that really necessary, Gunny?"

"Yes, ma'am. Doctor. It'll be a rough ride down."

"The pilot won't take it easy on the recruits?"

Torin secured the doctor's second boot and straightened. "The pilot will do everything he can to make them shit themselves."

"Oh."

"Yes, ma'am."

"Doctor."

"Right. This is your quick release." Reaching out with one finger, she tapped the gray plastic cylinder centered on the webbing that crossed the doctor's chest. "When Staff Sergeant Beyhn gives the order for Platoon 71 to snap-off, twist it hard to the left. Not now." Fingers around the doctor's wrist, Torin moved her hand away from the release. "If you snap-off before the order is given, you'll set off . . ."

The alarm was louder than Torin remembered.

". . . that," she finished as the echoes of the siren died down.

"Kichar! What the *sanLi* are you up to!"

"Sir, this recruit's release was resting a full three centimeters off center, sir!"

Torin couldn't see Beyhn's face, but she could almost hear him blink at that response. When he finally responded, it took a full sentence and a half before the disbelief left his voice.

"I will deal with you later, Kichar. Right now, strap back in and don't fukking move until I tell you to!"

"Sir, yes, sir!"

Hitting her seat at the same time as the senior DI, Torin was pleased to see that her ready light wasn't the last on.

"Release from NirWentry *in thirty seconds."*

Dr. Sloan's coat rustled as she shifted inside her webbing. Torin shared a glance with the major over her head and said, "You know you don't need the coat, Doctor. Between your bodyliner and the combats, you're ready for whatever this planet throws at you."

"I like my coat."

"Release in fifteen."

The doctor's knuckles whitened as she tightened her grip on her lower straps.

"I notice there's no corpsman dropping with us, Gunny."

Torin raised an eyebrow at the major. Corpsmen never went dirtside on Crucible. Part of the scenario was to test how much of the first aid training the recruits had absorbed—and in case they hadn't, all three DIs were qualified medics.

"Why would there be a corpsman?" Dr. Sloan snorted before Torin could answer. "I doubt there'll be anything a corpsman could handle that I can't. Or do you expect me to be taking readings off you 28/10?"

"I just thought . . ."

"No, you didn't."

"Release in five, four, three, two, one. Release."

The VTA shook as the clamps released with a sound like bolts tearing free, and they dropped away from the *NirWentry*, passengers in the troop compartment bouncing against their webbing.

"That was for effect, right?"

"Yes, ma'am."

She was shaken enough to let the honorific stand. "You don't think that's a little childish?"

"Just a little." Major Svensson sighed happily as they left the big destroyer's AG field and the zero gee kicked in. "But pilots on this rotation are glorified bus drivers; they're just trying to juice things up a bit."

"Childish," she repeated, slowly releasing her grip on the webbing. "So what happens if someone is seriously hurt after we land? Beyond what a medic—or I—can deal with? Dr. Weer discussed the *NirWentry*'s schedule with me, and his sick bay is gone eight days out of ten."

"There's a platform in low orbit," Torin told her at the major's nod. "It has a small VTA if we need an emergency dustoff."

"Doctors?"

"No, but six Navy corpmen and eleven Marines plus three full immersion tanks and a Susumi beacon able to punch a hole back to Ventris." The beacon took so much power it was single use only, but since it was a high-tech equivalent to an emergency flare, that didn't much matter.

"If you're going to puke," Staff Sergeant Beyhn announced, glaring around at the double row of recruits, "use the bags. That's what they're there for. And *if* you puke, don't think for one moment that your buddies will ever let you live it down."

Sakur leaned over Hisht and muttered, "If you're going to puke, Kichar, do it by the numbers."

"There's numbers for puking?" Hisht demanded, head turning from one to the other. "I never remember that!"

Kichar shot the di'Taykan a disdainful glare. "You're not funny."

"He makes a joke?"

"He *was* making a joke," Sakur corrected. "Your Federate still needs work, buddy. You should get Kichar to help you. Might give her extra ass kissing points with the DIs."

"But you say di'Taykan like ass kissing."

"Different kind of ass kissing. Are you trying not to smile, Kichar? You are." Sakur's eyes darkened to almost fuchsia as more light receptors opened. "I can see a muscle jumping in your jaw. You know, Marines are allowed to laugh; if we weren't, they'd have never let Hisht here join up."

"He is right," Hisht agreed. "I am here to be the light in your life."

"You are here to be a Marine," Kichar snapped as Sakur snickered and bumped Hisht's shoulder with his elbow.

The Krai stared up at her, eyes narrowed. "Are your underwears in a knot again?"

"Underwear. Singular. And no!" She shifted inside her webbing so that she was pointedly looking away from them—it was as much as she could do under the circumstances. Two tendays with the two of them in her fireteam would definitely test her resolve. From where she was strapped in, she could just see Gunnery Sergeant Kerr's profile, and she locked her gaze on it, vowing that no matter the provocation, she would be worthy.

With only one Marine to worry about, and he didn't need supervision at the moment, Torin turned her mind to the upcoming scenario. They had 340 kilometers to travel in twenty days which meant a minimum of seventeen k a day—a morning stroll under righteous conditions. Taking the terrain, the simulated attacks, and the fact she'd done this once already into account, she knew there'd be days when they traveled a lot farther and days when they went nowhere at all. Seventeen kilometers with a civilian could easily seem like a hundred, although the doctor's choice of treadmill program was reassuring.

"Now this is like an SAC drop," Dr. Sloan observed happily. "Smooth but fast."

"Atmo in five, four . . ."

The major snorted. "Hold that thought, Doc."

". . . two, one."

Torin had been through worse atmospheric buffering but not for a while. Either they were diving through one hell of a storm, or the pilot was going for a new dive to dirt record. "It helps if you keep your teeth together, ma'am. That way you don't bite off chunks of your tongue."

"Thank you, Gunny."

"Sergeants!" Staff Sergeant Beyhn managed to make himself heard over the rising ambient noise. "Have your squads sound off by fireteams!"

"What about *their* tongues?" Dr. Sloan demanded through clenched teeth.

"Their tongues belong to the Corps, ma'am."

The VTA rocked sideways. Hard.

"This is ridiculous!" Dr. Sloan's eyes were open painfully wide and there was a dark spot of color high on each cheek. "And unnecessary!"

"Could be worse, ma'am." Torin blocked a yawn. "We could be jumping in."

The doctor's head snapped around. "Jumping?"

"Three-minute freefall with a fifty k weight to make sure you fall fast enough to clear the VTA's AG field before it sucks you up. Not a problem if you're one of the last out, but all those weights dropping after the three count are a pain in the ass for the jumpers already on the dirt in the DZ."

Dr. Sloan stared at her like she was studying a new and unexpected life-form. "You have got to be kidding me."

"I don't think gunnery sergeants come with a sense of humor," the major pointed out.

"Officers jump first," Torin told the doctor solemnly.

"Pull the other one," she snorted but settled back in her webbing with a smile.

Torin accepted the major's silent *well done* with a nod. The story was essentially true although fifty k of fine particulate released onto the wind was more annoying than dangerous. Some officers jumped first, some anchored the line—it depended on their jump experience.

"Jonin!" Sergeant Jiir's voice rose above the din. "I said, sound off!"

"Sir!" The anonymous voice sounded impressed. "He's asleep, sir!"

"Are you sure he's asleep and not unconscious?"

"Sir, he's snoring, sir!"

"Well, wake him the hell up!"

What would be nerves of steel on a Human was probably no more than a di'Taykan using time with no sex to rest up for sex later. Regardless, Torin appreciated the recruit's ability to snooze in the midst of chaos. It was a skill all Marines needed to learn eventually, and it seemed like Jonin had it nailed. Apparently di'Taykan aristocrats developed interesting skill sets.

"Two to dirt. Temperature outside minus three degrees C."

"You heard the pilot!" Beyhn bellowed, slapping his helmet on. Helmets rose down the line of recruits as his platoon followed suit. "Check your environmental settings. On my release, 71 will retrieve packs and weapons. When that door opens, and I give the word, you will disembark in pattern 42Alpha. Major Svensson!"

"Staff Sergeant!"

There was a distinct snap in the major's voice, Torin noted with amusement. It seemed a good DI threw all ranks back to basic.

"Sir, you will disembark when landing site is called secure."

"Roger, Staff!" He reached into an upper vest pocket and pulled out a gray plastic wafer about a centimeter square. "Doc," he said, pressing it onto her forehead with the ball of his thumb, "this is for you. Don't worry about losing it; you'll need a special solvent to get it off. I want you tight to my left side," he continued as Dr. Sloan ran her fingers over the observer's chit. "As long as you can keep up, we'll leave you to move on your own."

"As long as I can . . . And if I can't?" she demanded.

In answer, he looked over her head. "Gunny?"

Torin tightened her chin strap. "Not a problem, sir."

"What?" Dr. Sloan's attention jerked back and forth between them. "She'll carry me?"

"She'll carry you."

"It *won't* be necessary."

He nodded. "Good. Gunny, you're on our six."

"Yes, sir."

The lights in the troop compartment flashed. *"Dirt-side. No enemy sighted!"*

"Release!"

Torin was on her feet and into her pack before Dr. Sloan got clear of her webbing.

"71, go! Go! Go!"

With the sound of thirty-plus pairs of boots slamming against the deck ringing in her ears, Torin hung her KC-7 around her neck, grabbed the doctor's shoulder, and turned her so that she was facing the major. With her other hand, she hauled her pack off the rack. "Give me your arms!"

Dr. Sloan thrust her arms back, and Torin slid the straps up them into the major's grip. He settled the pack and, still holding the straps, started moving the doctor toward the door.

"Secure!"

Torin hit the dirt on the doctor's heels, heard the door close behind her, and raced for the trees where the platoon had gone to ground. She was pleased to see that Dr. Sloan was right at the major's side as they passed the fireteams holding a defensive position at the edge of the woods. Safely inside the perimeter, the major stopped running and put out one hand to catch the doctor. Torin spun around in time to see the VTA scream out of sight. Her helmet scanner registered only empty landscape; she knew the scenario had no attack planned until the morning of day two but she kept her weapon up and ready until Staff Sergeant Behyn gave the all clear.

They'd landed in a field, open but for a few scrawny leafless trees, some clumps of thorn bush, and a scattering of small evergreens—half a dozen of them crushed by the weight of the VTA. Golden spears of dead grass stabbed up through the eight centimeters or so of hard snow, and the dark gray clouds over the trees to the south promised more snow to come.

From where she stood, in mixed deciduous forest 19.5 meters from the landing site, Torin's scanner put a similar forest 2.2 kilometers to the east, 233.7 meters to the south, and 167.2 meters to the west of the clearing.

"The pilot said the landing site was clear." Dr. Sloan slumped back against a tree, yanked off her toque, and used it to fan her face. "Why the mad dash for cover?"

"If they know we're incoming," Torin told her quietly, "the Others occasionally hide snipers under an electronic camouflage the scanners don't always penetrate."

"Don't always penetrate?" The doctor's brows rose. "But sometimes they do? So these snipers sit out here . . . there . . . and risk being spotted and killed from the air. Why would anyone do that?"

"Because sometimes it works." Confederation forces occasionally did the same thing. For the same reason. "About a third of all Crucible scenarios used to include an immediate attack upon landing, but Command deleted that from the programming about eight years ago. Too many VTAs were taking damage."

Dr. Sloan pulled off a mitten and touched her observer's chit. "Couldn't Crucible be programmed to miss the VTAs?"

"They weren't taking hits from Crucible, ma'am."

It didn't take her long to work it out. "Oh, wonderful," she sighed. "Here I am in the woods with a group of barely trained Marines who, precedent suggests, would be likely to shoot at their own transport if under attack. Tell me that my little bit of plastic will protect me from them, too."

"Sorry, ma'am. You're under the same danger from friendly fire as the rest of us."

"What's friendly about it?" she demanded pulling mitten and toque back on as she cooled down from the run.

"Not much," Torin admitted as the major rejoined them.

She stared at the major's combats, then at Torin's, then at the rest of the platoon. On board ship, they'd been mottled gray, urban camouflage; here they were white with pale shadows zigzagging across them. "Chameleon fabric?"

"Within certain very limited parameters, yes." Major Svensson grinned at her. "You stand out a bit, Doc."

"It doesn't matter," Torin explained hurriedly as the doctor sighed and began unfastening her bright blue coat. "The system only sees the chit, and it's best to give this lot as few opportunities for mistaken identity as possible."

"So this isn't why you mentioned my coat on the VTA?"

"No, ma'am. If I thought you'd be safer without it, I'd have said exactly that."

She zipped up and shot the major an exasperated look. "Forewarned, Major. I have laxatives with me and I will use them if you keep yanking my chain."

Squad One, Team One had been assigned the first scout position. When one/one gave the all clear, a kilometer northwest of the landing site, Staff Sergeant Beylin put the remainder of the platoon into a narrow diamond pattern, tucked his three extra personnel into the center, and gave the order to move out. Torin thought his warnings to be careful went just a little over the top, but on reflection she realized that perhaps she'd gotten too used to Marines who'd been blooded and who, in turn, had done some damage of their own.

The woods were quiet, the sounds of thirty-six Marines and one doctor almost completely muffled by the snow. In the summer, the underbrush would have dragged at feet and equipment, masking poor footing, but most of it had died back and what hadn't was leafless and easy to get through. The few evergreens were low and avoidable. The walking wasn't quite as easy as it would have been out in the open, but it was close. With scanners preset to Crucible's true north and 337 degrees keyed in, it was impossible to go off course; a minor deviation showed as a red line, anything more than five degrees sounded alarms. Late in the scenario, Torin knew the scanners would be taken out by a particularly nasty piece of programming used by the Others on Arim's Moon and reverse engineered by Corps R&D. The recruits would be dependent on the equipment between their ears instead of on their heads so, given that their heads were still cluttered up with the kind of preconceptions that would kill in a combat situation, Torin had every intention of enjoying the certainty of tech while she had it.

"Looks like we're about to run out of woods."

Kichar signaled for quiet and indicated they should remain in place while she went forward to have a look. Tucked behind the largest of the remaining trees, she peered out across a clearing her scanner marked as

827.3 meters and, also, completely empty. Scanners could be fooled. Carefully moving out into the transitional growth, she swept her gaze left to right, marking a disturbance in the snow at about twenty-two degrees, three meters east, and visually confirming her scanner's data.

No enemy in sight.

"All right . . ." Hours of practice alone on her bunk put her voice just over the edge of her PCU's ability to read. ". . . come on up."

The rest of her team approached a lot less quietly, but then, she'd told them it was safe.

"We're not going to get around that," Sakur noted, leaning out far enough to see that the clearing was actually an extended east west break in the trees. "We'll have to cross."

"Two by two, double-time; covered from the trees first on this side . . ." Hisht waved across the open ground. ". . . then from over there."

She nodded. "Last one sweeps the trail in case the Others have air support and do a flyover."

Sakur snorted. "That's a little paranoid."

"We're supposed to be paranoid."

"We gonna check out the tracks?" Lynne Bonninski, the fourth member of the team and currently carrying the KC-9, shifted her grip on her weapon. "Because I'd just as soon not double any farther than I had to."

"Hisht and I will detour to check them out on our cross. You and Sakur take the shortest points. Sakur, you . . ."

"Sweep, yeah, I got it. With what?"

"This." Nose ridges nearly shut in the cold air, Hisht reached down and snapped a branch off a sprawling evergreen.

"You didn't scan that, did you?" Kichar sighed. "You have no idea if it's poisonous."

"Isn't." Proving his point, Hisht shoved the collar of

his bodysuit down and bit the end off a branch. "Prickly, though," he added after chewing a couple of times.

"But you're handing it to a di'Taykan, not another Krai, and he's not wearing gloves under mittens."

"I've scanned, I'm good." Sakur snapped his slate back in place and took the branch. "But you'd better move before you have to ping group and tell Staff Sergeant Beyhn there's been a delay. You don't want him crawling up your butt."

Since she couldn't argue with that—the staff sergeant had been very clear about no contact unless the body of the platoon had to be warned about the route. "Hisht."

"I come."

Her stride longer, she reached the tracks seconds before Hisht and stared down at them, hoping for some kind of insight into the species who had made them. "They look like . . ."

"Cloven hooves," the Krai announced, catching up.

"Not Others, then. At least not Others we know."

"Not Others. Look." He pointed at a cleared bit of earth. "There they scrape the snow away to get at grass. Grass eaters. *Chrick*."

"What don't you consider edible?" Kichar wondered as they started moving again.

"Rocks. Most rocks," he amended thoughtfully as they reached the trees.

"Of course," Bonninski muttered a few moments later, "we had to follow your tracks, or the mad sweeper here couldn't delete them, could he?"

Kichar felt her cheeks flush. "I never . . ."

"Nice to know all those times the Staff gave me cleanup duties paid off," Sakur declared as he backed under cover and tossed the branch away. "I have completely obliterated any chance of us being identified by our footprints. What?" He looked from Human to Human, then grinned. "Ah, Bonbon mentioned your fuk-up. Good on you. You need more of them."

"Fuk-ups can get Marines killed," Kichar growled. "Tag and let's move out." She didn't bother waiting to make sure he'd thumbed the marker onto one of the trees at the edge of the clearing. Sakur might be an annoying pain in the ass, but he did his job—which was more than could be said for her right now. *Stupid. Stupid. Stupid.* Gunnery Sergeant Kerr would have never missed anything so obvious. She'd just have to try harder.

After checking for the scouts' tag, the bulk of the platoon double-timed across the clearing in four lines, recruits of three/three sweeping away identifiable footprints. If the Others did happen to stumble over their tracks, they'd have no way of knowing how many Marines were dirtside. The scenario knew exactly how many, of course—not only were they under constant satellite surveillance but their stats had been programmed into the sector so that any injuries severe enough to set off a med-alert would immediately ping the OP.

Setting the recruits to sweeping, therefore, had no intrinsic use particularly since in this part of the scenario Crucible had no air support. The ability to keep this kind of information to themselves more than anything convinced Torin she'd never make it as a DI—she'd have the whole platoon moving slick and sloppy, trying to throw the system off by getting them to an unexpected camp and then, in case that didn't work, setting up an ambush for the scenario's attack. Winning quickly and decisively meant fewer casualties.

"What is that?"

Torin followed the doctor's pointing finger and, pulling off her mitten, scooped a dark brown pellet about a centimeter in diameter out of a small pile. "Herbivore shit," she said, squashing it between thumb and forefinger as she walked. "Not that old either. It wasn't quite frozen through."

"You're a woman of many talents, Gunny."

"I grew up on a farm. You shovel enough shit, you remember things about it." She tossed it away, rubbed her fingers on her leg and frowned as once again a mitten rose to rub against the chit on Dr. Sloan's forehead. "Is that bothering you?"

"No. Yes. It's just a little obvious."

"It's supposed to be," Major Svensson interjected from her other side. "It's to keep you from getting shot. It can be read from under your clothing, but I'd rather not take the chance that the signal might be blocked."

"And I appreciate that."

But Torin noticed she continued to rub at it every now and then.

After an hour and forty minutes of walking, they caught up to the scout team at the east end of a narrow lake where they already had a hole through the ice and their spare canteens filled. After confirming their new azimuth with Staff Sergeant Beyhn, they started out again while the rest of the platoon dropped packs and topped up their water supplies.

"Are you sure this is safe?" Dr. Sloan asked, sliding her backpack down her arms and arching her back. "There are alien microbes in that water, after all."

"Any microbe that can survive the purifying process inside our canteens deserves to have a chance at the inside of a Marine."

"These canteens can take pretty much any liquid with more hydrogen than oxygen in it and turn it into water," Torin explained, tightening the lid as Dr. Sloan shot the major an exasperated look. "It's the same tech as in our HE suits, so purifying actual water is fairly rudimentary."

"Still, if we need water, we're surrounded by snow. Wouldn't that be cleaner?"

"Takes energy to turn snow to water," Major Svensson told her as they walked off the lake. "We'll use it if we have to, but . . ."

Torin missed everything after the *but* as she headed over to Staff Sergeant Beyhn. Standing where he could see the lake and both trails, his cheeks were flushed a deep red and, based on the flicker of water vapor by his face, he was breathing heavily. When she got close enough, she saw that the ends of his hair were in constant motion under the edge of his helmet. Trouble was, they weren't moving in unison.

When di'Taykan hair grew that agitated, the di'Taykan in question was laboring under some strong emotion.

She considered and discarded a number of tactful ways to find out what she needed to know and finally figured, screw it; they had thirty-six recruits humping packs across a frozen landscape assuming every moment they were going to come under fire. This was no time for good manners.

"You okay? You look like shit."

"This is my last group." He turned pale eyes on her, glare off the snow shutting down most of his light receptors. "My last set of recruits. Once I get them through, once I know they're safe, I can go home."

Ah. "You're going to retire?"

She couldn't read his expression. "It's time."

"You're not sick?"

"Me?" His posture changed subtly, any softness, any uncertainty disappearing. "I have never felt better, Gunny, and I plan to run your major's ass ragged from here to the pickup point."

"Glad to hear it, Staff. He needs the workout. Oh, and . . ." She shifted her weight as she recognized her body's reaction. ". . . you might want to turn up your masker. Even at this temperature, you're a little potent."

Hand to his throat, he flashed a strangely triumphant grin and strode toward the ice. "Back in position, 71! We're not gathered here for *Mon gleen*; get ready to move out!"

Feeling the pinprick of someone's regard between her shoulder blades, Torin pivoted on one heel and caught Jonin's gaze before he looked away. A gesture held him in place and, after a quick glance to ensure the staff sergeant was still out on the ice, she walked quickly to his side.

"What's wrong with him?"

"You're not a di'Taykan, Gunnery Sergeant."

"Tell me something I don't know, Recruit. What's up with the staff sergeant?"

"I'm very sorry, but I'm not able to tell you."

He looked miserable but not as miserable as he was going to look if he kept crucial information from her. "Why not?"

"Because the information concerns the di'Taykan as a people, not the Corps. If I told you, and the other di'Taykan in the platoon discovered that I had acted in such a culturally insensitive manner, then they would . . ." He sighed. "Actually, they *wouldn't*."

"Wouldn't?" Torin felt both her brows rise in unfeigned astonishment. If di'Taykan didn't bother defining a physical activity, they could only be referring to one thing. If Jonin discussed the staff sergeant's problem, they *wouldn't*? Critical injuries barely stopped the di'Taykan. This was big. "If it affects the Corps, Recruit, it's no longer a di'Taykan matter."

"I'm aware of that, Gunnery Sergeant Kerr. If it becomes a Corps matter, I promise I'll come to you. I should never have said anything on the ship."

"Too late now."

Jonin shrugged, the gesture elegantly saying in spite of combats and pack: *We all make mistakes.*

Torin watched him a moment longer and was impressed in spite of herself by the way he met her eyes. "Go on," she said at last, jerking her chin toward the rest of the platoon, "your fireteam's forming up." As he doubled across the snow, she wondered if the other di'Taykan in the platoon had given him trouble after he'd come to her. Probably not. In the Taykan class system, di'Arl Jonin, with a three-letter family name, socially outranked the rest and since that wasn't a reaction that ever completely vanished, even from Marines with significantly more experience, these recruits would be unlikely to buck the system.

She didn't like not knowing what was going on—and she was damned sure Beyhn's impending retirement was not the whole story—but there was nothing she could do to force the issue. No point in informing Major Svensson until she had intell a little more concrete than *it's a di'Taykan thing.*

Three hours of easy humping later—low ground was significantly easier to cross when it was frozen solid—they caught up with the scout team and broke for lunch to the south of a small woods. With good lines of sight in the other three directions, they set only aerial pins in case of an enemy flyby.

Dr. Sloan watched with interest as Torin expanded the sides of a ration pouch, poured in a little water, snapped the heating filament, and peeled the flap back to expose a thick chicken stew with three large dumplings. "This isn't bad," she murmured chewing thoughtfully. "Your packaging must be quite complex to reconstitute with this much flavor."

"Yes, ma'am." Seemed like the safe answer. The packaging wasn't Torin's concern unless it stopped working.

The piece of meat on the doctor's spork steamed in the cold air. "Can I assume this has never been anywhere near an actual chicken?"

"Would that be a problem?"

"No, just a surprise. The civilian equivalent is a little tastier, but as it contains the liquids already, it's also a bit heavier."

Torin shrugged and scooped up a bit of gravy. "*A bit* weighs up when you've got other gear to carry."

"I'm sure. You know, you could get all your nutritional and energy requirements from a capsule which would be even lighter to carry."

"We're carrying those, too, ma'am, and emergency ration packs, and the scenario has us using both before we're done, but research has shown that Marines like to eat." Out of the corner of her eye she spotted the two Krai recruits taking turns to sample bits of the local flora. They'd sample the fauna, too, if they could get their hands on it. Sergeant Jiir, sitting with the other DIs, was stirring his coffee with a stick and morosely biting the end off it every now and then. He'd likely be less morose if he'd been allowed *sah*, the Krai stimulant of choice, but given its highly illegal effect on the Human nervous system, the Corps no longer permitted it in uncontrolled environments.

"All right, people, let's haul ass. Sunset's at 17:41 and we've got twenty-three k to go." Staff Sergeant Beyhn got to his feet and the platoon followed. "Two/one, you're scouting this afternoon. Do you know where we're supposed to end up?"

"Sir, yes, sir!"

It was a ragged but confident response from the four recruits in the fireteam.

"You sure?" His hair whipped back and forth over his ears so quickly it looked like a fan-shaped wave. Torin noticed that none of the di'Taykan were looking directly at him. "I don't want you getting lost out there."

"Sir, we're sure, sir." Piroj, the Krai who'd been so fond of the issued toque, seemed to be team leader.

"Move out, then, but be careful. We don't want to lose you. The enemy knows we're here, so proceed accordingly."

"Sir, yes, sir!"

As two/one checked their azimuth and moved out, the rest of the platoon gathered up the garbage and dropped it into a bag held by Sergeant Kim Annatahwee.

"Does she carry the trash the rest of the way?" Doctor Sloan asked just as the sergeant activated the molecular charge and the bag flattened. "Never mind."

"It's a variation on our body bags," the major told her. "Only slightly less respectful," he added as the sergeant shook the fine dust out onto the breeze. "We carry our Marines back with us."

Torin touched the part of her vest designed to hold the metal capsules in individual pockets and said a short prayer to whatever gods looked out for the Corps that, this trip, those pockets would stay empty.

Twenty-three kilometers in four hours and forty-one minutes meant an average speed of just over their standard hump speed of 4.8 kilometers an hour. Not exactly a sprint but still intended to cover some ground. On relatively flat terrain—which their maps indicated this would be—and with no interest from the enemy—which everyone but the platoon and Dr. Sloan knew wouldn't happen until morning—it was an easy enough speed to manage. The plan was to cover the maximum distance possible on the first day to take the edge off the recruits and to make up for days later in the scenario when they'd be pinned down.

Major Svensson had decided to keep the doctor in the dark about the scenario for a couple of reasons. The first because he wasn't one hundred percent positive she wouldn't let anything slip to the platoon and the second because he had a truly warped sense of humor. The second reason was Torin's, but she suspected the major would happily agree with it as he seemed to be enjoying the way the doctor peered suspiciously at every shadow.

Camp that night was just across the narrow isthmus that connected the peninsula they'd been crossing to the mainland—the geography enough of an explanation to the recruits for the distance covered. The scout team had located a hummock of higher ground back from the water and set perimeter pins. It was the logical place to make camp for the night—it was high enough to be defensible, clear enough to have good lines of sight but with enough cover to shield the platoon from the air. Because it was the logical place to make camp, it was where the enemy would mount their first attack.

The di'Taykan sealed their shelter halves together to create one large, albeit low, communal quarters. Most of the rest stayed in fireteam combinations—although the two teams that had each lost two di'Taykan got together. Because they were a unit within a unit, Major Svensson suggested that the three of them combine halves to increase body heat. Torin was fine with that—recruits dumped most body issues by about day two or they didn't last to day three, so hers had been gone for some time now—but she was unsure about the doctor's response.

Dr. Sloan snorted. "I'm molecularly familiar with the major's body, Gunny, but isn't that fabric heated? I could have ordered a single shelter that would maintain seventeen degrees C indefinitely."

"They're heated," Torin told her, snapping the three pieces of smart fabric together and activating the seal. "But they're also so well insulated that body heat will keep them comfortable with less risk of the enemy picking up the energy output." The fabric had been designed to prevent thermal imaging; with no power running, they were almost invisible to enemy scans. She stepped back, keyed a color code into her slate, and nodded as the shelter blended almost perfectly with the surrounding snow.

"Remember where it is," Major Svensson warned. "The children should be tired from their nice long walk, but they'll still be jumpy and they're armed and you don't want to crawl into the wrong tent."

"Key your slate to recognize this location and to vibrate when you get close," Torin said as the doctor stared around at the nine nearly identical mounds, growing even harder to see as the sun set.

The tenth mound, the di'Taykan shelter, cycled through a few vibrant colors before Staff Sergeant Beyhn growled something they were too far away to hear and the fabric blended like the rest.

"Interesting that the staff sergeant seems to be sleeping alone."

Torin frowned as she watched Beyhn set up a single shelter. "He's a DI, sir; they're recruits." But it sounded like a question even to her own ears.

"When has rank ever mattered to a di'Taykan, Gunny? Where'd he sleep when you were here?"

"Communally."

"I think I'm going to go have a word with him."

She watched him walk away, then she watched him walk back. "He didn't quite tell you to mind your own *ninLi* business?"

"Got it in one, Gunny." The major frowned down at a loose thread on the cuff of his mitten. "So, what do you suggest we do?"

"Watch and wait, sir. So far, whatever it is isn't affecting the Corps. When it does, we'll deal with it."

"And if it's something you can't deal with?"

Torin stopped watching the staff sergeant long enough to lift an eyebrow in the major's direction.

Grinning, he spread his hands. "Sorry. Spoke without thinking."

That night, Torin woke as the major skimmed out of his sleeping bag and left the tent. He was gone for a little over an hour. She lay there, listening to the doctor sleep, and watching the seconds tick by on her sleeve until 0147 read 0251. He was gone long enough that her concern had begun to outweigh the certain knowledge he wouldn't want her going after him. Seconds from deciding she didn't give a good Goddamn what he wanted, he returned.

He shimmied back into his bag, sighed, and said quietly, "Still awake, Gunny?"

"Yes, sir."

"Well, if you're that concerned about my bowels, you should talk them over with the doctor in the morning. Right now, get some sleep."

"Yes, sir."

Since the first attack against Platoon 71 would happen in just over three hours, that seemed like a good idea.

SIX

SUNRISE WASN'T UNTIL 0709, but when Torin left the shelter at 0600, the predawn light, helped out by a minimal overnight freshening of the snow cover, provided sufficient illumination for personal hygiene and breakfast. Except for the self-heating pouch, oatmeal hadn't changed in millennia. Torin liked the connection to the past, liked the thought that Humanity had gotten some things right long before that first Confederation ship had shown up and made their offer of advancement for aggression.

Pouch of coffee held temporarily in her teeth, she pulled one for the major as he emerged looking bleary-eyed and slightly cranky and pulled another for the doctor a few moments later—pleased to see that they'd both snapped their bedrolls back to carry configuration. While they ate, she dealt with the shelter.

"Kids are doing a nice fast job of breaking down," Major Svensson observed, crushing his empty coffee pouch in one hand.

Dr. Sloan's gaze swept the camp, lingering in a professional way on each recruit. "They look tired."

"Tired?" The major snorted. "Not likely, Doc, it's only day two—their depilatories haven't even started to wear off. By day twenty they'll be scruffy and red-eyed and bruised and bleeding and crazy with exhaustion."

She raised a disdainful brow in his direction. "And that's a good thing?"

"That's when they start feeling like Marines."

She snorted. "And my question stands."

He grinned and turned his attention back to Torin. "Beyhn's got them hopping this morning."

"Actually, sir, I haven't seen Staff Sergeant Beyhn this morning." As she handed him his folded shelter half, she scanned the camp. The di'Taykan communal shelter had been broken down into sixteen packs, slightly darker rectangles of packed snow marked where the fireteams' shelters had been, and Sergeants Jiir and Annatahwee were both moving around the platoon. The new snow made it difficult to see the few larger shelters still up; had she not known where it was, the staff sergeant's small one would have been essentially invisible. "I don't think he's out yet."

"Giving his juniors a bit of a run?"

"That's possible, sir."

Neither of them believed it. Major's Svensson's tone made his opinion clear and, from the way the junior DIs kept glancing at their senior's shelter, Torin could see they were growing concerned. Before she could suggest she check things out, Jonin left a clump of di'Taykan and approached Beyhn's shelter. They watched while he dropped to one knee and leaned in toward the entrance.

"Can you hear what he's saying, Gunny?"

"No, sir." She could see his mouth forming words, but the angle was too tight for her to make any of them out.

"Hair's really moving."

"Yes, sir."

Hair still moving, Jonin stood and backed up, giving Staff Sergeant Beyhn enough room to emerge and rise to his feet. His own hair perfectly still, he pulled the recruit into a quick hug—not unusual for di'Taykan although less usual for drill instructors—and then set about packing up his shelter. Jonin stood where he was for a moment, his hair only marginally less agitated, then rejoined his fireteam.

"The question becomes, Gunny, how much do we interfere?"

Torin glanced down at her sleeve: 0708. "No time to interfere right now, sir."

Major Svensson grinned at her. "Oh, come on, you've got a whole minute. Loads of time to straighten this lot out. A senior NCO should be able to win the war in that much time."

"Thirty seconds less now, sir."

"Thirty seconds might be pushing it. Dr. Sloan?" When she glanced up from her slate, he waved at the chit on her forehead. "Just checking."

0709. The sun rose.

All hell did not break out.

"Any chance we read that wrong, Gunny?"

"No, sir. First attack was to occur this morning at sunrise, catching the recruits as they prepared to move out." She nodded to where Staff Sergeant Beyhn and his two junior DIs had their heads together. "I'd say they're also wondering what's going on."

"System failure or program glitch?"

"Second is more likely, sir."

"Why don't you . . ."

"See what the staff sergeant has to say? Yes, sir." As she walked away, she heard Dr. Sloan move up to take her place.

"You're molecularly active this morning, Major."

If the major had a reaction to this information on a macro level, Torin didn't catch it. Beyhn met her halfway, his hands spread.

"I am as confused as you are, Gunnery Sergeant Kerr, although I'm not disappointed to have the first attack postponed. It'll give this lot a chance to calm down a bit more before loud noises and bright lights gets them all geared up again."

Since the recruits knew attacks were inevitable, Torin couldn't see how waiting for the other boot to drop would calm anyone. As she remembered it, once the first skirmish with Crucible was over, Platoon 29 had settled down to the business of being Marines. Still, Beyhn knew Platoon 71 better than she did, so she'd take his word for it. "System failure or program glitch?" she asked, echoing the major's question to her.

"Program glitch," he snorted. "I told the lieutenant on the platform that the cold's likely messing with the node. They'll try and work it out on their end. I'm impressed with how that civilian of yours is keeping up," he continued. "Still, real test's how she acts when the shooting starts. Keep an eye on her." Then he nodded, spun on one heel, and headed back into the middle of the camp, yelling, "Two/one! You're scouting this morning! What's your azimuth?"

"Sir! 307 degrees for two kilometers, then 281, sir!"

"Well, what are you doing still standing here? Haul ass!"

"Sir, yes, sir!"

Making her way through the churned up snow back to Major Svensson and Dr. Sloan, Torin checked her sleeve. The temperature was holding steady at minus seven degrees; cold enough for Humans, miserable for the Krai, but not even close to a temperature that should bother a di'Taykan. She wondered why, in that case, Staff Sergeant Beyhn had mentioned only the cold as a possible reason for messing up the scenario.

And why he'd spent the night alone.

And why he'd been so slow to rise this morning.

And whether or not he was capable of reprogramming the node that was a mere 3.5 kilometers east along the shore of the bay. Given that he was the only one on Crucible who currently held the codes.

Maybe it's time I took some of that accumulated leave. Thanks to the Elder Races and Big Yellow, I'm starting to see conspiracies everywhere I look. But she couldn't shake the thought loose, and as they formed up to hit the trail, she kept at least part of her attention on Staff Sergeant Beyhn.

"Oh for fuk's sake, Lirit, what's the delay now?"

"I'm caught on a bush!" Tossing her helmet clear of the thick underbrush, impressively clingy in spite of the lack of foliage, Lirit jerked the KC-9 free and used the butt end to try and pummel her way free. "Why is it always me?"

"You're carrying a bulkier weapon than you're used to," McGuinty suggested, dropping down onto a fallen log and pulling a stim stick out of a vest pocket. Technically, they weren't illegal; vacuum jockeys practically lived on them, but that didn't mean he had any intention of allowing the DIs to see him indulging.

Pushing her own helmet to the back of her head, allowing the front half of her hair to spread out in an emerald-green fringe, Ayumi snorted. "Nine extra kilos. That shouldn't be a problem."

"It's not the weight." Lirit made a diagonal move into what looked like less dense growth. "Not just the weight," she amended, jerking it free again. "The magazine sticks out at a weird angle, and the scope won't stay locked down."

"That's not good about the scope." McGuinty chewed thoughtfully. "Should mention it to Staff Sergeant Beyhn when we meet up at noon."

In spite of Lirit's thrashing, the silence in the clearing got louder.

"Opens up, up ahead." Piroj tucked his slate back in his vest as he rejoined the fireteam a few moments later. "You get free here and it should be easy going for a while. Still no sign of the enemy." His nose ridges flared, the expression barely visible between toque and the raised collar of his bodyliner. His gaze skittered over the two di'Taykan and landed on the Human. "What?"

McGuinty swallowed. "I mentioned Staff Sergeant Beyhn." The di'Taykan had gotten progressively weirder about the senior DI over the last couple of tendays. The moment they'd hit Crucible, the weirdness had intensified.

"What the fuk is wrong with you guys? It's like he's suddenly gone all *revenk* and you lot are busily ignoring it."

"*Revenk*?" Ayumi wondered.

"Inedible."

"So, anything inorganic is *revenk*?" She had her slate out.

"Yeah, and stop trying to change the fukking subject. What's up with Beyhn?"

"Hey, instead of worrying about the staff sergeant, worry about me!"

"Oh, for *yinahay*'s sake, Lirit, it's just bushes! We all got through it, and Piroj couldn't even see over it." Ayumi lined up with Lirit's bright yellow head and began forcing the interlaced branches out of the way. "If they were shooting at us, you'd be totally baked!"

Lirit glared at the other di'Taykan. "Good thing they're not, then, isn't it. And I'm actually half a meter to your right. You're working at the thickest part!"

"You know, I think they want us to drop it," McGuinty said thoughtfully. He tucked the rest of the stim stick away and stood. "So, let's talk about how much their woodcraft sucks. And I'm station-born, so if I'm saying it sucks, it truly does."

Piroj pulled out his knife—one of the personal possessions he'd brought along—and flicked it open. "Ayumi, move. This is taking too fukking long; rest of the platoon'll be up our ass in a minute."

McGuinty frowned as Ayumi moved away without either argument or innuendo. The latter proved, more than anything, that the di'Taykan were dangerously distracted. It was getting to where he might actually need to have a few words with Sergeant Annatahwee over lunch—Human to Human. He hated to do it, though; talking behind the di'Taykan's backs seemed uncomfortably close to being a snitch.

He couldn't decide whether he admired the efficient way Piroj hacked Lirit free or if he was appalled by the destruction of habitat—knew he couldn't have done it, though. No station-born could. Real actual growing things were treated with all the reverence an oxygen producing system deserved and to take a knife to one . . .

For half a second he thought the explosions in the distance were the sound of station security charging through the decom doors and about to come down on them with both feet, then his brain caught up with the here and now.

"Incoming!"

"No, it's behind us!"

Lirit charged through the remaining bushes and whirled to stare back along her path. "The platoon!"

"But they're following us and there was nothing!"

"We *saw* nothing."

"That fukking sounds like something!"

"You need to contact . . ." Ayumi began, but Piroj cut her off hard.

"No! That'll give our position away. Platoon's walked into an ambush—enemy knows how far ahead scouts work, they think we're out of the picture. Lirit's kept us close enough we can haul ass back there and ambush the ambush. Scanners down, team. Let's haul ass."

Torin dropped to one knee and raised her weapon as a round blew through the eight centimeters of snow and still had enough left to kick up a spray of frozen earth. Angle said the shooter was in the trees. The only tree close enough to give that kind of cover was a huge evergreen at about forty degrees, so she fired five quick shots into the branches 3.5 meters off the ground. She could hear the DIs yelling orders, could hear the staccato slam of weapons fire, could hear branches and small trees blowing apart, but all she could see was the way those branches moved when shot, exposing the edges of a familiar energy signal to her scanner. Three more rounds and a blaze of red light as the drone tumbled out of the tree and slammed into the snow.

Three answering rounds from farther out on the right tumbled her back into the hollow where the major lay, half over Dr. Sloan.

"Right in the middle of our fukking formation!"

"Yes, sir! Good thing there was only the one . . ." A half rotted log exploded right by her face. Spitting out a bit of frozen fungus, she surged back up onto her knee and snapped off half a dozen shots. The second drone fell, surrounded by a shower of evergreen boughs. ". . . tree," she finished dropping down again.

"Might be more than two drones."

"That's why I'm still down here, sir. Doesn't look like it, though."

"If you can see them in your scanners, why didn't you shoot them first?" the doctor demanded, using elbows and knees to dig a little deeper down into the hollow.

"They took us by surprise, ma'am. That's the whole point behind an ambush."

"Why didn't your scouts see them?"

"This is just a guess, Doc, but I'd say they were hidden." The major rolled over onto his back. "Looks like you got them, Gunny. Left or right?"

"Right, sir."

"Do it!"

As they started to move, surprisingly strong hands locked around Torin's ankle and the major's wrist. "Just where," Dr. Sloan demanded, "do you two think you're going?"

Torin yanked her ankle free. "We're under attack, ma'am."

"Really?" She had to shout to be heard. "That explains all the noise."

"We're being attacked from both sides of the march," Major Svennson explained, signaling for Torin to stay put for the moment. "We three are in the middle of the march. The gunny and I can't fire from here because there are Marines between us and the enemy."

"And that's about you; what about me?"

"You're chipped. You're safe."

"Then wouldn't you be safer with me?"

"We'd be safer behind you, but it doesn't work that way, ma'am. We need to be part of this fight."

The doctor waved a hand toward the evergreen. "What were you just doing then? Never mind," she snapped before Torin could answer. "In this scenario of yours, you're protecting me, so if you want to keep to the scenario, you should stay here."

"Yes, ma'am, but this attack is off the scenario, so we need to be where we can do the most good and that's with the recruits."

"Off the scenario!"

When Torin rolled her eyes, the major waved her on. "You go. I'll explain."

"Yes, sir!"

The ambush had pinned the platoon in an area of second growth—probably growing up after having been shot to shit in a scenario some years earlier. They had very little cover and were, for the most part, attempting to become one with the ground, hoping their combats would make them look like just another mound of snow.

A well-armed mound of snow, Torin amended as she crawled toward the line on the right. She paused as the trunk of a sapling about three centimeters in diameter exploded beside her, splinters thudding into her pack like hail, the top of the tree blown back and hung up somewhere behind her. Okay. That wasn't good. The drones were programmed to keep from creating potentially deadly shrapnel near the recruits, but as she wasn't in trainers, she was apparently fair game. A quick scramble on elbows and knees brought her up to the fallen log Kichar and her fireteam were using to extend their cover and in under the protection of the recruits' combats.

About three meters away on the other side of the log, the underbrush got thicker and the trees got distinctly bigger.

A splash of red pooled around Lynne Bonninski's right calf. The drones fired nonlethal rounds but the meaty part of exposed extremities was considered fair game.

"Bonninski?"

"Just a crease Gunnery Sergeant! Hurts, but I'm fine."

"Good." The seal sprayed over the wound looked like it was holding, but she leaned forward and checked the readout on the recruit's sleeve. In the adrenaline rush of battle everyone underestimated wounds, and Torin had no intention of having anyone bleed out. Bonninski's combats agreed with her assessment of the injury, so Torin settled for tossing a double handful of snow over the red.

"Too visible," she explained when the recruit turned to look. "Blood on snow can give your position away."

A fist-sized chunk exploded out of the top of the log.

"I think they know where we are, Gunnery Sergeant!" Sakur yelled as the fireteam ducked.

"The time to duck," Torin snapped, "is before the hit, not after. *After* you shoot back along their trajectory before they have a chance to take cover. You!"

Hisht jerked, chin coming up out of the collar of his bodyliner.

"Load up your impact boomers!"

His hands responded before his brain did. He snapped the standard magazine out of the KC-9 and snapped the impact boomers in.

"On my three, we're going to lay down covering fire and you're going to blow the biggest tree you can see to hell and gone."

About to raise his weapon, Hisht froze. "I . . ." Nose ridges flared open as far as they'd go, he began to shake.

"Gunnery Sergeant Kerr, he can't . . ."

Torin shot Kichar a look that stopped the words cold. "Hisht!" She locked eyes with him, fully aware that, to the rural Krai, trees were home and food and safety and to destroy a living tree was one small step away from murder. Hisht was in the Corps now. "I guarantee there's something hiding behind that tree trying to kill your team! You hesitate, they're dead!" Reaching out, she turned his face toward the older growth forest. "Sakur, Kichar, aim high. On my three!

"One!

"Two!

"Three!"

Drones were programmed with the same instincts of self-preservation nonmechanical soldiers exhibited. Most living things wanted to stay that way, regardless of species. Blanketing fire from four KC-7s kept the drones down long enough for Hisht to aim and fire.

A glint of metal in the flying debris. Four shots and a sudden blaze of red light. Torin had no idea which of them had actually hit the drone, nor did she care.

"How did you know?" gasped Bonninski as they dropped back behind the log.

"If you can't see the enemy, you shoot at what you can see—the shit they're using for cover. Where would you have been if you'd been on that side shooting at us?"

"Behind that tree?"

"Is that a question?"

"No, Gunnery Ser . . ."

The grenade hit the snow by Kichar's boot with an ominous thud.

Torin ripped the grenade shield off her vest, scooped up the explosive, and flipped it back at enemy lines. "Down!"

It blew back behind the enemy position.

When she lifted her head, ears ringing, all four recruits were staring at her. "Never do that," she snapped, reattaching the shield to her vest. Instinct had kicked in before brain cells. "You slap your shield on the grenade, hit the anchors, and pile whatever's handy and inanimate on top. You pick it up, it could blow in your face. If I'd thrown it too close to a tree, a splinter in under the edge of your helmet would kill you too dead to tank."

"But that grenade was thrown from close in, so you knew you had more time because it had spent less time in the air. And a shield is only good once; it won't take a second cover, so using it like you did saves it for later when you might not have the opportunity of a return throw. Also, if their own grenade returned does enough damage to the enemy, they'll think twice about continuing to use them. Right, Gunnery Sergeant?"

Unable to decide if she was impressed or annoyed by Kichar's analysis, Torin snorted. "Essentially right. But until you get to a rank where you don't have to listen to me—which would mean you've stayed alive about as long—you use your shield the way the nice folks in R&D intended."

"It was just a thunderstick," Sakur snorted. "We've got the frag grenades, not the drones."

"You sure of that, Sakur?"

"The Corps isn't going to blow us up." He blinked at Torin's expression. "Is it?"

"No way of knowing, so you treat everything on Crucible like it can kill you because some of it can." She turned to Hisht. "You okay?"

His nose ridges were wide open; short, shallow breaths blew out a constant thin cloud of water vapor. "Yes, Gunnery Sergeant."

He didn't look okay, but she'd deal with that later.

"Rest of the platoon's pinned down in that thinned bit." Piroj adjusted his scanner and tried to pick up individual heat signatures, but with only the faces radiating it wasn't easy. "Doesn't look like they've taken a lot of damage—the trees are small, but they're screwing up the enemy's lines of sight. Our side's using impact boomers. Crucible isn't."

Elbows planted on the rock, Lirit kept the KC-9 pointed at the fight. "I heard a grenade, though—unshielded. Didn't sound like one of ours."

"Stupid to toss a grenade in a woods," the Krai grunted. "Fighting's too close. Wood shards can do us easily as them. You people always forget a pointy stick'll kill you just as dead as heavy ordinance."

"We people?"

"Non-Krai."

"I think if a grenade went off," Lirit snorted, "I'd be more worried about shrapnel from the grenade than bits of tree."

"Your mistake." He adjusted his scanner again and frowned. "If our guys stay down, they're not in bad shape. They're hard to see in all that uneven ground. Hard to see means hard to hit, and most of them seem smart enough to lay off the explosives."

"Were you asleep in tactics, then?"

He glared at her through the transparent overlay of the scanner. "What?"

"Why would the enemy hold a platoon stationary?" When he didn't answer immediately, she answered for him. "Air strike!"

"Fuk!" Turning, he slid down the outcrop of rock they'd been using as a vantage point, hitting level ground less than a meter from the rest of the fireteam. McGuinty staggered back, Ayumi brought her weapon up. When Lirit landed beside him a second later, startling them again, the profanity started. "Forget that shit," Piroj snapped, "there could be an air strike by any minute and that could take the whole platoon out!"

"An air strike?" McGuinty moved back in close. "How do you know?"

"The platoon's pinned, being held in place. Simple tactics."

"I told him," Lirit added.

"So we have to get them moving." Ayumi swept a skeptical gaze over the other three. "How?

"Easy." Piroj shifted his weight from foot to foot. "We make the enemy think they've been flanked. Ayumi and McGuinty, go left until your scanner says you're lined up with the drones. Lirit and I will go right. Ten minutes to get into position, then we all start shooting. The enemy won't be hiding from us, so that'll give us an advantage targeting. Take out as many of them as you can, but mostly bring down sound and fury."

Lirit grinned and snapped in her impact boomers.

"Air strike?" Sakur's eyes darkened to near fuchsia.

"Number one reason to immobilize the enemy. Make them a target for your air support." This part of the scenario wasn't supposed to have air support, but then, this part of the scenario wasn't supposed to have happened so Torin wasn't ruling it out. "Two responses. One, we move forward fast, out of the killing corridor."

"Not going to happen, Gunnery Sergeant!" Bonninski jerked her head toward the thicker trees, and almost in response another piece got blown out of the top of their log.

"It's not as easy as you think to hit a moving target

you can barely see," Torin told her. "On the other hand, once they realize we're moving, it's not a waste of ammo to spray the whole damned area. They'd be guaranteed to hit something. Marginally more survivable than an air strike, though."

"But if they're not firing lethal rounds," Sakur began. Paused. "One shot in the leg is nonlethal, half a dozen . . ."

"Could cut your leg off at the knee," Torin told him matter-of-factly, pleased that he was thinking.

"Swell," Bonninski sighed. "And the second response?"

"Take the fight to them. Charge them behind a spray of impact boomers. Hit them with the lighter stuff as they break cover."

"And we learn whose morale is stronger."

This time there was no question, Torin was impressed. "Exactly." She nodded at Kichar, whose cheeks darkened under her scanner. "If ours is, they run. If theirs equals ours, it comes down to hand-to-hand. To hand. Occasionally claw. And that is always more survivable than an air strike."

"What if they have more stronger morale, Gunnery Sergeant?" Hisht asked.

Torin snorted, glad to see he was taking an interest again. "That won't happen."

"Actually, Gunnery Sergeant," Kichar began reluctantly, "on Norton's Down, the . . ."

"I didn't say that it has never happened," Torin interrupted. "I said it wouldn't happen. Not here, not now."

They lay quietly for a few moments; the enemy kept up random fire, the recruits shot back enough to keep them from advancing. Torin saw no more of the red flares that indicated a drone had been taken down, but neither did she hear any of the screaming that suggested a recruit had. There'd be more small stuff, like Bonninski's crease—the point of Crucible was to teach proto-

Marines how to act under fire, and that didn't work if they knew they wouldn't be hurt—but as long as everyone kept their heads, they should get through this with minimal damage. Right up to and not including that possible air strike.

There had been a scenario a few years ago; a platoon had gotten pinned four days in and an air strike had knocked the lot of them out with gas bombs. They'd woken with headaches and *dead Marine* scrawled on their combat vests. Their DIs had not been impressed and had bounced the whole lot of them back to day one hundred. The second time through, they'd kicked Crucible's ass. Two of them had landed in Sh'quo Company, and Torin had to admit they were among the most motivated Marines she'd ever known.

If she, personally, got caught in a gas-out today, she was going to be very pissed.

"Gunnery Sergeant Kerr?"

"Kichar." Torin shot at a weird-looking shadow and dropped back down onto the packed snow.

"What would you do here?"

"I'm doing it."

"No, I meant, what would you do in response to this situation, Gunnery Sergeant."

"If I was your senior DI?"

"Yes, sir!" Her cheeks darkened again. "Gunnery Sergeant."

"But I'm not your senior DI, and this is his platoon. I'm therefore going to do what Staff Sergeant Beyhn tells me to do. Just like you are."

Sakur glanced up at the sky through the bare branches of the trees. "Staff Sergeant Beyhn hasn't told us to do anything, Gunnery Sergeant."

"And yet the entire platoon went to ground and returned fire . . ." Two quick shots at that same weird shadow. ". . . and are still alive."

"Yeah, but that's because we were trained . . ."

"By?"

"Staff Sergeant Beyhn." Sakur shook his head, took a quick shot of his own, and dropped down to grin at her. "Point taken, Gunny."

What the hell; they were pinned down together behind a rotten log, in a frozen forest, expecting an air strike, and—so far—no one in this particular group of recruits had done anything particularly stupid. She let the gunny stand.

"Gunny?"

"Major."

They were with Platoon 71 but not of it; the private channel reinforced that. The enemy's guns made it easier to keep her voice under eavesdropping volume in such close quarters.

"Not a lot of com chatter. Of any kind."

"No, sir, there isn't."

"You think the DIs are being a little too quiet?"

Officially, they had the codes for the group channel. She was pleased to discover that the major had picked up the codes the DIs were using as well. Not that those codes were doing much good right now. "I suspect they changed codes the moment we hit dirt."

"I sure as hell hope so."

So did she since other reasons for the silence were more disturbing, although they better explained the total lack of orders from Staff Sergeant Beyhn. DIs did not get injured on Crucible. But then, Crucible didn't change scenario parameters after the platoons were dirtside either.

"Gunnery Sergeant Kerr?"

"Kichar."

"Can't the enemy lock on your com signal?"

"Yes. Bare minimum of fifteen seconds to get a lock," she added as Kichar opened her mouth again. "And at that, they have to be actively scanning for a signal."

"Are you of knowing they aren't, Gunnery Sergeant?"

Hisht's Federate apparently took a beating under stress. "No, I'm not. That's why we kept it under fifteen. There's a time code on the upper left of your scanner; it reset automatically off the OP when we landed. Use it."

His eyes nearly crossed as he tried to look at her and his scanner simultaneously.

The unmistakable blast of impact boomers sounded from the trees to her left, near the leading edge of the platoon and then, a heartbeat later, from the other side.

Hisht's ridges slammed shut. "They rain destruction!"

Archaic but succinct. Also, wrong. "No, those are ours."

"Platoon!"

And here, finally, was the staff sergeant.

"Fireteams in the back half of the march, advance toward the enemy on my word. Give me sound and fury, but don't waste ammo! Go!"

"Hisht?"

"I can rain for my team."

"All right, then." Torin rose with the rest of the fireteam under cover of the impact boomers.

"Gunnery Sergeant Kerr?" Kichar had to shout to be heard as they advanced. "Why only the rear fireteams?"

"Why do you think, Kichar?" Something slammed into her combat vest, but no alarms sounded, so she ignored it.

"Because the front teams would walk into the fire from whoever flanked the enemy."

"Whoever?"

"The scout team?"

"Don't ask me questions you know the answer to, Kichar. It's annoying."

"How do you program morale?" Major Svensson asked, a coffee pouch in his right hand and his left under

Dr. Sloan's slate. "That's got to be skirting close to that old AI issue."

"Well, I don't blame them for running. Wheeling. Hovering. Whatever it is they do."

"They have legs and feet, so mostly they run."

"Good for them." Hands shoved deep in her pockets, the doctor paced seven strides away, seven back. "I'd have run if I'd had any idea of where to go!"

"You were perfectly safe, ma'am." Torin would rather have been circulating around the fireteams with the other NCOs, but from the look Beyhn had shot her when he'd discovered both she and the major had been in the thick of the fight, she suspected she wouldn't be welcome. "The drones were programmed to miss you. You did the right thing, staying where we left you."

"And at the risk of being annoyingly repetitive, you left me!" Color burned high on each cheek. "You were supposed to be protecting me."

"In the old scenario."

She turned on the major, pulling off a mitten to jab a finger at him. "I am not a scenario!"

Major Svensson shrugged carefully so as not to move his hand. You weren't in any danger, Doc."

They *had* gone back for her when the platoon had started doubling away from the killing corridor, tucking back into formation and staying beside her as they made the best time possible over the rough terrain until the scout team had led them down into a rough gully where a rock overhang would give them cover in the event of enemy air support. Where, between the rock and their gear, they'd be invisible from the air. Wounds were tended, all of them too small to require the doctor's involvement. Pain killers and stimulants were pulled from packs as energy levels sagged with the fading of adrenaline.

"Gunnery Sergeant Kerr."

Torin looked up to see Beyhn and the two sergeants

standing together at the edge of the gully. It took a moment for her to realize what was wrong—all three had their helmets off and one of them, probably Beyhn, was subvocalizing into his implant. "Staff Sergeant."

"A moment of your time."

That didn't sound like a request. Interesting.

"Sir?"

"Go ahead, Gunny. You want me to come with?"

"Forget it," Dr. Sloan snapped. "You're staying right here!" Crouching, she checked the screen on her slate. "Adrenaline seems to cause an interesting response in the polyhydroxide alcoholydes."

The major frowned down at what he could see of his hand. "Define interesting?"

"I can't yet. But they're still remarkably active on a cellular level, perhaps even more than they were last night. How badly does your head hurt?"

"It doesn't."

She folded her arms.

"It's no big deal." When her foot started to beat out an impatient rhythm against the snow, he sighed, took a swallow of his coffee, and looked up at Torin. "I guess I'm staying here."

The three DIs were quiet as Torin walked up to them. They shuffled closer when she stopped, and indicated that she should remove her helmet. "You want to make sure Major Svensson isn't listening in," she said as she slipped it off.

Beyhn's eyes darkened. "Is that a question, Gunny?"

"Not really, no." Helmet tucked under her arm, she scratched under the edge of her toque, then nodded at the brilliant blaze of the staff sergeant's hair. "Bad example for the other di'Taykan, Staff, and noticeable from above."

"The enemy has no air support in this part of the scenario."

"Do you know that for certain? The scenario has already been changed, and that attack seemed air strike specific."

"Forget about the air strike! There was no air strike!" It took a visible effort for him to lower his voice. "The question is: who changed the scenario?"

"This morning you thought the cold had fukked with the program."

"A failure of an attack program to launch is one thing," he snarled. "A whole new attack is something entirely different."

"Can't argue with that." He expected her to, though; Torin could see it in his face and, in spite of the cold, she was still getting a pheromone hit off him. This time, she was close enough to see that his masker was on the highest setting. Time to change the subject. "I think your masker's broken, Staff."

"No." Looking miserable, Sergeant Annatahwee shook her head. "This one came off one of the recruits. Worked there but not on him."

"*He* is standing right here!"

Annatahwee shifted her weight. "Sorry, Staff."

Pushing past the rising desire, Torin forced herself to concentrate. "Check to see if one of the recruits is carrying a spare. Maybe two in tandem will work."

"Good idea!" Sergeant Jiir began to peel away from the group, but Beyhn grabbed his shoulder and pulled him back. Nose ridges completely closed, he still reacted to the staff sergeant's touch but managed to stop himself before he rubbed up against the much larger male's leg.

"Do it later," Beyhn snapped. "I think an unscheduled ambush is higher priority than your species'—both your species'—inability to control its biology. The ambush has convinced me that the changes are a test."

Torin filed the first part of his statement away for future reaction and concentrated on the second. "A test? What kind of a test?"

"There have been rumors that some of the DIs have been giving the scenario specifics away to their recruits. The recruits have fewer screwups, the DIs look good. You look good enough and you'll move up the promotions list."

Stand on the front lines and you'll move up the promotions list, Torin thought as the staff sergeant continued.

"Too many platoons look too good, and it sets off alarms. Eventually, Command does something."

"This is a dangerous something," Torin pointed out, breathing shallowly through her teeth. "If the DIs don't know what's going on, there's a good chance recruits will get hurt. Badly hurt."

No one disagreed with that assessment.

"Have you contacted the OP?"

"If we're being tested," Beyhn snarled, "that's the last thing we want to do. We take whatever they can throw at us and we don't go crying to our *sheshan*."

"They have to tell you what they're up to, Staff Sergeant."

"Do they?"

Torin didn't actually have an answer for that.

"We need to see the scenario you downloaded," Annatahwee told her. "To see if it's the same as ours."

"You think I may be the safety?"

"No," Beyhn declared, his tone unarguable. "I think you and the major are part of the test. Observers to see how we react when things are changed."

"I'm not." Unless she didn't know she was. She could be here to be exactly that, an observer sent in to allay the suspicions of Command, unaware of it until her debriefing back on Ventris. If they'd sent her in with orders to observe, that would have been one thing, but putting her in another position to find out what was really happening after the fact, after Marines died, that really pissed her off. "I don't mind following orders," she growled as she pulled out her slate. "But I hate being manipulated." Two taps on the screen pulled up the scenario. She passed it over to Beyhn, and the three DIs huddled over it.

"*Chreen!*" Jiir snarled a moment later, showing teeth. "Identical download."

"What about Major Svensson?" Beyhn handed the slate back. "He has the download?"

"He does."

"Can you get a look at it?"

"The major was as surprised as I was this morning when that attack never came."

"He would be, wouldn't he?" The staff sergeant focused past her shoulder, and Torin knew he was watching the major and Dr. Sloan. "Crucible seems like a strange place for physical therapy."

"He came out of combat, he's going back into combat. Crucible lets Dr. Sloan run tests under controlled combat conditions."

"Not as controlled as they should be."

True. "All right. I'll check the details of Major Svensson's download, but I still think you should contact the OP and find out what's up."

"Is that an order, Gunnery Sergeant?"

Beyhn's tone was aggressive enough it pulled Jiir's lips back off his teeth. "It's your platoon and it's your scenario," Torin told him flatly. "It's a suggestion." The *for now* was heavily implied. With no intention of blemishing Beyhn's spotless record last trip out before retiring, Torin would pull rank all over his ass the moment she thought he was actively putting his recruits in danger. It was weirdly easy not to think of his ass. The pheromones seemed to be down to more normal levels and those in the air had dissipated.

"The OP will be observing the test—think on that."
His lip curled. "I'm sure they have orders to lie to any
DI who asks too many questions."

"Then let me have the codes, and I'll ask them some
questions. You won't come into it at all."

"I will not be left out of it!" Hair whipping back and
forth, he pivoted on one heel and stomped off. It wasn't
much of a stomp, given the combination of inherently
graceful di'Taykan body language and the snow, but the
intent was clear.

Torin slid her helmet on and smiled at the two junior
DIs. "What the hell is up with him?" she demanded as
Annatahwee took half a step back and Jiir closed his
lips over his teeth in a conciliatory movement.

"I wish we could tell you, Gunny." The Krai sergeant
pulled his helmet back on over his toque. "He's been
touchy lately—not in a di'Taykan way, but . . ."

"Yeah, I get it." She rolled a mittened hand in the air,
indicating he should move on.

"We thought it was just the thought of retiring. He
doesn't want to, this has been his whole life, but he got
a message from home and, well, it's making him . . ."

"Slightly crazy," Annatahwee put in dryly. "We've
been cutting him all kinds of slack, but . . ."

But, indeed. Most Marines never lost their trained reaction to a senior DI—even those currently working with
him. Command would have made sure that neither Jiir
nor Annatahwee had gone through in one of Beyhn's
platoons, but, other than that, they were on their own.

"What about the pheromones?"

"They're strong. Or they don't exist at all. We figure
they're tied to his emotional state and, you know, we
live through it."

"The Corps needs more female Krai," Jiir moaned.
Looked up at the other two. His nose ridges snapped
shut. "Sorry."

Torin waved it off. "I've heard it before. Has Jonin spoken to either of you?"

They exchanged glances and shrugged.

"He's a leader among the di'Taykan recruits," Annatahwee offered.

"Three-letter last name, I'm not surprised. There's something going on with him and the staff sergeant."

"Something about their families?"

"Could be." Taykan hierarchy didn't usually cause problems, but if Beyhn was being forced to retire by his family and Jonin's family were their direct superiors . . . Torin could see how that might be trouble.

"Jonin's in my squad. I'll talk to him."

"Jonin's not who we need to talk to," Jiir snorted. "We need to talk to the guy in the sky, and the staff sergeant's refusing. Stupid fukking system that only gives the codes for the OP to the senior DI. What the hell is up with that?"

"The Corps moves in mysterious ways," Annatahwee muttered.

"Should we need to, and I'm not saying we do," Torin added, "can we contact Staff Sergeant Dhupam and get her codes?"

Jiir's nose ridges flared. "The platoons are deliberately isolated. All necessary contact would be made through the OP. And we can't contact the OP because we don't have the codes unless the staff sergeant's med-alert goes off."

Right. She knew that. The last part anyway. The odds were good that at the moment both sergeants were considering the placement of nonlethal wounds.

"If you're finished with my sergeants, Gunny, I need them back." Back on his PCU, Beyhn sounded almost jolly.

Torin figured there were two ways she could approach Major Svensson about his download . . .

"Sir, may I examine the scenario in your slate?"

... but the direct approach seemed best.

"In case I've got a download of what's actually happening?"

"Yes, sir." It was a conclusion anyone with more than three functioning brain cells might come to.

Shifting his weapon away from his body, he took his slate from his vest and passed it in front of the doctor. "Is this what you four were doing back in the gully?"

"Yes, sir." The footing was secure enough she could split her attention between walking and scrolling through the major's scenario. Point by point, it was identical to hers. "Dr. Sloan?"

"I don't have a scenario of any kind on my slate." The doctor stepped up on a fallen log the other two had been able to step over, shifted the weight of her pack, and stepped down. "And I guarantee no one could have put one there without my knowing."

"He should call the platform," the major mused, gaze seeking out Staff Sergeant Beyhn walking up ahead. "See what they have to say."

No mention of *his* name to attract attention. Torin wondered how long the OP would attempt to contact Staff Sergeant Beyhn before they sent the VTA down to find out what the hell was going on. "And if the OP says things are proceeding as planned, sir?"

"Then at least we know there's a plan, however fukked, and no one changed things on the fly last night. It's unusual for di'Taykan to sleep alone," he added as Torin leaned around the doctor to look at him.

"His pheromones *are* a bit off."

The major flushed. "Yeah, noticed that, too. I could order him to contact the platform. You think it may come down to me taking command of the platoon, Gunny?"

"It had occurred to me, sir." Essentially.

*　　*　　*

That night, they camped 16.2 kilometers from their first camp in a heavy copse of trees next to the large lake they'd been paralleling all day. Although the ambush had delayed them, the original scenario would have delayed them as well, so they were within the five-kilometer adjustment of where they should be. They drew water from the wide mouth of a small creek and set up shelters in a random pattern within the area covered by the perimeter pins. The di'Taykan set their communal shelter up against a rise in the land; by the time they finished, it had become part of the landscape.

"The di'Taykan know how to work with snow," Major Svensson acknowledged, accepting his meal with a not entirely hidden grimace. "Let's hope none of them get lost on their way back from the latrine, or they'll never find it again," he added, waving off Torin's offer to switch meals.

"No maskers inside the shelter, sir, so I doubt it."

"I'd like to take some readings as it gets colder, Major." Dr. Sloan stared suspiciously at her peppered noodles, before winding one around her spork. "Do you think you could keep your mitten off for—oh, say—forty minutes?"

"After I eat."

"Of course. But before you spend another hour behind a bush."

"An hour?" Torin asked, not liking the sound of that considering how long he'd been out of the shelter less than eighteen hours earlier.

The major sighed. "I wasn't behind a bush for an hour."

"Fine, you chatted with a few recruits after you finished. You were behind a bush for fifty-five minutes." Waving a spork of noodles, the doctor continued before he could protest again. "I'd also like to take a few readings on your bowels. We regrew your lower intestine from scratch, and while it doesn't involve any new technology, it could be . . ."

"Dr. Sloan!" All three of them rose as Kichar charged through the trees toward them. "You're needed ma'am! Staff Sergeant Beyhn is having a seizure!"

SEVEN

TORIN ROCKED TO A STOP almost on Dr. Sloan's heels and stared at the fifteen di'Taykan surrounding Staff Sergeant Beyhn's shelter. Just under half of Platoon 71 was di'Taykan, standard numbers for infantry, and grouped together they made an imposing—and colorful—barricade. Somewhere in the group, Masayo could be heard praying; Torin hoped she was praying that the whole multicolored lot of them would come to their senses before bad things happened.

Sergeants Jiir and Annatahwee appeared to the left of the shelter, skirted the outer di'Taykan, and hurried around to Torin's side.

"They won't let us in," Jiir snarled, his lips all the way off his teeth. "I don't want to start anything, but . . ."

"But we can hear the staff sergeant in there, and he doesn't sound good," Annatahwee finished. "His med-alert went off about fifteen minutes ago, but the readings don't make any sense."

"Give it to me!" Dr. Sloan threw out an imperious hand.

When the major nodded, the sergeant handed Dr. Sloan her slate.

"Yes," she muttered a moment later, staring down at the screen, "Saying these don't make any sense is an understatement." Her head snapped up at the sound of an extended moan. "That's it. I'm . . ."

"I'm sorry, Dr. Sloan." Jonin stepped away from the others—far enough for separation but close enough to maintain the protection of numbers. "We can't allow you to come any closer."

"Don't be ridiculous." She took a step left, then a step to her right, a substitute for forward motion. "If the staff sergeant has had a seizure . . ."

"It wasn't a seizure. Staff Sergeant Beyhn's condition is purely a Taykan matter."

"Staff Sergeant Beyhn is a Marine, and that makes it a Marine matter." Major Svensson pushed past Torin to stand at the doctor's side as another moan rose from the tent in the center of the ring of recruits. "Move."

"No, sir!" Jonin came to attention but stayed where he was, hair flipping randomly around his head. "I'm sorry, sir! But we can't."

"Can't?"

"Jonin . . ." Torin drew his attention before he could answer. Everyone involved in this standoff was armed, and the di'Taykan looked spooked enough to do something stupid. Stupider. And their vision was significantly better than either Humans or Krai in low light. ". . . is this what you were worried was going to happen?"

"Yes, Gunnery Sergeant."

"You knew about this, Gunny?" the major demanded without taking his eyes off the massed di'Taykan.

"Not exactly, sir." She wasn't happy about Jonin not coming to her when this became a Corps matter, as it had the moment Staff Sergeant Beyhn had become unable to do his job, but now wasn't the time.

A third moan twisted and became a pained wail.

"Dr. Sloan, have you had Taykan patients?"

"Of course I have!"

"Jonin, Staff Sergeant Beyhn obviously needs medical attention. You lot aren't able to provide it, or you wouldn't all look scared shitless. Let Dr. Sloan through. No one else needs to go in."

"This isn't . . ."

The wail slid sideways and lifted the hair on the back of Torin's neck. It was hard to tell, given the lack of light, but the di'Taykan closest to her seemed to be breathing heavily.

"Jonin!" The pale pink hair made Sakur easy to spot in the dusk. "We don't know what to do! Maybe the doctor does!"

"What would a Human know?" Jonin demanded angrily, whirling to face this breach in solidarity.

"How the fuk would I know?" If Jonin sounded angry, Sakur sounded desperate. "I'm not a doctor!"

"Jonin!"

He turned and refocused on Torin.

"What do they say about corpsmen?"

"About . . . ?"

"About corpsmen, Recruit! Or weren't you listening during training?"

"Sir!" After 122 days of training, he responded involuntarily to the tone. "That corpsmen have no species, sir!"

"Neither do doctors. Now let her in."

For a moment, Torin thought he was going to refuse. Then his hair flattened, he nodded, and stepped aside. Behind him, the living barricade split. Every movement she made expressing her very negative opinion of the situation, Dr. Sloan stomped toward Staff Sergeant Beyhn's shelter. The barricade closed behind her.

"You might want to mention at some point," Major Svensson growled by Torin's ear, "that I outrank you."

"They're recruits, sir," Torin reminded him at the same low volume. "Officers are beyond their experience. NCOs, they understand."

"Your thoughts on what we should do about this?" He jerked his head toward the massed di'Taykan.

"I think we should break it up, sir." The longer it continued, the worse it looked to the rest of the platoon.

"It's all yours, Gunny."

"Thank you, sir." She meant it, too. The major stepping back made her job easier. "All right; Jonin, Sakur, Lirit—take up perimeter positions around Staff Sergeant Beyhn's shelter! The rest of you . . ."

The southwest perimeter pin went off.

". . . rejoin your fireteams, now! Defensive positions! Move!"

They moved. Inanimate objects moved when she used that tone.

Southwest was the lake.

"Sergeant Jiir! Light it up!"

She heard the sergeant yell, *"Stone!"* and a moment later a flare exploded over the ice.

"Holy fuk!"

Torin didn't recognize the voice, but it was a fair response. What was a tank doing out there? Squinting into a freezing wind, she searched her scanner for air support or drones. Nothing. So the more relevant question would be: why was a tank out there all alone?

The first shell went long. One of the sergeants must have activated the screamer in the northeast perimeter pin and messed up the shell's guidance system, but even half a kilometer on the far side of the camp, the explosion was still nearly deafening.

"Son of a fukking bitch!" Major Svensson rose up onto his elbows to stare over the rock they'd dropped behind. "That was no thundershot!"

Thundershots, a much larger version of the grenades thrown by the drones, were sound and fury and impressive pyrotechnics but essentially harmless if everyone kept their heads.

"Sounded like an HE antitank round, sir."

"You hiding a tank you're not telling me about, Gunny?"

"No, sir."

"Then what the hell is going on here?"

Her scanner picked up no life signs. The tank was essentially a big drone. "Seems like Crucible's trying to kill us, sir."

The second shot blew a hole in the woods to the west.

Breathing heavily, Sergeant Jiir dropped to the snow beside her. "*Serley* thing's firing antitank rounds! There must've been a screwup in the load commands."

"Why does the Crucible even have HE rounds in a training area?" the major asked tightly.

"We use them sometimes to make a point, sir."

"You might want to rethink that, Sergeant."

"Yes, sir. What do we do?"

"We stop it," Torin growled.

"With sevens and nines? No way, Gunny! Not at that distance!" Scanner down, Jiir nodded toward the tank. "There's a 20 mm machine gun top mounted. We get close enough and it'll read the trainers and pop us off."

"Then we don't take out the tank; we take out the ice."

"With what?" Jiir rose to gesture out at the ice, remembered why that was a bad idea, and ducked back down again. "It's holding a tank! A grenade won't crack ice that thick, and we'd be sitting *vertak* getting close enough to set a demo charge."

"Give me a perimeter pin. Stone!" Prone behind a ridge of frozen beach gravel, the big Human turned his head at the sound of his name. "I need your 9."

Jiir pulled a pin out of his vest as Stone cleared two meters of open shoreline between one heartbeat and the next and dove behind the rock.

"Activate the pin, Sergeant." Torin handed Stone her KC-7 and hooked the KC-9's strap over her shoulder. Plucking the activated pin from the sergeant's palm, she dropped it down the barrel.

"Never do this," the major mentioned conversationally as she got to her knees and raised the weapon to her shoulder. "The barrel's likely to explode."

"But . . ."

A third shell exploded in the trees southeast of the camp. Given the tank's firing pattern and their position outside the southwest pin, they'd just run out of options.

"The Gunny's done this before. Heads down!"

Problem was, if the pin jammed, the barrel *could* explode. It wasn't likely given relative sizes and the stupid-proof construction of the weapon, but it was possible. Weighing that possibility against the certainty that the tank would wipe out the camp and everyone in it with its next couple of shots, Torin aimed low and pulled the trigger. A spray of ice six meters in front of the tank and seventy degrees off marked where the pin impacted. "Set the screamer!"

"Impact probably destroyed it," Jiir muttered, jabbing at his slate.

"There's a chance," Torin admitted. The pins were Marine-resistant, but very few things were built Marine-proof. She watched in her scanner as the tank's big gun pivoted around to the right searching for this new perimeter pin. Confused by the screamer, it fired.

The shell slammed through the ice.

The recruits holding defensive positions along the shore were completely silent.

Water and ice together muffled the explosion.

Half a heartbeat later, sounding like a platoon's worth of KC-7s all firing at once, the ice began to crack. With a boom that echoed off the trees, the rear of the tank dropped.

The tracks spun, grabbing air and spraying water up over the tipping slab.

Three seconds later, it was all over. The only sound on the lakeshore was the sound of waves slapping against the hole in the ice.

"On Carlong," Major Svensson said into the silence,

"there was a big old ice wall holding back a river. Gunnery Sergeant Kerr fired a perimeter pin at it, and the enemy's mortars took it down, wiping out the leading edge of their advance. Bought us a few hours where no Marines died. She was a staff sergeant then, of course."

"Of course," Jiir muttered, staring out at the spreading patch of open water. "Aren't tanks supposed to be waterproof?"

"Not as much as they'd like you to think. I'll keep this for a while," Torin told Stone, gesturing with the KC-9 as the recruit got slowly to his feet. "I want to make sure I didn't damage it. All right, people!" She raised her voice, letting the sound lift the surrounding fireteams up onto their feet. Beyhn was out and Crucible was using live ammo; she'd be damned if she was giving way to a pair of sergeants. "I want a tightened perimeter and damage reports. Move!" She turned to the major. "That last shell sounded too close to the camp—the firing system had probably started to compensate for the screamers. We may have injured." Had she been part of the platoon, she'd know because the medical information on every recruit would have been in her slate. As it was, she knew the major hadn't been hit, and that was it.

"Deal with it, Gunny." He turned back toward the camp. "As soon as I get the codes out of Beyhn's slate, I want a few words with our eyes in the sky!"

"Yes, si . . ."

"Gunny?"

Momentarily unable to form the words, Torin pointed past his shoulder at the rising streak of light drawing a gleaming, deadly line against the night sky.

"That can't . . ." He shook his head. ". . . can't be what it looks like."

"I hope you're right, sir." Because it looked like a surface-to-air missile.

A moment later, pieces of the OP began to rain fire through the atmosphere; shooting stars against the darkness that represented the deaths of the eleven Marines and six Navy corpsmen who had been on board when the missile hit. There could also have been up to a dozen wounded recruits from the other three platoons dirtside in the sick bay—no way to tell watching from the ground as the station fell and burned.

All along the shore, Marines who'd been on their way back to camp stood and stared at the sky.

Torin took a deep breath and when she was certain nothing but what she intended would show in her voice, snapped, "I could have sworn I gave you lot something to do!"

"They blew up the Orbital Platform, Gunnery Sergeant!"

"Someone did," she allowed. "And there's not a damned thing we can do about it, but we can do something about a blasted perimeter and possible casualties, so *move!*"

They moved.

When it was just her and the major on the frozen beach, Torin glanced at her sleeve. "They timed the missile for just after the *NirWentry*'s jump to Susumi." She forced her teeth to unclench, forced her tongue away from her implant. The upgrade had reserve power, but who the hell was she going to talk to. "Eight days before another ship's in system."

"The OP had a Susumi beacon," Major Svensson said in the same quiet voice. "They might have had time to get a message off."

"Yes, sir. That's possible."

But neither of them believed it.

A splintered branch about twelve centimeters long and less than one in diameter had been flung like a dart under the edge of Recruit di'Lammin Oshyo's helmet, into and through her right eye socket, and then her brain.

"There's no exit wound." Torin straightened and wiped wet hands on her thighs. "Probably splintered further when it hit the back of her skull."

"You keep telling them to keep their helmets on," Sergeant Annatahwee muttered. "Like it fukking matters sometimes."

There was nothing Torin could say to that, so she moved on. Soon Sung Cho, the recruit positioned next to Oshyo, had taken a facial laceration from a second piece of flying debris. It had opened his cheekbone deep, but Cho had pinched the wound closed and sprayed a layer of sealant on it. A handful of snow had scrubbed the blood from his combats. One injury, one death, one tank; it could have been a lot worse.

Perimeter pins had been reset and teams two/one and two/two—less Lirit who remained at Beyhn's shelter— were standing the first four-hour watch, individuals placed close enough together that their lines of sight overlapped. If tanks were out there firing live rounds, bets were off on what else might show up. Perimeter pins might no longer be enough. Moonlight and starlight reflected off the snow, and the sentries navigated the bands of shadow between the trees with their scanners down, using as little light as possible.

"Camp is secured, sir."

"Good." Major Svensson glanced toward the lake, just barely visible through the trees. "What the hell do you think is going on, Gunny? This is more than just a glitch."

"Best guess: someone has hacked Crucible's system, sir."

"The Others?"

Torin thought a moment before answering. When the Others came into Confederation space, they invaded to advance their perimeter. If Crucible was suddenly in contested real estate, then the Corps had a lot more to worry about than the loss of its training facility. If the Others had developed a new battle plan, however, a plan to take out the Marines at the source . . . "This is a little subtle for them, sir, but they are who we're fighting. There's no ship in system eight days out of ten; if they timed it right, they'd only have the Orbital Platform and its satellites to avoid—easy enough for a good pilot in a small VTA. Once down, they find the nearest CPN . . ."

"Not exactly difficult," the major grunted, pulling off helmet and toque as one unit and running a hand back over his head. "The damned things aren't more than a day's march apart."

"In case something goes wrong."

He raised a pale brow. "Where wrong isn't referring to antitank rounds being fired at recruits?"

"Yes, sir. The nodes can't be too well hidden, or they wouldn't be very useful in an emergency. Once the Others have cracked the system, they wait until the Navy's gone, then they blow the OP and control the satellites with an uplink from the ground. They have surveillance, the tank proves that—they know where we are—and at least some control of the peripherals."

"Which the tank also proves."

The tank gave the Others the most firepower for the least amount of reprogramming.

"Yes, sir."

"If it's so easy for the satellite to find us, why the hell didn't it spot *them*?"

"Easier to hide from someone who isn't looking for you, sir. Not to mention," she added dryly, "the ETGs mean we've got a platoon of recruits with BFFMs built into their combats." To a certain extent, all combats carried enough tech to act as a *Better Fukking Find Me*. The trainers just went the extra distance.

"Not to mention: do we strip them down?"

"Maybe we should hold that in reserve, sir."

"Right." Headgear back in place, he sighed deeply, blowing out an impressive plume of air and nodded toward the center of the camp. "Well, while we're contemplating fighting a war in long underwear, let's tackle the more immediate problem."

"Staff Sergeant Beyhn."

"You read my mind, Gunny."

"Just part of the service, sir."

There were ten di'Taykan around Beyhn's shelter—of the original fifteen, one was dead and three were on watch, so that meant one was likely in the shelter. Dr. Sloan emerged as Torin glared a path clear to the entrance.

"He's essentially stable," she said, then focused on the two non-di'Taykan as she pulled on her mitts. "Everything okay?" She'd seen to the wounded, complimented Cho's quick thinking, and then returned to the staff sergeant.

"For certain values of the word *okay*," the major told her. "What's wrong with Staff Sergeant Beyhn?"

"Well, he's an idiot." One of the di'Taykan growled. Before Torin could respond, the doctor snarled, "Don't even go there. I'm not telling you anything you don't already know!"

"Nice someone knows," Major Svensson said pointedly.

"He delayed the change," Dr. Sloan snorted. "Used mail order drugs to repress, thus my diagnosis of idiot."

"What change?"

"He's becoming qui."

"Qui'Taykan?"

"No, qui sera sera! Of course qui'Taykan. And because of the aforementioned drugs and repression and idiotic-acy, it's not going well."

The Taykan had three distinct biological divisions

over their life span: the di'Taykan, the qui'Taykan, and
the tir'Taykan. The qui'Taykan were the breeders—
temporarily fertile, extremely conservative, and seldom
if ever seen away from territory the Taykan claimed as
their own. And that essentially summed up everything
Torin knew about them. They weren't part of the Corps,
so they weren't her problem. So they previously *hadn't
been* her problem.

"Jonin."

"I couldn't . . . I wanted to . . ." His hair spread out
from his head in a cobalt corona, a visible indication of
how upset he was. "We don't talk about it. It isn't done."

Behind him, the other di'Taykan shifted—the movement eerily coordinated.

"It's going to be done now," Major Svensson growled.

Torin had never seen a di'Taykan look so completely
miserable, and she'd seen them covered in blood, missing their favorite body parts.

"Yes, sir."

"And put your damned helmet on!"

"Yes, sir."

"I thought I could detect a difference before we left
Ventris Station, certain variations in his scent. And then,
that morning when we formed up in the shuttle terminal, Staff Sergeant Beyhn was . . ." Jonin paused, searching for the word, ". . . softer, but by the time we left, he
was right back to being a . . ." The second pause suggested Jonin had remembered his audience and was re-
considering his initial description.

"Aggressive son of a bitch?" Major Svensson suggested mildly from the stump he was using as a command center.

Jonin nodded, hair under the edge of his helmet moving against the motion. "Yes, sir." He didn't look comfortable with the description, but then he was using a
formal aristocratic cadence that once again reminded

Torin of Lieutenant Jarret back at Sh'quo Company, and *aggressive son of a bitch* didn't exactly fit the tone. No matter how accurate a description of the staff sergeant it might be.

"Once we were on the *NirWentry*," Jonin continued, "there were other recruits in both this platoon and in Platoon 72 who began to notice changes in the staff sergeant's scent. Some of them came to me. I suspect all the di'Taykan had noticed the changes in scent at this point, but most of them kept it to themselves. Many of them probably denied even noticing. This . . ." He swallowed, took a deep breath, and kept going. ". . . to become qui is very private and personal. To speak of it even among ourselves goes against what we have been taught all our lives."

"But *some* spoke of it."

"Yes sir. There are always those bound less by cultural expectations than others, and some were beginning to consider this . . . situation more as Marines and less as di'Taykan."

"But enough as di'Taykan that they wanted you to do something about it."

"Yes, sir. I approached Gunnery Sergeant Kerr."

"And didn't actually tell me anything," Torin pointed out.

"I . . ." He glanced down at his hands, the long fingers laced together, then back up again. "No, I didn't." One foot shifted, digging a hole in the snow, but he offered no excuses. Torin respected that, even through her annoyance. "Usually, when the change comes upon you, you return to your family and go into seclusion with those of your closest *thytrins* who have already changed. They assist in the process. No disrespect intended, but Staff Sergeant Beyhn waited too long."

"That's a little too obvious to be disrespectful," the major noted.

"Yes, sir. Anyway, it kept getting worse. The staff sergeant's decision making began to be affected."

"The delay in coming to a decision when we were pinned down . . ." The major glanced at his sleeve. ". . . this morning."

The Crucible day had been divided into twenty-seven hours, sixty-six minutes—as close to the twenty-eight hour cycle on the stations as the Corps could manage. It was only 2240. Still the second day of a twenty-day scenario.

"Yes, sir. The qui don't . . ." He swallowed and kept going, his eyes so light Torin doubted he could see through them. He couldn't close them, not while talking to a superior, so he did what he could. Torin didn't entirely blame him. ". . . deal well with risk."

"Wonderful." Running both hands up under the edge of his toque, Major Svensson turned his attention from Jonin to the doctor. "But the staff sergeant isn't qui yet?"

Dr. Sloan shook her head. "No. Like I said, the drugs he used to delay the change have messed up his system. He's changing now, but it's happening slowly and painfully."

"Is he functional?"

"Define functional. He's breathing on his own, his heart is beating. We can get liquids down him, but I'm not so sure about solids."

"Can he walk?"

"No."

Under the circumstances, that wasn't unexpected.

"All right, we move him on a stretcher."

"I'd rather not move him at all, Major."

"Unfortunately Doctor, staying here isn't an option." The major forestalled further protest by turning his attention back to Jonin. "How does the staff sergeant's *condition* affect the di'Taykan?" When Jonin paused a little too long before answering, the major sighed. "We just had a single species mutiny, Recruit. There's obviously an effect. What is it?"

"We have to protect him, sir."

"Have to?" Imperatives with the Taykan took only one form. He nodded toward Jonin's masker. "New pheromones?"

"Yes, sir."

The major's attention shifted to Torin. "Did you know about the pheromones when you ordered this one, Sakur, and Lirit to stand guard?"

Torin shook her head. "No, sir, but they obviously weren't going to leave him alone, and that seemed the best compromise."

"Good call." He drew in a long breath and let it out slowly. Information gathering had finished, Torin realized. Time for decisions. "The staff sergeant's masker isn't enough to block the effect?"

Torin frowned as Jonin's hair stilled. "You've taken the masker off him, haven't you?" she asked.

He straightened; shoulders squared, chin up. "It's wrong."

"For the qui'Taykan to wear a masker?" Major Svensson looked less than thrilled, and Torin didn't blame him. In accepting three different species into the Corps, Command had realized it would have to make certain concessions, but some of those concessions were damned inconvenient.

"Yes, sir."

Interesting that Jonin's tone suggest he didn't quite agree with the party line. It sounded to Torin like he was looking for a way out. "Major?"

The major sighed. "Go ahead, Gunny."

"It is entirely possible Oshya died because she was distracted by Staff Sergeant Beyhn's situation. This stopped being training the moment that tank showed up. This is combat now. If the di'Taykan want to protect the staff sergeant, they have to have their wits about them. They have to be Marines."

Jonin's eyes began to darken. "We can protect him better if he's in the masker."

"Yes."

He stared at her for a long moment, his eyes almost cobalt again. Then his shoulders relaxed and his hair began to move, long slow sweeps front to back. "Permission to give that as the rationale for your order to the other di'Taykan, sir?"

Major Svensson snorted. "Do it. And then get the masker on Staff Sergeant Beyhn. Double it if you have to."

"Even with the masker, one of us will have to be with him at all times, sir."

"As long as he's not walking, I'll make sure the stretcher bearers are di'Taykan."

"Thank you, sir." He stood and took a step away.

"Jonin."

"Sir?" Startled by the steel in the major's voice, he stopped.

"Do not forget that this is a Marine Corps problem, not yours alone. If you ever try to take matters into your own hands again, I will personally see to it that you are not only brought up on charges leading to, at best, a dishonorable discharge but given a good swift kick in the ass on the way out—and when I say you, I mean every di'Taykan in this platoon. Do you understand?"

"Yes, sir!"

The salute was pixel perfect. Torin had no idea how he managed to pivot on one heel in ankle-deep snow, but he managed it. "That went better than he'd expected," she said quietly as Jonin rejoined the other di'Taykan at Beyhn's shelter.

"You gave him an option he could work with as both di'Taykan and Marine. Nice work, Gunny."

"Thank you, sir." The di'Taykan aristocrats who became Marines tended to head for officer training, and Torin realized she'd just been shown why that was very much to the benefit of the Corps. They'd been raised to lead and some of them had been well raised, indeed.

"I'm not sure about calling it the staff sergeant's condition though."

"Seems a better choice than calling it the result of the staff sergeant's dumbass behavior, sir." Just for that moment, Torin didn't bother hiding her disgust. Maybe the situation with the Elder Races had left her feeling a little sensitive about betrayal, but by putting his own desires ahead of the Corps, Beyhn had abdicated his responsibility for the Marines under his command—and that was the one thing she couldn't, wouldn't forgive.

Major Svensson stared at her for a long moment, his expression unreadable.

Torin honestly didn't care if he thought she was being too hard line. She only hoped he wasn't going to suggest she try to be more understanding of Staff Sergeant Beyhn's motives because that would definitely put a crimp in their working relationship.

"I think we'll stick with condition," he said at last. Folding his arms, he stretched out his legs and crossed them at the ankle—a parody of relaxation. "So, what do we do now? We're not in what anyone would call a defensible position, and once the Others gain better control of Crucible's systems, we'll be thoroughly fukked. It'll take time. I'm betting the Corps' programmers were sufficiently paranoid to layer security on the scenarios and even the drones themselves, but a few decent techs, given enough time, could take out every Marine on the planet. Zero risk of retaliation and they're gone by the time the Navy gets back."

"We need to know how far their control extends," Torin said, frowning. "If we could get into the closest CPN . . ."

"Not without Staff Sergeant Beyhn's codes."

"They'll be on his slate."

"Behind heavy encryption," the major snorted. "If those codes get into the wrong hands . . ." His voice trailed off into irony given whose hands currently held the system.

"I think I can deal with that, sir."

His brows rose up to meet the edge of his toque. "You have hacker skills I don't know about, Gunny?"

"Not exactly, sir." Since the Others had the satellites, they had the ability to pick up the signals from the PCUs—all dirtside frequencies were logged with the Orbital Platform on approach. Easy enough to fix by changing frequencies and setting up eavesdropper alarms, but, for the moment, keeping their location secret was worse than pointless. Torin switched from group to the NCOs' channel. "Sergeant Jiir."

"Jiir here. Go ahead, Gunnery Sergeant."

"A moment of your time."

"On my way."

The major looked intrigued. "Sergeant Jiir has hacker skills I don't know about?"

"No, sir. He has . . ." As Jiir chose that moment to jog up, Torin turned her attention to him. "Sergeant, who's the best hacker in the platoon?"

"Gunny?"

She could hear the concern in his voice and smiled. "By the time a platoon hits one twenty, there're always a few recruits trying to crack the system." Back in Sh'quo Company they had a lance corporal who could not only crack the system but break it into bits and make those bits march in straight lines. Torin wished Ressk was here right now. "Which one of them were you watching in case they actually managed it?"

"That would be McGuinty; he's station-born, been in and out of all kinds of systems his whole life. But . . ."

"He's not in trouble, Sergeant. In fact, he could very

well save our collective asses. Have him pick up Staff Sergeant Beyhn's slate and bring it here."

McGuinty shoved his helmet back on his head and frowned at the major. "You want me to hack into the staff sergeant's slate and get the codes that give access to the CPNs, sir?"

"Is that a problem, Recruit? Sergeant Jiir said you were close to cracking the Ventris codes."

"Did he? That's great, sir."

"Not exactly," Major Svensson pointed out dryly, "but since we're about to take advantage of your skills, we'll let that slide."

"Sir! Yes, sir!" When the major raised a brow, his thin cheeks flushed. "Sorry, sir. Won't Staff Sergeant Beyhn be furious about . . . that doesn't matter, does it, sir?"

"No."

Cautiously, looking ready to dive for cover with the slightest encouragement, McGuinty glanced over at the slate now slaved to Torin's. "When do you . . ."

"The moment the gunny finishes transferring what she needs. Which would be right now," he added as Torin tapped out of the connection and passed the staff sergeant's slate back to the recruit.

He looked from the major to Torin and back to the major again. "Will the two of you be watching, sir?"

"What part of *now* are you having trouble understanding, McGuinty?"

"None, Gunnery Sergeant!"

"So get to work."

"Yes, Gunnery Sergeant."

Torin sighed, put her hand on his shoulder, and pushed him down into a sitting position on the other end of the major's log. He gave a muffled squeak, and keeping his eyes locked on the screens, pulled out his slate and slaved it to the staff sergeant's. After a few minutes, he looked up.

"I'm going to have to open . . ."

"Open what you need to," Torin interrupted. "If any information gets out that shouldn't get out, I'll know who passed it on."

"Yes, Gunnery Sergeant!"

She went reluctantly when the major beckoned her away, fully aware that her presence was intimidating but hoping to use it to speed things up.

They didn't go far, stopping at an old stump where the major sank down and sat staring up at the stars, right hand absently working the muscles of his thigh.

"I was just thinking."

Torin waited. A thinking officer wasn't always a good thing.

"With Staff Sergeant Beyhn down—we've got the codes allowing us to contact the OP." Torin tracked his gaze as he stared up into the sky, at the empty space between the stars where the Orbital Platform had been. After a long moment, he sighed. "All right, then." Pulling off his mittens, he rubbed his palms together. "They change the scenario, we change the scenario. No more games, no more moving from point A to point B. Our mission now is surviving until the Navy gets back. Huddle with the sergeants, they know this place a lot better than we do, and find us something we can hold."

"Yes, sir."

"Dunstan Mills." Sergeant Jiir tapped his screen, and everyone's maps scrolled north. "It's set up like a colony that's been taken by the Others. Training platoon has to get it back. Sergeant Dleer's group ran it just before they reset this section."

"So it's full of drones just waiting to be activated," Annatahwee sighed. "Why is it we'd want to go there?"

"It's set up like a colony," Jiir repeated, like that should make his reasoning obvious.

Torin, born and raised on Paradise, the first new

world the Confederation had settled Humans on, smiled. Every year growing up, she'd been forced on a pilgrimage to the First Landing Historical Site. "You're thinking it'll have an anchor."

When the Confederation set a colony of the Younger Races down on a new planet, the first building, the anchor, was a cross between the Marine Corps packets and a large Vacuum-to-Air transport. Thirty meters by twenty meters by six meters, it could withstand both the rigors of space and an atmospheric entry. It held everything the new colony needed to get started and once emptied became a community center, a hospital, and—if necessary—a fortress.

"I grew up on Sacurr," Jiir told them. "And every year we went to the Festival of First Seeding and I'm telling you, seventy-one years later that anchor was still in great shape. The *verrkark* things are indestructible."

Annatahwee frowned at her screen. "And Dunstan Mills has one?"

"Should have."

"But you don't know for sure?"

"It's set up like a colony . . ."

"So you keep saying," she interrupted sharply. "But why would they waste one of these indestructible anchor things on Crucible?"

"To teach Marines how to do their jobs," Torin said before Jiir could answer. "Any colony the Corps is sent to defend—or retake—will have an anchor. Therefore, any colony used in training needs to have an anchor as well. It won't need to be completely tricked out, but it will need to have the same structural integrity. If Dunstan Mills is set up like a colony, it will have an anchor, and when we can get to it, we can hold it for as long as we need to."

Annatahwee shook her head. "They know where we are, and they'll know where we're going."

"They'll know that no matter where we go, so we might as well head somewhere that's worth the trip."

*   *   *

"You want me to what, sir?" McGuinty stared up at the major with wide eyes.

"There's a CPN at ninety-seven degrees and 1.3 kilometers; use the map on the staff sergeant's slate to find it, then use his codes to gain access. If the Others aren't in control, shut it down. If they are, take the system back."

"The system? The whole system? Sir, if the Others are in control, taking the system back won't be easy. They'll have encryptions, sir. Alien encryptions. Those'll take time to break." His gaze turned inward, his brows nearly touching over his nose. "Maybe a lot of time," he muttered.

"Did I say it would be easy, McGuinty?"

The brows snapped apart. "No, sir! How long do I have?"

"We're moving out at dawn."

"Dawn. Right." He glanced up at the sky as though the stars would give him some hint of when dawn would be. "I'll disable the staff sergeant's slate so it can receive but not send. That'll isolate it, and I'll use it to back up my work. If you get me to another CPN, I can pick up where I had to leave off." The silence pulled his attention back to his listeners. "Uh, if that's okay, sir."

"By all means, disable the staff sergeant's slate." The major wasn't bothering to hide his amusement. "And we'll see what we can do about getting you hooked back up if you have to bail tonight. Take another recruit with you—someone who *won't* be fascinated by what you're trying to do and will therefore actually keep watch and keep an eye on the time. They're to check in with the gunny once you've got to the CPN and, if you can't immediately shut the node down, every hour after."

"Yes, sir."

"Well, go!"

"Sir, yes, sir!"

*   *   *

A few minutes later, as Torin brought the information on Dunstan Mills to the major, there was just enough light to see a pair of shadows heading for the trees; McGuinty and . . . had to be Piroj. The lack of height made it a Krai, and Piroj was in McGuinty's fireteam.

"I'll tell the sergeants to take McGuinty and Piroj's team off watch and scouting rotations," Torin said as the shadows deepened and she lost sight of the two recruits. "If Lirit and Ayumi become the primary stretcher carriers for Staff Sergeant Beyhn, that'll put all of two/one on special duties and make it easier to draw up a fair rotation."

"What do you figure the odds are he can use the staff sergeant's codes to shut down this node and keep the drones off us for this sector at least?"

"Honestly, sir, not high."

"Oh? How do you figure, Gunny?"

"Because that would be just too damned convenient, sir."

Finding the CPN wasn't the problem; it was exactly where Staff Sergeant Beyhn's map said it would be, tucked in behind a false front on an outcrop of rock. And access wasn't a problem with the staff sergeant's codes.

"That's interesting . . ."

"Interesting how?" Piroj demanded from his position on top of the rock. "Interesting where you can shut it down and we can haul ass back to camp? Or interesting where I'm standing around here all night watching you try and try and win the war by using your ten precious fingers to rearrange a few ones and zeros?"

"Interesting where this CPN has definitely been tapped and once you get inside a bit, it looks like the Others are using a weird variation of Marine security encryptions." McGuinty bent closer over the screen, bare fingers flying over the surface from one input to the next. "It isn't. It can't be. But it looks like it could be."

Piroj snorted. "Isn't. Can't. Could."

"I almost cracked Ventris."

"Yeah and *almost* right now is going to get our asses bagged." He turned slowly in place, data flashing across his scanner. No enemies. No wildlife either, though that was no surprise, not with the damage that tank had done to the woods. He came from Naalirk, the largest city on Kraiyn, had grown up on streets close enough to the spaceport that he could feel the ground shake whenever one of the shuttles lifted off, but even he felt the pain of those shattered trees. He'd hate to be Hisht, who came from far enough upcountry that he'd probably never even touched ground until he was considered an adult.

The trees here were in one piece, not too big, though, with the rock so close to the surface. The snow had been disturbed around the base of the outcrop when they'd arrived and something had gone charging out of the clearing. Maybe more than one something—all the wildlife he'd ever seen had been in bars after payday. He guessed that for real wild animals, 1.32 kilometers was still a little close to all the explosions.

"It's the almost that makes this a fukker," McGuinty muttered. The screen flickered, then steadied, then flickered again. "Convinces you that you think you know what you're doing, then after an hour or so kicks you in the nuts and runs off laughing."

"I think you need to cut back on the stim sticks, McGuinty." Sighing, he settled into the most comfortable position possible. "I'll let the gunny know we're going to be here for a while."

McGuinty and Piroj were young—pulling an all nighter wouldn't hurt them. It'd certainly hurt a lot less than having every drone on Crucible suddenly show up to pound the shit out of them. Torin had learned through experience that when facing another long hump on no sleep, perspective was everything.

Since she was up, she made a fast, silent circuit of the sentry positions. She wouldn't have bothered with more seasoned Marines at the posts, but this lot were on their first time out and it wouldn't hurt for her to check up on things.

No one was sleeping and no one shot at her—things were going better than she'd anticipated. The night was quiet beyond the perimeter. The Others seemed to have blown their offensive capabilities with the sammy and the tank.

"Gunny?"

Torin turned toward the quiet voice. "What is it, Sergeant?"

Her face a flare of red on the scanner, but otherwise nearly invisible in the dark, Sergeant Annatahwee stopped close enough for them to talk without waking the camp. "I'm not sure we're doing the right thing, moving off the scenario."

"We're moving off because we're five days from anything we can hold against a determined assault if we stay on."

"A determined assault by what, though? If the Others are on Crucible," she continued before Torin could respond, "the odds of them showing up in this section and facing off against us are pretty slim. They have a whole planet to cover."

"I'm more concerned with their control over the planet's armaments than I am with them personally," Torin pointed out. "You agreed we'd be better off heading two days' north to Dunstan Mills."

"I know, Gunny, but I've been thinking. If the Others have cracked the surveillance satellites . . ."

"Which the tank seems to indicate they have."

". . . then they'll know where we're going as soon as

we start to move. Dunstan Mills is the only possible destination on that heading. They could easily have the drones in the colony reprogrammed and waiting for us."

"Easily?"

"All right, not easily, but . . ." Annatahwee glanced around, as though expecting a protest or support from an outside source. Torin wondered if she'd been talking things over with Jiir. "We're supposed to keep moving. That's what this scenario is about; moving the platoon to where it's supposed to be."

"I'd say that standard operating procedure blew with the OP." Seemed Annatahwee didn't like having her scenario messed with.

"But, as *Marines*, we're supposed to keep moving," she insisted.

Torin bit back a suggestion that the sergeant not tell her what Marines were supposed to do. "If we weren't dirtside playing silly bugger, then, yeah, we'd continue in our assigned AO, but since there's no actual reason to keep moving west and thirty-six very good reasons to find a place we can defend, we're heading for Dunstan Mills. And the anchor." Her tone suggested that was the end of the discussion, and if she still had doubts about there being an anchor, she should keep them to herself.

Fortunately, Sergeant Annatahwee caught the subtext and kept face and voice carefully neutral as she asked, "Will you be taking Staff Sergeant Beyhn's squad?"

"No, divide his fireteams between you. I'll handle the platoon; you two keep handling the pieces. You know these Marines, I don't."

"Recruits."

"Sorry?"

She stiffened disapprovingly, the shadows that marked her shoulders lifting and squaring in place. "You called them Marines, Gunny. Until they finish Crucible, they're still recruits."

"Crucible changed the rules, Sergeant. This is now a combat situation and, for that, we need Marines."

"Saying they're Marines doesn't make them Marines." Sergeant Annatahwee took a step back as Torin smiled.

"It does if *I* say it," she growled.

Torin slid out of vest and boots and into her bedroll thinking that the shelter seemed empty with Dr. Sloan spending the night watching over Staff Sergeant Beyhn. Perspective was a funny thing since, with all three of them in residence, the shelter had been on the crowded side. With one less body, it was definitely a little cooler, but she'd slept in worse and so had Major Svensson, who was snoring softly, left arm thrown up over his eyes to block the dim light from her sleeve. As she flicked it off, his nails glowed green and then faded so quickly, she wouldn't have seen it had she not been looking directly at them as darkness fell.

I wonder if he knows they do that? Making a mental note to ask him in the morning, Torin dropped off to sleep.

With Staff Sergeant Beyhn semiconscious and strapped to a stretcher, doped to the eyeballs with a tranquilizer Dr. Sloan insisted was safe at any stage, Jonin stepped forward as the senior di'Taykan. While the sergeants had been seeing to the breakup of the camp, Torin had taken him aside and explained what he needed to do.

His hair spread out from his head, ends trembling slightly, he stared down at the body bag with dark blue eyes. "*Fraishin sha aren. Valynk sha haren.*"

Pushing his left mitten down, Sergeant Jiir bit a small piece off the base of his thumb, chewed, and swallowed. "*Kal danic dir k'dir. Kri ta chirkdan.*"

"We will not forget. We will not fail you." As he finished speaking, Major Svensson nodded, once, and

Torin dropped a knee to the packed snow, activating the single charge in the bag.

The bag stiffened, then flattened. When Private di'Lammin Oshyo had been reduced to ash and that ash contained, Torin picked up the small metal cylinder and slipped it into one of the measured pockets in her combat vest. She was the senior NCO, and it was part of her job to see that *all* her Marines made it home.

"Move them out, Gunny."

"Yes, sir." She swung her pack up over her shoulders and buckled it down. "Listen up, Marines! As of last night, this became a combat mission; Crucible's stopped playing by the rules, so we need to reach a position we can defend until the Navy finishes its latte and sashays on back here. You've got the new route and our destination on your slates. Sergeants, move your squads into position and let's haul ass."

EIGHT

YOU WERE RIGHT.

That got his attention. He checked again, but the message had indeed been sent by Gunnery Sergeant Torin Kerr to Civilian Salvage Operator Craig Ryder, point of origin the *CS NirWentry*. His codes had opened it, and the ship's security protocols had verified hers. A little worried about just how, exactly, he'd been right, Craig propped his heels up on *Promise*'s control panel and kept reading.

Those I've spoken to—people who should know about the escape pod—seem to have forgotten it ever existed. The brass has forgotten . . .

General Morris. Only brass it could be for Torin. Interesting that she wasn't mentioning names.

. . . and says it wasn't in my report or anyone's report, and not one of the team mentioned it in their debriefing. His aide agrees with him. Nothing unusual about that last bit except that I believe both of them believe what they're saying.

A yeoman and a member of Lieutenant Commander Sibley's deck crew off the B. also believe the escape pod doesn't exist.

She was paranoid enough not to spell out *Berganitan* but figured that Sibley, being dead, was safe. Safe from what? Respecting the paranoia of a professional, he cranked his security protocols up a notch.

Memories have been wiped and not by the military— civilian watchdogs would never allow us to develop that kind of tech.

True enough. A military of any kind gave most members of the Confederation bleeding piles and a good portion of those members would—if not for the aggression of the Others—happily stuff Humans, di'Taykan, and Krai back onto their home worlds and blockade them in. Had even the hint of a rumor of either branch working on mind control tech slipped out, shrill shrieks of hysteria would have filled known space; deafening and impossible to miss.

Logically, it had to have been done by one, or more, of the Elder Races—there's something about Big Yellow's escape pod they don't want us to know.

As Craig remembered it, it wasn't that great an escape pod—a smoothly featureless gray sphere with a padded interior designed for multiples of a smallish species or something Human-sized with no friends. Nothing about it seemed worth hiding. And mind wiping? What the hell was the point when everyone knew about Big Yellow? The alien ship had been all over the vids for days after they got back. What was so different about the pod?

Maybe that they *had* the pod.

Maybe the Elder Races didn't want tests run. Who knew what shite would be discovered?

He wished Torin had sent voice instead of text; he couldn't read emotion into words on a screen. That strong emotion prompted her to message, well, that was obvious. No other way Torin would have ever admitted he was right and she, by implication, was wrong. But which emotion. Fear? Anger?

Actually, if there was something in known space Torin

Kerr was afraid of, he didn't want to know about it. Anger, then. Much safer. The Elder Races had betrayed the Corps, which meant they'd betrayed Torin personally, and she was righteously pissed.

"Bloody, fukking hell." He rubbed both hands back through his hair and tugged hard enough to stretch his scalp. He'd just wanted Torin to check on his salvage, not find a conspiracy and then put things in motion to take it down.

The big question seems to be: Why weren't you and I wiped?

"Yeah, you think? Because I'm thinking who, specifically, is doing the wiping is a little more important."

What's different about us?

"Besides a donger even the H'san envy?"

And it has nothing to do with your dick.

Mind reading was apparently part of her job description. He wasn't sure how he felt about her ability to read him. Although, in all fairness, that had been a giveaway.

I believe they couldn't memory wipe us because we were deep scanned by Big Yellow. I believe the alien ship may have changed our brain wave patterns in some way. There's only one way to be sure about this.

His eyes widened as he realized where she was going. "Please don't."

There's only one other person deep scanned by Big Yellow who survived. You're going to have to find Presit a Tur durValintrisy and see if she remembers the pod.

Moaning, Craig dropped his face into his hands. The Katrien reporter was not one of his favorite people—she was an arrogant, self-absorbed show pony. Although, in all fairness, she thought he'd crawled out of the arse end of the universe, too. Eventually, because not looking at it wasn't going to make it go away, he lifted his head and finished the message.

If she remembers, tell her what I've told you and let her

blow this wide open. Classifying the pod is one thing, screwing with memories is something else again. If they've wiped out knowledge of this, what else have we forgotten? If they can adjust the memories of the Corps, what have they told us to do that we don't remember doing?

Yeah. Anger.

If all goes well, I'll be back on V. in about twenty-four days.

"What if it doesn't go well, eh?" he asked the screen. "What if this mind wiping *they* of yours catches on that they missed you and tries take you out on Crucible? What then?"

Then I get annoyed and kick their collective unnamed asses.

Even at this point in their—whatever the hell it was they had—it wasn't difficult to fill in Torin's responses. Bottom line, once past all the tougher than any four H'san shite she waved around, she was an uncomplicated person. An uncomplicated person who hadn't asked him to look up that yappy little reporter but had told him he was going to *have* to find her. Not only find her but get her to shut up long enough to listen to what he had to say. Fine. But did he have to stick around while Presit took on the Elder Races? No, he bloody well did not. He'd find a nice safe place to watch the shite hitting the fan.

Because what if that mind wiping *they* of Torin's caught on that they'd missed him? What then? Unlike Gunnery Sergeant Torin Kerr, he didn't have the Marine Corps at his back.

Compressing the message, he tucked it in behind his strongest encryptions. The thing that pissed him off most about Torin's expectations was that he kept trying to live up to them.

"You had me at what else have we forgotten," he muttered as he dropped his feet to the deck and began the search for Presit a Tur durValintrisy. "No bloody need to add well-armed amnesiacs to the problem."

"Mined?"

"Yes, sir."

The major glared down at the spray of blood and tissue across the snow. "Looks like we've got evidence the Others are keeping an eye on us. Hell, even if they haven't the capacity to watch all of us, all the time, on this heading, this is our likeliest route and they'd have been playing the odds to switch the mines on the moment they got our first heading. The swamp's frozen, but too exposed, and following the top of the ridge would be dangerous." He turned and squinted at the uneven spill of rock. "An ankle breaker without a stretcher. With one . . ."

"Yes, sir." Factor in ice and crevices masked with drifts of snow and even the di'Taykan would have difficulty taking that particular high road while carrying Staff Sergeant Beyhn. The thirty meters of flat land between ridge and swamp was the best route north. Low evergreens, their needles sharp enough to cut through exposed skin, hugged the base of the rock. Spindly trees—so close to willows in appearance and habitat that Torin applied the name even though they were an entirely different species on an entirely different world—grew in sparse clumps between the evergreens and the swamps. The land itself—probably boggy in the summer—was mostly flat and easy to move over.

At the moment, however, the most distinguishing feature of the area was the hole left by the mine—earth and rock and bits of bloody flesh spread out in a two-meter radius. By heading nearly due north since before dawn at the fastest possible pace the stretcher bearers could maintain, the platoon had moved far enough off the path of the training scenario that the mine field hadn't been marked on anyone's download.

There were plenty of high-tech ways to do soft tissue damage, but mines were cheap and so basic a construction that they couldn't be disarmed from orbit, requiring the significantly more dangerous physical contact. While it was a truism throughout most of known space that the shortest distance between two points was a straight line, it was equally true as far as the Corps was concerned that the shortest distance between two points had probably been mined. Both sides used them and although the Corps PR insisted the Others had used them first, Torin wouldn't have been willing to swear that was the case.

No way of telling when these particular mines had been planted although they'd undoubtedly been serviced the last time NHS19 had come up for maintenance. DIs bringing their platoons this way, knowing the mines were part of their scenario, would use them as teaching tools and object lessons; blowing them for the best effect.

Activating them wouldn't require reprogramming but merely the flipping of an off/on switch. Even with only partial control of the systems, the Others could easily manage that.

One/one had been on point, a minimum distance out in front.

"We're in bizarro land now, Gunny, keep them close," Major Svensson had told her as the team moved out. *"We can't take a chance on having a team cut off."*

Torin had agreed with the major's assessment.

In the lead, Hisht had been hugging the bushes, desperate enough for green that he was willing to put in the extra work to avoid the clumps of needles that capped each branch. He hadn't noticed the stubby-legged herbivore until he nearly stepped on it. He jumped back as the animal rocketed up out of its nest, tripped over his own boot print in the snow, and fell flat.

Pieces of the animal, chunks of dirt, shards of rock

and shrapnel from the mine passed harmlessly over his head.

Sakar was hit twice on his way to the ground, but his vest absorbed most of the impact.

Kichar's helmet deflected a rock that would have caved in the side of her skull.

Farthest from the blast, favoring the leg that had been creased in their first skirmish, Bonninski hadn't been hit by anything either large or solid enough to do damage.

Major Svensson looked at the four imprints of bodies in the snow, then over at the Marines who'd been bruised and frightened but were still very much alive. "Sometimes the gods smile," he grunted.

"Yes, sir."

And sometimes they kick you over and stomp you flat.

The major knew the corollary as well as Torin, so she didn't bother mentioning it.

Doctor Sloan, who'd gone through the shelling with considerable aplomb for a civilian, had reached her limit on explosions. She quickly checked bruises and inconsequential lacerations while keeping up a steady stream of snark about the sort of people who'd leave explosives lying around for other people to step on interspersed with a detailed list of just what exactly said explosives were capable of doing to Human, di'Taykan, and Krai bodies.

Sergeant Annatahwee started toward her, intending to shut her up.

"Let her talk." Torin blocked the sergeant's path.

"I don't think the recruits need to hear the gory details of what'll happen to them if they step on a mine."

"I do. A few gory details now could stop a lot of gore later."

"She's freaking them out."

"She's freaking you out; at least half of them seem fascinated. Let her talk."

Annatahwee stared past Torin's shoulder for a moment, then she nodded, spun on one heel—not an easy maneuver given the snow—and stomped away.

"Trouble, Gunny?"

"No, sir."

He pushed his helmet back on his head and scratched under the edge of his toque. "Options."

"The mines have no energy signature for the scanners to read, and while I have a reader on my slate, I don't have a wand." She paused, one brow up. The major would have a reader on his slate as well, she'd bet her pension on that. The only question was—would he have one of the filaments that actually swept the ground when the original scenario had not included mines?

"Reader," he nodded. "But no wand. You always forget to pack something. I probably left the lights on, too."

Running the mines without a wand had a survival rate just above suicidal.

"We'll be exposed out on the swamp, but the snow isn't deep and we'll make good time. We won't be as exposed on the ridge, but we'll move a lot more slowly."

The major squinted up at the top of the rocks. "And there's something to be said for having the high ground."

"Yes, sir."

"Mind you," he continued, "with this particular high ground what's likely to be said is, 'Help, I'm falling.' Odds of trouble from above?"

Torin glanced up at a pewter colored sky. "Likely, if you're talking about snow. Total crapshoot if you're talking about Crucible coming at us from the air. We're moving blind with no way of knowing what the Others have available to activate in this sector."

"All right. Without wands, the straight and narrow path is out. I don't like the idea of this lot having to fight the landscape as well as an unknown enemy, so that knocks us off the ridge. Looks like we're sprinting up the frozen swamp, Gunny. Any chance it's mined, too?"

"A slim one, sir. And if it is, we'll be able to pick it up on the scanners."

"We will?"

"Crucible is a classroom, sir. If there's a mine in the swamp, it's just there to reinforce the lesson these mines have taught. If a path is obvious to you, it's obvious to the enemy," she added when he indicated she should expand on just what that lesson might be. "And you should always watch where you walk."

"What if, in this case, they're teaching us that you can't get there from here?"

"Then we're screwed, sir." But the subtext said, *Stop being an ass just because you can. Sir.*

He heard the subtext and grinned. "Move 'em out on the ice, Gunny. We've got miles to go before we sleep."

Presit a Tur durValintrisy worked for Sector Central News, their main offices for this part of the sector at MidSector Station. Craig liked MidSector Station. It was a short Susumi jump away, it usually had a few cheap berths open, and there was a decent chop shop at sub27 where he could get a few parts for the *Promise* at an "I see no removed serial numbers" price.

Unfortunately, Presit, who considered herself an investigative journalist rather than a fuzzy pain in the arse, wasn't at MidSector Station. Fortunately, Craig had been with her on Big Yellow while she covered the top news story of the year; that plus his best smile and a little heavy charm convinced one of the office PAs to spill.

"She's where?"

"Presit a Tur durValintrisy are in orbit around Rosenee." The Katrien on his screen scrunched up her very pointed muzzle in distaste. "There are being riots on a gas mining platform."

"Is she likely to be there for a couple more days?"

"Easily. Apparently, she are getting to the bottom of things."

Craig grinned at the tone. Presit hadn't made herself too popular around the station, it seemed. "Let's hope I get there before someone shows her the bottom of a gas tube, then."

"There are no need for you to be hurrying."

"Any other time I'd agree with you, but this time I need to chew over some old news with her. Thanks for the info."

"You are welcome, Mr. Ryder. But if you are please not letting her know how you are finding her."

It took him a moment to untangle the syntax.

"Don't worry, darlin'," he told her at last. "I won't let on who gave me the drum."

She might have looked relieved, but it was hard for a nonfurbearing species to tell for certain. After he signed off, he called up all current Susumi equations for Rosenee, a gas giant out toward the edge of the sector's y-axis. As the basic equations would need specific adaptations for his ship, he poured himself a fresh cup of coffee and settled down at the console to do some basic math.

Bigger ships, ships with crews, had Susumi engineers. He had a good program, a head for numbers, and a basic desire to survive the trip.

"Sergeant Jiir! Long-range scanner's got an energy signal at 193 degrees!"

Jiir jogged over to the Marine's side. "Show me, Stevens."

"I don't . . ." Stevens tipped her head left, then right. "Damn."

"You've lost it?"

"It was at the edge of the scanner's range," she explained, continuing to try and coax the reading back. "It was barely . . . There! 193.77 degrees!"

From his lower angle he might have seen a flicker of something at 193.77, but he wasn't sure. At 193.84, though, his scanner showed a fuzzy point of contact. "Don't lose it again," he snapped. "And let me know the moment you get better definition." Stepping away from her position, he tapped his com with one mittened hand. "Gunny, we've got incoming on our six."

"How many?"

"Still too far back to get separate signals."

Long-range was relative with the basic helmet scanner. Marines were infantry and generally not particularly interested in anything they couldn't shoot with a KC-7—on the other hand, they were very interested in what might be showing up to shoot at them. Had they been carrying any artillery, they'd have had an actual long-range scanner. As it was, they could grab an energy signal at five kilometers under optimum conditions. Fortunately, the total absence of any ambient energy in the area made the current conditions about as optimum as it got.

"Let me know the moment we get a number."

"Sergeant Jiir! I have three signals, Sergeant."

He stomped back beside her and squinted through his scanner. "They're still at the edge of scanner range, Stevens. I'm only seeing one."

"They've split and come back together a couple of times. Never more than three contacts, though. There! See the split? Three contacts."

His nose ridges flared. "For maybe half a nanosecond. Are you sure?"

"Sir! Yes, sir!"

"Three," Torin repeated. "Good work, Sergeant. All right, people, let's pick up the pace!" As the platoon began to move faster over the frozen swamp, she trotted forward to tell the major.

"Three drones against thirty-six of us?" he snorted as

she fell into step beside him. "The Others never struck me as that bad at math."

"Nor me, sir, but it's likely taking them some time to program the CPNs. It's easier to free up the long-range drones the way they freed up the tank—they're throwing what they can at us while they work at gaining enough control over Crucible to destroy us." She pulled off a mitten and thumbed a map up on her slate. "We're off the scenario, so there's no telling what resources each CPN has, but . . ." A touch on the screen and the node they were approaching lit up. ". . . if we camp in tight, we can not only give McGuinty another chance to crack the system but extend the node's no fire zone over the platoon."

"No fire zone?"

"None of the scenarios I downloaded ever included making camp right on top of a node. Every camp has been a minimum of one kilometer away. It looks like the drones have safety protocols that keep them from firing near their controllers and by camping tight and forcing the Others to work through that on top of everything else, we'll delay them gaining control of this specific CPN."

"Unless they've already got control and we're walking into an ambush."

"We'll watch for that, sir."

He scratched his throat under the collar of the body-liner. "Or during the night they could gain control of everything but the safety protocols and ambush us in the morning."

"That's possible, sir. We'll take that into account when we move out."

"Business as usual, then, Gunny? Stay sharp and out of the bag?"

"Yes, sir."

"And the three drones behind us?" He jerked his head.

Torin turned, looking past the Marines, past the thick tufts of rushes stuck up through the ice, drifts of snow fingering out from their leeward side. She smiled. "We've got three Marines who shot Expert, sir."

Silver-gray sky, silver-gray snow; Stone checked his sights again and thanked any gods who were listening that the drones were not silver gray. At least the drones they'd seen so far hadn't been. These could be, of course.

A rustle to his right.

"Calm down, Cho," he murmured, eyes on the sky. No point in shutting down all energy systems if the drones sensed movement.

"They should be here by now. What if they changed heading?"

"Gunny said to give them an hour. Said if they haven't passed by then, they won't."

"Well, how long's it been?"

"Twenty-seven minutes."

"Seems longer."

He wasn't arguing. It had been the longest twenty-seven minutes he'd ever spent lying camouflaged in a snowbank.

"What if we can't see them," Cho muttered. "Snow and sky's the same color."

"Not to me," Lirit snorted from Stone's left. "I can see . . ."

"Incoming." He shifted slightly to better track the center drone. "Twelve o'clock."

"Got them."

"They're moving fast."

"Yeah, but right toward us."

"On my word." Gunnery Sergeant Kerr had put Stone in charge. *Because someone has to be,* she'd said. *And you're marginally the best shooter. You have to hit them simultaneously; if they start evasive action, you'll be*

SOL. It wasn't exactly shooting at a moving target; it was more like shooting at a target that kept getting bigger. The question became: how much bigger should they be allowed to get?

"Stone . . ."

"Wait for it."

The center drone filled his gunsight: triangular wings clearly visible, folded extremities a shadow against the main casing. He refused to look up and see how close it actually was.

"Acquire your target."

"One acquired."

"Three acquired."

"Two acquired." Maybe he didn't need to say it. He wasn't sure. "Fire on silent three count."

Deep breath on one. Hold it on two. Squeeze the trigger on three.

Three shots so close together they sounded like one. An instant after that, the echo bounced back off the ridge.

Two drones flared red and dropped out of the sky.

The third drone hit the ice and didn't bounce.

The crack as it broke through sounded like a fourth shot.

The sounds as the ice continued to crack brought up memories of a sinking tank and Stone threw himself back out of the drift, tripped over the rushes and landed in a tangled pile with both Cho and Lirit who had, evidently, done the same damned fool thing. The di'Taykan got to her feet first. Head cocked, she held up a hand for silence.

The other two Marines complied. The ice continued to crack.

"Son of a fukking . . ."

And then it stopped.

It was suddenly so quiet, Stone thought he could hear his nose hair freeze.

"Didn't come this far. We're okay."

Crack.

"Not that humping our butts out of here isn't a damned good idea!"

As the only Marine besides the major with recon experience, Major Svensson had put Torin on point with one/three—moving one/one, too jumpy to be sharp, into the body of the moving platoon.

"From here on in, we teach these Marines how to stay alive and that means we utilize all that government training we've benefited from over the years." He swept a pale gaze across his NCOs. *"Since we've got a whole platoon of greenies under attack, we'll all be getting our hands dirtier than we might be used to."*

Dirty wasn't a problem—cold, though, that was making things a bit dangerous as Torin, on her stomach, cheek pressed against the snow, both arms buried almost shoulder-deep, had begun to lose feeling in her fingers. On the other hand, the cold—or more specifically an eddy in the vapor plume her breath made in the cold air—had given away the position of the upper filament just before her shin would have hit the lower, so she had no plans of complaining too loudly.

"All right, Ashlan . . ." She worked her right hand free. ". . . give me back the scarab."

"I still can't believe you saw that line," he muttered as he set the tool back in her hand, waiting until her fingers had closed around it before he let go.

"I didn't see it." She carefully worked the blades back into the spool's access hole, right hand pressed against her left arm as it moved lest she cut anything better left in one piece. "I saw a pattern I couldn't identify."

"But you knew what it was," he insisted.

"Experience is the best teacher, Ashlan; everything on Crucible has been faced by Marines in combat more than

once. Next time, *you'll* know what it is." It had been almost seven years since she'd run into this particular bit of
nasty business—although *run into* was a bad choice of
words since not running into it was the preferred choice.
Once seen and the spool found, it was still a tricky bastard
to disarm. Unfortunately, it had been longer than seven
years for the major, Annatahwee had only worked on
simulators, and Jiir's arms were too short. "Nobody
move."

Working in micro movements that made the muscles
in her forearms ache, she touched the blunt edge of the
blade to the first line of tension, then the second, and
cut the third, careful not to even touch the fourth. She
was close enough to be safely under the filament's
rewind path, and if the other four stayed where she put
them . . .

Someone cried out.

No point in asking who'd moved when turning to
look would answer the question. Snapping the scarab
closed as it cleared the hole, she slid it into her combats
as she rolled up onto her feet.

The handful of snow Lumenz held against his chin
turned rapidly red. His expression as much embarrass-
ment as pain, he fumbled in his vest with his other hand
for a tube of sealant. Even Marines able to wade ankle-
deep through battlefield gore could freeze at the sight
of their own blood and Torin was pleased to see Lumenz hadn't.

As he tossed the snow aside and sprayed the slice
closed, she stepped closer. He stiffened, waiting for a
reaming out, but she only nodded as he spat out a
mouthful of foul tasting chemical, and said, "You're
lucky you didn't lose your nose."

On either side of an impressive protuberance, his
cheeks flushed.

"Bury the bloody snow." Swinging her weapon

around into her hands, she double tongued her implant to let the major know the path had been cleared. "All right, one/three, let's move."

"Gunny?"

"Lumenz."

"Why couldn't we have marked the trap for the platoon and walked around it?"

"Because the filaments don't always kill." She allowed the rage, present since she'd identified the trap, to rise. "They . . . *wound* indiscriminately." She hated the damned things; not only because of the damage they could inflict on their actual targets but because of the wild animal lying legless and still thrashing beside the first one she'd ever seen. Swearing in all three of the Corps languages, her sergeant had slit its throat and then disarmed the trap. No one in the squad mentioned that they were losing time and every one of them saluted the animal as they passed, its torment having saved the Marine on point a similar fate.

"But, Gunny, the time . . ."

"Fuk the time." They were racing the Others' ability to hack the security on the drones, and any time spent not moving toward Dunstan Mills might come back to kick their collective asses later. To his credit, the major had left the decision of disarming the filament up to her. Even knowing that the Others were activating lessons in the shittier parts of war all along the trail, and that they couldn't safely make up the time, she still couldn't, *wouldn't* leave that fukking thing up.

Considering what they'd already run into, she circled around an old piece of deadfall rather than stepping over it, one/three following carefully behind like heavily armed ducklings. *Tentative* heavily armed ducklings.

"Caution, not fear," she snapped.

"Yes, Gunnery Sergeant!"

In unison. While they might be afraid of what they'd face on the trail, they were definitely afraid of her. Not good. She dialed the rage back, packed it down until she could stuff the memory back into the compartment marked *do not open* it had been dragged out of. A deep breath of cold, damp air. These Marines were here on Crucible to be taught, so she'd teach them.

"Ashlan . . ."

The di'Taykan lengthened his stride until he was beside her. "Yes, Gunnery Sergeant."

"How do we know this trap was rigged recently?"

"Um . . . because we just got here? The enemy's either watching us on a satellite feed or they're extrapolating our path from the topography," he added hurriedly when she raised a *what the hell are you talking about* brow. "They couldn't have figured out we were going to choose this particular gully until two or three kilometers after we came off the swamp, so they had to have rigged the trap recently."

"Granted. But not the answer I was looking for. Thing is . . ." Another deep breath. ". . . specifics change, so you want to keep things as simple as possible. Filament is always rigged right in front of pursuit because it's indiscriminate; dead or injured wildlife will give its position away."

The silence had a different feel now. The Corps had little use for Marines unable to connect the dots and she could almost hear these three making connections.

"Gunny . . ."

No, she was not filling in details. "If you run into filament—and trust me when I say I mean that euphemistically—it means that you're climbing up the enemies' butt. It could mean they want to slow you down while they set up an ambush in better terrain or that they're heading for somewhere they think they can defend, and they're slowing you down to make sure they can get there."

"But today . . ."

Torin shrugged, cutting off the question. "Today it's

probably nothing more than a simple 'if, then' statement. If Platoon 71 goes this way, then we'll activate this. If it goes that way, then we'll activate that. And as soon as we've reprogrammed enough drones, we'll drop everything we've got on them and wipe them off the planet."

"They may not."

"Yeah, they will." A triangular crack in the rock ahead and to the left was large enough for a drone. She brought the team to a stop, sent Lumenz to check it out, and kept a light on it as they passed. "Because it's what I'd do."

"If they know we're here, then they know where we're going. On this heading, there's only one logical place to make a stand." Ashlan seemed to be thinking aloud.

Torin appreciated that—both for the thinking and the aloud. "And?"

"And they'll have baked a *crif*," muttered a dry voice from the rear.

Kaimi, the second di'Taykan in the squad, had a cynicism unusual in her species. It made her seem remarkably Human in spite of the lavender hair and eyes, but Torin had long since learned not to fall into the "sounds like must be like" trap. Ducking under a low hanging branch, she snorted. "Even so, knowing when and where the battle's going to be beats planning on the fly."

The di'Taykan's mittened hand came into her peripheral vision as he reached out to move the next branch along. "You make it sound so simple."

"Well, it's war; it's not rocket science." Then the memory of what had once been accomplished by three Marines with a surface-to-air missile launcher, a game chip, and the guts from a field kitchen twisted her mouth into a grin. "Usually," she repeated.

"It's good to be more than just an observer, isn't it, Gunny?"

Torin, watching Sakur and Jonin carefully moving Staff Sergeant Beyhn from the stretcher into his shelter, wondered how the hell Major Svensson expected her to respond to that. As far as she was concerned, she'd never been an observer. Her job was to fulfill mission objectives while keeping those Marines she was responsible for alive. She had been responsible for the major and Dr. Sloan; she was now responsible for the major, Dr. Sloan, and Platoon 71. Her hand rose to touch the small metal cylinder holding the remains of Private di'Lammin Oshyo—it was nothing more than a matter of degree.

Was it good to be back in actual combat instead of playing silly buggers against a system that guaranteed only the extraordinarily stupid or inordinately unlucky could get hurt? Actually, yes. Everyone liked their work to have meaning.

And no.

Given the present circumstances, only a fool or an optimist would assume they'd seen their final KIA, and Torin was neither.

Fortunately, the major kept talking. "I hated being sent to Crucible while Marines were fighting a war. If I was combat ready, I wanted to be back in combat. You know?"

She did. "Yes, sir."

Which did not mean that he wanted the war to come here just so he could be back in the thick of it. Too many officers liked to make it all about them, but Major Svensson knew there was war enough to go around.

They'd kept moving through dusk and into early dark in order to make it to the theoretical safety of the next CPN. Torin had half expected the drones to attack at their closest perimeter, and when that attack never happened thanked any gods listening that they'd beaten the Others' reprogramming. She only hoped that the other three platoons of recruits spread out over the planet were doing as well.

Fumbling his slate back onto his belt, the major sank down onto an ancient rockfall at the base of the cliff and almost, but not quite, made it look as though his legs hadn't nearly given out under him.

Torin watched him as she set up their shelter and because he had a bit of color back in his cheeks when she rejoined him she asked only, "How's the hand, sir?"

He had his mittens off, thumb of his right hand digging into the palm of his left. "Itches. The part I hate most about healing."

"Dr. Sloan . . ."

"Is busy dealing with the staff sergeant. Trying to get enough information to deal with the staff sergeant," he amended as an incredulous shout of *"You have got to be kidding me!"* rose out of the middle of a cluster of half a dozen di'Taykan.

Lirit stumbled back as the doctor pushed past her, the cluster opening to watch the doctor stomp away, a dark slash of blue against the gray-on-gray the uniforms and the snow had become after sunset. If Torin had to guess, based on body language and the movement of their hair, all six of them were embarrassed. And that was a description she couldn't remember ever having applied to a di'Taykan.

"They really don't know anything," Dr. Sloan announced the moment she was close enough, where *close enough* meant she obviously didn't care who overheard, "when that blue hair . . ."

"Private di'Arl Jonin," Torin interrupted.

"Right. Fine. When Private Jonin said his people don't talk about this, he meant it literally." She dropped her volume slightly as she planted her boots in front of Torin and Major Svensson, but only slightly. "I have only theoretical knowledge of the change, and even I know more details than these

Marines do. This is going to happen to their bodies someday and the only information they have is that they should head home at the first indication the change has begun."

"A Taykan heading into qui while still in the Corps gets an immediate medical discharge," Major Svensson told her quietly.

"And that's a big help now. Staff Sergeant Beyhn has been having a series of small seizures as his brain chemistry adjusts to the new *normal*." The doctor sketched mitten-thick quotation marks in the air around the final word. "But, unfortunately, since I don't know where things are supposed to end up, I can't actually define normal, so any response I make is based on a less-than-informed guess."

"Come on, Doc, you do experimental procedures all the time. A lot of that is guesswork."

"It's the less-than-informed I'm having trouble with," she snapped. "And speaking of . . ." She pulled her slate from one voluminous pocket. "Let's see your hand."

He held out his right hand.

Dr. Sloan looked down at his palm and her brows dipped. That was enough to pull his left hand around to join the right.

Torin was impressed; she couldn't have done it better herself.

As the screen lit up with numbers and what looked like a small graph, the doctor frowned at her slate. "You're still very active on the molecular level and the temperature in the surrounding tissue is up one fourteenth of a degree."

"And that means?"

"That you're still very active on the molecular level and the temperature in the surrounding tissue is up one fourteenth of a degree." Moving the scan up his arm, her frown deepened. "The join is holding, but I need probes of . . ."

"Doctor!" All three of them turned to see Jonin half out of the staff sergeant's shelter. The four di'Taykan who had assigned themselves guard duty on first watch brought their weapons up. "It's happening again!"

"What's happening again?" the major demanded as Dr. Sloan started to move and Torin made a gesture that suggested those weapons be lowered immediately or they'd end up somewhere extremely unpleasant.

"Could be a lot of things. This is me off to my next learning experience." She stopped four strides out and half turned. "Are we likely to be attacked tonight?"

Torin shook her head. "The odds are against it, ma'am. We're right on top of the CPN, and they're too expensive to lose."

The noncombatant chip rode up and down on her forehead as she frowned. "The Others care about the Corps budget?"

"No, ma'am, but they'd have to reprogram each drone individually and crack a number of safety protocols to bring the drones in this close."

"And that's not likely to happen because? I mean, since they're clearly already able to hack the system?"

"It would mean that of all the Marines on Crucible, they're choosing tonight to focus all their reprogramming attention on us. Possible, but as I said, the odds are against it. And even if they are, hacking through safety protocols takes time."

"Good." She snapped out the word like it was the final one on the subject and continued on her way to the shelter.

Torin watched as she dove inside, saw the sides of the shelter bulge and shook her head. "That's got to be a little crowded in there."

"I think the doc can handle it, Gunny."

And Sakur emerged right on cue, his hair whipping

back and forth as he stood and glared down at the door he'd just been summarily backed out of.

"So all that screwing around with the staff sergeant's slate that you were doing today . . ." Piroj shuffled left, then right, then finally gave up attempting to see around his teammate. ". . . I'm guessing you were beating his high score in *Delaysu Tong*."

McGuinty's gaze flicked between his slate and the node's screen. "What the fuk are you talking about?"

"You're not in, are you?"

"What was your first clue?" He scowled at the scrolling lines of code, frustration level rising, and touched the screen, freezing the numbers in place.

Piroj juggled his weapon from hand to hand. "Fact I'm still standing here freezing my ass off and not in the shelter, boots off and starting to warm up, that gave me the first clue. Fact you're still playing with that thing gave me the second."

"Oh, yeah, playing. This is fukking fun and games." The Others might not have gotten around to reprogramming Crucible's drones, but they definitely controlled the system, locking him out with encryptions that weren't just alien, they were *weirdly* alien, and that was distracting because he kept thinking they weren't alien at all—and then they were again. But numbers were numbers and code was code, and he'd been so close to cracking the insanely-more-complicated Ventris security when they shipped for Crucible that he should have been able to get this. Except he wasn't. It just . . . kept . . . slipping . . . by. "Crap!" Slate shoved under his arm, he began working the screen with both hands as the light in the niche began to pulse.

"Ah, shit, look at the lights. Are you doing that? McGuinty?"

"Shut the fuk up!" The CPN, built into a niche carved

out of the wall of a steep-sided gully, was identical to the previous CPN, and both were kissing cousins to the station consoles he'd grown up with. The weird alien encryption did not—thank God—extend to the security protocols. This sudden cascade, he could stop. Probably.

"McGuinty! What's happening?"

"What part of shut the fuk up don't you get?" This wasn't especially complex, it was just moving fast. The trick was to get ahead of it and . . . "Got it!" The pulsing stopped. The light settled back down to the traditional dim glow, and his heart settled with it. He really wanted a stim, but he didn't dare risk it with the rest of the platoon so close.

"You said you disconnected the security codes!" Piroj smacked the barrel of his KC-7 against McGuinty's shoulder.

"I did!" As his bodysuit sucked up the sweat, McGuinty turned his back on the node and smacked the barrel away, glaring at the other Marine. Piroj's nose ridges flared, his lip pulling up off his teeth, and McGuinty forced himself to calm down. He needed all his fingers. "All right, so I missed one. If I hadn't stopped it, we'd have lost the core."

"The data storage?" With no challenge to respond to, Piroj's ridges snapped closed with one final puff of water vapor. "That where the command codes for the drones stay when they're home?"

"Yeah. No. Sort of."

"If the drones don't have commands, what happens to them?"

"I dunno. I guess they fall out of the sky."

The words hung between them for a moment, then Piroj shrugged. "So, I'm not raised in a can, techie-type, but wouldn't that be a good thing? Least while we're up this node's tree?"

. . . in this node's territory, McGuinty translated, and

then the implications smacked him in the chops. "Crap. Crap. Crap!" Whirling around, he stared at the screen. Stopping the core dump had been instinct. Station kids learned early on that hard vacuum was unforgiving of mistakes and that hacking any system on station meant small, careful, *specific* changes. Control maintained at all times. That control had nearly given him Ventris. "But we're not in a fukking vacuum now," he muttered. His intervention had knocked him right back to the beginning, tossed him out through the layers of encryption he'd already broken. The Corps' crest, the only thing currently on the screen, seemed to be mocking him.

"Problems, Marine?"

He snapped to attention at the sound of the major's voice, heard Piroj doing the same.

"Sir! No, sir!"

"Glad to hear it. As you were."

Backing up until he was beside his teammate, McGuinty wished Major Svensson had stopped about two meters farther away. *Probably intentionally looming. Officers probably do that.* He wasn't quite as short as the Krai—*Not quite as good looking either*, Piroj had pointed out toothily—but the major was tall enough, and close enough so that distinction became moot.

"So . . ." Major Svensson frowned down at the node. "This is as far as you've gotten?"

He actually felt his ears heat up. "No, sir! I got tossed trying to prevent a critical error."

Beside him, Piroj shifted his weight from boot to boot.

"Well, why don't you two relax for a moment while we see if I can get us in a little further." The major paused, right hand raised, bare fingers nearly touching the screen. "I assume I need to disable the security codes?"

"Yes, sir, but only because I . . ." *Marines don't make*

excuses, Recruit! He could all but hear Staff Sergeant Beyhn's voice. "Yes, sir."

Major Svensson moved one-handed through the first few layers of security. He seemed to know what he was doing.

But then, my eight-year-old niece could get this far in.

After a few more minutes, the major made a speculative sound, pulled off his other mitten, and began to work two-handed. If he could work the screen two-handed, he definitely knew what he was doing. Speed mattered when breaking systems. McGuinty wondered if the major was station-born.

And then he just wondered what the major was doing since his chance of seeing the screen through the broad shoulders now blocking it was zero to zilch. He'd have moved in on another guy in the platoon, but one twenty days of training suggested officers got shitty about being crowded.

When he glanced over at Piroj, the Krai gave a been-there-done-that kind of shrug.

Major Svensson worked in silence while McGuinty wondered how long they were going to have to stand there. It had been a long, hard hump, and if the major thought he was going to break the node, then maybe other people could go get some sleep. Not that the major was going to break the node or anything because McGuinty was into his second night of tearing through the both the Corps' encryptions and that weird alien shit and he hadn't even found the drones' programming yet, and he knew how good he was.

He was just working up a good head of resentment for officers who showed up and showed off and kept people who knew what they were doing from their jobs when the major jerked, muttered, "What the hell?" and stepped away from the screen. When he turned, rubbing his head with the heel of his right hand, he looked as frustrated as McGuinty felt.

"It was . . . There was . . ." He turned just enough to glare at the node. "Well, at least I . . ." The pause was almost too long then he shook his head. "It's all yours, McGuinty, and good luck."

"Yes, sir."

He stumbled as he walked away, catching his boots on the deep footprints others had left in the snow banked against the side of the gully, and McGuinty remembered how recently he'd been detanked.

"Major's not doing too bad considering he was a floater not so many tendays ago."

Piroj seemed to be reading his mind, and that was just fukking scary. "He got five screens in, that's not too bad. At least there's a bunch of really basic crap I don't have to redo."

"Oooo, bite!" The Krai snapped his teeth together and McGuinty grinned.

"Gunnery Sergeant Kerr? Can I speak with you?"

"No one's stopping you, Kichar." Torin took another pull on her pouch of coffee. Under her earnest expression, the young Marine looked even more tightly wound than usual. Given the events of the day, it wasn't hard to figure out why.

"It's my helmet, Gunnery Sergeant." In the reflected light of moon and stars, the helmet in question was a rounded blur—built-in camouflage darkening with the setting of the sun. "Damaged equipment is to be reported to the senior NCO."

In previous, albeit limited conversations, Kichar had tended to sound like a vid Marine—all clichéd gung ho. Right now, she sounded like a twenty-year-old whose fireteam had detonated a mine that had thrown up a rock that had nearly killed her. Easier to process Private di'Lammin Oshyo's death—it had happened to someone else. Torin held out her free hand. "Let's see it."

Kichar glanced around the camp, pulled the helmet off her head, and reluctantly passed it over.

Given the light levels, the damage wasn't a lot easier to see up close and personal but a rough, palm-sized patch on the right side indicated where the photovoltaic covering had been destroyed. Although she knew very well what had happened, Kichar needed to talk about it with someone who wasn't all *Oh, my God, you nearly died!* "Let's hear the report, then."

"Gunnery Sergeant, the helmet was damaged at 10:13 this morning when one/one detonated an anti-personnel mine, probably a L08 on the trail. During the subsequent explosion, a piece of rock about six centimeters in diameter slammed into this Marine's helmet."

"More of a glancing blow than a slam." Torin turned the helmet upside down on her knee and checked the inside. She couldn't feel any damage and assumed one of the sergeants had checked it while they still had the light. "Good thing these weren't built by the lowest bidder." Dark brows drew in over a raptor's nose as Kichar responded to her quip. "Are you all right?"

The brows were reluctantly lifted. "Yes, Gunnery Sergeant."

"Did you have the doc check you out just in case?"

"Yes, Gunnery Sergeant."

"What do you think I should do about your helmet?"

"It's damaged, Gunnery Sergeant. I had the suggested diagnostic chip in my pack, but I can't repair the photovoltaic cover."

"Uh-huh." A little more coffee seemed called for. Torin took a long swallow. "Kichar, in a combat situation, which this is, there's really only one response I, as senior NCO, can make to this kind of damage." She saw Kichar square her shoulders, waiting for the reprimand, and had to remind herself that Platoon 71 was technically still in training where rules were rules and sergeants were vengeful gods. She'd probably find a little yelling comforting, but Torin was neither her mother nor her DI. "This kind of damage . . ." Torin tapped the rough spot. ". . . seems a fair exchange for a functioning brain."

"Gunnery Sergeant?" Kichar seemed more confused than relieved.

"Equipment gets damaged in battle, Private, no way around it. However," she added dryly passing the helmet back, "if you see a rock coming at your head, it's still best to duck. Easier on your headgear."

"Duck, Gunnery Sergeant?"

"If you see it coming—where *it* applies to anything damaging coming at you. Sometimes, it's rocks. Did you see this rock coming?"

"No, Gunnery Sergeant."

"Then ducking couldn't have helped you." Torin shoved the empty pouch in her pocket. "R&D comes up with new weapons all the time," she said as she stood and stretched. "And yet, in spite of new tech, in spite of all that time and money they spend teaching Marines how to be Marines, we can still be taken out by something as simple as a rock."

"A rock!" Kichar spat the word at the night, reaction breaking through her tightly wrapped control as anger. "I could have been killed by a rock!"

"And you wouldn't be the first."

"We can be killed by rocks, Gunny!"

"Yeah, it's insulting."

"Insulting?" Torin admired the way her voice had begun to rise on the second syllable and got dragged back down to a lower volume on the third. The dark brows dipped in again. "You don't think that after all this tech and all this training, it would be *humbling*?"

"Not likely." The snort conveyed Torin's feelings perfectly in a situation where facial expressions couldn't be seen. "Nothing humbles a Marine, Kichar, or we'd have packed this shit in long ago. You're not on watch, so you should get some sleep. It's another long, fast hump tomor . . ."

"Stop him!"

"What the hell?" Naked di'Taykan weren't unexpected in the Corps, or anywhere else in known space, but Torin had never seen one bounding up the side of a snow-covered gully before. Out of uniform, uncamouflaged, Staff Sergeant Beyhn was easier to spot than the rest of the Marines—there wasn't enough light to see hair color but as Dr. Sloan was doing the shouting, Torin went out on a limb and made the identification. Half a dozen clothed and helmetless Marines were right behind him but unwilling to reach out and grab the closest body part.

And that's a hesitation I never thought would apply to a di'Taykan.

Given how protective they'd all gotten, she assumed they didn't want to hurt him.

Unfortunately, the staff sergeant didn't share their warm and fuzzy feelings. He turned at the top of the gully and kicked out, catching his closest pursuer in the chest, sending her plummeting along with the di'Taykan directly behind her.

It was a hard enough shove that they only bounced once before they hit the packed snow at the bottom.

Torin, Kichar hard on her heels, was there before the impact blizzard settled. "Lirit?"

"I'm okay," she gasped, struggling to her knees, arms sinking past her elbows into the snow. "We have to catch him, Gunny!"

Torin met the major's eyes over Ashlan's still body. "No argument here."

It took nearly three hours, and they might not have found him until dawn had the wind not shifted, blowing the staff sergeant's scent back over the searching di'Taykan and sending them into a fresh frenzy.

He was unconscious when Sakur and Jonin carried him back to his shelter.

So was McGuinty, lying crumpled to one side of the smoldering node, bits of hot metal having melted a pattern into the snow around him.

NINE

"**I WAS WORKING THROUGH ONE** of the new encryptions, not the Corps stuff but one the Others added that was kind of wound through the Corps stuff, and the pattern just kept sliding away. See, everyone's got a pattern, Gunny. Krai, di'Taykan, Human; if you're even a little plugged in, you can look at Corps code and figure out what race laid it down. Mictok, they're base eight, so I can't crack their shit but I can finger it, you know?"

"No, I didn't." It made sense, the Mictok having eight legs and all, but the giant spiders weren't in the Corps, so their math wasn't Torin's concern. "Focus, McGuinty."

"Sorry, Gunnery Sergeant. I . . ." He blinked bloodshot eyes and stared over Torin's left shoulder like he was looking for answers on the inside of shelter. "Is Piroj in trouble? I convinced him to go join the search for Staff Sergeant Beyhn."

"McGuinty!" Her voice pulled his gaze back to her face. "I will deal with Private Piroj. You will tell me what happened at the node."

"I don't know, Gunnery Sergeant." His shoulders rose and fell within the confines of the bedroll, and he sounded both miserable and guilty. "I was concentrating on what I was doing and then I was opening my eyes, only the light was too bright, and Dr. Sloan was asking me to pull her finger."

Years of practice kept Torin's reaction dialed back to a single blink. "I think she was asking you to *follow* her finger." She waved her index finger in front of his face, stopping as belated understanding dawned.

"That makes more sense," he admitted. "Is the CPN destroyed?"

"You remember that?"

When she raised a brow, thin cheeks darkened and he said, "No, Gunnery Sergeant. I heard you and Sergeant Jiir talking after the doc brought me round. It wasn't me. I never triggered something that would cause it to explode."

"I know."

He blinked and swallowed. "You know?"

"Dr. Sloan says you were taken down by a choke hold." This wasn't exactly what the doctor had said but rather the translation into Marine. "That's not something a piece of flying debris could manage. You don't remember being grabbed?"

"No." One hand struggled up from the depths of the bag to touch his throat. Torin could just see the tips of pale fingers against the darkening bruise. "But they'd have grabbed me from the back, so even if I did remember— and I don't—I wouldn't have seen them. How did they destroy the node?"

"I have no idea, McGuinty. Come morning, you can tell me."

"Yes, Gunnery Sergeant!"

Smiling slightly, in spite of everything, at his attempt to give the trained response, Torin backed away from the bedroll. With the injured Marine alone in the shelter, there was room to turn, but the last thing he needed right now was an accidental boot in the head. Besides, discipline tended to suffer when senior NCOs waved their asses in the face of their Marines. *di'Taykan excepted*, she amended, watching McGuinty's eyes close.

As her feet pushed through the shelter's flap, his eyes snapped open. "I'm better when I have a roof, Gunny."

"I hear you," she told him, allowing her smile to show. "I'm better when I have something to shoot at. Get some sleep, McGuinty."

As she settled her weight back on her heels, pulling her upper body through the flap, his eyes closed and his breathing deepened. Rocking up onto her feet, Torin stroked off the light on her sleeve, then pulled on toque and helmet as she turned.

"You were right," she said to the waiting doctor. "He was a little loopy."

"Did you find out who did it?"

"No, ma'am. He doesn't remember."

"He might eventually."

Torin made a noncommittal noise, then asked about the staff sergeant.

Dr. Sloan folded her arms, the puffy sleeves of her jacket making the motion awkward. "No change; although it's a good thing the Taykan have a lower body temperature to begin with."

"Private Ashlan?"

"Concussion. I've got him in the shelter with the staff sergeant. They both seem calmer with the physical contact, and I'll be able to get more sleep. Speaking of sleep, Major Svensson's out for the night. He covered a lot of ground today, more than may have been smart, and his headaches are back. I doubt tonight's is the first on Crucible," she continued before Torin could demand details, "but it's the first he's come to me about. Don't worry, Gunnery Sergeant, he's had worse."

"Worse?" Torin prodded. Her eyes had finally adjusted to the ambient light provided by starlight on snow and what she saw on the doctor's face was not reassuring.

"For a while, right after he came out of the tank, he was losing almost an hour a day. Then a few minutes.

Then there was a pain and pressure but nothing entirely unexpected given the extent of the damage. When I cleared him for this . . ." She waved both hands in the universal sign for *I have no idea what the hell this is.* ". . . he'd gone days with a clear reading. Tonight, well, like I said, I've seen worse, but I'm reading dilation of blood vessels, *major* stimulation of the trigeminal nerve and the subsequent release of sensitizing chemicals; there's a series of neuronal clusters—in the sensory ganglions, the brainstem and the thalamus—that are . . ." She stopped, took a closer look at Torin's face, and sighed. "You don't really care about this, do you, Gunnery Sergeant."

"No, ma'am."

"All right, short form: he was in pain, he's been in worse. I've given him a sedative and, best case scenario, he'll be at least as mobile as Ashlan and McGuinty by morning."

"Worst case?"

"He'll wake up feeling the pressure of each single hair like a knife blade into his scalp. If that's the case, I'll up his serotonin levels until he's functional."

"Thank you, Doctor."

As Torin started to pass, Dr. Sloan reached out and grabbed her arm. "That throat grip that incapacitated Private McGuinty; could you have done it?"

Torin shook her head. "I'm not really about precise application of pressure, Doctor. I could have killed him, but I'm not sure I could have just knocked him out."

"Then who?"

"I don't know."

"I was thinking that these recruits didn't spring fully formed from the head of Zeus."

"Ma'am?" It had been a long day and a long night and Torin was four downed Marines and a body bag past having the patience for riddles.

"These recruits had lives before they became Marines."

"We do a security check, ma'am. The Confederation has rules about not giving weapons to those likely to abuse them."

"Of course." As she still held Torin's arm, Torin waited while she gazed around at the cluster of nearly invisible shelters, then up at the stars, then at Torin. "The idea was to test the major's recovery under controlled conditions. I'm beginning to think it was a bad idea."

Piroj was waiting for her by the destroyed node. He came to attention as she approached.

Torin stopped about two meters away and stared down at his face—any closer and she'd have been staring down at the top of his head. Height differences created distinct difficulties with getting in the face of the Krai.

Although he had his bodyliner pulled up over his lower face, she knew his lips were up off his teeth in an instinctive reaction to threat. She locked his gaze with hers and waited. It didn't take long for clouds of water vapor to start thinning as his body realized challenging would be a remarkably suicidal thing to do and his nose ridges closed. Behind the bodyliner, his teeth were now covered.

"Private Piroj."

He twitched. "Gunnery Sergeant!"

"Stop shouting, it's the middle of the Goddamned night."

"Yes, Gunnery Sergeant."

"You were watching Private McGuinty's back."

"Yes, Gunnery Sergeant."

"And yet when Private McGuinty suggested you join the hunt for Staff Sergeant Beyhn, off you went."

"He convinced . . ." Her expression cut the protest dead. "Yes, Gunnery Sergeant."

"You deserted your post, Private McGuinty was attacked, and our chance of controlling Crucible in the immediate future was sabotaged. Did I miss anything?"

"No, Gunnery Sergeant."

"You're damned lucky you weren't *ordered* to watch McGuinty's back, Private, because then we'd be talking about more than an error in judgment." And one just as likely to be made under the same circumstances by Marines a lot less raw, but she wasn't going to tell him that. "What is the best time for the enemy to infiltrate an encampment?" She whipped the question at him hard enough to hurt.

"When the functioning of the camp has been disturbed by a diversion either presented or taken advantage of, sir!" His nose ridges opened and closed. "I mean, Gunnery Sergeant."

"Right out of the book. Try to remember it next time." Moving up beside him, she crouched and swept her light over the ground. The snow around the node had been alternately churned up and packed flat by half a dozen sets of boots before she'd put Piroj on guard. "I hope you haven't let anyone disturb the site, Private, because that *was* an order."

"No, Gunnery Sergeant. I mean, no one has disturbed the site."

Not that it mattered. She had as much hope of finding an enemy track in that mess as the teams out circling the camp looking for access tracks did. The hunt for Staff Sergeant Beyhn had provided the perfect cover. Straightening, she switched her attention to the remains of the CPN. Given the pattern of the debris, it had obviously been destroyed from within. A self-destruct to prevent recruits from messing with their scenarios? Turning components and housing to slag seemed excessive.

"Private Piroj, I am now giving you an order to watch McGuinty's back." The packed snow immediately in front of the node where no slag had spattered marked where McGuinty had fallen. "He's still our best bet at regaining control of the system, and nothing gets in the way of that. He doesn't take a crap without supervision. Understand?"

"Yes, Gunnery Sergeant."

"Good." Stepping back, she caught his gaze again and didn't let hers soften although her voice was kinder when she said, "Dr. Sloan says McGuinty'll be fine by morning. No lasting damage done. He's already asleep, so you might as well be, too. Go."

"Nothing. No tracks; no signs of any kind." Sergeant Annatahwee smothered a yawn with the back of her fist. "No surprise. We made a mess of the perimeter searching for the staff sergeant and if the Others made it to the ridge, well, there's a lot of bare rock. If we had a scout—hell, if we had something besides a platoon of greenies . . ." No need to define how they could use a scout. They all knew.

"And we have no idea of what we're looking for," Sergeant Jiir put in, shifting his weight from foot to foot. He looked fidgety, but it was more likely a psychological reaction to the cold—movement equaled warmth even when environmental controls did the actual warming. "The Others have put fourteen species in uniform and for all we know, this group that infiltrated Crucible could be a fifteenth."

Torin nodded because neither sergeant had said anything she disagreed with. "The sammy that took down the OP, that didn't go up from our immediate neighborhood. Same hemisphere, sure, but not so close we needed to be expecting callers."

"They must've known someone was fukking with their programming. All they had to do was use the observational satellites to see who was standing by the CPN being fukked with," Jiir muttered into the neck of his bodyliner.

"But a physical attack makes no sense when they're

so far away. And there's another three training platoons down here, with their senior DIs still in charge. They must be trying to access the nodes as well."

"Then maybe one of the Others got bored with surveillance and was sent out for some one-on-one shit disturbing before they caused trouble at the base."

"But why sent to us?"

Jiir shrugged, a Human motion the Krai had picked up. "Why not? One in four chance, those are pretty good odds."

"Not so good as all that," Annatahwee corrected. "There's always armored and artillery down here. And R&D has a couple of setups, too, though I don't know if they're dirtside now."

"Then there'll be a ship back before the *NirWentry*?" The moment the Navy cleared Susumi space and discovered the Orbital Platform had been destroyed, the Others still dirtside would have no chance to run. With the system free of the enemy's ships, the Navy would have no distractions to keep them from finding the Others, even with a whole planet to search. Torin wondered if she could swing a posting on the team sent in to take the nest of Others out.

"Sorry, Gunny," Annatahwee broke into her thoughts, "but the *NirWentry*'s got transport duty all to herself. Back every eight days, like clockwork. Sometimes it's just us; sometimes we've got a whole artillery company packaged up with us."

"Sergeant, if you know where you can get us a whole artillery company . . ."

"If they're dirtside, they're not even in this hemisphere, Gunny. They've got this massive desert just below the equator that they practice blowing up."

"So given the size of the planet and the number of Marines scattered across it, we're looking at ridiculously long odds when we consider that the Others chose our camp to dance into when they were nowhere near us a little better than twenty-seven hours ago."

Jiir frowned up at her. "So what are you saying, Gunny?"

"These recruits had lives before they became Marines."

If the Elder Races could wipe out the memory of Big Yellow's escape pod, they could fake a past for a recruit and get it through the Corps security. Which hadn't been what Dr. Sloan'd meant, but that didn't make her observation any less relevant. And there was nothing to say they hadn't set this operation up years ago; Annatahwee and Jiir could as easily be compromised as any of the recruits. Hell, even Beyhn wasn't off the hook. His conditioning could have been what drove him up onto his feet. He could have doubled back and taken out McGuinty and the node while the di'Taykan were searching the woods for him. Major Svensson? Dr. Sloan? Unlikely, but given that she was considering an Elder Races mind fuk on a galactic scale, the line leading to *unlikely* had already been crossed.

"Gunny?"

She forced both hands to unclench. "Just thinking about ridiculously long odds, Sergeant." Get her people to safety, take out whoever tried to stop them—conspiracy theories weren't going to be much help. "Sunrise is at 0711. Get them up at 0530. We've got just over eleven hours of daylight, and I want us moving the moment there's enough light to keep the stretcher bearers from breaking an ankle."

"One/two is scouting tomorrow. Will you be going out with them?"

"As it stands right now." And all three turned toward the shelter where Major Svensson slept. "Makes more sense than sending them alone," Torin continued.

"They're short one."

Torin touched her vest. "I know."

*   *   *

"Gunnery Sergeant."

"Dr. Sloan." Torin handed the doctor the pouch of coffee she'd just opened for herself and pulled another one out of the kit. She'd seen the camp locked down, then grabbed a couple of hours' sleep, years of practice getting her out of her bedroll and then out of the shelter at 0515. The air had started to lose a bit of its bite and was so still she half wished she'd gotten up earlier to enjoy the peace a little longer. No birds or animals stirred, no breeze rubbed branches or rustled evergreen needles; the only sound she could hear was the faint, rhythmic creak of a sentry's boots against the packed snow and that was more a comfort than an intrusion.

Dr. Sloan settled beside her on the rock, swallowed, and sighed. "Nice morning," she said after a minute. "When can we expect the fireworks?"

"Hard to say. With the CPN destroyed, the drones it controls are either inoperative or locked into their last commands unless the Others managed to reprogram before the destruction, in which case they could attack at any time."

"Either. Or. Unless." The doctor shook her head. "So you have no idea?"

"I know there's nothing showing on my scanner." Torin savored her first mouthful of coffee.

"Small mercies," the doctor muttered, then added in what Torin had come to recognize was her professional tone, "Did you get any sleep?"

"Enough. You?"

"Enough." She cocked an eyebrow as Torin gave a disbelieving grunt. "It may interest you to know, Gunny, that your profession is not the only one capable of functioning through high stress, life-and-death situations with little sleep."

It seemed safer to murmur an apology than to mention that few life-or-death situations were low stress. "Staff Sergeant Beyhn?"

"Back to yesterday's semiconsciousness, occasionally seizing delirium."

Tucking her coffee pouch into its pocket on her vest, Torin pulled out her slate. "Ashlan's stats are reading near normal."

Dr. Sloan glanced down at the screen and snorted. "Normal post-concussion; no blood vessels torn, but no guarantee there won't be problems later. I'd rather he wasn't about to exert himself."

"It's a fast twenty-six kilometer hump in full pack over rough terrain with the possibility of enemy action," Torin told her blandly. "That's hardly exertion for a Marine."

"Then I guess it's a good thing he hit his head." She nodded at the slate. "Have you got everyone's stats in there?"

"Yes, ma'am. But I can't access them unless their med-alerts go off."

"Because that would be invasion of privacy?"

"That's what they tell me."

"What does it say about Major Svensson?"

"Major Svensson's alert never went off."

"So by Marine Corps standards his pain wasn't debilitating enough?" She turned her attention to her coffee so deliberately she was clearly buying time to calm down.

Torin returned to her own coffee. The odds were good that because the major's pain hadn't been caused by trauma the med-alert hadn't recognized it—headaches were considered ignorable and brain aneurisms fatal. It was possible the program needed a little tweaking in the middle ranges.

"Does the military even have a position between going all out and casualty?" Dr. Sloan wondered—her thoughts apparently having been following the same paths.

"Yes, ma'am. We in the Corps refer to that position as being in the Navy. If you want to check on the major while he's still lying down," she added, glancing down at her sleeve, "you've got less than a minute to get into the shelter before he's on his feet requiring a coffee and a Sitrep."

"You'd be surprised at what I can accomplish in less than a minute, Gunnery Sergeant." Tucking her coffee into an inner pocket, she strode toward the shelter and disappeared inside.

As Marines began emerging and the camp took on the appearance of a somewhat ghostly anthill in the pale predawn light, Torin grinned to hear the major's voice rise loud and clear over the ambient noise.

"For pity's sake, Doc, can I deal with my bladder before you start messing with my head?"

He was fine. And he'd just let the camp know it.

"Staff Sergeant? Can you hear me?" Jonin slid his arm behind the staff sergeant's shoulders and lifted him until he was supported against his chest. His eyes closed and his hair still, the older male twitched and shuddered and turned to drive his head against Jonin's chest so hard that his vest had to absorb part of the impact.

"You okay?" Sakur asked as Jonin grunted.

"Fine." He shifted just enough to move the staff sergeant's elbow out of his crotch—two maskers cranked up full couldn't prevent a response, not with physical contact in the equation. "Give me the pouch."

Sakur passed it over, then took one of the staff sergeant's hands between both of his and gently rubbed the chilled skin, murmuring soft words of comfort in a Taykan dialect Jonin didn't know although he found the cadence of home soothing.

"Staff Sergeant Beyhn, you have to eat." Slipping the nipple between slack lips, he squeezed some of the nutrient up out of the pouch. "Please, *comti*." Maybe it was the old endearment, one his *sheshan* had used to him when he was small, maybe it was nothing more than hunger induced by the taste of the paste, but the staff sergeant began to suck and swallow, one hand working the fabric over Jonin's thigh, rhythmically crushing and releasing his combats.

"Should his face be so flushed?" Sakur wondered quietly.

"I don't know." He kept telling them he didn't know, but falling back on Taykan hierarchy was a comfort in uncertain times. *Unless you're the one fallen on.* "Careful, *comti*," he murmured, lips against the staff sergeant's hair. "Not so fast."

"You think he took damage last night?"

"The doctor says no."

"We should've found him sooner."

"He's not helpless. He remembers what it is to be a Marine, or we *would* have found him sooner." But the words warred against the thought of *qui* out alone in the woods, unprotected, and the memory ached.

Not the only thing aching.

Pouch emptied, Jonin gently lowered Staff Sergeant Beyhn back down on the stretcher. "Let Ayumi know we're coming out," he told Sakur as he secured the straps. He heard a low murmur at the entrance to the shelter and turned to see a wide open triangle, the fabric of the shelter framing legs and boots and snow.

Given his condition, it was awkward guiding the stretcher out into the predawn light and from the careful way Sakur moved, he seemed equally affected.

Ayumi, every light receptor open, the dark green of her eyes nearly black, took the handles of the stretcher from him as they cleared the shelter, took one look at him as he straightened and shook her head. "You're going to have to do something about that before we move out."

"No shit," Sakur snorted. He jerked his head down the gully toward a clump of evergreen bushes. "Jonin?"

The staff sergeant's pheromones weren't as overpowering out in the open, the cold air aiding the maskers, but that was irrelevant really because twenty minutes of close, closed-in contact had left him nearly keening with need. His only answer was to start for the bushes. Raw and open, he could sense every di'Taykan in the camp although that eased a little when Sakur fell into step beside him and his arousal blanketed the awareness of the others.

"Where the hell are you going?" Sergeant Annatah- wee stepped in front of the two di'Taykan, halting their progress toward the edge of the camp. "We're moving out in fifteen. Do not tell me you're taking the time for a quickie."

"We were in with Staff Sergeant Beyhn," Jonin began. "Two maskers aren't enough to . . ."

She held up a hand to cut him off, a sudden flush of heat defining the problem for her. "Yeah. I get it. And you're working yours overtime, too." A glance down and she shook her head. Given they were wearing body- liners under their combats that had to be painful. "Fine. Go. But make it fast!"

"Yes, Sergeant!"

"You could come with, Sergeant," Sakur suggested as they passed.

"You could hump that along with your pack if you don't move it," she snapped, barely resisting the urge to follow. "And put your Goddamned helmets on!"

McGuinty peered into the melted interior of the node then straightened and shrugged. "Massive power surge?"

"Are you asking me?"

"No, Gunnery Sergeant!" He flushed, picked at a bit of plastic until it came off in his hand, stared at its sharp edges for a moment, and shoved it into a pocket on his combat vest. "It's the only thing that makes any sense."

"Nice that something does," Torin muttered.

*   *   *

"I feel fine," Ashlan protested, sitting on the indicated stump and frowning as Dr. Sloan held her slate to his temple.

"Uh-huh. Your hair's not moving." She flicked it with her fingertips, and it fell to lie inert against his skull. When she flicked it again, he shuffled just enough sideways on the stump that he could rub his shoulder against her. "Not an invitation," she sighed.

"Half a platoon of hysterical di'Taykan running around the woods is a little fuzzy, which is probably a good thing for all concerned, but I remember the rest." Major Svensson looked up from tightening the straps of his pack and caught Torin's eye. "It's long odds that the Others are playing personally with us given they've got the whole planet to cover."

"Yes, sir."

"Long, but better than the alternative."

Interesting emphasis on the last word. Torin thought back to their conversation in the gym and wondered if the major believed the Elder Races had placed a saboteur in the Corps. Or, because the possibility made her so furious, was she reading more into his tone than was there?

"Is there any chance Staff Sergeant Beyhn, not being in his right mind—or at least his usual mind—is responsible for what happened at the node?"

"I'm not ruling anyone out, sir."

"From now on, no one goes anywhere alone. Tell the sergeants it's for the troops' own safety—which has the added benefit of being the truth."

"Yes, sir."

"So . . ." He straightened and grinned. "When you say you haven't ruled anyone out, are you on your list, Gunny?"

She returned the grin and pretended she didn't notice

the way his left hand was trembling. "That would be ridiculous, sir."

"Gunny?"

"Private Cho." Torin moved out and around rather than under one of the big evergreens, scanning the dark recesses between the branches as she went. They were an hour out from the node and still no energy readings. She was beginning to think that McGuinty's massive power surge had grounded the drones.

"Do you think we'll make Dunstan Mills tonight?"

"Yes."

A few paces more, then a tentative protest from the Marine on her left.

"Don't you mean that if we're lucky, we'll make Dunstan Mills tonight?"

"Afraid I'll call bad luck down on us, Stevens?"

"No, Gunnery Sergeant! We make our own luck in the Corps!"

Had to be said, but Torin was just as happy she hadn't had to say it.

"It are surprising to be seeing you here, Mr. Ryder." Presit a Tur durValintrisy smiled up at the waitress, her teeth a flash of pointed white within the dark fur of her muzzle, and wrapped a small hand around the pinched waist of her glass. Against the glossy black of her fingers, her nails looked like they'd been chromed. "I are not knowing there are salvage out by Rosenee."

"There isn't," Craig told her, shooting a smile of his own at the waitress. *What's a couple of battlers like us doing in a place like this?* it asked her. When she set his beer down, her breasts pressed against his shoulder. Tactile sympathy.

Presit cleared her throat, the sound not quite an impatient growl. "Then this important story we are needing to talk about are not being about salvage?"

"It's not, it's . . ."

"Good. Because I are knowing nothing about salvage." She stroked her whiskers, left side then the right. "So when I are getting your message that you are here at Rosenee and you are needing to be talking about an important story with me, I are not imagining what you are needing to be talking with me about."

"Big Yellow."

Her exaggerated shock was so perfect—both hands in the air, her eyes wide, ears up and swiveled forward, the tip of her tongue very pink against dark lips—that Craig forgot how much he disliked the chattering little furball and actually laughed.

"Yeah, okay, I get it, you're not surprised." He took a drink—whoever was brewing the local beer had half an idea of what they were doing—set the glass back on the table, and leaned forward although between the ambient noise and minimal volume the Katrien's acute hearing required there was little chance he'd be overheard. Presit paused, a piece of skewed fruit from her cocktail halfway to her mouth, and leaned in to meet him. "I hauled ass out here beyond the black stump," he said, "because we need to speak about the escape pod."

Then he waited.

"Why?" she asked and ate the fruit.

"You remember the escape pod?"

Even in the minimal illumination of the bar, the silver edging the dark fur of her shoulders rippled with highlights as she sat back and plucked another skewer of fruit out of her drink. "Oh, yes, I are just saying to myself this morning, I are wondering what are happening to that escape pod from Big Yellow." Presit sighed heavily, ate the fruit, and fixed him with a flat, black stare. "I are remembering the escape pod," she told him, her tone suggesting he get to the point. "Why?"

"You didn't mention it in your broadcasts."

"You are having seen my broadcasts. How sweet."

Chromed claws stroked through her whiskers again. "I are not mentioning the escape pod in my broadcasts because General Morris are been asking me not to, in return he—and the military—are guaranteeing me exclusive rights when the story are breaking."

"No one remembers the escape pod."

She sighed. "No one remembers because it are never mentioned on vids."

"People who were there don't remember."

Her nails sounded metallic against the plastic table. "You are remembering. I are remembering."

"Yeah, and Gunnery Sergeant Kerr are . . ." He fought his way out of the Katrien syntax and started again. "Gunnery Sergeant Kerr remembers. No one else."

The impatient tapping stilled as Presit's upper lip curled. "Gunnery Sergeant Kerr? That are higher than staff sergeant." When Craig agreed that it was, the lip curled higher. "She are having been promoted, then."

"Listen up, you bloody *galah*, she's also the one pointing you at the biggest fukking story of your career, so let the old shit go and ask yourself why no one but the three of us remembers. Why only us?"

"We are not in common . . ." Her eyes narrowed and although the thick fur made it difficult for him to tell for sure, he thought she was frowning thoughtfully. "We three are being together on Big Yellow . . ." Without looking, she picked out the last skewer of fruit. "Many are together on Big Yellow, though, not only us." She slipped the first piece of fruit off the skewer and chewed slowly. The soft gray fur on her throat moved as she swallowed. "We are not getting on or off together." The second piece of fruit followed the first. "We are not being alone together . . ."

"Oh, for fuk's sake, we were all sucked through the floor and brain scanned!" He returned a glare from a neighboring table. "Don't even go there, mate," he wearily warned the young turk in the suit that probably cost as much as his Susumi drive. "I'm having one fuk of a day."

"You are having a worse day if you are getting me thrown out of here," Presit hissed. "This are the only decent restaurant on station!" She thumbprinted the bill and slid off her chair, glaring up at him in a way that made her seem a lot more dangerous than anything a meter high should. "We are talking elsewhere. Now."

Craig sighed and stood. At least she hadn't expected him to pay for the drinks.

"There are being no evidence that the Elder Races are erasing memories."

Craig stretched out his legs, the only comfortable way to sit in a chair with his ass barely up off the deck and shrugged. "Who, then?"

"We are only having Gunnery Sergeant Kerr's word for it that the memories are gone," Presit snorted. "Perhaps she are wanting me to be breaking this story and be made a fool."

"Yeah, not entirely an unattractive prospect, but if you break this story, it'd bring some bad news down on the Corps and she'd never go there."

After a long moment, the reporter heaved an exaggerated sigh. "You are being right. She are totally a pawn of the military structure."

"Not a pawn . . ."

Silver-tipped ears swiveled forward.

It didn't seem worth the energy to argue a losing position. This was a conversation where he had to pick his fights. "Yeah, all right, she's a little overly invested."

"I are not so much concerned with there being no memory of the escape pod," Presit murmured, her attention dropping to her slate, "as there being other memories tampered with. The military must not be having given a hidden agenda."

"Having given?"

She ignored him. "You are trusting her word, I are not having to. I are a reporter, I are only interested in the facts. Ah!" Trilling in Katrien, she turned her slate toward him.

Craig snorted. Light levels in Presit's quarters were low enough he could barely make out the screen let alone the information on it.

"I are finding three Katrien scientists who are having been on the *Berganitan* when it are investigating Big Yellow."

All but two of the scientists who'd been *on* Big Yellow were dead.

"If they never left their labs, what are the odds they even heard about the escape pod?"

"One are being a structural components engineer—she are hearing about it, I are guaranteeing! I are messaging her for being interviewed. If she are not remembering . . ." Her teeth gleamed as she grinned. ". . . then we are having a story."

"All right, then." He stood, remembering this time to hunch forward and not slam his skull into the low ceiling.

"I are having a few things to be tying up with my very important story here, so we are leaving tomorrow, then."

That jerked him erect. "We?" he snarled, rubbing the back of his head.

"There are being no commercial flights from here to Cetem—they are being at the university there. I are having to be traveling Coreward and then be transferring two, maybe three times. That are taking too long."

"No."

"You are not being my first choice either." She waved off his protests. "I are remembering your ship and how *scented* she are being, but you are being here. I are messaging Sector Central News, and you are being paid."

"It's not about being paid, mate."

She shrugged. "You are not liking others in your space. *Retri serintare heh*—stop grooming yourself. This are about the story. You are saying Gunnery Sergeant Kerr are asking questions. She are not a reporter. She are not know how to ask questions. If there are being mind wiping, and she are asking the wrong questions, then maybe they are knowing there are memories they are missing. We are not having time to be dealing with you having issues!"

Both hands pressed hard against the ceiling in a valiant and bloody futile effort to keep it from coming in on him, he sighed. It was hard to argue with the same position that had sent him looking for the reporter in the first place. "You have a point," he admitted reluctantly.

Crossing the room, she patted him on the knee. "I are always right. You are remembering that and we are doing fine."

They stopped at midday only because they had injured.

"We're not making the kind of time I'd like."

Torin kept her gaze moving over the platoon and not on the purple-gray half circles under Major Svensson's eyes. "We're moving into deeper snow, sir. It's only to be expected, but we'll make Dunstan Mills before full dark."

"Think there'll be a welcome there?"

"I expect there'll be something, sir."

"Think we'll run into whoever attacked us last night?"

That hadn't occurred to her. "We haven't seen any tracks, sir. They might be following, but I very much doubt they're out in front. Not when they still control the system." McGuinty and Piroj were sitting a little apart from the others, and McGuinty had the staff sergeant's helmet balanced on his knee.

The major followed her line of sight. "So what's tech support up to now?"

"I'm seeing if he can pull some particulars off Staff Sergeant Beyhn's scanner. According to the sergeants, the senior DI gets a better look at the drones."

"Going to spread the program among the troops?"

"If McGuinty can get it off, sir."

"Socialist move there, Gunny."

"Knowledge is power, sir."

"Yeah, that was kind of what I meant." He grinned and massaged his left hand through the mitt. "Still no sign of any local drones?"

"No, sir." The di'Taykan not on watch were clustered around the staff sergeant's stretcher. Torin wondered if they'd determined a minimum safe distance, or if they just didn't care about taking a hit from his pheromones. They were damned well going to walk with the consequences, so she hoped they'd thought it through. "I'm a little surprised there've been no more long distance drones moving in."

"With this CPN out, they'll have to take the scenic route." She turned to look at him then, and he smiled. "The long-distance drones navigate from node to node. Last night's meltdown means that instead of following us from point a to point b . . ." He reached down and drew a straight line in the snow. ". . . they'll have to take the scenic route around."

"So whoever blew the CPN last night did us a favor."

"Somehow, I doubt they intended to." As he straightened, he used his right hand to move his left out of the way.

"Sir?"

For a moment, it looked as if he might not answer, then he lifted his head and snorted. "Just a weak arm, Gunny. The rest of me's fine. No head pain, no memory loss, no need to fret."

"Has Dr. Sloan . . ."

"Dr. Sloan's been a little busy. Don't worry," he said as he stood, "I can keep up with a couple of concussions and a stretcher."

"Yes, sir. Where . . ."

The major sighed. "To take a piss, Gunny. I'll let you know if I have any trouble."

She topped his sarcasm with sincerity. "Thank you, sir."

"Did you eat?"

"I ate."

"Must've inhaled it. How are you feeling?"

"Like I've acquired an obnoxious growth I can't get rid of," McGuinty snapped turning to glare at the Krai sitting beside him. "Back off!"

"Can't do that." In the gray light of day, with his heartbeat back to normal and the fear that he'd fukked up badly enough to be sent home fading, Piroj hadn't been thrilled about his baby-sitting duties. They weren't, however, completely without amusement value. "Gunnery Sergeant Kerr said I was to watch out for you, and that's what I'm going to do."

"Well . . . fine." Gunnery Sergeant Kerr trumped annoyance. "Can you do it from a little farther away!"

"Nope. Went away last night and look what happened." He considered resting his chin on McGuinty's shoulder but tossed the idea as being too di'Taykan. Also, his chin didn't quite come up to McGuinty's shoulder regardless of how close to a normal height the Human was. "What are you doing?"

His attention dropped back to the helmet. "Gunny asked me to separate out the staff sergeant's drone identification program. Apparently, he can see them better than the rest of us."

"Yeah, didn't do him much good."

"Wasn't a drone took him down, Piroj—it was biology. If it was tech, I could fix it."

"Like you fixed the CPN last night?"

"Fuk you, man."

"Hey!" Hands up, Piroj carefully kept his teeth covered. "Just asking."

"I didn't melt the fukking node!"

"Okay, then."

McGuinty sighed. "I didn't."

"Okay."

"I had a worm running, something that might slide in deep enough to get me the data I needed, but it got fired. I figured I could refine a copy of it, but then Gunny put me on this . . ." He tapped the helmet. ". . . and I haven't had time."

"Can you walk and separate?" When McGuinty frowned up at him, he jerked his head toward the larger mass of the platoon on its feet. "Looks like we're getting ready to move out."

"Oh, great . . ."

Piroj swung his pack up onto his shoulders and frowned at the soft white flakes drifting past his nose. "Hey, it's snowing."

"Shoot me now," McGuinty moaned slipping the slate into his vest, reaching for his pack. "I hate weather."

Barely visible behind a curtain of falling snow, Dunstan Mills was a cluster of prefab buildings within the curve of a frozen river. There was a small hydroelectric power station—a dummy but a good-looking one—thirty or forty individual dwellings and a two-story building that, with any luck was exactly what they were looking for.

Lying flat on one of the ubiquitous ridges of rock, Torin adjusted her scanner and tried for more detail. A dummy anchor, built like the power station as a prop, would do them no good. They needed a real anchor, one used by Marine engineers to put this fake colony into place on Crucible and then left as part of the scenario.

It looked good, but she could only be a hundred percent certain by getting up close and personal, and that, unfortunately, wasn't going to happen right away.

Sliding down to rejoin one/one, who'd taken point after the break, she frowned at the data scrolling across her scanner from the EYE she'd left up on the vantage point. Too small to be read by the enemy and useless more than three meters from a scanner, it was having a little trouble with the snow. Calibration helped, and the blip from the nearest sentry reappeared where it was supposed to be.

"You don't post sentries unless you're expecting trouble," Kichar declared. "The enemy has the town."

"Looks that way," Torin agreed. Another time she'd have been amused by Kichar's certainty.

"Activated or reprogrammed, Gunny?"

"Activated. If they'd reprogrammed, they'd never have positioned a sentry."

"Because when we saw the sentry, we knew they had the town."

"I think we've all got that, Kichar."

"What about the Other that blew the CPN and took out McGuinty, Gunny?"

She ran the scan one more time just to be sure. "There's no life signs anywhere in the settlement. Only drones, so now we need to figure out how to beat the scenario."

Sakur's eyes lightened as he drew his focus in to his scanner. "We don't know what the setup is."

"Sure we do. First, it's supposed to teach you lot something."

"Teach us what?" Sakur muttered.

"Good question. We figure that out and we've beaten it. In this scenario the enemy has attacked the planet Dunstan Mills is on. They've attacked the planet, Bonninski, because the Others don't attack a single town and they're our only enemy."

"How did you . . . ?" Bonninski flushed as Torin raised a brow. "Never mind."

"A platoon of Marines—platoon because that's the recruit training size—has been sent out to either protect or evacuate the people of Dunstan Mills, but they arrive too late and trap the enemy in the town."

"And we know the enemy is in the town because we've seen the sentry."

"Kichar . . ." Torin sighed and let it go. "That's right. But there'll be *sentries*." She stressed the plural. "There, and there at least." She positioned them in the sketch on the snow. "Logically, here as well if you're defending all approaches. The enemy in the town feels that they have a defensible position, and so they make a stand. The recruits' mission is to take the town back in as close to one piece as possible—probably for the sake of the power station."

"What about for the sake of the townspeople, Gunny?" Hisht asked quietly.

"The Others don't take prisoners. If they're in control, the townspeople are dead."

For a moment, only the soft hiss of snow.

"Enemy scanners will see a platoon coming." Using a twig, Sakur drew in the scan overlap between the sentries. "There's no way to get into the town without being seen. What's that supposed to teach?"

"I'd say the futility of war," Torin told him. "But as we generally like you to discover that on your own, the scenario's got to be set up so there *is* a way into the town. I'd say a diversion here, big enough so it doesn't look like one." She poked another hole in the snow by the map. "Then the bulk of the platoon comes in from here . . ." A line along the edge of the river. ". . . and infiltrates the power plant where the majority of the enemy has gone to ground. Two reasons I think they're in the power station," she said before they could ask. "First, if they're in the anchor, there's no way to get them out and we're back to the futility of war. Second, the power station is why they're here, and so they'll protect it. Now, experience tells me that the scanners right on top of the station are a little wonky—because the recruits are moving and the enemy isn't, they can use that to their advantage during the attack. Once the enemy's security has been breached, they'll scatter, and the exercise becomes a vicious house-to-house fight for the remainder of the two tendays. From the scenarios I've downloaded, the Corps never puts drones and small buildings together without it becoming a vicious house-to-house fight."

"If that's the scenario," Hisht said slowly, staring at the sketch as if he could see answers in the snow, "what happens differently in the real world?"

Torin grinned. "In the real world, we don't give a crap about the power plant and we know that drones in scenarios don't shoot to kill. And we've got Dr. Sloan."

"So, if we're injured, she can patch us up?" Bonninski asked a little wide-eyed as the rest of the platoon caught up to their position.

"Dr. Sloan," Kichar said gleefully, before Torin could answer, "is wearing a non-combatant chip. The drones can't shoot at her. The drones can't even see her."

TEN

"YOU WANT ME TO DO WHAT?"

"Walk through the settlement to the power station." Crouched in the lee of the rock, bootheels tucked up under her butt, Torin traced over the route with the point of her stick, gouging it a little deeper into the snow. "Confirm that a majority of the enemy is inside, place the charges where marked on the schematic I'll download into your slate, and get back here as quickly as possible so that they can be detonated before the Others have the opportunity to reprogram the scenario."

Dr. Sloan shook her head, smiling tightly. "You misunderstood the question, Gunnery Sergeant. I wasn't asking for clarification, I was asking if you were insane. I'm not walking into that." She gestured toward Dunstan Mills, outlines of the buildings barely visible behind a gently falling curtain of snow. "I'm not a soldier, I'm a doctor!"

"If you don't do this, Dr. Sloan, you'll have plenty of chances to practice your trade." Torin straightened, never taking her eyes off the doctor. "In the time it would take us to crack this scenario, the Others will have their chance to take control of the drones."

"Major . . ."

"Sorry, Doc." Major Svensson frowned down at

Torin's sketch. "There may be a better way to do this, but we don't have the time to think of it. We need a position we can fortify—and we need it now. The last thing we want is to be caught in the open between the drones from the settlement and any long-distance drones that might be on their way. If we had any more of those chips . . ."

"Fine." Yanking off her mitten, she shoved her thumbnail up under the lower edge of the plastic square on her forehead. "You can have this one."

"You're going to hurt yourself," the major said quietly after a moment, grabbing her wrists and pulling her hands down to her sides. "Remember, I told you it wouldn't come off without a special solvent. You'll be saving lives, Kathleen," he added, sliding his grip down to her hands and wrapping his fingers around hers.

"You also told me that the drones in an operative scenario don't shoot to kill, and you . . ." She freed a hand to point at Torin. "You told me this is an operative scenario. So why can't we wait until morning?"

"For now this is an operative scenario," Torin agreed. "The Others know we're here—they turned it on. You need to destroy the drones before they can be reprogrammed to shoot to kill."

"And we wouldn't ask you if there was any other way," Major Svensson assured her.

She stood for a long moment, the snow beginning to pile up on the bright blue shoulders of her jacket, then she sighed. "Do you guarantee the drones won't notice me?"

"Just to be on the safe side, you'll maintain comm silence, but that chip renders you invisible until the Others reprogram," Torin told her. "After that, we can't guarantee anything but a fight we might not win."

"I thought Marines didn't know the meaning of defeat."

Torin kept her hand from rising to touch the cylinder

in her vest. "We don't like it, ma'am, but we know what it means."

Her gaze flicked down, as though she'd sensed the movement Torin hadn't made, and she sighed again. "All right, let's get it done, then. First, how do I confirm the enemy is inside? Send in a questionnaire?"

"No," Torin told her as the major grinned, "we'll load one of our scanning programs onto your slate."

"You can just do that?"

She believed they could *just do that*, Torin realized, and she didn't like it. The irrational fear that the military could mess with civilian lives became no more legitimate just because someone was messing with the military.

"Gunny?"

She'd paused just a little too long. Unclenching her jaw, she faked reassurance. "No, ma'am. We need your security codes first. You can just put them into my slate," Torin added holding it out, "and I'll never see them."

Lips pressed into a thin line, Dr. Sloan did as Torin suggested.

"You can change them later," Major Svensson reminded her.

"Don't think I won't." She frowned at her screen. "This is it? MAR-SCAN?"

"Yes, ma'am, and there's a mapping program as well."

"Which will?"

"It's dark and it's snowing, Doc. You might need a little help staying on course."

"I might need a lot of things, but I doubt I'm going to get them," she told the major tartly. "Let me have it, Gunnery Sergeant. And it had better not mess up any of my diagnostic programs."

"We're one hundred percent behind that as well, Doctor. If you'll check your screen . . ."

Backlit, it was a small rectangle of light in the gathering dark.

"This is where you're supposed to go," Torin explained as the green line on the doctor's screen flashed. "This is you." At one end of the line, a red light blinked slowly. "You don't need to see your surroundings; you only need to see this."

The edge of a mittened hand brushed snow off the screen. "Oh, joy."

"And this is where you place the charges." The image changed to an outline of the power plant. "We don't know how the drones will react to our communicating with you—they'll pick up the signal even if they can't crack the code, and we'd rather not draw any more attention to you than absolutely necessary."

"Thank you." Definitely more sarcasm than gratitude.

"Because you'll be on your own, we've designed things to be as simple as possible. Just match up your red dot with the yellow dots showing on the outline of the building, unwrap the charge . . ." Torin held up the small cube of explosives and mimed stripping off the back of the paper cover. ". . . and press it to the nearest hard surface. You activate it by ripping off this tab."

"Lovely." Dr. Sloan turned a cube between her fingers, carefully not touching the tab. "These little things will be enough to drop the roof?"

Torin nodded. "Set in the right places, yes. Once they're activated, they'll link up, blow simultaneously, and the pressure wave will collapse the walls."

"That seems almost too easy. Shouldn't it be harder to blow things up?"

"That depends on what side you're on, ma'am." The pack of explosives dangled off Torin's hand for a long moment before Dr. Sloan took it and hung it off one shoulder.

"Don't worry about being seen or heard," Major Svensson told her. "I know you've walked a long way today already, and I'm sorry, but speed is your only criteria."

"It's almost dark."

Torin reached out and tugged the sleeve of the doctor's borrowed combats out from under her jacket, thumbing the cuff light on.

Dr. Sloan snorted and turned on the much stronger light in the cuff of her jacket.

"We really need a look at that catalog, Gunny."

"Yes, sir."

"She's past the sentry," the major announced. As darkness fell, the EYE had switched to reading heat signals. "A noncombatant chip is a wonderful thing, Gunny, although, I have to admit, it feels a bit like cheating."

Her back against the rock, sheltered from both the snow and the enemy's scanners, Torin watched the red line spooling out beside the green across the screen of her slate. "It's not cheating to use all available resources, sir." After a moment, the silence lifted her attention to the major's face. His expression confused her. "Sir?"

"Whatever it takes to get the job done, Gunny?"

"Yes, sir."

"Fulfill the mission objectives; see that you kill as few Marines as possible?"

Because he'd phrased it as a question, she answered. "No, sir, that's your job. My job is to fulfill the mission objective in such a way that my people survive."

"Semantics."

"Perspective. Sir."

To her relief, he smiled. It wasn't a happy smile, but his mouth moved in roughly the right directions. "I stand corrected, Gu . . . Son of a bitch!"

"Sir?"

Eyes clamped nearly shut, both palms at his temples, he scowled up at the falling snow. "Damned low pressure system is playing hell with my head."

And their doctor, his doctor, was trudging through a fake settlement carrying enough explosives to flatten the very real walls of the fake power station.

"Are the fireteams in position?"

"One/two and three/one are still on the move sir. Both teams have a ways to go yet . . ." She glanced down at the doctor's position. ". . . but they'll be there in plenty of time."

"What about the staff sergeant's drone ID?"

"Sorry sir, McGuinty hasn't been able to tease it out yet. He's still working on it though and with any luck we can upload it to the rest of the platoon before we move out."

He watched Dr. Sloan's progress a moment longer. "Which won't be happening any time soon."

"No, sir."

"Hurry up and wait. Hurry up and wait."

Torin waited in turn for some sort of punch line, but it never came. Collar up and scanner down, Major Svensson settled down in the snow like the rest of the platoon—pack on, weapon resting diagonally across his body. Combats and bodyliners would keep them warm and dry, and field rations required nothing more than a free hand. The only difference between the major and the platoon was that they watched the sky darken and the snow fall while he watched her, the shimmer of his scanner barely visible across his face.

Seemed like a good idea to ignore him.

"Ayumi, put your Goddamned helmet on."

Three/one moved around the south edge of Dunstan Mills, heading for the river and the third sentry Gunnery Sergeant Kerr had marked on her sketch of the settlement. It was a long way to hump based on the gunny's assumption that there'd be a drone at that point needing removal, but then, Stone figured other Marines had humped farther based on other gunnery's sergeants' assumptions, so no harm, no foul. And, besides, the one thing he'd learned for certain after 120-odd days of training was that the gunny's job was to know things and his job was to do what he was told.

Technically that applied to sergeants and above, but specifically it was all about the gunny.

Given the size of the trees around them, it was a good bet that the nearly knee-deep powder now covered more soil and less rock. The branches overhead, in spite of being bare, were interlaced thickly enough to keep out most of the falling snow which, unfortunately, also kept out a lot of the ambient light.

Scanner down, Stone felt like he was back in the quarry, dust forcing him to operate his loader by way of the readout on the screen. The scanners the Corps used were more complex but essentially the same, and it had surprised him a little that a number of recruits washed out because they couldn't adapt to seeing their immediate surroundings through a tech filter.

Up ahead, Vega on point and Jonin right behind her showed on his scanner outlined in a nice friendly green, camouflage and light levels making them nearly invisible to the naked eye even though Jonin was almost close enough to touch. On the lower left corner of his screen, his scanner noted that another Marine followed three paces behind. He knew it was Alison Carson, the fourth member of the fireteam, even if the scanner didn't.

Stone frowned as Jonin stumbled, boots catching on something under the snow. Not good. Picking up his pace, he closed his hand over the di'Taykan's shoulder and shook him none too gently. "Hey. Get your mind back in the game."

Jonin twisted out from under his grip and turned just enough to glare. "I'm not . . ."

"You are," the big man told him calmly as Vega stopped and came back six paces to see what had stopped them. "You're walking like you're Human, covering ground with your head up your ass."

"Up Staff Sergeant Beyhn's ass," muttered Carson from behind Stone's shoulder. When Jonin switched his glare to her, she snorted, "Oh, come on, Jonin, I'm not telling you anything you don't know."

"We've got some distance to cover before we're in position," Stone continued, ignoring the interruption, "and I think we need to know now if you're fit to go on or if it'd be safer for all concerned . . ."

"That being us," Carson added.

". . . if you head back."

"To Staff Sergeant Beyhn."

"Shut the fuk up, Carson. I know it's some kind of biological imperative thing you guys have got going," Stone continued, his scanner showing that Carson had taken half a step back, "but if you can't get past it—well, I'm not dying for your biology."

Jonin's eyes were dark—hardly surprising given how many receptors he'd need open to see—and he was wearing the *I'm a hot-shit aristocrat* expression that training had pretty much slapped out of him by day seventeen. Being the focus of the other di'Taykan in the platoon had not been good for him.

"You've got to put the staff sergeant down," Stone said levelly, wondering if the gunny had sent three/one on the long hump not because they were the only intact fireteam with a shooter but to get Jonin away from species issues. "Gunnery Sergeant Kerr seems to think you're good to go or she wouldn't have sent you. Now, if she hadn't, I don't know if she'd have sent us out one short or if she'd have sent another team, but me, I wouldn't want to be the one to tell her she was wrong because I have a feeling the survival rate for . . ."

"Shut up, Stone." His eyes were lightening, and the di'Taykan aristocrat had been replaced by someone who looked tired and pissed off about equally. "You made your point. Quit beating it to death. I can do this."

Now he could.

Stone nodded and said, "Okay."

"Well, McGuinty?"

McGuinty quickly swallowed the butt of his stim stick and shook his head. His helmet wobbled, sending clumps of accumulated snow falling down onto his shoulders. "Sorry, Gunny. It'd take me weeks to separate out the staff sergeant's program for the drones. It's wound in and around too much other crap."

Torin tucked Beyhn's helmet under her arm. It had been worth a shot, worth taking the time from the attempt to regain control of the CPNs. But now . . .

"I'm back on it, Gunny." He held up the staff sergeant's slate before she could speak.

"Good work, Marine."

Temporarily attached to one/two, Duarte followed in Cho's footsteps, the indentations of his boot prints in the snow showing briefly, palely green in her scanner. di'Lammin Oshyo was dead and she had replaced her in the fireteam and that was just a little creepy.

Oshyo is dead, and I am her.

No one was supposed to die on Crucible. Wish they were dead, yes. Actually die, no.

Her boots felt like they weighed ten kilos each and her nose was running again. She wiped it next to the frozen snot already on the back of her mitten and wondered if being chosen for the walk around to the north side of the fake settlement actually meant anything, or if she had just been standing closest to the three remaining members of one/two when the gunny'd had to make a choice.

Each of the three potential sentries—and two of them would remain potential until two/one and three/one had gained their positions and marked them—had been assigned one of the recruits who'd shot Expert. Stone, Cho, and Lirit. Kichar was fine with that; it made sense that Major Svensson and Gunnery Sergeant Kerr were making use of the skills they had available. She, herself, had shot three points under Expert and that might have had some bearing on why her team had been chosen to back up Lirit who was on her own what with McGuinty still working the staff's slate trying to crack the system and Piroj ordered to stick to McGuinty and Ayumi staying with the Staff Sergeant.

The only problem was that Lirit's target was the sentry first spotted by Gunnery Sergeant Kerr, the sentry closest to the platoon's position. The team would be going in well within range of the gunny's scanner.

Gunnery Sergeant Kerr would be watching her . . . their every move.

They could have been sent to one of the farther positions if not for Hisht, but the Krai's short legs had made the day's march harder on him than anyone but Piroj and Sergeant Jiir. Kichar glanced over at Hisht, the pouch of rations he was eating giving away his position without her needing to use her scanner to determine which of the mounds of snow and camouflage was him. It probably hadn't helped that Krai weren't fond of the cold.

She was not going to turn and look at Gunnery Sergeant Kerr although she thought she could feel the gunnery sergeant looking at her.

Inside her mittens, her palms were sweating.

"Gunnery Sergeant Kerr, this is Private Stone. Three/ one is in position and have targeted enemy eyes. Over."

"You've got about a half an hour if Dr. Sloan maintains speed. I'll ping you before the fireworks start."

"Roger, Gunny. Out."

Nice to know the other two sentries were exactly where she expected they'd be. It raised the odds they'd be right about the rest of the drones gathered in the power station.

It turned out to be closer to forty-five minutes, Dr. Sloan visibly tiring as she covered the final kilometer back to the platoon, the circle of light her sleeve cast on the snow skittering sideways at odd moments, the red line looping to both sides of the green. The moment she was far enough from the sentry, Major Svensson went out to meet her, nearly carrying her the last few meters.

Torin had objected and then shut her mouth about it. She hated waiting, too.

"Next time," Dr. Sloan panted, dropping onto the rock ledge the major had cleared of snow, "you can just go yourselves and get shot. I honestly don't care."

"Next time," Major Svensson agreed, dropping to one knee so he could look into her face. When he was satisfied with what he saw, he handed her a canteen.

She took a long swallow, wiped her mouth on the back of her hand, and said, "You know you have a bunch of Marines down there by those trees, right?"

"They're at the ZP," he told her. "The Zero Point. Any closer and the enemy sentry would have to do something about them."

"What? The drones know we're here?" Leaning forward, she punched him in the shoulder. Torin glared at the watching Marines until they stopped smiling. "I thought the whole point of my little trek through the twelfth circle of hell was so the drones wouldn't know we were here."

"No, it was so they wouldn't know we were planting explosives. They know we have Marines at all three ZPs. They know these Marines won't attack because attacking a sentry over that distance, a sentry that's aware of you, is stupid at best and suicide at worst. While we're covering the distance, they'd have nothing to do but shoot at us."

"I thought they couldn't kill you."

"They can't. But the ETGs only ensure nonlethal until the programming changes, and we don't know when that'll happen, so we can't risk ..."

Dr. Sloan raised a hand, cutting him off. "I get that we don't want the programming to change," she said wearily, "and I'll take your word for the rest."

"Sorry. The point is, they're dug in and defensible, they can afford to be lax."

"They're not lax," she sighed. "They're programmed. They're drones."

"Ah, but they don't know that."

It took her a moment. She frowned as meaning pushed past exhaustion. "You people ..."

When she let it lie there, the major patted her arm—not unsympathetically, and stood.

"Make it happen, Gunny."

"Yes, sir." Torin turned to face the settlement. It wasn't necessary; she could detonate the charges no matter which way she faced, but she preferred to look the enemy in the eye—or sensor array—even if the gesture was purely symbolic because of the dark. A tap on her comm to make sure the entry teams were listening. "Heads up, people ..." Behind her, she could hear the sound of Marines readying their weapons. ". . . we're about to blow."

Both sergeants, Torin, and Major Svensson had all done demolition training—although only Torin and the major had applied that training in combat. A quick run over their options and they'd agreed to err on the side of caution and use all the available charges. Training platoons didn't travel with an abundance of explosive power; privately, Torin hoped they'd have enough.

The sound wasn't as loud as she'd expected; a series of distant bangs when she'd been hoping for *blam*.

Turned out the *blam* had been momentarily delayed. The power plant lit up the night sky, painting the settlement with streaks of orange and red.

"Holy crap," someone observed.

Either the drones were extraordinarily explosive with only a little encouragement or the charges had gotten stronger since she'd taken her last course.

Three squads at the ZPs. Another three ready to move in a direct line to the anchor. Get it. Hold it. The final three squads, including the walking wounded, to remain in place, guarding the doctor and injured. Torin and the major were going in with the second wave. It only made sense; together they had more combat experience than everyone else in the immediate area combined, and if the bulk of the drones hadn't been destroyed with the power station or if the Others managed to reprogram before they had the platoon under cover, they needed to be on the scene and able to make the necessary decisions.

Individually, they had more combat experience than everyone else in the immediate area combined. Using the information Torin sent him, the major could make the necessary decisions safely back beyond the ZP. Unfortunately, the major didn't see it that way.

Jiir lost the toss and remained with the reserve squad.

The explosion was not only intended to destroy the majority of the drones but also to pull the enemy sentries out of their defensive positions. In Torin's experience, there was nothing like an attack inside the perimeter, the sudden, explosive evidence of failure, to throw sentries off their game.

The distinctive crack of KC-7s proved her point.

"One/two reporting target down. Moving in."

"Three/one reporting target down. Moving in."

"One/one reporting target down." Torin could hear the relief in Kichar's voice and she grinned. *"Moving in."*

"All right people, let's go."

* * *

The first surviving drone nearly took off Sakur's head. Would have had Hisht not knocked the di'Taykan to the snow as a round slammed into the building behind him, spraying them with smoking debris.

"Ablin gon savit!"

"Highly welcome," Hisht yelled back, rolling clear.

Sakur scrambled up to his feet, heart pounding, hair stinging his cheeks as it whipped around under the edges of his helmet. "I thought they were programmed not to kill us," he snarled knocking the snow from his weapon.

"You have not died," the Krai pointed out as Lirit caught the drone in a short, sharp burst and blew it to bits.

The second surviving drone came around the corner of one of the buildings they'd already searched and moved out onto the road behind them. It got off three fast shots before Kichar took it down with a single shot of the KC-9.

Sakur's vest absorbed most of the impact of all three enemy rounds. "Why me again?" he demanded, wincing as his vest lost its defensive rigidity.

"Your sparkling personality?" Kichar offered, smacking him on the shoulder as she caught up. "Let's move."

"No sympathy?"

"For bruising?" she snorted. "Not likely. Now move, we have another eight buildings in this sector."

"You can't . . ."

"I can," she growled, glad of the mittens that hid the way her fingers were trembling. "The gunny put me in charge of this team. Now move!"

The third, fourth, and fifth surviving drones were together in a building on the north side of Dunstan Mills not far from the sentry's position. With one/two keeping up steady but random fire, Stevens crawled forward to toss both her grenades through one of the broken windows near where her scanner showed them as red circles behind the barrier of the wall. As she moved, the distance registered kept changing.

Just like we practiced on the range, she told herself, hissing through her teeth as melting snow dribbled down the inside of her cuff. *These things can't kill us. Unless the Others had reprogrammed in the last few minutes. And they could have. Shut up, brain!* The first grenade made a perfect arc through the broken window. As the second grenade left her hand, a three count after the first, she turned and raced back toward a low wall. Still counting, she dove for cover—she'd made the move a hundred times back on Ventris. Could almost hear Staff Sergeant Beyhn yelling at her to hustle.

Four of the five rounds fired from the building hit the wall.

The enemy killed the first grenade. But not the second.

"Textbook example of using an adrenaline rush against the enemy," Ioeyn said smugly as the rest of the team dropped down beside her, kicking up a spray of snow.

"Hardly surprising," Cho snapped at the di'Taykan. "This is a classroom." Then he took a good look at Stevens' position. "Are you all right?"

Stevens stared up at him with wide eyes, then twisted around, trying to examine her right cheek. "They shot me in the ass! When I went over the wall, they shot me in the ass!"

"No one ever died from getting shot in the ass," Duarte observed, her heart pounding so loudly she could barely hear her voice over it. "And your med-alert didn't even go off."

"It fukking hurts!"

"It bounced off you. It didn't even go through your combats."

"I got shot in the ass!"

"Then you left your ass up where they could shoot it! This isn't an exercise! Didn't Oshyo teach you that?"

"Oshyo?" Stevens glared at Duarte. "Don't even talk to me about her!"

"Not the time to be talking, period," Cho growled, grabbing her arm. "We have to finish clearing this section. Can you walk?"

"It fukking hurts!"

He rolled his eyes. "Can you *walk*?"

"Yes, I can walk!" Sucking cold air past clenched teeth, she stood. "Still hurts."

"Still not going to die," Duarte murmured as she passed. Oshyo had died.

Torin could hear the entry teams taking fire, and prayed that the Others hadn't reprogrammed.

Grenade!

One of theirs. And only one. Odds were good it meant that one of the teams had taken out a small enclave of drones.

Torin tried not to think about the odds in combat. That way led to hard liquor and an early body bag.

Head down, staying close to the major's left side, she pounded along the streets that gave them the fastest path to their chosen building.

"Definitely the anchor," Major Svensson panted by her left shoulder as all three squads paused, pressed tight up against the buildings closest to their target. "Let's hear it for the anal retentives in Parliament who insist every colony starts the same way, thereby ensuring that the anal retentives in the Corps drop an anchor into their training colonies."

Two stories tall, set back from the river, it commanded a good view of the entire settlement—which was very likely why the scenario included at least one drone on the roof.

"Son of a bitch!" The Marine on point dove back toward safety as rounds from the roof kicked up a spray of snow.

Being able to see the drone as a red circle a meter in from the edge seemed a bit moot. They knew it was there.

"Any way to be certain they're still targeting non-lethal areas, Gunny?"

"Only one I can think of, sir."

"Not sure walking out there and letting him shoot you is a good idea, Gunny."

"Hadn't intended to let him shoot *me*, sir." Although she had given it a moment's consideration.

Safest decision was to act as if they could die at any moment and the anchor had to be reached anyway.

They crossed one at a time, broken pattern running, trusting to the night and to camouflage and to whatever gods they personally believed in. Unless the shooter was very good or very lucky, moving targets wearing combats designed to fool the eye were damned near impossible to hit with a personal weapon. Unless the Others were in control of the drones in which case the trainers worked remarkably like a targeting beacon.

Torin crossed first, only because she had the best odds of identifying and disarming any traps on the doors. *And being one of the only grown-ups is getting old fast,* she sighed as she sprinted across the open ground, twisting, turning, and adding about another fifteen meters to the run. Her boots seemed to have been gaining weight all day and now felt like dragging a full-grown Krai around on the end of each leg.

The outer doors were unlocked and open about six centimeters, snow drifted across the threshold and into the air lock entry. The inner doors were wide open. The scenario had left the explosive equivalent of a bucket of water propped on one of the outer doors, and Torin had it disarmed before the next Marine arrived. Annatahwee had sent two/two over with orders to take out the drone.

"Remember that if it's on scenario, the Others don't surrender. It'll self-destruct. If it's been reprogrammed, it'll just try to kill you," she told them as they passed. Because she hadn't been intended to hear it, and because she hadn't told them anything they didn't already know, she ignored Ducote's murmured, "Yes, Mother." She had no idea how Staff Sergeant Beyhn had survived a career of taking new Marines to Crucible. After only three days, she had to constantly fight the urge to shove them out of the way and do things herself.

Of course, the staff sergeant's recruits had never been in any real danger.

A spray of snow chased Kirassai to the building.

"Break the pattern up!" she yelled, grabbing the di'Taykan's arm and hauling her up onto the step. "Keep it fresh and keep it moving!" Pushing Kirassai to the left edge of the door, she snapped, "Watch 90 to 180! Shoot anything you see that isn't one of us."

"Ducote!" Sergeant Annatahwee on group channel as the last of the second squad started toward the anchor building. "Is there a particular reason why that bastard drone is still shooting at us and not at you?"

"Yes, Sergeant! We can't get onto the roof. We'd need a demo charge to get through the door."

And the charges had been used.

Three/two was across. The drone still had a shot at Major Svensson, the sergeant, and three/three as well as the three squads working their way in from the sentry positions.

"One/one, one/two, three/one—we have a shooter on the roof of the anchor. Repeat a shooter on the roof of the anchor. Advance with extreme caution."

During shipping, the access to the roof had been sealed between two pieces of spaceship hull. The colonists would cut out the inner piece, open the door, cut out the outer—the door opened in and couldn't be locked from outside. If two/two couldn't get through it, the drone had fused it somehow.

Another learning experience, as Dr. Sloan liked to say.

Major Svensson was across. Then Sergeant Annatahwee.

Then Meir slipped on ice under the snow and landed hard on his back. The drone had a clear shot at his face, the one uncovered part of his body. A guaranteed lethal shot. Meir jerked at the impact, then scrambled to his feet and raced for the doorway, blood seeping up from the crease across his left bicep.

"It's still a scenario," Torin declared as the sergeant nearly dragged Meir off his feet getting him up and into the building. "That means somewhere inside is the way to get through that door!"

"On it!" Handing Meir off to Leford, the sergeant ran inside, yelling for Ducote and crew to leave the door and start searching the upper level for a cutting tool.

"Hope it wasn't in the power station," the major murmured quietly enough so only Torin heard.

When the last two Marines made it across, Torin followed them into the anchor, leaving Kirassai at the door on watch.

Straight ahead, a wide hall led to another set of doors. Almost directly to the left, through a wide break in the interior wall, was a large rectangular room with long, narrow windows taking up nearly the entire far side. It had probably started as storage for construction supplies and become the community hall when it emptied out after the other buildings were built.

"Three bennies in a weapons locker, rear of this floor, near what looked like holding cells," the sergeant announced, grinning broadly as she rejoined Torin and the major. "Ducote's team are cutting the door out now."

"Good work." Major Svensson pushed himself up off the wall and walked past Torin into the community hall. "Let's get the rest of the building secured."

Torin answered Annatahwee's worried frown with a noncommittal shrug and followed. The major might be reaching the end of his reserves, but until he fell over, she could do nothing about it.

Her light picked out a pile of objects in the middle of the room just as her nose recognized the familiar smell of rot. The hair lifted off the back of her neck. She could hear the major's breathing hitch and then speed up.

"Meat bags," Sergeant Annatahwee said quietly. "They set them out under a stasis field when they set up the scenario. When it's activated, the stasis field is turned off. It's to get the recruits used to . . ."

"I know." Torin cut her off. "Get them used to what you find because the Others don't take prisoners."

"Yeah. I'll have the di'Taykan put their nose filters in," the sergeant added. "We'll move these out once we know . . ."

Three quick shots.

"Gunny . . ."

For one long moment Torin thought the next words out of the major's mouth were going to be *with me*, and she had a vision of him charging forward and falling flat on his face.

His expression suggested he was having the same vision.

". . . take care of that!"

"Yes, sir!" She pounded the length of the room and through a small door in the middle left of the building's center wall. A quick turn, and she was in the lower level toilets. As she ran past the open stalls, the Marine by the sinks whirled around, weapon up, just as the rest of her fireteam piled through the door in the other end of the room.

"What the hell is going on . . ." Two more long steps and Torin could see the Marine's face. ". . . Vaughn?"

"Sir! I saw something, sir!"

"Don't call me sir, Vaughn."

"Yes, Gunnery Sergeant."

The shattered mirror made it fairly obvious what she'd seen.

When the major grinned, the rest of Vaughn's team took that as permission to ride their teammate mercilessly. Torin let it go on for about thirty seconds.

"All right, people, that's enough. Is the building secure?"

Vaughn looked relieved to have the teasing interrupted. "No, Gunnery Sergeant!"

"Then unless you were planning to take a dump on company time, what the hell are you doing in here?"

"We were drawn by . . ." Iful frowned, tangerine eyes darkening. "That was a rhetorical question, wasn't it, Gunny?"

"Yes, it was. Now, move!"

The anchor held nothing of note but the bennies—still in use at the roof access—the meat bags, and a supply cache holding both food and ammo.

"Makes sense," Major Svensson observed, tossing a H'san Style Chicken short of the pile. As Torin bent to retrieve the package, she used the new angle to watch him work the fingers of his left hand against his thigh. "If this scenario was a full exercise, the training platoon would probably be running short right about the time they took the anchor. With this lot, we can settle in for a long winter's nap." He shone his light around the communal kitchen, squinting in the reflected flare of the stainless steel. "Map's got the CPN in the anchor, so where the hell is it?"

"I doubt it's in the kitchen, sir." Torin said as she straightened. "Since the training platoon using this scenario is supposed to end up inside, it's probably very well hidden."

"Sergeant, we're through to the roof."

"Advance with extreme caution, Ducote. If the drone decides to self-destruct, there'll be shrapnel."

"Roger that."

"I could go up . . ." Annatahwee began, giving voice to the words in Torin's head.

"No." Major Swensson dragged off his toque and dug his fingers through sweat-darkened hair. "Let two/two handle it."

One shot. The KC-9.

"Sergeant, Bynum just blew it to shit."

"Good work, Re . . ."

Torin caught her eye.

". . . Marines. Bring all the pieces down. We want to make sure there's nothing left to reprogram."

"Roger, Sergeant. On our way."

"So that's that." The major shoved himself up off the wall, swayed once, and steadied. "Let the teams coming in from the sentry points know the shooter's been taken care of and then let's get this place squared away."

One of the upper windows had been smashed by a piece of debris from the power station, the roof access was now a hole with edges still steaming slightly in the cold, and the outer air lock door closed but no longer sealed—otherwise, the building was in good shape.

"I wonder if the toilets work."

"Only one way to find out, sir."

There was no power—lights, heat, toilets were nonfunctional.

"Sergeant Annatahwee, put two Marines on the roof and then start clearing out those meat bags. Once the common room is empty, start dismantling the inside wall—they made it by snapping the exterior shutters together, and we need to get them reinstalled."

The sergeant's eyes flickered once toward Torin—fast enough, Torin hoped, that the major had missed it. "Sir, we don't have the right tools."

"They're in here somewhere, Sergeant. I'm betting the scenario includes securing this building, and you can't do that without those shutters."

"Yes, sir."

"Gunny, you and I are going to check out the power station. I want to be sure none of those drones survived."

The power station wasn't far and moving might be better for him than remaining still since he couldn't collapse until all the teams were in. "Yes, sir."

A twist of his lips let her know he knew what she was thinking.

"Any chance that explosion left any drones in one piece?" he asked as they headed slowly toward the main mass of rubble.

Torin kept her hand on the trigger guard of her KC-7. "Long odds, sir."

It had stopped snowing although cloud cover continued to block both moon and stars. Their boots whispered through the snow on the ground. Distant sounds were muffled and indistinct. At least no one seemed to be doing any more shooting.

The power station walls had looked to have been about four meters high before the explosions. If they were a third of meter now, Torin would be very surprised. The few larger pieces of the heavy metal roof lying across the rubble looked as though burning fists had punched through it from below.

"Built-in charges," Major Svensson said suddenly. "The training platoon was supposed to save the power station. The charges might have been Crucible's way of reinforcing what a bad idea it is to use explosives around a building you're supposed to save."

"Makes as much sense as anything," Torin muttered.

"Why, thank you, Gunny."

"Sorry, sir. I didn't mean that the way it sounded." Although given that training platoons weren't exactly bad-idea free, it didn't make as much sense that they'd risk the loss of the drones to one. As she swept her light over the wreckage, her scanner registered residual pockets of heat but no power signatures. The data retrieved from Dr. Sloan's scan showed thirty-nine drones had been inside the station.

"Looks like the doc got them all, Gunny."

"Yes, sir."

It was always easier when the enemy didn't bleed.

The major bent and grabbed a piece of metal only to have it slip through his fingers and clatter back down onto the wreckage. "Damn mitten, can't get a grip . . ."

The mitten made it hard to tell for certain but, to Torin, it had looked more like he hadn't had strength enough in his hand.

They got back to the anchor just as three/one emerged from between two of the south buildings, visible as green sketches on the scanners. Major Svensson headed across the open ground to meet them, so Torin followed although she wasn't happy about it.

He opened up the beam of his cuff light and familiar faces appeared between helmets and vests. Carson had a bit of frozen snot on one cheek. "What do you have for me, Private Stone?"

"Sir, scans show no active drones in any of the buildings in this sector, sir."

"Good work. Drop your packs with the others in the common room and lend a hand getting that wall down. We need those windows shuttered before that building's secure."

"Yes, sir." Stone beckoned to his team, and although they clearly would have preferred a chance to sit down and get a little rest, they followed him over to the anchor. Torin couldn't decide if he was a natural leader, or if the other three were tired enough they didn't really give a shit about who was telling them what to do as long as they didn't have to think for themselves.

She checked her sleeve. Twenty-three forty-two. It had already been a long day—and it wasn't over yet.

"Gunny, check on the other two entry teams. If they're within thirty, then give Sergeant Jiir a heads up."

"Yes, sir."

The other two teams put their ETA at under fifteen. Jiir sounded relieved to be contacted. *"I was beginning to think you'd forgotten about us, Gunny."*

"We were just making the beds and putting the mints on the pillows, Sergeant. Bring them in."

As she signed off, four Marines emerged from the anchor carrying the first of the long metal shutters out the double doors. Impossible to tell who they were given the distance and the dark except that two of them were obviously di'Taykan.

Torin flicked her light in their direction. "Kirassai! Iful! Get your damned helmets on!"

"But the drones have been destroyed, Gunnery Sergeant. And there's enough light for us to see."

"Did that sound like a request, Iful?"

"No, Gunnery Sergeant!"

"It's late," she sighed a moment later as the shutter crashed to the ground. Both di'Taykan had released their grip and grabbed for their dangling helmets at the same time. Profanity made it clear that no one's feet had been under the heavy slab. "And they're new at this."

The major snorted. "And you scared them."

"They need to get over that."

"No one ever gets over that, Gunny. Come on, let's give them a hand or we'll be at this all night."

Around a decimeter thick, the shutters were heavier than they looked, and the length made them awkward. It took all six of them to maneuver the first shutter into the southernmost window embrasure.

"Essentially," the major grunted as it finally snapped into place, "you're looking at a removable piece of spaceship hull."

Torin took another look. "I think I was happier believing there was more than this between me and vacuum, sir."

"The inside of the window enclosure is filled with expanding foam."

"Well, that makes all the difference, sir."

With two Marines keeping pressure on the shutter, a quick search found a manual mechanism to lock it in place.

"It'll take one of the same tools we're using to dismantle the wall," Iful muttered peering under the faceplate. He straightened to find the other five staring at him. "Uh, some of my *thyrtins* have a *jurdingon* ..." He paused and glanced at Kirassai.

She shrugged and offered, "Repair shop?"

"... and I worked there when I wasn't at school."

"So you're saying you know tools?" the major asked.

"Yes, sir."

"Good. Go get the one we need."

"Yes, sir!"

They had the second shutter up by the time one/one came in from the east and the third was on its way out the air lock when one/two emerged from between the buildings to the north. Moving slowly and carefully, three of them were clearly matching their pace to the fourth.

"Stevens, you're limping."

"She got shot in the ass, Gunny."

"Is your name Stevens, Ioeyn?"

"No, Gunnery Sergeant!"

"Stevens?"

"I got shot in the ass, Gunny."

She said it like she'd come to terms with it, so Torin didn't smile. "Go drop your pack inside, then get a handful of snow against the skin. Now you're not moving, it's going to start to swell. And have Dr. Sloan look at it when she gets here."

They were shifting the last shutter into place when all six di'Taykan outside turned toward the east. Torin wasn't surprised to discover that was the direction of what might, by virtue of massive exaggeration, be called a breeze.

"Heads back in the game, people!"

They jerked, as one, and returned at least the visible part of their attention back to the final shutter.

It was 0146 by the time Sergeant Jiir, Dr. Sloan, Staff Sergeant Beyhn, and the final four fireteams made it into the anchor. Torin had seen to it that Humans stood watch on the roof and by the doors, allowing the di'Taykan to cluster around the stretcher in the common room. With the windows shuttered, it was pitch-black outside the overlapping circles of cuff lights.

"Playing favorites, Gunnery Sergeant Kerr?"

"Allowing a biological imperative a little leeway, Dr. Sloan. How's the staff sergeant?"

Eyes shadowed and a little sunken, the doctor yawned. "He had a bad moment when we first started moving, but the di'Taykan you left with us gathered around the stretcher and he settled."

"Good."

"For certain values of the word good, yeah, I guess. But he's still caught in some kind of hormonal systems failure, and I still don't know what to do about it."

"Ashlan?"

"He has a purpling lump the size of my fist on his head, but other than that, he's fine."

"You?"

"I had a nap in a snowbank, Gunnery Sergeant. I'm peachy." She yawned again and slumped against the wall. "What happens now?"

"Now, we block the outer doors, seal the inner doors, and—except for the team on watch on the roof—we get some sleep."

"And tomorrow?"

With body heat and insulation bringing up the ambient temperature in the anchor, Torin pulled off her toque and ran a hand through sweaty hair. "Tomorrow we fix the outer door, we find the node, we may send out teams to search the settlement for things other than drones. Mostly we wait."

"Waiting." A sweeping glance covered most of the Marines in the room. "Not what they expected from their Crucible trip."

"No, but they're getting a lot more realistic look at life in the Corps."

"Waiting?"

"We do a lot of it, ma'am. And it beats being shot at."

ELEVEN

"**CETEM INSTITUTE OF SCIENCE AND TECHNOLOGY.**" His hand resting on the top of the skimmer, Craig Ryder frowned up at the sign. "CIST? Yeah, a degree from CIST is really going to inspire confidence in prospective employers."

"It are being an example of why all universities should be having arts programs," Presit said dryly, adjusting mirrored sunglasses as she started toward the nearest building. "They are needing someone who are putting the letters into words. You are bringing the equipment."

"Yeah, yeah."

"Why should I be paying for strong arms to be carrying our equipment when I are paying to be traveling with you?" Presit had wondered.

"Because I'm not your bloody beast of burden!"

She'd shrugged. *"I are preferring to be with others of my species, and I are having crew here who are able to go, but I are not bringing them because you are not having room. If you are not carrying, then we needing to bring another with us and you are needing to put another in your ship."*

That wasn't happening—the seventeen-hour Susumi jump had been hell with just one small, furry, incessantly jabbering reporter on board. He'd finally locked her in the head to keep from spacing her. Two more and he wouldn't have made it. Easier by far to carry her gear.

Even considering that it included full editing capabilities, an enormous digital memory, and could beam a show onto the network from anywhere it could hit a Susumi beacon, the recorder was far larger than it needed to be. In an effort to keep the media honest, Confederation law stipulated that all recording equipment must be large enough to be easily seen by the general public and carry obvious network identification. It wasn't heavy—Craig suspected that half the casing covered nothing at all—but it was awkward.

He didn't ask what had happened to her previous set of strong arms or why Presit had shown up at his ship with a human-sized recorder. Not only did he not want to know, but he suspected he'd strangle the reporter halfway through the explanation. Sure, he was going to carry the damned thing, but a guy liked to be asked.

"Ryder!"

Dragging the recorder out of the back, he released the skimmer to the boarding platform and hurried to catch up. Given their respective leg lengths, it didn't take long.

Lifting her sunglasses, she leaned toward the door's security module for a retinal scan while snapping out, "Presit a Tur durValintrisy, Sector Central News!" as though the module would care.

When the door irised open, she shot Craig a look promising painful retribution if he didn't follow immediately—easily readable in spite of the mirrored lenses and the species differences. Reminding himself that Torin really fukking owed him big, he leaned into the scan and followed.

Gad a Tur durEdkabidge preened under Presit's attention, claw tips fluffing out the fur of her ruff as she explained the implications of her current research.

Craig had lost interest early on and, tucked safely behind the bulk of the recorder, was playing solitaire on one corner of the monitor. He'd begun to suspect that the size of the equipment had been chosen as much by the technicians who had to carry it as by political mandate. The memory held more games than he had on his ship, a truly eclectic selection of music, the most recent seasons of half a dozen Human-centric drama vids, and a partitioned section he couldn't access without a Guild membership.

"Fascinating!"

The frightening part, as far as Craig was concerned, was that Presit actually sounded fascinated. The reporter was clearly a skilled and well-practiced liar.

"I are just thinking . . ." Presit's small, sharp teeth gleamed as she continued. ". . . how much more you are being able to accomplish if you are being given a piece of the alien ship's escape pod to study."

"Escape pod?" The scientist snorted so hard her whiskers twitched. "There are being no escape pod! There are being no physical, actual piece of the alien ship to study. Our away team are all killed in the explosion, and no one else . . ." She stared at Presit pointedly. ". . . are bringing back samples."

"It are possible the military are hiding the escape pod."

"It are possible, but it are not happening. Our lab team are desperate for samples—we are knowing if there are an escape pod on board. We are not having allowed anyone to hide such a thing. If the military are saying they are hiding an escape pod, they are lying. And that," she added shrewdly, "are actually what you are coming here to ask me—if the military are hiding an escape pod. No." She sighed. "And it are too bad because Parliament would be making them give it to us."

"Is there a chance . . ."

"I are telling you, no. I are top in my field . . ." On the

other side of the room, three Katrien trilled. Craig had no idea if they were colleagues, grad students, or cleaning staff, and neither did he care. Gad a Tur durEdkabidge trilled something back and then ignored them. "I are knowing every structural components engineer they could be having called in—there are being not so many at a level to study alien construction. If there are an escape pod, I are knowing about it. I are not knowing, so . . ." She spread her hands. ". . . there are no escape pod."

"I are remembering an escape pod." Arm tucked so close into her side that the fur blended into the fur on her torso, Presit drummed her claws against a bit of hard plastic on the skimmer's door. She had insisted that Craig set the recorder on the opposite seat and that he share hers. Given that he wanted to retain some hearing in the upper registers and the reporter was growing increasingly shrill, he'd given in. Even given how tiny she was, the two of them sharing a seat left little room for movement. "You are remembering an escape pod. Staff Sergeant . . ."

"Gunnery Sergeant."

Her lip curled. ". . . Torin Kerr are remembering an escape pod. Everyone else are being made to forget. We are having been deep scanned by Big Yellow. Everyone else are not. It are not too large a leap to be assuming that the scan are having done something to keep our memories from being erased. That are what we know. What we are not knowing is who are erasing memories."

"It has to be one of the Elder Races."

"Why?"

"Because they'd raise high, holy hell if it was someone else."

"That are undeniable," she admitted toothily.

Craig could understand the teeth. The Katrien were among the Mid Races along with the vast majority of those who made up the Confederation and, like many of

them, believed that the Elder Races were just that—
elder. Not better; older. They resented the influence the
founders of the Confederation still wielded and resented even more the fact that those founders were, at
the very least, more intellectually, scientifically, techno-
logically advanced. *Ethically* more advanced was a topic
of hot debate on all the Mid Race worlds.

"*Why* are being nothing more than speculation. How
are important only for scientists watching. Which of the
Elder Races it are being, that is the story!" She craned
her head back to stare up at him. "We are going to Ventris Station."

"I'm not exactly popular at Ventris right now."

She waved that off with a single flick of her small
hand. "You are not being important. General Morris are
being at Ventris Station, and General Morris are liking
me very, very much. General Morris are being ranking
officer affected, so he are who we are needing to speak
to. I are convincing him, he are finding the escape pod,
I are exposing paternalistic alien autocracy!" The possibility of exposing paternalistic alien autocracy had her
bouncing in the seat. "I are winning the Retrenzic
Award for this!"

He'd never heard of the award, figured it must be
some kind of journo thing, but the thought of winning it
definitely got Presit stoked. "It's going to take some fast
talking to get me a berth at Ventris."

"You are leaving that to me."

"When I say fast, I don't mean speed." Most Katrien
languages sounded like a cat fight on caffeine.

"Am I looking like a *vortzma*?" she snarled.

No seemed to be the right answer.

As they pulled into the disembarking platform at the
space station stop, Craig froze half out of his seat.
"What if we're the ones whose memories have been
tampered with? What if Big Yellow planted the memory
of the escape pod in our heads?"

Presit stepped out onto the platform. "I are liking to see it try," she snorted.

Wrestling the recorder out of the cramped space, Craig couldn't decide which he found more disturbing—that he found her certainty comforting or how much Presit was beginning to remind him of Torin.

At 0711, Torin watched the sunrise from the roof of the anchor and wondered how long it would be until the Others brought in drones to replace the ones destroyed with the power station. With all of the section to pull from and their destruction the only logical desired result, they'd soon be facing more than they had to date.

A single tank? Three long-distance drones? The activation of a couple of stationary trail busters?

Pathetic.

Granted it had been luck alone that no one had died in the minefield, and if the major hadn't sent her out on point, the filament would have taken out one or maybe two of the lead team, but given what Crucible had on tap, they should never have survived the first night. Weapons that were no more than a challenge when the senior DI knew when and where and how to shut them off were lethal in the hands of the enemy.

It was hard to believe that the Others had gone to all the trouble of inserting a team this far behind the front lines and not included a hacker good enough to crack the individual security codes on the drones. Granted, that soldier could have been taken out of the action in any number of ways—probably not by suddenly going through puberty cubed; Staff Sergeant Beyhn would likely be the sole owner of that distinction for a while— but any number of other ways. And it was also entirely possible that the Others knew exactly how much time they had until the Navy returned and they were having a little fun. It wasn't likely; Torin had fought against the

Others all her adult life and wasn't in the habit of demonizing the enemy, but it was possible.

Scanner down, she swept the horizon one more time. Nothing.

Something about this didn't feel right.

"Gunnery Sergeant Kerr!"

"What is it, McGuinty?"

"We've found the CPN!"

"I'll be right down." She studied the sky to the southwest a moment longer, then nodded to the sentries and went inside.

Jiir met her in the upper hall. Although body heat and kickass insulation meant the anchor had begun to warm up, the three Krai still wore their toques although Jiir at least had pushed the collar of his bodyliner down in under the edge of his combats. "We were overthinking it," he said as they headed to the stairs, Torin matching her stride to the Krai's. "There's an admin office in this building, right? Kitchen, lockup, medical centre, community hall, and admin office. And what do you find in an admin office?"

"A desk?"

"A desk," he repeated, standing aside to let Torin enter the office first.

Although the small window high in the outer wall remained unsealed, most of the light in the room shone up from the surface of the desk.

"The desk works?"

"The desk is the CPN." Perched on the edge of an absurdly ordinary office chair, McGuinty grinned. Like the Krai, he was still in his toque. In spite of the dark circles under his eyes, made even more prominent by the lack of light, he looked both excited and confident. "It was all Major Svensson."

"What was all Major Svensson?"

"He found it, Gunny. He got it to work."

A week ago, Major Svensson couldn't operate a therapeutic chair.

"Where is the major?"

"Major's with the doc," Piroj put in from behind McGuinty's left shoulder. Torin was pleased to see he hadn't assumed his duty'd ended now they were inside. "Said getting the desk working made his head hurt. She took him up to the medical center."

"The big room on the second floor full of junk?" She'd gone past on her way down but hadn't looked in.

"Says medical center on the door, Gunny. Seems like that's good enough for the doc."

Torin couldn't really blame Dr. Sloan for trying to find a little normalcy in her situation, even if it was nothing more than a sign on a door. She walked into the room and ran her fingers along their reflection in the inert plastic trim of the desk. "So the Others still control the system?"

"Yes, Gunnery Sergeant." McGuinty sounded surprised by the question. Then his brows drew in as he realized what it meant and *surprised* became *mildly insulted*. "You thought a Marine in one of the other platoons might have cracked it? Gotten control back?"

"It was a possibility." And one she had no intention of apologizing for mentioning. "What else is in here?"

"Nothing. It's just a CPN hiding in plain sight. I already have the staff sergeant's slate slaved in—software was a little dicey, so rather than screw around, we're on a hardware link—and as soon as I get in a little farther, I'll download a worm I created to . . ."

Torin's raised hand cut him off. "I don't need to hear it. You know what you're doing, and that's good enough for me. Let me know when you've got results."

"You know," Jiir said quietly as they walked away, "Staff Sergeant Beyhn's always saying that Marines don't do if, they do when."

"I know." She knew because that was where she'd learned it.

The staff sergeant was still in the community hall—

any space smaller and the attending di'Taykan were unable to cope with the strength of the pheromones.
They'd slept piled around him and as it had calmed
him—more than anecdotally, the doctor's scanner had
confirmed it—they kept as many hands touching him as
possible. Hands because Torin had point-blank told
them to keep their combats on.

*"When those drones attack, they won't wait ninety sec-
onds for half the platoon to tuck their collective asses
back into their uniforms. You don't keep him calm by
risking yourselves or the rest of the Marines in this anchor, and if he was in his right mind, Staff Sergeant
Beyhn would tell you that himself."*

With the big windows sealed, the only light in the hall
came from the units embedded in the combat sleeves.
One of the shelter halves had been rigged up over the
stretcher, and the staff sergeant's light pointed up at it
so its inner surface could reflect and diffuse the beam,
illuminating the immediate area. The rest of the room
was dark, most of the di'Taykan having chosen to keep
their lights off. There were three, no, four around the
staff sergeant, Ashlan and Kaimi were on the roof on
watch with their fireteam, Iful was cannibalizing parts
of the kitchen to ensure that the outer doors could be
secured, three more were with their teams searching for
the pieces removed to open up the smaller windows,
and Oshyo was dead. That left four of the original fifteen unaccounted for, but as only orders would move
them out of sight of the stretcher, she had no doubt they
were somewhere in the darkness.

Standing in the doorway, in her own circle of light,
Torin frowned. The staff sergeant's condition had di-
vided the platoon on species lines and that wasn't good.
If Platoon 71 came out of this thinking they were
Human or di'Taykan or Krai rather than Marines, then
the Corps'd lost all thirty-six recruits, not only the one
Torin carried out in her vest. Odds were excellent that

when the drones attacked, combat would focus them and 120 days of training would reassert itself, but—in the meantime—she needed to keep this rift from growing.

"Gunnery Sergeant Kerr."

"Private Jonin." He might have intended to startle her by appearing suddenly out of the darkness—he was still very young, and youth was a constant, mostly unconscious struggle to find a place in the pack—or he might have merely walked quietly across the hall while her thoughts were elsewhere. As it had been close to a dozen years since she'd been startled by anything short of heavy artillery, and that rarely, Torin decided to give him the benefit of the doubt.

"We were wondering if Ashlan was well enough to be standing sentry duty."

We? And the benefit of the doubt lasted—she glanced at her sleeve—nearly seven seconds. After barely six hours in the safety of the anchor, it sounded as if they'd gone from a platoon of Marines with an injured NCO to a group of di'Taykan and everyone else.

"We thought that maybe one/three could come in and instead two/three could . . ."

"You thought?" Her tone made it quite clear that she doubted he had the capacity for thought. "Two/three gear up and join one/three on the roof," she snapped, CPU on Group Channel. "We're sending teams out to check the closer buildings and we'll need better coverage. Three/one . . ." She locked eyes with Jonin as she spoke. ". . . and one/one gear up and meet me by the airlock in two."

"Gunnery Sergeant . . ."

"Little less than two now, Private. And you've still got to retrieve your helmet."

That would leave two di'Taykan with the staff sergeant and give the rest a new species to concentrate on.

And as long as she didn't hear what they were saying about her, Torin was fine with that.

"Sounds like things got busy for a minute there, Gunny." Sitting up on an examination table, vest off and combats pooled around his waist, Major Svensson looked up from his slate and around Dr. Sloan. "Anything you wanted to tell me?"

"I sent a couple of teams out to check the closer buildings, sir. There's extra coverage on the roof."

"I heard that. What do you expect them to find?"

"I don't expect them to find anything, sir, although they might. If the scenario *was* set up as a house-to-house . . ."

"And that would be the logical assumption based on the way the Corps has used settlements like this in the past."

". . . then there could be items of value in some of those buildings intended to be found."

"Wasn't the entire settlement checked last night?"

"Only for drones, sir."

"I see." He sucked air through his teeth as Dr. Sloan unsealed the front of his bodyliner and ran an extension out of her slate along his collarbone. "That's cold."

"Yes, it is."

When that seemed to be all the response he was going to get, he sighed and returned his attention to Torin. "After two days' hard humping, you wouldn't think you'd need to keep this lot busy."

Torin glanced at the doctor and chose her words carefully. The problem was not one a civilian needed to be advised of. "Marines need to be Marines, sir."

A pale brow rose. "Do they?" He stared at her for a long moment, and she thought she saw understanding dawn. He was too good an officer not to have seen what was happening. "I leave it in your hands, then, Gunny.

Not that I could get involved even if I wanted to—Dr. Sloan is giving me a full workup before we start getting shot at again. She seems to think I'm flagging a bit."

If flagging meant running on nearly empty, stressing new body parts, and likely to fall flat on his face at an inopportune moment, then, yeah, Torin could agree with that. And if he'd been up early enough to get the CPN running, he hadn't gotten much sleep.

"It's hardly a full workup," the doctor snorted. "I'm sure you remember what those are like, Major, and this is a lot less intrusive." She sounded as if she regretted that.

He indicated his slate. "While I was being molecularly dissected, I got a head start on writing up my report. How would you prefer to be referred to, Gunny? As rising heroically to meet the situation head-on or more than a little pissed about the whole thing?"

"Somewhere between the two would be fine, sir."

Neither of them mentioned that the major's slate might survive where they didn't and anything he wrote would have to tell their story for them. Neither of them had to.

As the two sergeants came into the room, the major set his slate aside and caught Dr. Sloan gently around the wrist with his good hand. "That's it, Doc. All we've got time for."

She frowned, first at his hand then into his face. "I'm not done."

"Bookmark it, then, because I need to meet with my people."

"I'd rather finish."

"And I'd rather be on Ventris drinking a cold beer and fairly certain no one was going to try and blow me up. Unfortunately, neither of us is going to get what we want." He continued to hold her wrist until she moved the slate away and then he released her.

"You're still my patient," she pointed out sharply.

"And their commanding officer," he told her, nodding toward the line of NCOs. "Right now, and until the *Nir-Wentry* returns, that comes first."

As the major pulled his combats back up over his shoulders, Dr. Sloan turned to Torin, clearly about to plead her case. Whatever she saw in Torin's face both snapped her mouth shut and propelled her toward the door. Where she paused. "I want to go on record as opposing this interruption. Your health . . ."

"Is not more important than my Marines, Doctor. If there's time later, I'm at your disposal."

No mistaking the dismissal. Dr. Sloan pivoted on one good-to-forty-below heel and stomped out of the room.

All four of them remained silent while her footsteps echoed in the stairwell and then disappeared on the lower level. Torin figured she'd gone to check on Staff Sergeant Beyhn and wondered if patients who didn't talk back counted as spending quality time.

Major Svensson glanced over at the window in the second-floor medical center—empty of anything that might be considered medical and then trashed by the "Others" as part of the scenario—and then back at the NCOs. "So, what do we do when the drones arrive; do we hunker down and assume the anchor can take anything they can throw at us for the next seven days, or do we stand up and fight?"

Both sergeants looked to Torin. "Unfortunately, sir, as much as I might prefer to have the platoon sit safely undercover waiting for the *NirWentry* to return and put the fear of her not inconsiderable guns into the Others—not to mention let loose two squadrons of vacuum jockeys bored out of their tiny minds by flying exercises around a transport run—that can't happen. The anchor has weaknesses that the drones will exploit."

"Which are?"

"We still haven't found the rest of the plates that reseal the windows—both up here on the second floor and the smaller ones on the first floor. Debris from the explosion at the power station smashed through one of them, proving that high impact polymer or not, they'll still shatter with the right incentive. Also, they open and that weakens their structural integrity."

"Open windows aren't unusual in a new colony," Annatahwee put in. "Low-tech solution to the ventilation problem."

Torin nodded. "True, but I'm surprised the Corps bothered installing them in an imaginary colony."

"Perhaps they picked the anchor up surplus with them already in place," the major offered.

Jiir's nose ridges flared. "More likely that they were expecting recruits to shoot out them during the scenario, sir."

"Then in fine Marine Corps tradition, we'll just have to exceed expectations." He glanced over at Torin. "Were the windows our only weakness, Gunny?"

"No, sir."

"The fact that the outer doors no longer seal is really moot as long as we don't take the anchor into space."

"Yes, sir." She smiled politely. Even good officers, officers who were in every other way a joy to serve under, wanted their attempts at humor acknowledged. "Private Iful is certain he can secure it without making it unusable."

"Go Iful."

"Yes, sir. Our biggest problem concerns the hole in the roof." She handed off to Annatahwee.

"We know there's fliers in this section, sir—we were due to run into one on day fifteen, and I've heard of at least two more in other section scenarios. Three definitely, maybe more. When they pass over the anchor, they're going to read the hole."

"And having read it, will return and drop something explosive in it. What's your solution? Can we put the hatch back in place?"

"No, sir, the bennies were drained cutting it out. But we have a team dismantling the metal stalls in the non-operative latrine."

"And one of those pieces will stop what a flier can throw down? That's one high-tensile crapper."

"Not exactly, sir." One of those pieces couldn't even stop the round from a KC-7 that Torin had shot into it. "We're going to stack two pieces, work them through on the diagonal, then wrap them in a shelter half before laying them over the hole."

"And the shelter half is for ... ?"

"Camouflage, sir. To hide the fact that the pieces aren't actually a part of the roof."

"You think that'll work, Gunny?"

She wouldn't have ordered it done if she didn't at least hope it would work. "Yes, sir."

"So . . ." Torin turned with him to look at the sergeants. ". . . what's coming at us?"

"Shouldn't be that much of a problem, sir." Jiir glanced over at Annatahwee who indicated he should continue. "We've never run into a flier in a scenario that had more than a five-tube, light-weight launcher. Crucible usually uses air support to make a point, and once that point's made, then it's all small caliber chaser rounds—no real danger unless a platoon's caught in the open."

Torin gave him the chaser rounds, but . . . "You can make one hell of a point firing five rockets. And in a scenario, the fliers wouldn't be shooting to kill."

"Yeah but most of those rockets are flashbangs."

"Most," Torin repeated. "And the rest?" Because if most were, then some weren't.

"Gas if the platoon holds a position long enough to be taken down, incendiaries sometimes and . . ."

"And sometimes Crucible goes for the big bang," Annatahwee finished. "Blast fragmentation warheads with impact det fuses."

Major Svensson stared at her in astonishment. "Fired at training platoons."

Torin felt as appalled as the major sounded. She'd seen the damage those things could do, and the thought of recruits coming under fire from their own side . . .

"They're not generally fired at the recruits, sir." Annatahwee explained a bit defensively. "Just near enough they get the idea."

"And what's the idea?" he demanded. "That sometimes artillery makes you shit yourself?"

"Yes, sir."

"Sorry, I asked."

"If the fliers are packing actual heat, there's never been more than one in five, sir."

"I think one in five is sufficient, thank you, Sergeant. And given that our friend the sunken tank seemed to be carrying an unlimited supply of high explosives, I'm not counting on the fliers to be shooting blanks."

"Not exactly easy to hit a meter-square window moving at speed, sir."

He snorted. "Even the bad guys get lucky occasionally, Gunny. Any other surprises we should know about. High-heat, high-pressure thermobaric warheads maybe?"

The sergeants blinked in unison. "No, sir."

"Glad to hear it."

"The drones won't be able to reload sir," Jiir put in quickly. "Once they've fired their five, that's it."

"But we don't know how many are on the way," Torin reminded them. "At least three—and that's fifteen chances we'll get a BFW—but no top number. We could get waves of them as they're pulled in from progressively farther into the section. Or pulled in from other sections."

The major turned to stare at her. "Thank you, Gunny."

"You're welcome, sir."

"How adaptable are these fliers, Sergeant?"

Jiir glanced at Annatahwee and answered. "Sir?"

"The Others won't have programmed in the specs of the building. If they just fly to where they can get a lock on the building and fire, then it's a crap shoot if they hit anything they can penetrate, but if they take a bounce at the building and analyze the structure on a flyby, then they'll be aiming at the windows and the hole in the roof." Sliding off the exam table, he picked up his vest. "Not a problem if they're firing training rockets, but . . ."

". . . if they're firing a frag rocket, then we're in trouble." Torin finished when it became clear he wasn't going to.

"You're a joy to work with, Gunny." Together, they turned their attention on Sergeant Jiir. "Adaptable," the major prodded.

"Yes, sir. In scenarios, the fliers are able to determine where the recruits are so as not to hit them."

"Then if they've been order *to* hit the recruits . . ."

"They can find them, sir."

So instead of being camouflaged, the platoon would be going into battle with a nice big target painted on them and they had nothing big enough to jam the flier's scanners. Scanners . . . Torin frowned. "What's the range on most of these things, Sergeant?"

"Depends on the scenario," Annatahwee answered. "There's training benefits to having them roar in up close and personal, and there's benefits to having them fire from maximum range and just having the rockets appear as if . . ."

"By magic," the major finished dryly.

"Yes, sir. But they fire from maximum range in response to one or more of the recruits sending up an energy signal that can be read by the enemy. It's a cause-and-effect part of the training."

"Intended to teach them not to send up energy signals that can be read by the enemy?"

"Yes, sir. If we give them no reason to fire at distance, then they'll roar straight in close for maximum psychological effect."

"And the maximum psychological effect is once again getting them to shit themselves?"

"Sir." *Don't poke at the sergeants,* Torin's tone said clearly. *What happens on Crucible isn't their fault.* "When you say straight in," she asked Annatahwee, "do you mean no evasive maneuvers? Just . . ." She drew a line in the air. When the sergeant nodded, she grinned. "Then close in is better for us. If the fliers are in range of our weapons before they fire rockets, we have a chance to take them down."

The major's brows rose and both sergeants turned to stare.

"You packing a sammy you neglected to mention there, Gunny?"

"No, sir. If they're coming in a straight line, the scanners can plot their course and massed fire from the nines . . ."

He nodded. "Good thing we found that ammo. Best shooters from each team on the roof, and we try to take the bastards out. What kind of armor are these things wearing?"

"Not much," Jiir admitted. "They're drones, and weight is an issue. Even if a recruit gets off a shot during a rocket attack, a single 7 or even a 9 won't do much."

"Since we'll be using all nine heavies, that's good news for us."

"Sir, all the drones adapt to being shot at and if I were reprogramming them, that's not something I'd change." Jiir's nose ridges had closed tight. He obviously wasn't happy. "If the fliers aren't destroyed, they'll target the roof. We'd have to be very lucky to not lose everyone up there."

"If the flier isn't destroyed and it's packing anything

more than a training rocket, we run the risk of losing everyone in the building, so let's assume the fliers will be destroyed." Major Svensson ran a hand back over his head and sighed. "Gunny."

"Sir?"

"Assumptions make a lousy battle plan. Come up with a contingency in case the fliers aren't immediately destroyed."

"Yes, sir."

He could see the southwest corner of the anchor, which meant he could see the southwest corner of the big common room where Staff Sergeant Beyhn lay fighting the change. It was wrong, it was so wrong that a qui would be here, in danger. Even more wrong that he wasn't over there with him, protecting the future of the . . .

And that was where it got weird. He'd never spent time with a qui who wasn't a member of his own family, either by blood or by ritual. Just what, exactly, was he protecting the future of? The Taykan? Fuk that. There were plenty of Taykan around. Staff Sergeant Beyhn's family?

Frowning, he drummed his fingers against his weapon.

"Sakur!"

He jumped and turned away from the window to find Hisht staring up at him, the lower half of his face actually out from under the bodyliner.

"I asked you what you look at."

"Sorry. I didn't hear you." Another glance out the window.

The Krai moved closer. "You are worried for the staff sergeant?"

"About the staff sergeant. Yeah. I was thinking . . ."

"That explain it," Hisht snorted. "I smell burning and I thought to myself, must be Sakur thinking." Grinning, he easily ducked under the di'Taykan's swing, but as he straightened, he sobered. "The whole platoon is worried."

"It is?" It hadn't occurred to him that the staff sergeant's condition was affecting anyone but the di'Taykan.

Hisht sighed, all nose ridges open, and nearly disappeared behind a plume of water vapor. "Not the same worry with not the same biology, but that doesn't make our worry less than yours. He was strong like a *harshak* in a gale. Tree," he added when Sakur frowned. "Very big strong tree; we build our cities in them. No matter the wind, they never fall." He shrugged, one shoulder and then the other, the Human gesture still needing a little work. "Until they do, and then no one can believe it."

"For fuksake, Hisht, that makes less sense than you usually do."

"It's hard to believe some things can fall. Some people. If he was someone else, it would not be so hard to believe."

Sakur glanced out the window, then back at his teammate. "You're saying the di'Taykan are overreacting because of who Staff Sergeant Beyhn is."

Hisht shrugged again. "I'm saying the di'Taykan are not the deepest thinkers in known space, that maybe it would help if you used your nose filters while you're inside, and that we'll all be glad when the staff sergeant is on his feet again."

Before Sakur could decide if he—and his species—had been insulted, Kichar appeared in the doorway of the inner room.

"Is there any particular reason you two are just standing there?" she demanded while, safely out of sight behind her, Bonninski rolled her eyes. "We've cleared this building, there's nothing here, so let's move ass."

Hisht shifted his grip on his weapon. "And I will also be glad when this is over and that one is alone with her water dreams of Gunnery Sergeant Kerr."

"Wet dreams, brother." Sakur rapped his knuckles against the top of the Krai's helmet. "And I hear you."

They regrouped outside the building as Kichar marked a large white X, a 1/1, and a zero on the door.

"Okay ..." Sakur leaned against the wall, cradling his weapon, legs crossed at the ankles. "   I get that the X means the building was searched, I get that 1/1 refers to us—the team at the top—and I get that the zero means we found nothing except artfully adorable ..."

"Adorable?" Hisht murmured to Bonninski.

She snorted. "He's just being an ass."

". . . tableaux set up to make us think that the occupants of the house had been dragged out by the Others without putting up much of a fight, but you know what I don't get?"

Kichar waited expectantly.

"I don't get why you packed a permanent marker."

She frowned. "It was on the alternatives list. It's not just for marking buildings but for marking trails and leaving messages for the platoon if you're scouting."

"Kind of low tech," Bonninski muttered.

"Exactly. You can't hack writing on a rock." Kichar slipped the marker back into a pocket on her vest. "And it luminesces under a sleeve light."

"It what?"

"Glows in the dark," Sakur told the Krai who was staring at Kichar in confusion.

"This is fukking stupid."

Stone shrugged and continued rolling another layer onto the already sizable ball of snow.

"We're marking searched buildings with snowmen!"

"Look, Carson, if you packed an indelible marker, then whip it out." He set the ball on top of the larger one sitting directly in front of the building's door. "If you didn't, we'll just continue using the material at hand."

"It's a snowman!" she protested again.

"And a damned fine one," Vega added as she snugged the third and smallest ball down on the pile. "We're just lucky the temperature's up a bit and this stuff's packing."

"I hate snow." Pulling off her mitt, Carson held her hand against the snowman's head. The white of the snow made her skin look even darker. "I stand out. That sucks when things are shooting at us."

"Stand behind Stone," Vega suggested. "He's big enough to provide cover for the whole squad."

Carson nodded, poking her finger into the snow and making a pair of eyes. "True."

"We're wasting time." Hair moving under the edge of his helmet, Jonin returned from pacing and glared down at the snowman. "We need to call this building cleared and move on."

"So you can get back to the staff sergeant."

He transferred his glare to Carson. "I should be there."

"Not if we're out here," Stone said quietly, brushing snow off his mittens. "Are we going to have to have that talk again?"

"No, but . . ."

"No buts." He closed his hand over Jonin's shoulder. "There's half a dozen di'Taykan with him. Right now, you're with us. Or you're not with us. Choose."

The silence went on almost too long.

His eyes gradually darkening, Jonin stared down at Stone's hand. "I can think of better things you could do with that," he said at last.

"He's back," Vega snorted.

Eyes narrowed thoughtfully, Stone waited a moment before he let go. Jonin's tone hadn't been completely convincing, but the words were completely di'Taykan—he just wasn't sure that was a good thing right now. "Hand me that bit of broken flashing off the edge of the

window. I want to leave our snowman with a weapon."
When Jonin passed it over, he twisted the bit of metal,
set it in place and stepped back. "There, that's the . . ."

"Private Stone, what the hell are you doing?"

The team turned as one to see a figure, indistinguish-
able at that distance from any other Marine, on the roof
of the anchor.

"Marking this building as searched, Gunnery
Sergeant."

*"Not like that you're not. The weapon goes up to the
snowman's right shoulder."*

As the other three exchanged silent but speaking
looks, he bent and fixed it.

"Better."

There was still no sign of the enemy. Torin moved
away from the edge of the roof hearing herself explaining to Command why the platoon had been moved off
the designated scenario after the appearance of a single
tank and a distant surface-to-air missile that hadn't
been aimed at them.

"Gunny!" The amount of teeth snapping Piroj managed in that single word was not a good sign. *"We've got
a problem!"*

She was running before he finished. "What kind of
problem?"

"With the CPN!"

No point in calling him on the lack of details in his report; if it was a tech problem, she'd be in the room before he could finish explaining.

When she got there, both Piroj and McGuinty had
their hands around the staff sergeant's slate—although
technically Piroj had his hands around McGuinty's—
and seemed to be trying to pull it from the port. "What's
happening?"

"I sent in a worm," McGuinty grunted. "It came back
with something that's destroying the slate."

Every screen on the desk seemed to be open, code moving across them all too quickly to read. "It's wiping the data?"

"Yeah, that, too. But it's also frying the hardware. Not so totally fried as last night, but . . . shit!" With a smell nasty enough to slam Piroj's nose ridges shut, the slate came free. Both Marines stumbled back, bouncing off the outside wall. McGuinty pulled his hands and the slate from Piroj's grip, glanced down at it, and tossed it away. "It's toast, Gunny." Bending, he flicked on his scanner—for the magnification, Torin realized—and shone his light into the port. "This is fused. Unusable." Scanner off, he ran his thumb down the nav bar along the side of the desk then tried each screen in turn. "And I'm completely fukking locked . . ."

The desk made a deep, whining noise and every screen went blank.

McGuinty smacked his palm down on the glossy black surface.

Nothing happened.

"That's that, then,"

"That's what?" Torin demanded. His hand left a print behind, but that was all.

"The CPN is slagged. Maybe they added too much juice last night, but this . . ." Another smack. ". . . may not be melted but it's just as dead."

"Last night was a practice slagging?" Piroj snorted. "How'd they do this one? Hijack an ObSat?"

"Probably." McGuinty sighed and pulled off his helmet. "I'm not sure what all that code was, Gunny, but I can tell you one thing, there's one fuk of a lot of something on the way."

"When we are moving out of Susumi space, I are sending this message to Ventris that instant." Cradled in the pilot's chair, Presit swung away from the board and flashed a mouthful of sharp teeth in Craig's direction.

"Parliament are not allowing the military to be keeping the press away. If you are showing legitimate press credentials, then public relations officers are needing to find your ship a berth. Even if your ship are not one they are wanting to be seeing back again. Why are the Marine Corps not wanting to see your ship back again, Mr. Ryder?"

"The Corps," Craig told her from where he sat on the pulldown bench by the cabin's one small table, "didn't like me asking about classified information."

"But why are Big Yellow being classified to you?" She combed chromed claws through her whiskers, first one side then the other. "You were there, so they are overreacting."

Craig blinked. That last sentence had been in fluent Federate. Seemed like there might be some basis to the theory that the Katrien could unscramble their syntax, but they enjoyed pissing off the rest of the Confederation too much to bother. He supposed that at less than a meter tall and covered in plush fur they needed every advantage to keep the larger races from considering them almost unbearably cute.

Personally, he found the Katrien's size an advantage. The amount of room taken up by the Susumi drive meant that salvage vessels the size of the *Promise* had next to no living space. Smaller lungs needed less oxygen and extrapolating from lung size and body weight, he could calculate her diffusing capacity and from there her absorption rate, but if he took the percentage down from twenty-one to say, nineteen then it would last . . .

"You are wearing your *there are too many people in here* face," she said, not unkindly. "Be taking a deep breath."

"Just what I don't want to do," he muttered, took a mouthful of coffee, and made a face as he swallowed the cold, slightly greasy liquid. Carrying three injured Marines, two Katrien, and an elderly Niln away from

Big Yellow in an area barely more than fifteen square meters had kicked his phobia about sharing space right in the arse, but it hadn't kicked it entirely out of his head.

And this trip, Presit spent most of her time in the cabin instead of spending it locked in the head with the landing party's only surviving Katrien scientist grooming and bitching.

Grooming and bitching.

He frowned.

Katrien were a very social species and they didn't like being on their own. Presit had been the only Katrien on Rossenee Station—the station's OS had been very clear about that when he'd had it comm her. He had thought that meant she was working with a non-Katrien crew, but now he realized that made no sense, not given species preferences and the fact that Sector Central News was predominately Katrien staffed. She'd said she had a crew with her, but he suspected now that she'd lied. More telling, she'd taken commercial transport to get to the station when she'd arrived at Big Yellow in a news ship.

Which she'd damned near destroyed. Might as well have destroyed since the military had confiscated the pieces.

Her crew had been killed in the explosion.

A lot of very expensive gear had been lost.

The story she'd returned with, while exclusive, had been very limited in scope both because she'd had to rely on the military for all her visuals and because they'd left Big Yellow knowing little more than they had going in—unidentified alien ship, constructed of polyhydroxide alcoholydes, interior able to take a number of shapes, capable of performing detailed brain scans although probably only with contact. Four points; that was it.

Presit a Tur durValintrisy was no longer Sector Cen-

tral News' fair-haired girl—or silver-tipped female—
and she wanted that position back. She'd been willing to
travel out to Rosenee in search of a story big enough to
put her back on top. No wonder she'd jumped at a
chance to investigate the missing escape pod.

It also explained why she'd curbed her ego enough to
keep him from wanting to dump her out the air lock.

"You are stopping staring at me! Now!"

Most of the time.

Having seen some truly bizarre things during her
years in the Corps, things beautiful and terrible, Torin
was able to school her expression as she came out onto
the roof. But it was close.

"This happens every time she comes up here?" she
asked Lirit quietly.

"Every time, Gunny. They're nesting on the roof of
that building there." Lirit pointed and, dialing her scanner up, Torin could see piled mud and entry holes and
an impressive amount of bird shit. "When she's not
around, they go back, but as soon as she appears
again . . ."

They looked as much like pigeons as it was possible
for a nonpigeon to look. The details were wrong, but the
overall resemblance was uncanny. And they seemed to
love Dr. Sloan. She stood in the middle of the roof, staring off at the dense cloud cover that had filled the sky
to the west, blatantly ignoring the circle of birds bob-
bing and strutting around her feet. Where the snow
hadn't been packed tightly enough for them to walk,
they'd flap a few paces before settling down and walking again.

"She used to run at them, try and chase them off.
Hell, we tried, too, but nothing works. Shooting them
seemed a little over the top although Sergeant Jiir did
wonder how they might taste."

The Krai had a simple response to wildlife. If it got

close enough, and it was moving slowly enough, they tried to eat it. Torin made a note to keep the sergeant off the roof at the same time as the doctor.

Wondering what would happen if she got closer, Torin walked forward.

The circle of birds parted around her and closed up again as if she were a rock and they were a stream and by the time she reached the doctor's side, she'd become part of the core of the pattern.

"Dr. Sloan."

"Good afternoon, Gunnery Sergeant."

"Any ideas?"

Dr. Sloan turned, slowly, and stared up at Torin through narrowed eyes. "About what?"

"I'm sorry, had you not noticed the birds?"

"Oh, ha." Arms folded, she resumed staring to the west. "I'm not doing anything, they just keep coming back."

"Maybe your jacket . . . ?"

"Is what? Stuffed with birdseed? Emitting mating coos on a frequency only these birds can hear? Looks like their big blue mother? You're so good at getting various and varying species to do what you say, you tell them to shoo."

"Shoo?"

"Fine, pick a tougher word."

No longer bothering to hide her smile, Torin leaned slightly forward and said, "Scram."

The birds took off almost as one bird, their wings chopping at the air. Torin felt something scrape across her helmet, then they were gone and the last set of tail feathers disappeared surprisingly quickly into the nest.

"Okay. That was . . . interesting." Turning on the spot, Dr. Sloan examined the empty circle. "Is this something the Corps teaches all their NCOs, or is this a talent you alone possess?"

"It wasn't me."

"It sounded like . . ."

"They didn't look up at me. Just before they took off, they looked to the west." Torin adjusted her scanner, quickly running through the available audio frequencies when visual gave her nothing. When she finally heard the hum, it was almost too late. Grabbing the doctor's arm, she began dragging the other woman toward the access hatch. "Incoming!"

Marines on the roof opened fire as the drone dove out of the cloud cover, rapidly becoming a wicked looking wedge. A heartbeat later it swooped low and, too far from the hatch for safety, Torin threw the doctor down and threw herself on top of her as cover, trusting her vest would protect both them both. Extremities could be patched. Rounds splattered into the roof, one smacked into the center of her back, and then the drone was moving on. Rolling clear, she brought her weapon up but didn't pull the trigger. She didn't have a hope in hell of hitting it and had no desire to waste ammo she'd need later.

The drone circled wide around the anchor, then disappeared back into the cloud cover heading west.

"Cease fire! You can't fukking hit it if you can't see it!" Torin's ears rang in the sudden silence. "Anyone make contact?"

"I hit it, Gunny . . ."

Lirit. That made sense.

". . . but it wobbled and kept flying."

"Nice try." And she meant it. "Unfortunately, we're past the point where that means anything." And she meant that, too. Dr. Sloan was still flat on the roof, staring at her arm lying bent and bright blue against the snow. "You okay, Doc?"

Eyes wide, she slowly lifted her arm. There on the roof was a rough line of impact that traced the angle of her elbow, the snow pack having kept the rounds from ricocheting and doing the kind of random damage no tech could prevent.

"Well, that answers that question. The system's still honoring your noncombatant chit."

Dr. Sloan smiled tightly. "Oh, joy. Correct me if I'm wrong, but if I'm impervious to bullets doesn't that mean I should be lying on top of you?"

A very good point. Torin grinned. "I'll try to remember that the next time, Doc."

Breathing heavily, Lirit held down a hand. "What was that, Gunny?"

"A scout." She let the private pull her to her feet and stood working her back, checking for bruising, but her vest had done its job. "About a third the size of a flier, too light to carry anything but low caliber rounds that probably wouldn't have pierced your combats. It was just making a point before the main force arrives."

"What point?"

"That the main force is about to arrive." She switched her comm to Group. "Major?"

"I heard. Get ready for them, Gunny."

"Yes, sir." Only the foolish and the insane looked forward to combat and Torin was neither but, just the same, it was impossible not to feel relieved that the other shoe had finally dropped. "Marines, battle stations! This is not a drill!"

TWELVE

"**WHY SEND A SCOUT?**" Kichar asked suddenly. "They've warned us that they're on their way in time for us to get ready for them. According to everything we've been taught, according to everything I've read, that makes no sense."

There was a moment's silence in the second-floor room as the three remaining members of the team thought about that.

"Maybe they're taunting us," Sakur suggested. He pulled his helmet off and his hair expanded out to surround his head in a pale pink halo. "Maybe there's so much coming at us, it doesn't matter that we know. We don't stand a *hurfil's* chance in *sanLi* of surviving."

"I don't want to die on a training run," Kichar muttered. "That's just all kinds of wrong."

"I said maybe," Sakur pointed out.

"Maybe you should put your helmet on!" She leaned forward and peered down into the street, one hand splayed flat against the glass.

"Is she still team leader?" Hisht asked Sakur quietly.

The di'Taykan sighed as he replaced his helmet. "The gunny didn't say different."

They had two windows in one of the second-floor rooms in the middle of the west wall, both about 1.3 meters from the floor and a little under a meter square. The lower section slid up and over the upper, the overlap barely visible until the window was opened. Both windows had been tested, opened and closed to make sure the cold or the Corps hadn't messed up the simple track system. Sakur and Hisht were at one, Kichar at the other. Both windows were now closed.

Bonninski had asked to carry the KC-9.

"I don't mind the extra weight, Gunny," she'd pointed out, "and if we're going to be shooting, I'd just as soon get the bigger bang for my buck."

Sakur, as the only di'Taykan in earshot, had made the obvious comment.

"Didn't seem that much bigger to me," Bonninski had snorted.

Torin had mentally compared Bonninski's scores on the range to the rest of her team. Kichar's were marginally higher, but Bonninski's were high enough that her desire to carry the heavier weapon made up the difference. Maybe the H'san could turn shit into shine, but in her experience, heavy gunners were born, not made. She'd nodded and Hisht had traded the 9 for a 7.

Standing on a broken footlocker in order to see out the window, Hisht used his sleeve to rub off the fogged circles built up by exhalations, thought of Bonninski on the roof, and was just as glad it wasn't him. "The drones have been reprogrammed, that is right?"

"That is right," Sakur repeated agreeably.

"Is their are changed or only their do?"

Kichar leaned out to get a better look at Hisht while Sakur shook his head as though he was trying to jiggle the question into making some kind of sense. "That sounded like Federate," he muttered.

Hisht sighed. "Drones have been brought from all over this sector, perhaps this whole section, and are now programmed to attack us. This is right?"

"Following you so far, big guy," Sakur told him.

"Some of those drones were once programmed to act like the enemy's infantry. If we wound, they act wounded. Like we would be wounded if they hit us. I ask: are they still infantry or only drones? It's harder to hurt machines."

"Is their are changed or only their do?" Kichar repeated, eyes wide. "That's one damned good question."

Torin thought so, too. The Others had taken the silly bugger part of Crucible to a whole new level. Layers within layers and each of them making her job more difficult. "McGuinty, you get that?"

"Got it, Gunnery Sergeant."

She waited a moment, then prodded, "And?"

"And . . . ? Oh. Did the Others *change the core programming? I don't know."*

"Best guess, McGuinty."

"Uh, probably only their orders have been changed, but their core programming will remain the same. Unless that's what took them so long to get here; the Others *were changing the core programming. Except, I don't think they did because that would be a stupid waste of time except that Hisht is right, it is harder to hurt machines, so it might be worth the trouble."*

"So, basically, we'll know when they get here."

"Sorry, Gunny."

"Hey, same old, same old." Her tone was an audible eye roll designed to let her listeners know she was, at worst, mildly annoyed by the situation. "You never know what's going to show up until it arrives." Jiir and Annatahwee hadn't seen combat since they'd made corporal and Major Svensson's last meeting with the enemy had maxed out his tank time, which didn't exactly inspire confidence in raw troops—the platoon would be taking their cues from her. If she lost it, the whole house of cards could come tumbling down. Fortunately, she had no intention of losing it; it would take too damned long to find it again, and she didn't have that kind of time. "Stay sharp, people, and sing out the moment you've got a locked sighting."

The major had set up a command post in the admin office, using the glossy black surface of the inert desk as a mapping station. He'd sketched out the anchor and placed the teams. Torin frowned down at the desk.

"You brought a soluble white marker, sir?"

"Not me." He grinned, the expression momentarily lifting the strain from his face. "Kichar. She's been humping half a support base in her pack. If she wasn't so stiff necked, she could be one hell of a black marketeer."

"The day is young, sir." She glanced up at the wall behind him. "I see Iful got the window sealed."

Disassembling parts of the kitchen to secure the air lock's outer door had given the ex-mechanic new perspective on the anchor's construction, and after passing it a dozen times, he'd realized that the counter separating the outer lockup from the hall had been made from window panels.

"Said you told him to do it first."

Fortunately, all the remaining windows on the first floor had the same profile, so no time had been lost sorting out which panel went where. Unfortunately, they all had to be sealed from the outside, and not even the di'Taykan were tall enough to set the panels without help. Three/two was still outside hauling a storage cube from window to window, closing up the north wall.

"Didn't want to chance you being taken out, sir."

"I appreciate your concern, Gunny, certain as I am that it has everything to do with your concern for my well-being and nothing at all to do with you needing a place to pass the buck." As Torin gave the quip about as much of a smile as it deserved, he ran a hand—his right hand, she noticed—over the pale bristles of his hair. "That scout was way too far out in front."

"Good news for us, then, sir. I think the lag between scout and attack means we're facing only a basic programming change," she explained when he indicated she should continue. "The scout got here when it did because that's how much faster it is than the other fliers. My gut says the drones have been pointed at us and told to attack, nothing more. No strategy, no tactics—they're just to overwhelm us by sheer numbers."

"And that's good news for us because?"

"Because those minimum three fliers will be hitting us sequentially not simultaneously, and because numbers mean squat against a group of well-led, motivated Marines."

He stared at her for a long moment. "You've been here before."

One moment the surrounding low hills were merely an empty purple horizon. The next they were crowned with Silsviss. The thrumming from a thousand throats grew louder and ended in a bass note so deep it continued to buzz through the silence that followed.

"Yes, sir." There were, unfortunately, a limited number of ways to fight a war. Surrounded by a superior number and holding until the Navy showed up just happened to be one of the ways she'd regrettably become familiar with.

"You won last time."

Once again, she kept her hand from rising to touch the cylinder in her vest. "I lost thirteen of my people, sir."

"Our people, Gunny."

His tone was mild and his expression neutral. She watched him rub his left hand with the fingers of his right and remembered why he'd been tanked for so long. "Yes, sir."

He heard the apology and nodded, accepting it. "McGuinty seems to think he could use his slate to jam their scanners if he could bounce it through something with a strong enough signal. If you go down, I told him he could crack your jaw for your implant."

"Happy to help the cause, sir." If the fliers fired from as close in as the sergeants seemed to think, then the much greater range of hers and the major's implants wouldn't be necessary, even the sergeant's implants would be strong enough. Not that it mattered as she doubted even Dr. Sloan would be able to extract them from the jawbones of their owners. And except for the implants . . . "The desk."

"Gunny?"

"It's not working, but it's not slagged either, and the CPNs are in communication with both the OP and whichever of the ObSats the Others have taken." When the major nodded, eyes bright, she touched her CPU. "McGuinty. Admin office, now."

"On my way, Gunnery Sergeant!"

After only four days in the snow, cold had become relative. Yesterday, during the first part of the hump to Dunstan Mills, it had been freeze-nostril-hair cold. Then, it had snowed and that had brought the temperature up and, this morning, it had been comparatively balmy. If Stone leaned forward slightly he could see one of the snowmen they'd built still standing guard.

"You see something on the ground, Stone?"

He snapped his head up. "No, Sergeant Jiir." He wished now he'd taken his toque off before he'd come up to the roof; his scalp felt damp and itchy, and he couldn't take his helmet off to scratch it. Shouldn't have been looking at the snowman either. When the fliers finally showed, they'd roar in close before firing their rockets and the 9s would have almost no time at all to get enough rounds in front of them to stop them. If he let his attention wander, almost no time became no time at all.

One flier showed—they all fired.

Two showed—half fired at each.

Three showed—a third.

He knew his half, he knew his third, and he suspected he should have taken a piss before coming up here.

If the fliers had been reprogrammed to fire at their maximum range, well, then the nine of them on the roof had the best seats in the house for the light show.

Jonin refused to believe that taking responsibility for his people had been a bad thing. Staff Sergeant Beyhn's transition had destabilized them, thrown them right out of the Corps and their training, and they needed to be given the stability of home.

He was di'Arl. His family understood responsibility.

Weapon braced against the edge of the window, he slid his bare finger in through the trigger guard and looked through the scanner, all light receptors open, then at the scanner, most of them closed. Then through. Then at.

He was cold, and that was ridiculous.

He was di'Arl and he understood responsibility well enough he suddenly found himself relieved that Gunnery Sergeant Kerr had taken it away.

"Morning we left, I got a ping from one of my *thytrin.*" Ayumi leaned against the window frame and grinned down at Piroj. "She bet me her Crucible would be worse than mine."

"How much do you stand to win?"

"I didn't have time to take the bet. We'd already been ordered to the shuttle bay."

Piroj shifted his grip on his weapon and, balanced precariously on tipped crate, rubbed his right foot against the back of his left calf. "Too *serley* bad for you."

"Tell me about it. So, why'd the gunny want McGuinty?"

"No idea. Maybe she wanted him to change the ring tone on her implant."

*　　*　　*

McGuinty squatted by the ruins of the desk, lifting one tiny piece after another and holding it to his scanner. When they hadn't been able to find the actual way inside, Torin had made a new one. Like many things, the desk had proved to be Marine-resistant but not Marine-proof.

"I can do it. My slate to this unit." The piece held up in McGuinty's pale fingers looked like any other as far as Torin was concerned. "This unit amplifies the signal and bounces it at the enemy. The signal jams their scanners."

"What kind of range?" Major Svensson had saved the desktop, whole but for a cracked corner.

"Distance, pretty far. Area? No idea, sir."

"How long?" Torin demanded.

"As long as the power in my slate lasts." He blinked at her expression. "Right. How long before it's working. Don't know, easy bit of coding, hardware's all Marine issue, so hopefully no biggie getting them to snog ... and I should get to work, right?"

"Good call."

Any touch, skin-to-skin, seemed to help keep Staff Sergeant Beyhn calm, and that was a good thing because the di'Taykan had been ordered off to wait the way Marines waited for all hell to break loose—in whatever way that differed from the way normal people, non-Marines waited. Right hand lightly resting on the smooth skin of the staff sergeant's shoulder, Dr. Sloan looked around at her empty infirmary set up at one end of the common room and prayed that it would stay empty.

With the index finger of her left hand, she picked at the noncombatant chip on her forehead and thought how much more useful it would be were it attached to someone actually in combat.

"Three/two, talk to me." Torin's place was with the major until he said otherwise, and she knew the wisdom of not exposing command, but she hated being inside where she couldn't see. Especially now, when her gut said the party was about to start.

"Just sealing the last window, Gunny." Iful sounded slightly breathless. *"Latrine, west side."*

"Leave it."

"But . . ."

"Get inside, now!"

"Flier at 343 degrees Marine zero!"

Lirit's voice. Farther south on the roof, Stone shifted a little to the right and picked up the coordinates. At the absolute outside of the scanner's range, it was faith alone that translated the energy signature into a flier. And then it wasn't.

"One flier locked."

"No sign of the other two!"

"Fuk, it's fast!"

"Don't aim at where it is!" Sergeant Jiir's voice; the familiar DI cadence. "Let your scanner tell you where it's going to be."

Using a belt, rather than the fifty-round box mag, the KC-9 fired 600 RPM, 200 less than the lighter KC-7. Stone figured that from the moment his scanner told him to fire until he threw himself flat behind the low parapet of the roof maybe six seconds had passed. Little better than six rounds a second. Sixty rounds from each 9. Nine 9's firing. Roughly 544 rounds. Every tenth a boomer. Fifty-four boomers. All heading for the spot their scanners told them the flier was going to be.

The flyers were delta wings, a wedge no more than two meters along the back edge and a very little less along each side. In order to take it down, they'd have to damage the propulsion system tucked in just under the nose—where damage meant blow it the fuk up.

Fukking impossible to shoot down a flier that way.

Except it looked like it was heading down the same time Stone was.

He hit the roof, slid in tight behind what little shelter there was.

Impact.

It was one hell of a lot louder than he'd expected.

Impact but no explosion.

Debris slammed against the west side of the anchor, but the weight of the structure kept them from feeling the ground-shock effect.

"Three/two?" No way Iful and his team had time to make it the length of the west wall and then around the south wall to the air lock.

"Took the long way, Gunny. We're eastside at the northeast corner, we're good, and we're on our way in."

"Roger that. One/one . . ." Kichar's team held the center west position and with the flier coming in just slightly southwest. ". . . report."

"Both windows blew out. Snow mostly. Some . . . dirt? We're knee-deep in debris but no injuries."

"Two/two . . ." Second squad was in the medical center. They could spare a team. ". . . help them dig out." Torin glanced over at the major who nodded and said one word.

"Go."

"One/two?" She took the stairs three at a time. Chunks of snow spilled out the door of the west room into the hall. One/two had the room farther south, just off the direct impact.

"Lost both windows, but the south window blew out, not in. Ioeyn's bleeding, cut by something, maybe the window."

"I'm on it." Sergeant Annatahwee followed two/two out of the medical center as Torin reached the second floor. "If Ioeyn needs the doc, I'll pull someone from three squad to cover."

Torin nodded her thanks and continued up to the roof.

No way to get an accurate distance on point of impact since the flier had clipped one of the surrounding buildings and gone through another before hitting the ground. Forty meters out, maybe forty-two. Too damned close either way.

"Can't say I'm impressed with the workmanship," Jiir said as they looked at the shattered structure, pieces scattered along the trench the flier had subsequently dug in the ground.

"The Corps probably never expected anyone to drop a flier on it," Torin noted absently as she traced the trench to the west wall of the anchor. Half buried under snow and frozen earth and bits of building, the flier lay upside down about two meters from the wall. Only a very little of the debris had hit the roof. The Marines under cover had taken more damage than the nine exposed.

Jiir dropped to one knee on the parapet and leaned forward. "If this thing's only carrying training rockets, we're going to feel like idiots for doing all this damage to ourselves."

He had a point. The launch tubes had been twisted up on impact. The top two were clearly carrying flashbangs, but the rocket to the left, nearly buried in snow . . . The Corps tagged everything, but there might not be enough visible to get a firm ID. Torin pulled out her slate and tight pinged the tube. After a moment, specs scrolled up on the screen. "Cheer up, Sergeant, that's a blast fragmentation warhead."

"Nice to know we didn't achieve the impossible for nothing." He frowned down at the warhead. "BFWs are detonation on impact."

This seemed rather miraculous considering that the flier had completely destroyed a building, then flipped over and skidded along the ground for twenty meters or so except . . . "They're not armed until they leave the tube, and this one looks like it's still tucked in tight." Torin tossed in a quick silent thanks to whatever gods were watching over them. Maybe Private Masayo's praying had actually attracted some positive attention.

"I don't like this." Torin resisted the urge to grab the back of Jiir's uniform as he leaned farther out. The Krai knew heights, and he wouldn't appreciate the sentiment. "The drones have boomers, too, and if one them gets a shot in at that later on and it blows, we could still be in trouble—they don't call them big fukking warheads for nothing. An explosion could slam the bulk of the flier into the lower wall and buckle it."

"We'll just have to hope the drones aren't capable of that kind of lateral thinking."

Jiir blew a mournful cloud of water vapor through his nose ridges as he straightened and brushed snow off the knees of his combats. "Yeah, but I was assuming they'd do it by accident."

"Could they yank it out, arm it, and throw it at us?" Bonninski asked leaning out and taking a look of her own.

Torin and Jiir turned to stare at the private.

"That one is officer material," Jiir said at last.

"Flier at six degrees of Marine zero. Flier at minus forty-three Marine zero."

Lirit's voice, simultaneously on the PCU and echoing back off the surrounding settlement. The last time, although she'd hidden it well, Torin, listening down in the admin office, had been able to hear the strain in her voice as the first flier had been sighted. This time, she sounded cocky. Not surprising, considering that they'd brought the first flier down with no casualties, but the trouble with doing the impossible was that they now had to do it again. And again.

"Gunnery Sergeant Kerr! I've got it working. We can jam the flier's scanner!"

She turned as McGuinty appeared suddenly up through the access, his slate and the amplifier cradled in bare hands. What was that the Krai said? One leaf never falls but they all do. It looked like things were finally going their way.

"Dr. Sloan helped me connect some of the smaller pieces," he continued. "She's got a great eye for the little shit."

"Probably from surgery."

"No, she said it was from beading. It's a hobby," he added. "She makes jewelry."

Torin didn't actually care. "Sergeant Jiir, the fliers are yours. Private McGuinty . . ." she grabbed his shoulder and hauled him toward the edge of the roof. "Set it up and let it rip. Marines inside, move well away from the west side of the building. Take shelter against debris." Contingency plans had changed; it was obvious the fliers weren't supporting other drones.

Rocking a little as she let him go, McGuinty dropped to the roof and set the amplifier down on the top of the parapet. "I still don't know the area," he told her, aligning his slate.

"Then aim it at minus forty-three and hope it's wide enough to cover the other as well. Sergeant, flier at minus forty-three will be flying blind."

"Roger, Gunny. Let's do it again, people. Watch your scanners."

Torin's hands tightened on her weapon as the 9s started firing.

At 170 meters, the flier at six exploded.

The voice of experience suggested a boomer had set off BFW in the tube—the flashbangs wouldn't have taken out the flier.

Braced against the blast effect, minimal at the distance, Jiir shot Torin a quick grin and yelled, "What do you know; they *do* explode on impact."

The flier at forty-three went through the fireball.

"It's taking hits!" Cho yelled.

"Yeah, but is it taking damage?" Lirit.

"Hasn't fired rockets yet!" Bonninski.

"It can't see anything!" McGuinty whooped. "It won't fire at what it can't see."

Stone followed the changing coordinates on his scanner, leaning back and then dropping to one knee as, proximity beacon still apparently working, the flier pulled up and over the anchor.

Torin thanked those gods again.

It was maybe seventy-five meters straight up from Marine zero when it blew.

Ears ringing, thrown to her knees by the shock wave, Torin heard four flashbangs go off—after the initial explosion, and closer than seventy-five meters. The fifth . . . Not a BFW. Memory threw up Jiir's voice listing the flier's load.

"*. . . most of those rockets are flashbangs.*"

"*Most,*" Torin repeated. "*And the rest?*" Because if most were, then some weren't.

"*Gas if the platoon holds a position long enough to be taken down, incendiaries sometimes and . . .*"

"Filters!" She grabbed McGuinty's arm with one hand dragging him down to the roof as smoking debris began to fall from the sky while she used the other hand to rip the filter off her vest and slap it over her mouth and nose.

"Stay curled!" Jiir snapped out DI sure over the sound of a thousand small impacts. "Let your vest and helmet do their jobs!"

It honestly would not have occurred to Torin that Marines would need to be reminded of that.

A few of the impacts weren't exactly small, but, because of where and how the flier had finally blown, most of the larger debris had been flung out beyond the perimeter of the roof. So, besides the shock wave, the Marines had mostly had to contend with the bits of rockets that had gone up marginally after the initial explosion. Since both the flashbangs and the gas warheads were designed to be essentially shrapnel free, Torin had high hopes no one had been hit with anything bigger than vests or helmets could handle.

The gas, though . . . the gas was significantly heavier than the air it found itself in and was following the shock wave down. There'd be little or no dispersal.

One thing Torin had always liked about gravity, it worked fast. Lifting her head, she scanned the immediate area for debris and when none seemed to be falling, she stood. Without her support, McGuinty sagged over, curled around his slate, filter over his mouth but not his nose. With his helmet cocked sideways over his thin face, he looked about sixteen.

Kirassai had slapped her filter on too high, covering her nose and missing a full seal on her mouth. Her helmet had come off when she went down and her hair looked an even brighter fuchsia than usual against the snow. Even unconscious, she looked remarkably pissed off about the whole experience. Kneeling beside her, Lirit looked up at Torin as she passed.

"Will Kirassai be all right?"

"She'll be fine in an hour or two," Jiir answered as Torin kept moving.

Private Esteban Bynum, the shooter from two/two, hadn't got his left arm under his body in time, and the only sizable piece of the flier to hit the roof had come down on his left arm just above the elbow, breaking the bone. Torin keyed his med-alert quiet and then stiffened the arm of his combats to immobilize the break.

Panting, he stared up at her, pupils dilated. "Hurts."

"Of course it does," she told him. "It's a broken arm. Probably hurts like hell. If we get a buddy to help, do you think you can make it down to the doc?"

"I don't . . . know."

"Well, let's start with standing." Hand in the center of

his back, she gently lifted him into a sitting position.
Cheeks chalky behind his filter, he swallowed two or
three times, Adam's apple jerking up and down in his
throat. Torin held him steady until she knew he wasn't
going to puke. "Ebinger, if you could lend a shoulder . . ."

Ebinger, the shooter from two three tucked himself
under Bynum's good shoulder. "I've got him, Gunny."

Standing looked doubtful for a moment, but then
Bynum took a deep breath, nodded, and said, "I can do
it, Gunny."

"No shame in being carried if you can't."

He shot her the sort of look only a young man in pain
was capable of. "Didn't break my fukking leg, Gunnery
Sergeant."

"True enough." Leaving them to it, she crossed back
to McGuinty, tucked his slate and the amplifier safely
away in his vest, then hauled him up and tossed him
over her shoulder. "It's not like he weighs much," she
pointed out as she turned to see Marines staring. "And
I know you lot have better things to look at than me.
Eyes on the horizon, people. Stone, can you handle
Kirassai?"

"No problem, Gunny."

Stone was nearly as tall as the di'Taykan and consid-
erably broader.

Jiir paced her back to the makeshift hatch. "How did
you know it was gas?"

She shrugged the shoulder not holding McGuinty as
Stone and Kirassai started down. "I've heard a lot of artillery and I knew it wasn't a flashbang or a BFW."

"Could have been an incendiary."

"Could have, but it didn't sound like one. Besides,
wearing a filter without gas is infinitely preferable to
breathing gas without a filter. What's next?"

"If they're hitting us sequentially based on the speed
they travel, long-range drones probably."

"Well . . ." She grinned. "We know how to deal with those." With only her head and McGuinty's ass above the level of the roof, she turned to look out at the five recruits still standing. "Nice shooting, Marines. Well done."

"Three fliers down and three Marines taken out." Major Svensson shook his head as he led the way across the room in the west wall that had taken the brunt of the debris thrown up by the downed flier. "One for one is not the way I'd like to see this go."

Torin wondered if three for fifteen would make him feel any better, considering each warhead as a separate attack but said only, "Privates Kirassai and McGuinty will be up and around in about an hour, and Bynum made it clear he could fire one-handed if necessary."

"And what did Dr. Sloan have to say to that?"

"A few words I wasn't aware she knew, sir."

The major grinned, then sobered as he climbed the ridge of hard-packed snow and looked out the window. "This is not good."

Safely behind him, Torin rolled her eyes. "No, sir, it isn't."

The flier had thrown up enough debris to create a rough ramp from the wreck to the second-floor window, mostly snow but liberally mixed with dirt and pieces of the destroyed building. Solidified by heat and pressure, it would give the drones a road right into the anchor.

"We need to get this out of here, Gunny. Any ideas?"

"Two, sir. If we've got the time, we do a little hard shoveling."

"Registering six-long distance drones at maximum scanner range, minus six degrees Marine zero." Lirit again.

"And if we don't have time?" Major Svensson asked, dropping back into the room.

"One boomer fired straight down, drop a grenade in the hole."

"There's an unexploded BFW down there, Gunny."

"Unarmed, sir. You'd need to drop the grenade right on it to set off the detonators."

"Registering eight long-distance drones!"

Torin sighed, breath pluming as she stepped into the open window and looked west. "Private Lirit, is that eight new drones or a recount?"

"Uh, a recount, Gunnery Sergeant."

"Mention that next time."

"Yes, Gunnery Sergeant!"

And there they were, eight blips on her scanner—harder to lock onto from the second floor but on their way.

"Why only from the west?" the major wondered, eyes on his own scanner.

"Because we're near the far east edge of the section. Because it was easier for the Others to reprogram drones already activated for Platoon 71's scenario. Because the species of Others who landed believes the east to be sacred."

He shot her a look that said *stop being a smart-ass* so clearly he could only have learned it before he was commissioned. "You're allowed to not know, Gunny."

"In that case, sir, I don't know. But the second suggestion is the most likely."

"True enough." Blinking to help his focus adjust, he glanced down at the wreck. "Since we don't seem to have the time to shovel, looks like you're using that grenade. Try not to blow up the warhead."

"Yes, sir."

"And when McGuinty wakes up, have him teach the particulars of his jamming device to someone. He can't be the only one who knows how to use it."

"Yes, sir."

"You are being quiet."

Not entirely certain if that had been a comment or an

instruction, Craig ignored the reporter—a speedily acquired habit—and concentrated on the control panel. *Promise* wasn't as young as she once was, and a few systems were a little eccentric about fully shutting down after docking. Given how happy they'd been about seeing him gone such a short time ago, he had a strong suspicion that the Corps would view "a little eccentric" as grounds for kicking him the hell back into vacuum.

"I are doing all the talking."

Ah. An instruction, then.

"You are being strong and silent and are carrying the equipment unless you are being asked a direction question. General Morris are liking me, and he are being my best chance to be exposing the lie. You are brushing my back now."

That pulled his attention off the fluctuating temperature gauge. He spun the pilot's chair around to find Presit staring up at him, a stiff bristle brush held out in one small hand. "I'm what?"

"Well, I are not being able to do it," she sniffed, upper lip curled and showing teeth. "I are looking fine for spending time in tiny, smelly ship, but I are not looking fine to be seeing General Morris."

And Craig suddenly realized one of the reasons why the Katrien were such a social species—no matter how flexible the little furballs were, grooming parts of their own backs had to be pretty much impossible. Which led to the further realization of how much Presit needed this story to work out for her. Being on her own proved she'd fallen a lot farther than he'd thought.

"You are thinking too much!" she snapped. "Just brush!"

Or maybe she considered anywhere not at the top such an enormous step down that she was willing to put up with attention from aliens just to get back up there. He frowned at his reflection in her mirrored glasses and, as more teeth began to show, took the brush.

He had a feeling she was rolling her eyes as she turned.

Given their height differences, he had to bend at the waist, an awkward fold forward out of the pilot's chair, belt digging into flesh. At least when he'd been completely fukking freaked about having other people in his ship he'd managed to avoid being pushed around by a meter-high bottle brush. Telling himself it was a pity brushing, he set to work.

The outer, silver-tipped fur was silky sleek, sliding over his fingers like warm water, and her charcoal-gray inner coat was both soft and thick enough to sink a finger in up to the second joint. The Katrien were mostly fur. There were no mats, no tangles, and no real reason he could see for him to be brushing her, but she stood quietly while he moved the stiff bristles down the center of her back and maybe that was reason enough. It was very nearly the only time she'd been quiet since she'd come on board—curled up in a hammock strung across the small cabin, she even mumbled in her sleep.

He wasn't sure how long he was expected to continue brushing, and when the buzz of an incoming message jerked her away from his touch, he straightened gratefully.

"Promise, *this is Ventris Control. We require you to give over all security and system codes before you will be allowed access to the station.*"

System codes? Those questions about Big Yellow's escape pod really had stuck a wrench up someone's ass. Other visits, they'd never asked for more than basic security at docking. Before he got his mouth open to argue that he'd as soon let the Others have his system codes, a small hand grabbed a chunk of his thigh.

"Son of a . . . !"

"I are taking this," Presit purred.

Impressed by the number of sharp white teeth he

could see, he plucked her grip off his leg and silently slid the chair away from the console.

"Ventris Control, this are being Presit a Tur durValintrisy of Sector Central News. This ship are being for this time a registered media conveyance. According to article 471 of the Confederation Military Charter, you are not allowing more than basic security codes from any media vessel. Nor are you allowing to be interfering with any media access. Nor are you allowing to not be answering any media questions."

Most of known space could care less about most of the answers the media got from the military, but that didn't seem to be slowing Presit down.

"My viewers are wanting very much to know why you are refusing media's rights."

"Ma'am, it's security . . ." The voice cut off sharply.

Craig grinned. What was security for a civilian salvage operator they didn't much like wasn't just security for a media vessel.

"Promise, this is Ventris Control. Security codes will be sufficient."

"I are certainly hoping so," Presit sniffed. "You are reminding General Morris I are docked."

"Yes, ma'am."

"You are letting me know when Captain Stedrin arrives."

"Ma'am, it's station night cycle . . ."

"We are waiting." She drew a chromed claw through the fur of her throat, and Craig cut the connection.

"You're sure Morris will listen to what you have to say?"

"Of course—he are paranoid. He are military, and military are having a job that is to be shot at." She combed her claws through her whiskers. "If my job are to be throwing myself at death, I are being paranoid, too."

*   *   *

Two of the long-distance drones got through, landed, became standard infantry drones, and began returning fire. The good news, they didn't have a hope in hell of hitting anyone. The bad news, by late afternoon another forty-two drones had arrived and there were definitely more on the way. The anchor was surrounded and by dark, they'd beaten back two attempts on the air lock door.

The first attack answered Hisht's question. They fought like infantry, but they took injuries like machines.

All the windows on the second floor were gone by midnight, and the temperature inside began to fall.

They stopped the third attack around 0230 with a fifty-gallon pot of slushy water. Torin'd had two/two tear the pot out of the big communal kitchen, fill it with snow thrown in from the downed flyer's ground wave, toss in a couple of extra fire starters from Kichar's pack, and then dump it off the roof over the air lock.

The water almost froze on the way down, that's how cold it had gotten.

The drones moved so slowly as they retreated, there was plenty of time to aim, and it needed only single shots to take them down.

Torin nodded in approval as the last drone fell. Six days now until the *NirWentry* returned. She had a feeling that, even with the cache in the anchor, they were going to need the ammo.

The patch of ice at the south end of the building discouraged further attacks as soon as the drones accumulated enough data to convince them they'd been built with inadequate traction.

Machines didn't sleep.

At 0453 McGuinty jammed an incoming flier on approach, maintained the connection as it passed over the anchor, and directed it into explosive contact with the hills on the other side of the river.

"If I can keep contact long enough," he explained, "I can get in to its sysop and then it's like a big old remote control. Whoosh." He traced an arc in the air with his slate. "Bang!"

"And you didn't think to mention that before?" Torin asked, ignoring the orange traces of stim in the corner of his mouth.

He shrugged a little sheepishly. "It was a new modification, Gunny. I wasn't sure it would work."

"Uh-huh." Torin stared out at the burning wreckage. At least three of its warheads hadn't gone off in the crash. Something to remember. "You're heading straight for specialist training after Crucible, right, McGuinty?"

Thin cheeks darkened and he stared at the toes of his boots. "I hadn't actually thought about it, Gunny."

She grinned and gripped his shoulder as she steered him down off the roof. "I wasn't actually asking, McGuinty."

"Gunnery Sergeant Kerr. We need you on the roof."

Torin glanced over at the major, who nodded. "On my way."

When she joined Sergeant Annatahwee, she was surprised to see her facing south. In answer to Torin's silent question, Annatahwee said only, "Check 264."

Torin zeroed. Turned into the coordinate and swore. Even at the absolute outside edge of her scanner's range there was no mistaking what she saw coming up the frozen river. Tank. "Fukking wonderful," she sighed.

"At least there's only one of them."

"It's a *tank*, Sergeant, one's enough. And, if you'll recall, the last tank we faced was firing HE rounds."

"We don't know this one's been reloaded."

"We don't know it hasn't," Torin snorted. On the bright side, tanks were noticeable. There'd be no covert attacks. Not that the Others had been doing much more than the most basic surround-and-pound so far. "Is there a reason endemic to Crucible that it's not firing?" If they could see the tank, the tank could see them.

"They're used to train the recruits in antitank warfare so their programming has them moving in close before they engage."

"The last one fired on us from the middle of the lake."

"Not exactly the middle, Gunny." Catching sight of Torin's expression, she added. "But close enough."

The 20-mm top-mounted machine gun made it impossible for infantry to get close to a tank even with sufficient cover. Once again, they'd have to take it out from a distance.

"I wonder how deep the river is," Torin muttered, watching the tank's relentless grind forward. It was moving slowly enough they'd have a few minutes to come up with a solution. McGuinty would have to reconfigure his jamming program for the tank, and that would not only leave them defenseless against more fliers—she'd never liked the sound of defenseless—but wouldn't actually solve the problem of the tank. Better to let McGuinty get what sleep he could. "The drones don't actually see us," she said slowly, "they're targeting our combats—uniforms, vests, boots, helmets—everything that puts out some kind of a signal. If a couple of Marines stripped down to their bodyliners and went out with grenades . . ."

"The drones would read the grenade the moment it was activated."

"Good point." That also took Dr. Sloan and her noncombatant chip out of the equation. Not that Torin had been looking forward to suggesting the doctor take a brisk walk through three dozen or so drones and blow up a tank.

"And there's the problem of the drones charging the door if we open it to send a team after the tank."

Torin grinned as a plan came together. "Actually, Sergeant, I think I've got that covered."

Torin had to give Major Svensson credit for one hell of a poker face. He was showing at best polite interest while the Marines in the room all wore a variation on *"You have got to be fukking kidding me."* As identical an expression as varying physiognomies allowed.

"Let's just see if I have a handle on what you're suggesting. Someone strips down to their bodyliner, is lowered out this window . . ." His gesture at the blown window was admirably casual. ". . . removes the launch tube containing the BFW from the downed flier, and is pulled back inside with the tube. Did I miss something, Gunny?"

"No, sir."

"And then we launch the BFW and blow up the opposing tank."

"Yes, sir."

"I can't decide if that's crazy or brilliant."

"Do we get a vote, sir?" Sakur asked behind him.

Torin saw the ghost of a smile pull at the major's mouth. "No, Private, you do not. Gunny, what makes you so certain they're only targeting the signals from our gear?"

"They're not shooting at the doctor's pigeons, sir."

This time, he couldn't stop the smile. "Very convincing."

"Yes, sir."

"Not exactly good enough, though."

"I didn't think it would be, sir." She met his gaze, held it, and waited.

After a long moment, he sighed. "Go ahead."

Torin took off her mitts, handed Kichar her weapon—ignoring the blush that stained the private's high cheekbones—and bent to undo her boots.

"Sir, is the gunny . . ."

"Yes."

"I could help."

"You could be quiet, Sakur."

"Yes, sir."

Vest and combats took no time at all, then she set her helmet on the pile and stepped in front of the window. She felt lighter although her uniform weighed as little as tech allowed.

Nothing.

"Maybe they're not paying attention."

Her reply was to step back to the pile, pick up her vest, and toss it across the same space.

Four shots blew it across the room.

"Sakur, get that for me, would you. Stay low."

The major shook his head and started toward the door. "It's a crazy plan, Gunny. Go for it. I'll tell McGuinty we'll need the launch codes."

"Kichar."

"Gunnery Sergeant!"

With a nice solid piece of the anchor between her and the drones, Torin pulled her combats back on. "Go get that fifty feet of rope from your pack."

"Yes, Gunnery Sergeant!"

Kichar pounded off and Torin looked up to see the rest of the team watching her. "What?"

"How did you know she had the rope, Gunny?"

Torin thumbed the front seal closed. "It seemed to be a reasonable assumption since she brought everything else on the list."

"Gunny?" Hisht paused, one boot off. "I brought the rope, too."

"You willing to have Kichar in your pack?" When he nodded, she thumbed her PCU. "Kichar."

"Yes, Gunnery Sergeant!"

"Grab the rope out of Hisht's pack while you're down there."

"Yes, Gunnery Sergeant!"

"I don't suppose any of the rest of you brought rope?" she asked, bending to lace her boots. "Or maybe an antitank gun?" she added when there was no more rope in the offing.

Sakur snorted. "It wasn't on the list, Gunny."

Torin snorted right back at him. "I'm betting it will be next time."

"It may not *need* all three of us," Sergeant Jiir admitted, pulling off his boots and spreading long toes inside the liner. "But it'll go faster and easier with all three of us, and that tank is getting closer while we argue."

"We have three NCOs to thirty-five brand-new Marines," Torin reminded him. "We can't afford to lose you."

"And that's why you were on point, Gunnery Sergeant?"

Okay, she had to give him that one; they were also a little short on anything but basic skills. "Anything happens to you, and I'm going to get cranky."

He was too good to let triumph show in his smile. "I'll be careful."

Since in this particular instance, careful would actually count for something, she nodded and rejoined Hisht by the window. In next to no time, his fifty feet of rope had become a net with braided carrying handles. "I'm impressed."

His nose ridges flared and he ducked his head. "It is a high trees skill."

High trees. Krai for back country. "When we get out of this, I'll send a message to your *jernil*, thanking her for teaching it to you, because that net's going to make this one hell of a lot easier."

He looked up then. "You are not Krai. How did you know . . . ?"

"I'm a gunnery sergeant, Hisht. We know everything. Krai, Human, di'Taykan—if it's part of the Corps, we know it." Specifically, it had been a lucky guess. Seemed the sort of skill a grandmother would teach. "Piroj."

"Gunny?"

"The rope secure?"

"I'd send my *jernil* down it, Gunny."

"Too bad she's not here."

The drones didn't shoot at the rope—it had registered as inert, but Torin had long since learned not to take that kind of thing for granted.

The Krai's bootliners were a lot more flexible than either di'Taykans' or Humans' but not quite flexible enough to grip through. Liners and mitts shoved behind rope belts, they climbed with feet bare and slid the liners back on when they reached the wreck. Quickly clearing snow from the point where the launch tube connected to the flier required a little lateral thinking.

"Un, Gunny, are they doing what it looks like they're doing?"

"Does it look like they're pissing on it, Kichar?"

"Uh . . ."

"Then that's what they're doing."

Although it was difficult to clearly see what was happening, Piroj's voice carried. "Well, I'm sorry, Sergeant, but the whole long underwear, surrounded by a hundred drones programmed to kill me, standing next to a BFW thing has me a bit clamped up."

"Point and shoot, Private!"

"Sir, yes, sir!"

Torin was beginning to realize that instinctive responses to a DI had some advantages.

"Gunnery Sergeant Kerr."

"Sergeant Annatahwee."

"The tank'll be in firing range in three minutes."

"Roger that. Any idea what it's carrying?"

"Not until it starts shooting, Gunny. It doesn't have the weight restrictions the fliers do, so . . ."

"Yeah, I get the picture." She leaned toward the window. "Tank's within three minutes, Sergeant."

"Tube release is bent, Gunny. Hisht, hand me that hunk of . . . whatever the hell that is."

The first crack of metal against metal wasn't entirely unexpected. Unfortunately, neither was the reaction from the drones.

"*Chreen! Chreen! Chreen!* Fuk!"

Torin figured the single shot had been an attempt to elicit a response the drones could lock in on. "You guys all right?"

Jiir answered without looking up from the tube release. "Yeah. We're good."

"Good thing Hisht already emptied his bladder," Piroj snorted.

"*Gren sa talamac!*"

"I'm going to stuff this missile up your ass in a minute," Jiir growled. "On my mark, both of you pull. Three two one, mark! That's got it."

Tube and missile went into the net.

The drones took another three shots. One rang off the launch tube.

"I think they're going to notice it moving, Gunny."

This had always been the most dangerous part of the plan. "Get back up here."

Using hands and feet both on one length of rope, the three Krai were back inside almost before she finished talking while Sakur and Kichar hauled up the second length, launch tube dangling off the end.

The drones began firing. Marines along the west side of the anchor returned fire, hopefully keeping them from locking on the moving target.

"*Tank in one minute, Gunny.*"

"You heard the Sergeant, Marines! Clear the medical center!" The best defense usually included not being where artillery fire was going to land.

"Gunny, the warhead!"

Rounds were ringing off the metal.

Torin took the top off a drone rising up to aim. "There's no chance of them blowing it unless they get in a lucky shot with an explosive ..."

The explosion took out a piece of window trim.

"... round," she finished as the launch tube hit the floor, the clank barely muffled by the net. "Everyone all right?"

"Gunny, you're bleeding!"

She checked a cut on the edge of her jaw as she crossed to the net. "Minor. Everyone else?"

"Same kind of minor, Gunny."

"Good. And good work, Marines. Get dressed." She scooped up the net, tube, and missile. "I'll be on the roof."

Unfortunately, it took a little longer than a minute.

The tank's first shell slammed through the broken windows on the south side of the anchor. Torin stumbled as she stepped out onto the roof, recovered, and sprinted for the south end, dumping the net as she ran. At the south end of the roof, she dropped to one knee. "McGuinty?"

Yawning, he stumbled forward, touched a slate to the top of the tube, and peered down at the screen. "It's running."

"Whose slate?"

"Duarte's. Lots of room once I dumped her porn." He blinked. "I shouldn't have told you ..."

"I know what porn is, McGuinty."

"Right." He backed away. "As soon as the launch code locks, it'll fire."

"Tank's lining up another shot!"

"Thank you, Sergeant." Torin adjusted her stance slightly.

"Uh, Gunny?" McGuinty's frown tipped his helmet forward. "How are you planning to aim that thing?"

Eyes focused through her scanner at the tank, Torin grinned. "Point and shoot, McGuinty. Point and sho ..."

A heavy recoil on launch could knock a flier out of the sky, so a certain amount of movement had been built into the mechanism that joined the tubes to the flier. Missing that mechanism, Torin was flung back about two meters, landing heavily on her ass, ears ringing.

"Gunny! You all right?"

In the distance, the tank burned.

Tossing the tube aside, Torin grinned. "I'm good."

THIRTEEN

TORIN WATCHED THE SUNRISE through her scanner, habit marking the time and the temperature. The cold air was bracing—where bracing meant not quite cold enough to freeze her nose hair but cold enough to chase away the fatigue of a night on her feet. She'd cycled the fireteams in and out of the community hall all night, making sure everyone got at least a couple of hours' sleep. They were young; they could manage on next to nothing for a few days. Fortunately, when youth fled, experience took over. Torin and the major were old hands at grabbing a minute here, a minute there—combat napping—and both sergeants insisted that after years of shepherding recruit platoons through Crucible, they'd probably spent as much time awake in the field. Remembering her own Crucible and how the DIs never seemed to sleep, appearing when needed as well as when they were the last thing the recruits wanted to see, Torin believed them.

They'd passed the hundred drone mark around 0630. Fortunately, their programming seemed to consist of nothing more complicated than *this is the enemy*, *this is where the enemy is*, *shoot them*. While the drones were responsive to external stimuli to the extent that they refused to just stand still and be shot, they weren't able to plan anything complex enough to keep the situation from turning into a siege.

The *NirWentry* would be back in six days. They could survive a siege, but there were definitely more tanks coming and probably more fliers.

The snow squeaked under boot treads behind her, and she smiled. "Good morning, Dr. Sloan."

"I guess gunnery sergeants really do know everything," the doctor murmured as she came around to stand at Torin's right.

"Actually, ma'am, the scanner registered a presence behind me, and since you're the only noncombatant we've got . . ."

"Ah." She reached up under the edge of her toque to rub at the chip.

"Which doesn't, however, affect your actual statement."

The soft whuff of laughter was a welcome sound. "I'm glad to hear that, Gunny. You should let me look at that cut on your jaw."

Cut? Torin pulled off a mitt and touched her face. She'd forgotten she'd been hit. Remembering identified the pain that shot along her jaw when she'd yawned. "It's just a scratch, I'm fine. How are you?"

"Me?" She sounded surprised to be asked. "I'm tired, I'm not happy about what's happening . . ." A pause while three birds landed at her feet. ". . . and apparently I'm still irresistible to alien pigeons. You don't have to be here," she snapped as they gave her a chilled look. "You could be tucked up all safe and warm in your colony, so don't blame me if you're cold."

Torin heard a snicker from one of the Marines on the roof and turned to see Ebinger watching, a broad smile on his face. "You expecting those birds to attack, Ebinger?"

He started. "No, Gunnery Sergeant!"

"Then keep your eyes on the enemy."

"Yes, Gunnery Sergeant!"

"I don't see any drones." Dr. Sloan frowned and took a step closer to the edge.

"If you could see them, we could shoot them; so they tend to stay hidden."

"Ah. Makes sense." Arms folded, she sighed. "This must feel awfully familiar to you, Gunny, being surrounded by an overwhelming number of the enemy."

"We're not exactly being overwhelmed, Doc, but I take your point." She'd had that familiar feeling for a while now. It seemed she couldn't get away from the Silsviss. She'd come to Crucible to avoid talking about them and ended up practically reenacting the battle at the other temperature extreme.

"Well, you beat them the first time and you seem to be up to whatever they throw this time."

"We."

The doctor turned, brows drawn in. "Pardon?"

"We're up to it," Torin told her.

She glanced over at Ebinger who had his eyes locked on the nearest building. "Right. Sorry."

Feathers fluffed out, one of the pigeons bounced from boot print to boot print and gave a soft, mournful coo.

Dr. Sloan threw up her hands. "That's it; I'm going back inside. I have enough going on I can't cope with feeling guilty about these stupid birds getting chills because of me." She paused as she passed. "Oh, and the latest diagnostic data suggests something may be about to happen with the staff sergeant."

"Something?"

"Yes. Something. It's a medical term meaning I still don't know what's happening, but whatever it is, it's about to change. You hadn't asked, so I thought I'd better tell you."

"I figured you would. Has Major Svensson been informed?"

"I'm on my way to interrupt his report writing now."

"Thank you, Doctor."

Torin waited until the pigeons reached the colony—if the drones started shooting at them, she needed to know—did one last round of the Marines on the roof, then followed the doctor's boot prints toward the access hatch.

The sudden pain in her jaw snapped her head up and locked her knees. Eyes watering, she gained enough control of her tongue to punch the emergency response code into her jaw implant. The static sounded like she had a wasp's nest in her head, but the contact was so faint she couldn't adjust the volume.

"Shhhtzaft Sergeant Dhupam ... Platoon sevshshshtz two . . . using slate and implant to bounshshtz off shshshtzalitte . . ."

Gunnery sergeants and above had implants that could reach ships in orbit independent of an external sysop. Dhupam had a very handy Marine in Platoon 72 if he'd managed to boost her signal, hoping that either Torin or Major Svensson would pick it up.

"Ashshshzent on OP . . ."

Accident. They were in the wrong hemisphere to have seen the sammy go up.

". . . not effecting shshshhtzerio but with no shshshshzt of med-evac . . . have dialed back to shshshshstzing pattern."

Holding pattern.

". . . only shshshtzance . . . message . . . Staff Shshshshtzeant Beyhn changshshshtz . . ."

Another burst of static. Two nests of wasps. Angry wasps. And then silence.

Torin breathed as deeply as the cold allowed and fought the urge to beat her head against the nearest solid surface just to make it feel better. She scrubbed a mitt across her face, wiping off freezing tears and drying snot, and glanced around to see if anyone had noticed. No. Good.

So Staff Sergeant Dhupam thought she needed to warn them that Staff Sergeant Beyhn was changing. Apparently, she'd drawn the correct conclusions from his increasingly erratic behavior. Might have been more useful if she'd shared the information—or suspicion—before they'd hit dirt, but Torin would take that up with her later.

Platoon 72's scenario hadn't been affected by the loss of the Orbital Platform, but with no chance of medevac, Dhupam had dialed back to a holding pattern.

Therefore, Platoon 72 wasn't under attack.

Torin wondered if Platoons 69 and 70 were under attack. If, in fact, anyone was under attack except for them. And then she wondered why the Others would only attack one of four recruit platoons. Unless they were being significantly more subtle than Torin's experience showed them to be, they wouldn't.

So, if not the Others, who?

"General Morris." Presit swept into the general's office—force of personality substituting for size—and extended a hand. "I are so pleased to see you again. You are looking very distinguished."

Recognizing that the camera was at least recording and very likely broadcasting, the general stood and managed to get around his desk to her hand before it looked too much like he'd been planning on a less gracious reception. Peering into the monitors and pretending the camera's pattern recognition program wasn't doing all the work, Craig took a moment to admire the old goat's political savvy.

"Presit a Tur durValintrisy." He bowed over her hand. "To what do I owe the honor?"

"There are being things we must discuss."

"You know the Corps is more than happy to give the media the full disclosure mandated by law."

"Good." She took her hand back and smiled toothily up at him. "Please be retaking your seat."

He looked slightly startled. "My seat?"

Her smile broadened. "You are going to be wanting to sit."

"Very well." Still conscious of the camera, he returned back behind his desk. "Our data lists Craig Ryder as a Civilian Salvage Operator. When did he become part of your crew?"

"When I are asking him to."

The media was under no legal obligation to disclose anything to the military, and Craig gave General Morris credit for almost hiding what he thought of that. As Presit arranged herself in one of the faux wood-and-leather chairs, he set half the camera unit on a tripod, locked the focus on the general's face, and took the other half of the unit behind the desk.

"You are not minding Mr. Ryder back there, General?" Presit asked sweetly. "He are needing to capture my reactions. Because of the glasses . . ." One claw tapped the edge of her mirrored lens. ". . . it are delicate work."

"Of course I don't mind. You do what you have to."

Given the color rising on the general's broad face, Craig would have bet serious cash that he not only minded, he minded a lot. Craig didn't exactly blame him. His position had little to do with the camera and a lot more to do with making the general uncomfortable by putting someone he didn't exactly trust not only in his space but in his blind spot.

Good thing he's more politician than Marine at this point.

Had Torin been sitting in the general's chair, Presit would never have gotten away with it. And *he* might not have survived it.

Presit settled herself more comfortably, one leg tucked up under a fringe of silver-tipped fur. Her smile was genial and a little frightening. "So, General Morris, you are telling us why you are lying about the existence of the escape pod from the alien spacecraft that are being known to our audience as Big Yellow."

Inside the matte black of his uniform, the general's shoulders stiffened. Anticipating action, possibly violence, Craig shifted away until his back was against the wall. If the general happened to come up swinging, he wanted maneuvering room.

"There was no escape pod. I am not lying."

There was no action either, just more stiffening. Craig wondered if the desk was on and shooting a data stream straight to a watching cadre of Intelligence officers. It sure as shit would be had he been running the Corps.

Presit ran her claws through her whiskers. Right side. Left side. "But I are remembering an escape pod. So you are saying I are lying?"

"No . . ."

"I are not lying, then?"

"You are *mistaken*."

From the sound of things, the general had his butt cheeks clenched so tightly they were about to cut off all oxygen to his brain.

"And why are I being mistaken but you are not?"

Craig slapped at something tickling his ear, the gesture ingrained during a childhood on Vardie. The native bugs had very much enjoyed the imported food supply—proof the Elder Races weren't infallible.

"I assure you, Presit, I am not the only one who believes there was no escape pod."

"You are *believing*? But you are not having proof?"

He slapped at his ear again, turned, and saw only an expanse of pale gray wall broken by an ugly, darker gray plaque. The Corps didn't waste Confederation money on decorating, that was for sure. Still, it made sense to have the vid screen on the wall opposite the desk; no point in simulating a window the room's occupant couldn't see.

"As your audience is well aware, you can't prove a negative."

"You are being able to prove negative charges, negative balances, negative space . . ."

Paying minimal attention to the discussion being recorded, he tried to focus on what the damned plaque was actually for. Although the citation was definitely in Federate, individual letters were strangely unreadable. Craig reached out and rubbed his thumb over one corner. Plastic. And a little greasy.

"Fine. Then why, if you are not mistaken, if this alleged escape pod is real, do I not remember it?"

"You are having had your memory adjusted."

"By who?"

"Who are able?"

"I assure you that neither branch of the military is . . ."

"I are not speaking of the military," Presit interrupted.

General Morris' snort sounded almost relaxed. "Now, you're being ridiculous. There is no way that any of the Elder Races would use mind adjustment techniques on any member of the Confederation. That would be like asking the H'san to . . . to water-ski."

"I are not knowing what . . ."

"Actually, I think he's right." Craig turned in time to catch a pair of nearly identical glares shot his way. He ignored them and indicated the plaque. "Where'd you get this, General?"

"It was presented by . . ." The general stopped, flushed, and snarled. "What does that have to do with any of this?"

"Well, you're missing an escape pod and, while we were on board, Big Yellow shuffled itself around into any number of ace shapes, and this . . ." He pressed one finger to the plaque. As he pulled it away, a fine line of gray plastic followed, the end of the tendril reaching out to stroke his fingertip. ". . . knows me."

*   *   *

"Sergeant Annatahwee."

The sergeant turned, covering a yawn. "Gunny?"

"Two days ago, after the minefield when I went out on point, did Major Svensson leave the platoon at any time?"

"Why? Doc Sloan wants to know if he took a leak?"

Torin waited, her expression designed to stop further questions.

Annatahwee straightened, unaware she was doing it. "The major stayed within the bulk of the platoon the entire time you were gone."

"Thank you."

"Gunnery Sergeant Kerr! Stone on the south wall. We've got movement!"

"Don't tell me the damned drones are charging the fukking air lock again." The sergeant fell into step beside Torin as they ran for the stairs. "They may have minimal self-programming capability, but you'd think they'd learn they can't get in."

Torin snorted. "There's more of them now. They may be trying to overwhelm that specific defense with numbers."

The main room on the south wall had been a barracks, originally for the builders of the settlement and later for—actually, Torin neither knew nor cared.

Crouched below the window, Stone grimaced as the two NCOs pounded through the door. "Drones on the roof keeping us pinned, Gunny!"

"Thank you, Private. I'd noticed." Torin dropped to one knee as half a dozen rounds smacked into the wall behind her, provoking an answering volley from the fireteams on the roof of the anchor. "Sergeant Jiir?"

"We're on them, Gunny, but for every one we blow, another one moves in."

"There's a dozen—no, sixteen! heading for the . . . Holy shit!" Carson flattened as a round clipped her helmet. ". . . doors!"

After the last attack the drones had made on the air lock, Iful had loudly pointed out that grenades and flying bits of drone debris also damaged the doors, and he'd thank them to lay the fuk off with exploding things right next to his repairs.

A ricochet pinged off the room's door with a familiar metallic sound, scraping off a layer of blue paint. Torin tapped it with the butt of her KC-7 and grinned across the space at Anatahwee. "I think we just found two of this room's window seals, Sergeant."

Mitten off, Annatahwee scraped at the blue in the joint between the two pieces that made up the door. "I can't believe they bothered to paint them."

"Pin hinges." Torin pointed at the hinges in question. "Easy to take apart."

"A little hard to reinstall the window shields right now, Gunny!"

"Don't install them." Torin mimed lifting the door and shoving it out the window. Like the other parts of the spaceship hull, it would be damned heavy. "Drop the door on the drones."

"Gunnery Sergeant Kerr! Kichar on the west wall. We've got movement, too."

"Go ahead." Annatahwee's eyes gleamed at a chance to do some serious damage. "I've got this." Torin nodded and headed for the west wall as she yelled, "Three/one, get your collective butts over here and help me with this door."

"Uh, Sergeant, that'll leave no one at the window."

"So? It's not like you're shooting out it!"

There were drones on the roofs to the west as well.

"Could use some more shooters up here, Gunny!"

"On their way, Sergeant." Staying low as she crossed, Torin put her back against the wall between the two windows. "Two/three, get to the roof now!"

"On our way, Gunnery Sergeant!"

Four pairs of boots pounded past outside the room.

"Are they trying for what's left of the debris ramp again?" Torin asked as she joined one/one.

"Not this time, Gunnery Sergeant. There's thirty, maybe forty drones at the base of the building!" Kichar had her helmet scope up and over the sill. "It looks they're trying to get the sections out of the windows!"

Hisht leaned out far enough to stare at her. "I thought that needed special tools?"

"They're drones, you ass!" Sakur punched him in the arm. "They are special tools!"

"Iful! Can we drop grenades to the west?"

"Yes, Gunnery Sergeant! It's likely that any damage you do to the building will only cram those window sections in tighter."

Likely? "How likely?"

"I'd put serious money on it."

"Good enough." Torin gripped Bonninski's shoulder as the private began to rise up, grenade in hand. "Don't waste them. One per window, then get new intell. Bonninski, since you're so eager. Sakur." One/two held the other west room. "Ioeyn!"

"On it, Gunny!"

"Ready grenades, drop—do not throw, *drop* on my mark. One, two . . ."

In the pause there was a large explosion and some cheers from the south end of the anchor.

". . . three, mark."

No way of telling right off how much the snow amplified the red flare that still came off destroyed drones.

Kichar frowned at her scanner, one hand twisting her scope first left then right. "They've taken damage, Gunnery Sergeant."

"We dropped three fukking grenades on them. I sure as fuk hope they've taken damage!"

Torin agreed with Sakur's sentiment.

"They're still massing at the window sections."

"One more time, Bonninski, Sakur, Ioeyn, on my mark."

The explosions sounded louder. It was possible drones that had taken damage the first time took fatal damage this time.

Kichar pumped a fist in the air. "They're pulling back!"

"Drones are leaving the surrounding roofs, Gunny. Whatever they were trying, it's over."

"Thank you, Sergeant Jiir. Good work, Marines."

"Gunnery Sergeant Kerr?"

She paused in the doorway—wishing she could lean against it, knowing she couldn't. She didn't get to be tired until this was over. "What is it, Kichar?"

"I was thinking that if we secured the shelter halves over the windows, artillery might have a more difficult time targeting them."

The wall over the window was perfectly smooth. "And how do we secure them?"

"I have bonding materials in my pack, Gunnery Sergeant."

"Bonding materials?"

"Glue. And duct tape."

Glue and duct tape. Okay. "It's a good idea, Kichar. See that it's done."

She flushed. "Me, Gunnery Sergeant?"

"It's your glue and duct tape."

On her way down to report to the major, Torin met Annatahwee half carrying Stevens out of the south room toward the stairs, the private's left arm red and wet, a hole in her combats just under the shoulder.

"She took a round," the sergeant explained. "Missed the bone." Sealant glistened through the hole. "I told her that Doc Sloan'll patch her up as good as new."

"First I get shot in the butt and now this." Tears that all three of them ignored rolled down Stevens' cheeks. "Why me?"

"Roll of the dice, Marine," Annatahwee told her

cheerfully. "And look at the bright side, you've got a real doctor. Usually, on Crucible, we make do with the cheat sheets you lot downloaded onto your slates from your first aid course."

Stevens' expression suggested she didn't find the sergeant's comment even a little comforting. "Usually, on Crucible, the drones aren't shooting to kill."

"No one ever died from getting shot in the arm, Stevens. Can you make it to the doc on your own?"

"Yes, Sergeant." Adding in an undertone as she started down the stairs. "I didn't get shot in the fukking leg."

Torin grinned at the echo of Bynum's protest leaving the roof and then stopped grinning when she caught the look on the sergeant's face. "What?"

"Telling Stevens about the first aid on the slates reminded me. I don't know if it means anything, but that afternoon you were asking about, well, the major never left the bulk of the platoon, but he did have his slate out nearly every time I looked his way."

"While he was walking?"

"Yeah. The doc had to grab his arm once; he nearly walked into a tree. I figured he was probably helping McGuinty with trying to get the program back from the Others."

Figured. Torin noted the past tense, knew she'd caused it with her question.

Technically, Major Svensson was still on medical leave.

And Torin had been the second most talked about Marine on Ventris.

At what point did the pieces of the Marine put into the tank stop being a Marine and start being merely pieces?

The question was right there in Sergeant Annatahwee's eyes, and Torin didn't bother pretending she couldn't see it. "Major Svensson is one of the finest officers I've served under," she said.

Is.

Sergeant Annatahwee nodded, waiting.

"I have to talk to Dr. Sloan."

"And then?"

And then, if she was right, then the situation was going to get complicated very fast in very messy ways.

They were the only platoon under attack.

Gunnery sergeants and above had implants that could reach ships in orbit. Majors were definitely covered in the *and above*. If the implants could reach ships, then one could certainly reach the much lower orbits of the observation satellites.

"And then, we'll talk."

"No, you've been scanning the major; I need you to scan the polyhydroxide alcoholyde as though it was the patient."

Dr. Sloan stared at Torin as though she'd grown a second head. "Because you think I've put a piece of an alien escape pod in Major Svensson's arm?"

It sounded a lot more possible coming from the doctor than it had in Torin's head. "I think it's plausible. Interneural connections aren't built in a day. You'll find the molecular activity and heat you've been reading are bits of the piece in his arm heading into his nervous system."

"Gunnery Sergeant Kerr, I think you need to sit down and let me . . ."

"He's been working the slate with his left hand. Major Svensson is right-handed." When that gave the doctor pause, Torin continued. "You said it yourself. This feels . . ." Her gesture took in the anchor, the platoon, the surrounding drones. ". . . awfully familiar to me. But it's not the Silsviss. Not just the Silsviss," she amended because it was that, too, pulled from her memories when she'd been scanned. "Everything we've faced has been survivable—we just needed to find the way. It's a test. And the last time a group of Marines were tested like this, I was on Big Yellow."

The doctor sighed and scrubbed a hand up over her face. "You're sure it was Staff Sergeant Dhupam who contacted you? That it wasn't some enemy trick."

"I'm sure."

"And we're the only platoon under attack?"

"Yes, ma'am." Torin didn't know about Platoons 69 and 70. Nor did she care. "If I'm right, you can't let the major know you've seen it in the scan."

"Really? Because I was planning on leaping backward, hand over my heart, and exclaiming in horror that he had a piece of alien tech taking over his body." The doctor snorted. "Give me a little credit, would you; he won't be the first patient I've kept the details of a diagnosis from. The odds are good I won't even wake him up." She pulled out her slate, fingers moving almost reluctantly over the pad. "If you're wrong about this, Gunnery Sergeant, I'll want to scan your brain wave patterns."

I'm not wrong. She was used to being right. She knew how it felt. "Yes, ma'am."

"Twenty-seven percent of the polyhydroxide alco-holyde in the major's arm has migrated—primarily to his nervous system."

It was Doctor Sloan's turn to be stared at as though she had two heads—four, considering that both sergeants were involved in the expression.

In the kitchen, as far from the door to the admin office and the sleeping major as they could get and keep it in sight, as far from any of the platoon as they could get and remain in the anchor, Torin had told Jiir and Annatahwee what she believed and then had Doctor Sloan back it up with fact. It had been an effective one/two punch, leaving their audience reeling and unable to back away from the truth.

"You said primarily to his nervous system." Sergeant

Jiir's nose ridges opened and closed and opened again. "Where else?"

"His fingernails," Torin answered. "They allowed Big Yellow to access the CPNs directly."

"So he's been . . ." Jiir waved a hand, unable or unwilling to finish the sentence.

"Yes. And he's been using his implant to reach the ObSats and using the ObSats to beam down activation commands. Except for the rescheduled attack on day two, he's been making it up as he goes along. That's why everything's been so . . ." Not *easy*. She searched for another word. ". . . basic. He probably started reworking that first attack the moment we got the scenario and only had to get to the CPN to upload it."

"Probably added some kind of an interference program to keep the Orbital Platform from checking in," Annatahwee said slowly, running her thumb back and forth along the edge of the metal counter. "This time of the year, the weather's always a bitch. He only had to put them off for a few hours because . . ."

"Because that night, he shot them down." Jiir raised his head, his expression bleak. "Gunny, the major killed seventeen marines!"

"Eighteen." Torin touched the cylinder in her vest. "But it wasn't the major."

"There were times when he wasn't Major Svensson," Doctor Sloan explained hurriedly before Jiir could speak again. "Times when his consciousness was—let's say sleeping, for lack of a better word—and the alien was in control."

"So the alien tech . . ."

The doctor held up her hand, and all three Marines ignored the tremble. "You don't understand."

"That's for damned sure," Annatahwee muttered.

"It's not alien tech. It's the actual alien. The polyhydroxide alcoholydes are alive; each molecule is a separate entity. My theory is that working together they create a kind of hive mind within whatever shape they take. And the shape they're in now is inside Major Svensson."

According to the doctor's theory, Big Yellow hadn't been an unidentified alien spaceship, it had been an unidentified alien. Torin had to admit she wasn't exactly surprised.

"There's an alien inside Major Svensson!"

"Technically, a whole lot of aliens," Doctor Sloan amended. "But only one consciousness. I suspect they're—it's . . ." Her brows drew in. "Oh, great, it's fun with pronouns time again." She sighed. "I suspect the alien entity is probably observing the major, from the inside."

They all thought about that for a moment. Torin stared at her reflection in the brushed steel of the cabinets and wondered what the aliens would see.

"If there's not many of them," Annatahwee asked suddenly, "why aren't they all in his brain?"

The doctor rolled her eyes. "I like to think I'd have noticed if the lower bones in his left arm and his hand up and disappeared, Sergeant. As long as I continued scanning the major, they could hide what they were doing. It wasn't until Gunnery Sergeant Kerr had me scan *them* . . ."

Three pairs of eyes turned to Torin. She waited. It didn't take long.

"What do we do now, Gunny?"

"We shut the aliens down, and we get the major back." No doubt, no question. Statement of fact.

"Even if I had the facilities, I doubt I could remove the alien from his arm." Doctor Sloan glanced toward the admin office and lowered her voice. "The moment I began, it would know it had been discovered. And from his head . . ."

"It's in his brain!" Jiir pointed out.

"That's not a problem." She waved off the sergeant's

protest. "You'd be amazed at how much of your brain you can manage without. I'm more concerned with how much of it is in his spinal column. It might be easier just to keep the major sedated."

"Are you sure your drugs will sedate the alien?" Torin asked her. "Because if they don't, we're in the same place we'd be with you attempting surgery. It would know we were on to it."

"Yeah, but what could it do?" Annatahwee wondered.

"It'd run for the brain and threaten the major's life unless we left it alone." Torin looked around at the watching faces. "As far as I'm concerned the major is being held hostage by a hostile life form."

A moment of silence while that sank in.

"Then maybe we should negotiate with it," the doctor suggested.

"How?" Jiir demanded. "By letting it take over the major completely? Using his mouth, his ears?"

"Then we've lost the major," Annatahwee added.

Doctor Sloan looked to Torin. "It should be the major's choice."

"Except that we already know it can control the major. We wouldn't know who was making the choice, and if I was that alien, I'd vote to stay right where I am."

"Bonus points for thinking yourself into a polyhydroxide alcoholyde, hive mind alien, Gunnery Sergeant. But you don't know that."

"I won't risk that."

"You said this was a test, like the tests you faced on Big Yellow. You don't know the alien entity is hostile!"

"It's killed eighteen Marines. That's hostile enough for me."

"And me," Jiir grunted.

Annatahwee nodded.

"Dr. Sloan, if I understand you correctly, you believe the alien needs a certain critical mass to operate?"

For a moment, Torin thought the doctor wasn't going

to reply, but she finally sighed and said, "To operate the major, yes. Human beings are very complex. Which is not to say the Krai aren't complex," she added, glancing at Sergeant Jiir, "just that the aliens are in a Human currently, and . . .

Torin cut her off. "What happens if we take off his arm?"

The doctor blinked. "His arm?"

In answer, Torin raised her left hand.

"You want me to amputate his arm?"

"It's the fastest way to separate a large part of the alien from the major. Would it take the alien below the number it needs for control of the major's consciousness?"

"How the hell should I know?"

It was the first time Torin had heard the doctor swear. "Educated guess."

"I don't . . ."

"Yes, Doctor, you do."

She rubbed both hands over her face and sagged back against the cabinets. "Removing the major's arm will probably take the alien below functionality as the twenty-seven percent that has migrated is still connected to the seventy-three percent that remained behind. This seems to indicate that they're working together and not as two separate units. Happy? But you're out of luck," she continued before Torin could respond. "I don't have anything with me that will go through bone. I had hoped we were a little past battlefield amputations!"

Torin bent and pulled her heavy eight-inch knife from the sheath in her boot.

"You have got to be kidding me!"

"Actually, yes." The sergeants snickered as she resheathed the knife.

"Too bad the bennies are empty," Jiir muttered thoughtfully. "Cut and cauterize."

It *was* too bad. But they had a doctor with them, and Major Svensson had survived worse than an amputation. "Kichar has an ax in her pack."

"Of course she does," Annatahwee snorted.

"An ax?" Brows nearly touching over her nose, Doctor Sloan sounded like she'd prefer to take an ax to Torin.

"It has to be fast," Torin said flatly, "or more of the alien will move out of the arm and we'll lose the major. Sergeant Annatahwee."

"Gunnery Sergeant Kerr." Her wet boot soles squealed against the floor as she straightened.

"Get Private Kichar's ax." A raised hand held the sergeant in place while Torin worked through what had to be done. "And bring Private Hisht back with you."

"Back country boy." Jiir nodded in understanding as Annatahwee pounded up the stairs. "Barely down out of the trees."

Doctor Sloan's gaze shifted from Torin to Jiir and back to Torin. "What do you need Private Hisht for?"

"We need someone who can handle an ax."

Hisht examined the edge of the ax head and nodded. "It's sharp and heavy for its size." When he looked up, his eyes were shadowed. "But the bone will splinter."

"The doc will take care of that. Can you do it?"

"You do not order me?"

"No. I'm asking. Sergeant Jiir will do it if you can't, but you've got a lot more recent experience with an ax than he does."

"I thought . . ." He turned the handle between his fingers, nose ridges clamped shut. "A thing like this, I think you do it yourself."

She wanted to. It would make her life, not to mention Hisht's, a whole lot easier if she could. "A large part of my job is knowing whose skills give us the best odds of survival in any given situation. I haven't used an ax in almost fifteen years, so you're the major's best chance for a fast, clean cut."

"But you don't order."

"Not something like this, no." Although, to be honest, she would if she'd thought even for a moment that Hisht would refuse. Another large part of her job was knowing what the Marines in her charge were capable of—physically and emotionally.

"Gunnery Sergeant Kerr! McGuinty on the roof! Incoming flier!"

Torin touched her PCU. "Take it down, Private."

"Will do, Gunny!"

"Sergeant Annatahwee, keep the drones pinned, too busy to mount an attack. This would be a bad time for them to try anything."

"On it, Gunny." Annatahwee headed for the stairs, squeezing Hisht's shoulder briefly as she passed.

Hisht turned the ax around in his hands one more time, then he laid it gently on the counter and bent to unlace his boots. "I'll do it."

"Thank you. Sergeant . . ."

Jiir nodded. "I heard. I'll help keep the drones busy." He paused by Hisht until the younger Krai looked up. *"Ka sablin ser chrick. Deran heven Major Svensson."*

Hisht's eyes widened, then he laughed.

"What did the sergeant say?" Doctor Sloan murmured by Torin's ear.

"He said that no matter how good it smelled, Hisht wasn't to eat Major Svensson's arm."

When Torin entered the anchor's admin office, Hisht and the ax tucked in behind her, the doctor had Major Svensson perched on the edge of the desk chair, bare to the waist. In the harsh glare of the lamps from Doctor Sloan's medical kit, his skin still had the pallor of the recently detanked. Pebbled from the cold—the admin office was one of the warmer rooms in the anchor, but that wasn't saying much—he looked appallingly like a chicken recently killed and plucked. And not a sizable chicken either; in the last few days, he'd lost a lot of the weight he'd put on prior to leaving for Crucible. He definitely looked thinner than he had that morning in the *NirWentry*'s gym.

Where the rowing machine had been reprogrammed.

A test of how much control the alien had over the major's body?

". . . it's interesting to note that not one of the diplomatic attempts to negotiate an end to this war have ever included a member of the three races actually fighting this war. Since it all started before we got involved—and my we equals your us—all we have is the Elder Races' word for it that they don't know why the Others *are fighting."*

And how much control did it have over the major's mind?

If the Elder Races hadn't removed the knowledge of the escape pod, if the escape pod had done that itself as it shifted shape and spread through the military, what other memories had it changed?

She wasn't too worried about *why*—Doctor Sloan's smart-ass comment about thinking like a polyhydroxide alcoholyde hive mind aside, that wasn't her job. The Corps had battalions of xenopsychologists trained to translate motivations and reactions across species lines.

"Gunny?"

"Sir?"

He grinned, bending forward and shivering slightly as the doctor ran the head of her scanner up his spine. "You look like you're thinking deep thoughts. Cut it out."

"Yes, sir." Right now, her only concern should be getting thirty-five brand new Marines, three DIs, one doctor, and seven eighths of a major off Crucible alive. "You look like shit, sir."

There were deep shadows under bloodshot eyes, a

pulse thrummed visibly in his throat, and when he wasn't speaking, his lower lip hung slack, trembling slightly. "Interestingly enough, that's what the doctor woke me up to tell me. You sure you didn't go to medical school, Gunny?"

"I think I'd have noticed, sir." She was close enough now she thought she could feel the heat rising off his body. She couldn't—not through vest and combats and bodyliner—and this was a bad time to develop an imagination.

He was about to ask what she wanted, why Hisht was with her. She could see the question fighting its way through the exhaustion in his eyes. He wouldn't ask about the ax, though. He'd assume she had that covered.

Then Dr. Sloan took a step back to stand beside the desktop where the major had sketched out all the known positions of the drones as well as the crash sites of the flier and the shell of the destroyed tank. She held up the empty ampoule, and nodded. Reluctantly.

Major Svensson had been born on Earth. Torin was third-generation Paradise at 1.14 Earth gravity. Not enough difference to change the basic Human shape. Enough to kick the major's slate across the room and him down. Hisht balanced on his left foot, wrapped his right foot around the major's left wrist, braced his left hand against the major's left shoulder, and swung the ax. One blow, perfectly placed two centimeters above the point where alien pretended to be bone.

The sedative took effect almost before the ax impacted with the floor giving the major no time to protest, to struggle, to scream, before his eyes rolled back in his head and he went limp. Doctor Sloan bent over the stump and sprayed sealant and kept spraying as Torin flicked out a body bag and Hisht used his left foot to toss the major's lower arm inside.

Individual molecular entities or not, the alien

couldn't pass through solid objects easily or it would never have used Major Svensson's fingernails as a quick and dirty interface with the CPNs. The body bag, needing to withstand that one massive charge, was the most molecularly dense container they had and therefore the hardest to get through.

"You can be killed," Torin said grimly, her mouth by the lump in the bag. The di'Taykan scientists had accidentally destroyed a section of the wall during their initial investigation of Big Yellow by setting off an explosion. She was willing to bet that the charge in the body bag would have the same effect. "A single molecule of you leaves the bag, and I activate the charge. Stay where you are, and sooner or later we'll get to a trained negotiator."

"The polyhydroxide alcoholyde remaining in the major is no longer active," Doctor Sloan announced, still working on the stump. Her slate lay on the major's bare torso, reader pointed at his head. "Dormant. You've removed more than two thirds of the whole and taken it below critical mass."

"And the two thirds we removed?"

"What about it?"

"Is it dormant, or is there still a working consciousness?"

"How the hell should I know," she snapped. "Even if I'd had time while keeping Major Svensson from bleeding to death, I can't take a reading through the body bag." Both her hands were red. "Get his clothing back on him; his core temperature's dropping."

Torin slid behind the major and gently lifted his torso onto her lap, his head lolling against her shoulder. His skin was damp. Sedatives, or that split second when he realized what was about to happen? No way to know, but given the sharp, bitter smell, she'd guess the latter. She reached for his bodyliner and found Hisht's hands already there. "Are you all right?" she asked as together they skimmed the bodyliner back up over the major's good arm.

The young Krai sighed, nose ridges clamped shut. "What needed to be done was done."

"And it couldn't have been done without you. Not as cleanly," she amended. "Not as well."

Meeting her gaze, he attempted a shrug. "I am glad I didn't screw up."

"We all are." Both hands inside the left sleeve, Torin stretched the bodyliner out to three times its usual diameter, guided it carefully over the major's sealed stump, and folded up it over the remains of his arm. When she slid her hands free, the fabric conformed to its new dimensions.

An explosion off the east wall rocked the anchor. Torin curled forward to shield the major's upper body.

A moment of silence, then the group channel came alive.

"Nice flying, McGuinty."

"Sorry, Sergeant, it almost got away from me."

"But it didn't, which is why I said nice flying. Teams on the east wall, check in."

With the windows already empty, there were no injuries, although a piece of burning debris had slammed through three/two, leaving a thin line of char on Masayo's helmet. She declared the gods had saved her. No one argued.

"What will you tell the rest of the platoon?" Hisht moved away from the major and pulled his bootliners out from where he'd stuffed them in behind his vest and slipped them on, some of the tension leaving his face as his feet began to warm.

"The problem's been taken care of." According to the major's med-alert on her slate, the major had taken massive trauma but was now stable and sedated. "I'll tell them the truth."

"Taken care of?" That brought Doctor Sloan's attention up off her kit. "You have an alien life-form inside an amputated arm—and I use the word amputated in its broadcst scnsc—inside a body bag. In what universe is that a problem taken care of?"

"Major Svensson is no longer under the control of said alicn lifc-form." Torin grabbed his toque off a protruding bit of disassembled desk, laid it on the floor and gently set the major's head down on it.

"You had his arm chopped off!"

"And that solved thc only problem I'm really concerned about." She stood, crossed the room, and picked up his slate lying half propped on the wall where she'd kicked it. The ready lights were on, so she clipped it to her vest—Marine Corps slates were built to stand a lot more than an applied boot.

"Gunnery Sergeant Kerr?"

"Privatc Hisht."

"When you tell them, can you not tell them I did thc chop?"

"Your team will figure it out. It's Kichar's ax."

"Figuring it out cannot be the same as telling. I'm not sorry, I just . . ." His shrugs were getting more Human.

He wasn't sorry, but he didn't want them to think he was bragging about it either. Chopping off a major's arm was, well, pretty major. Torin clamped down on a totally inappropriate grin. "I won't tell thcm."

"Thank you."

"Rejoin your team. Leave the ax. I'll clean it and return it." She held his gaze until he nodded and watched him leave the room, picking his way carcfully around puddles of melted snow. Then she turned to the doctor who'd just finished cleaning her hands. "When you've laid out his bedroll in your infirmary, I'll carry Major Svensson in."

"You can do that? Of course you can. What about . . ." She gestured at the body bag.

"Eithcr it stays where it is and becomes someone else's problem, or it doesn't and it becomes no one's."

"It's an intelligent life-form, Gunnery Sergeant!"

Torin pitched her voice to carry to the outline of the major's arm. "That depends on whether or not it stays in the bag."

There were molecular disturbances in General Morris' brain.

Watching the old guy toss chunks when he realized that, while he'd been working on his desk, alien bits had been slipping into his cranium from the plaque on the wall kept Craig from taking advantage of the straight line so neatly provided by the situation. Although honestly forced him to admit it had less to do with sympathy and more to do with there being no one around who'd appreciate the joke.

Apparently, there'd already been some discussion among the Corps' geek squad that Big Yellow had been a living organism and that, combined with the way the general's plaque reacted to both him and Presit, had got Ventris Station hotter than a H'san on chilies.

Presit had dug in her claws and demanded the Katrien Parliamentary representative be present before she'd submit to even the most minimal noninvasive procedure but had been quite happy to volunteer Craig for anything up to and including vivisection just as long as she could keep her cameras running.

"Cameras off! This is a matter of Confederation Security!" The Intelligence officer snatched his hand away from the controls as Presit bared her teeth. *"You can't broadcast this!"*

"I are broadcasting this," she growled. *"I are broadcasting from the moment we are leaving Craig Ryder's ship. You are recalling laws of full media disclosure, or you are turning me off in front of entire galaxy. You are choosing. Smile,"* she added as he hesitated, *"it are likely your maternal is watching."*

As he'd been given a choice between having a hysterical hissy fit in front of half of known space or cooperating fully, Craig had agreed to cooperate with both Intell and the geek squad—sequentially and simultaneously—as long as Presit and the cameras were never more than a meter away. Presit may have been kidding about the vivisection, but he knew his own species well enough not to discount it.

The one thing that had made the whole experience bearable was the certain knowledge that whatever he was going through was nothing compared to what General Morris, Captain Stedrin, and anyone who'd served on the *Berganitan* was facing.

On the other hand, there were limits.

He caught the wrist of the Krai medical officer, stopping her hand and the instrument she held out away from his body. "Sweetheart, you're buying me drinks before you probe me again."

"But this . . ."

"No. You've already found the protein marker Big Yellow left behind." He crossed bare feet at the ankle and winked at the camera. "Everything else is original equipment."

"But . . ."

"I said no." He waited until she nodded before he released her.

"I told you we should have strapped him down," she muttered to her assistant as she turned away.

The assistant's eyes lightened. "I'll buy him the drinks."

There was something vaguely comforting about how predictable di'Taykans could be in any given situation. *Vaguely*, Craig reiterated silently as a whole new group of officers entered the lab. The Corps weren't big on fruit salad, so it was hard to tell rank from a distance, but something must have cued Presit that this lot was more important than the last since she abandoned the Intelligence officer she'd been grilling in the corner and reached his side with the other camera at about the same time as the half dozen Marines.

"High Tekamal Louden, we are thinking you are taking this seriously now."

The Commandant of the Corps inclined her head. "Presit a Tur durValintrisy, the Corps is taking this very seriously indeed. Mr. Ryder . . ." Her eyes within a fine network of lines were the same pale gray as the walls of the station. ". . . do you know who Lieutenant di'Fegarin Shylin is?"

Craig frowned. "Lieutenant Shylin?" When he closed his eyes, he could see the Jade move into the path of the bug fighter, see one escape pod ejected, see the explosion that saved the lives of the Marines in his cargo pod and probably his own as well. When he opened his eyes, Louden's expression had softened slightly, and he wondered what his face had told her. "She'd be Commander Sibley's gunner."

"That's correct. She's been wrapped in what the doctors call a separation psychosis since Commander Sibley's sacrifice."

"Out of her mind with grieving, then."

"Yes. Essentially. There are ways to . . ." Words were examined in the pause, and Craig gave the commandant credit for sticking with the basics. ". . . force coherency. It isn't something we care to do, but she was on the *Berganitan*, and, as we have checked on every other crewmember not separated by Susumi space, I spoke to Admiral Kirter, and he agreed that this kind of a potential foothold situation called for extreme measures."

"Potential foothold? We are thinking it are much, much more than potential."

The commandant silenced Presit with a look. "I just received a message from the physician in charge of Lieutenant Shylin's case on Dirinate Station. She remembers the escape pod."

"If you were looking for one of your own to remember ..."

"Gunnery Sergeant Kerr is not here, Mr. Ryder, and given the circumstances you shared, it is likely she also will have the protein marker left behind by the alien scan. Lieutenant Shylin however, does not. Nor does she have the differing protein marker everyone else on that mission carries from the ..." A glance around the lab and a moment of irony in her voice. "... probing. We are now certain that your memories were not the ones adjusted."

"I'd think the plaque playing patty-cake might have given you a clue on that, but ..." he raised a hand. "... I get that you're paranoid. And you know, given that you've got maybe point zero, zero, zero one of that escape pod's mass accounted for ..." He flashed the commandant his best smile. "... I can understand why you would be."

One of the officers behind her, a colonel wearing Intell tabs, opened his mouth, but she raised a hand and cut off his protest before he could give it voice. It was the sort of trick Torin would pull, and Craig bet that the commandant had been promoted out of the ranks. "Our initial scans have determined that the plaque is not, in point of fact, alien technology, but a polynumerous molecular species."

"Now that are something my viewers are being interested in." Presit moved forward. "High Tekemal, are ..."

"The H'san shut your broadcast down some time ago," the commandant said bluntly. "And I have neither the time nor the inclination to pretend any longer. Be silent, and you may continue recording. Do you know what I mean when I say polynumerous molecular species?" she asked Craig, ignoring Presit's sputtering but essentially silent protests.

"Lots of little aliens making up one life-form."

The colonel, who had been quieted, looked startled.

"Not just a pretty face here, mate. The scientists on Big Yellow said it was like an organic plastic. What stands out like dog's balls to me now is that it's more organic than plastic and that the whole shape-shifting thing was just the bits reconfiguring. If you can reconfigure into what you want, you can slip a molecular-sized probe into people's heads off a plaque or a collar tab . . ."

Every hand but the commandant's rose to their collars.

Craig grinned. ". . . or a beer stein. Which means that even when there's not enough of them to be conscious, each piece can carry out orders."

"You've given this some thought."

He laced his fingers over his stomach. "I've been sitting here for a while."

"We're going to have to scan every piece of plastic on the station." The colonel didn't seem happy he finally got a word in.

"On the station?" Craig snorted. "Dream on. You're going to have to scan every piece of plastic in known space."

FOURTEEN

"YOUR BEST BET TO GET IN will be with the codes you've been working up to crack the CPNs."
McGuinty looked down at the major's slate, one thin finger, the nail bitten down almost to the quick, rubbing along the casing. "So the alien that was in Major Svensson's arm, it was like, organic plastic?"

"Similar." There were weirder things in known space. Torin had never met any of them personally, and, frankly, didn't want to, but in the grand scheme of things, sentient organic plastic made up of molecular-sized pieces at least made a certain logical amount of sense—which was more than could be said for at least two members of the Methane Alliance.

"It's just that when I checked the CPN that blew, you know, the night Staff Sergeant Beyhn went running around naked in the snow and . . ."

"I know what CPN you're talking about, McGuinty."

"Right. Sorry, Gunny, it's just . . ." He reached into one of the front pockets on his vest and pulled out a dark shard. ". . . I picked this up out of the debris. It didn't look melted like the rest."

Torin held out her hand, and he dropped it into her palm. Holding it between thumb and forefinger, she frowned down at her reflection in the familiar glossy, charcoal-gray surface and remembered.

"*. . . the material at the back of the hole is different. The explosion changed the organic part—in layman's terms, we cooked it. I'm extrapolating a bit from available data, but if we smack this stuff hard enough, it's going to shatter.*"

This particular piece looked very much like it had shattered.

"Okay, McGuinty, two things. First, tell me the Corps' position on picking up battlefield souvenirs?"

His cheeks flushed. "Don't do it."

"Succinct and to the point. Don't do it." Not that there was a hope in hell of stopping it, but the Corps' position was clear. "Second, you're one lucky son of a bitch." Holding the shard between thumb and forefinger, she snapped it easily into two long narrow pieces, the sound strangely loud in spite of background noises that included the drones wasting ammunition firing through the broken windows. "These particular bits of alien are dead, which is why they haven't slipped through that scrape on your knuckles one molecular strand at a time and taken up residence in your brain."

The flush vanished as he blanched. "I don't think molecular strand is actually . . ."

"You're missing my point, Private." She handed him back his bits of dead alien. "If you don't know what something is, don't touch it. If it tries to touch you, don't let it. If you can't stop it any other way, shoot the fukker. Because if it comes to it, in order to save the rest of your platoon, someone is going to have to cut your arm off. Am I making myself clear?"

"Yes, Gunnery Sergeant!" McGuinty was so obviously not staring at the dark stains on the floor of the admin office that they became the dominant feature in the room.

Torin didn't look at them either. "Take the major's slate up to the second floor where you've got some decent light and try to work out how the hell he managed to upload the changes in the command codes through his implant. If we can get that, we can use my implant to shut the damned drones down."

"Yes, Gunnery Sergeant." His bootheels shrieked against the wet floor as he pivoted. "Uh, Gunny . . . ?" He paused in the doorway and turned, titling his helmet back off his face. "What happens when Major Svensson wakes up?"

"I imagine he'll be a bit pissed off."

"Because I'm trying to crack his slate?"

She couldn't stop the corners of her mouth from twisting into something very like a smile. "Trust me, Private, you're going to be way down on his shit list."

"I'm getting no *brain wave* patterns off the remaining alien . . ."

"*Brain wave?*" Torin interrupted, reproducing the emphasis.

Dr. Sloan sighed. "I could explain the specifics to you, Gunnery Sergeant, or you could accept what I'm telling you and save us both the aggravation. It's not *thinking* in any way I can register it, but it is moving."

She couldn't stop her hands from tightening on her weapon. "It's what?"

"Moving. Returning to his arm. At this rate, it'll all be at the edge of the stump in about six hours."

"Moving without thinking." Not a question. She'd seen Marines do it often enough—their brains shut down, reacting to external stimuli. "They're following orders. They've been discovered, so they're retreating. They're trapped inside the major, so they're looking for a way out and heading for the place where his physical integrity has been breached in a big way."

"Uh-huh." Eyes narrowed, arms crossed, Dr. Sloan stared up at her. "You got all that from *moving?*"

"It makes sense."

The doctor snorted. "Maybe in your world."

They'd brought the body bag into the infirmary and laid it out near the major. A bit macabre, perhaps, but efficient. The doctor was the only one who could set up the kind of molecular monitoring system Torin needed to ensure the alien stayed in the bag, and, at that, she had to monitor the bag, not the alien.

Although Staff Sergeant Beyhn remained oblivious, everyone else in the common room—everyone else who came up with an excuse to be in the common room— alternated between staring at the major's stump and staring at the major's arm. Even the di'Taykan sitting with the staff sergeant was paying at least as much attention to the other drama playing out.

The Berganitan *brought back an escape pod from Big Yellow.*

All of known space had seen the vids of the alien ship.

Turns out Big Yellow wasn't an alien ship but a shape-shifting alien, and the escape pod was a piece of it. Once inside the Berganitan *it shifted into one hell of a lot of different pieces and one of them eventually ended up inside Major Svensson's arm. Using a type of alien mind control...*

Accurate as far as it went.

... it hijacked the major's knowledge of Crucible and turned the drones against us. We solved the problem by removing the arm and the remaining seven eighths of the major is fine. There will be no new reprogramming of the drones, so let's concentrate on dealing with the old shit. And yes, flinging all our gear a few kilometers away would draw the drone's fire. If you can figure out a way to build a catapult with what we currently have in the anchor, let me know.

After 120 days of training, there was still a lot these new Marines didn't know, but one thing they were certain about, the one thing that had been downloaded over and over into the heads of all three species from the first day they stepped onto Ventris Station, was that every word out of their DI's mouth was the Corps' own truth. This was one of the many reasons Torin had no interest in ever ending up in RTC. If successfully completing the mission and getting her people out alive required a lie, she'd lie.

Fortunately, Platoon 71 didn't know that and had accepted her Sitrep at face value.

Alien. Amputation. All clear.

Torin dropped to one knee beside Major Svensson's bedroll and frowned at the stump of his arm. The sealant was semipermeable—if the alien wanted out, she had a strong feeling that the sealant wouldn't be able to keep it in.

"Gunny . . ."

"Major." She turned her attention from the stump to his face. He still looked like shit and didn't smell much better. Because the room couldn't have fallen more silent if someone had flipped a switch, she could hear the rough rasp of breath moving slow and shallow through his mouth.

Peering up at her through a sedative haze, he managed to pull his brows into the approximation of a frown. "You had my arm cut off."

"The artificial bone turned out to be an alien lifeform, sir. Just dealing with a foothold situation."

"Just?" It might have been a snicker, it might have been a cough. She lifted his canteen to his mouth, and he drank gratefully. When he finished, and she tried to move the canteen away, the fingers of his right hand closed loosely around her wrist. "The headaches and the memory lapses? The alien?"

"Yes, sir."

"Did I . . . ?"

She thought about deliberately misunderstanding but only for a moment. "No, sir. The alien did."

"In my body."

Torin snorted. "At the risk of sounding overtly di'Taykan, Major, you're not responsible for the actions or reactions of another species while it's in your body."

That time, definitely a snicker. "I've never had any complaints."

She glanced at the body bag and decided not to mention the exodus happening under his skin. "You may this time, sir."

"You cut off the major's arm. With *my* ax."

Only Kichar's emotional emphasis on the second statement kept Hisht from flinching. He peered through his scope, swept his sector for drones and said, "It is a good ax. Sharp. I was impressed by the edge."

She leaned out just enough to see him around Bonninski. "Thank you. I take care of my tools."

"It shows."

"Well, there's no point in carrying something if it's not in the best condition possible. And you," she added to Sakur, "you said I'd never use it."

"You didn't use it," Sakur snorted, eyes pale in the glare off the snow. "Hisht did. Obviously, the best man for the job."

"Still, if Gunnery Sergeant Kerr had counted on the contents of your pack, she'd have had to gnaw the major's arm off."

"No," Hisht sighed, his mouth flooding with saliva at the thought, "I'd have done that, too."

The snowball slammed into his torso, nearly knocking him over. The drones took a couple of shots at the movement, one/one sent a few rounds back at the drones, and when silence fell again, Bonninski muttered, "Let's not talk about eating people. That's just gross."

"Eating officers," Kichar corrected.

"Grosser," the other woman snorted.

"What happened to the arm?" Sakur wondered.

Hisht shrugged. He thought he was getting better at it. "Sergeant Jiir told me not to eat it."

The second snowball missed.

"High Tekamal Louden . . ." The major had clearly not expected Craig to be in the room with the commandant. She slid to an undignified halt and dramatically lowered her voice. ". . . we have a situation."

"Go ahead."

She glanced at Craig, who smiled and waved. Mostly just to see that vein pop on the major's forehead. "Commandant, it's . . ."

"If it's about the alien," Louden snorted, "then speak up. As Mr. Ryder had to tell us it was here, I don't think we're in any position to keep secrets about it from him, do you?"

"No, sir." Although she clearly did. "The plaque that was in General Morris' office? It's . . ." A deep breath and a visible girding of metaphorical loins. "It's disappeared."

"Disappeared."

It wasn't a question, but the major answered it anyway. "Yes, sir."

"How?"

"Probably broke into its component molecular parts, skittered away, and re-formed into a couple of dozen new and exciting things a few seconds later." As both the major and the commandant turned icy gazes in his direction, Craig shrugged. "Just a guess."

"High Tekamal Louden, we . . ." The colonel came to a halt just inside the door, his expression as identical to the major's as differing physiognomies could make it.

"We have a situation?" the commandant suggested. "What is it, Colonel?"

"Some of those who have the marker indicating

they'd been tampered with . . . they've sent coded messages into space."

"Break the code."

"We're working on it, sir."

"And track the messages."

"We can't, sir. They were sent into *space*. No actual coordinates."

"That's going to complicate the search." Three pairs of cold eyes this time. Craig shrugged again. "Space is big."

After a moment, Louden nodded. "He's right."

The major made a sound that could have been a protest. The colonel, with a few more years' experience, managed to remain both silent and expressionless.

"If we're going to stand even a chance of finding all the pieces of that escape pod," Louden continued, "we're going to need all the help we can get."

"Gunny!"

Torin straightened, held McGuinty at the door with a raised hand, and crossed the common room to his side.

Nearly bouncing in place, he started talking as soon as she was close enough. "I've isolated the code Major Svensson used to access the satellites, and I think I can figure out how to patch it through your implant . . ."

"You think?"

"It's a little funky." He tapped the screen. "I wouldn't have recognized it, but the major had the actual ObSat codes in a separate file, and I recognized the sequencing. I can't do it the way he did it—the way the alien did it—I don't think that way because you know, it's alien, but it's also sort of Marine codes like I thought at the beginning, so I'm pretty sure I can work something out."

"You don't need to tell me that you're working, McGuinty. I know you are." Years of practice kept her from patting him on the head. "Just let me know when you've got something."

"I've got something. Okay, I *found* something, Gunny. On his slate." He waved it.

Torin snorted. "If you found the major's porn, McGuinty, I don't need to know about it."

"He has porn?" Thin cheeks flushed. "I mean, no. I didn't. I found messages that weren't going to the Ob-Sats, they were just going out into space."

"Missing the ObSat?"

"Well, yeah, but on purpose. There was no destination; he was just jacking them off." Torin had never actually seen anyone turn that red, that fast. "Uh . . ."

Another time she might have let him muddle through an explanation, but his skills had a good chance of saving their collective butts, so she took pity. "It's all right, McGuinty. I understand the reference." A sudden spat of weapons fire from the south wall while she considered the new information. "Okay, wrap the messages and everything to do with them as securely as you can and transfer them to your slate and Piroj's." Storing them in a couple of other places might ensure they actually got back to the geeks at Command. "Concentrate on putting together that uplink. Once we shut this shit down, we can concentrate on the less-than-immediate danger."

"How?" He stared up at her like she'd have an answer.

Having the answers were part of her job.

She grinned. "If I told you, I'd ruin the surprise. Back-ups, upload, then the fun stuff."

"Yes, Gunnery Sergeant." He half turned, then turned back again. "Is it okay if I work on the roof? It's just easier if I'm already up there if another flier gets spotted."

"Do I look like your mother, McGuinty?"

"Uh . . ."

Suddenly suspecting she might, Torin cut him off. "Do

your job and don't get shot. I don't give a H'san's ass about where you do either. Got that?"

"Yes, Gunnery Sergeant!"

She hid a smile as he started toward the stairs and then remembered something. "Hey, McGuinty, I thought you worked better with a ceiling."

"Kind of smells in here, Gunny."

After only three days? It was a good thing for McGuinty's station-born sensibilities they weren't going to be there for the full two tendays, then. Torin had heard of station-born Marines who, with adrenaline fading, had passed out from the combined odors in the retrieval VTA. Possibly apocryphal, but even with wastes sealed into empty food pouches and stored in the useless latrines, the anchor was beginning to hum a bit.

"Gunny?"

"Sir."

Nothing like thirty-six unwashed Marines to make a place smell like home, she thought returning to Major Svensson's side.

He closed his eyes when she told him of McGuinty's discovery. "What have I done?"

"Not a damned thing, sir."

"You think the Corps is going to see it that way, Gunny?"

"Yes, sir."

Opening his eyes, he fought the painkillers to focus on her face. "Why?"

"We have the alien, sir."

"And we have my scans identifying it as an alien consciousness within your body." Dr. Sloan crouched at Torin's left. "Privates Bynum and Stevens want to know when they can return to duty."

Major Svensson dropped his head to the right and frowned through the shadows at the young Marines, both of them standing with one arm held immobile by their combats and strapped up against their chests. "He has a broken arm, and she got shot in the arm."

"That's right."

"Broken arm. Shot in the arm." A small wave of the stump. "There's some kind of smart-ass comparison kind of remark to make about that, but I just can't get hold of it right now. Remind me to try again later, Gunny."

"Yes, sir."

"And tell Bynum and Stevens that the Corps has a policy on letting Marines doped up on painkillers fire live rounds."

"Yes, sir."

"As a general rule," he added sotto voce to the doctor, "we try to discourage it."

"I'd be happier to hear that if it didn't imply it occasionally happens anyway." Reaching for her slate, Dr. Sloan bent over the stump. "They're starting to pile up at the edge of the . . . at the edge. Pile up being a relative statement, of course, given their size."

"The aliens remaining in your body appear to be trying to leave," Torin explained to the major.

"If they make it out, don't let them get away."

Torin wasn't entirely certain how she was supposed to stop a molecular-sized, shape-shifting alien but something would probably come up. "Yes, sir."

Sitting back on her heels, Dr. Sloan ran a hand up through her hair. Something about her looked . . . *off,* although Torin couldn't pinpoint what. "Look, Staff Sergeant Beyhn is stable, my other two patients are sulking, and you two would probably be happier if I was elsewhere, so you could discuss this, fighting person to fighting person. As I'm an accommodating person just generally, I'm heading up to the roof for some air."

"You don't have to go, Doc . . ."

"I won't be gone long, but I need to . . ." A quick wave

at the sealed wall of windows. ". . . look at the sky for a moment or two. I promise I'll stay out of everyone's way. And besides, you'd have to wrestle me to the floor and clap me in irons to stop me."

"Got irons, Gunny?"

"Not on me, sir."

"Guess we can't stop you, then, Doc." His eyes tracked her as she stood and Torin was reminded again of how long he'd been under the care of the medical profession. For a man who'd been as severely wounded as he had, Doctor Sloan's presence probably helped him feel secure now he was wounded again.

"McGuinty seems to think things are getting a bit whiff," Torin offered as the doctor disappeared up the hall.

The major made a sound halfway between a snort and a laugh. "This? We're here for another five days until the *NirWentry* returns. His delicate sensibilities are in for a shock." His mouth twisted as he stared at his stump. "Did we have fighting person talking to do, Gunny?"

"I was thinking that after McGuinty gets the upload specs worked out, and we shut the drones down, he can cannibalize the desk and try to give the alien a voice. We can find out where . . ."

There was a small gray square on the center of the stump.

"Gunny?"

She bent forward, gently slipped a fingernail behind it, and pulled it free. A small line of gray plastic came with it, but whether it was going into the major's arm or coming out, she had no idea. As the square elongated and curled around her finger, stroking it in a way that almost seemed content, she realized what it was.

Doctor Sloan's noncombatant chip.

The *something* that had looked off.

* * *

The sky looked close enough to touch. The clear, cold blue of the morning had become pale gray clouds hanging over the settlement promising more snow. The way Stone saw it, more snow was a good thing. The drones weren't infinitely adaptable, so eventually they had to bog down. He checked his snowman, fired back at the drone that had exposed itself to fire at him, rolled back up onto his feet, and realized his scanner had gone hinky.

He turned, saw McGuinty fiddling with something by the access hatch. Wondered if he'd screwed up his jamming thing. Saw Dr. Sloan emerge, blinking in the thin light. Saw her speak to McGuinty and laugh ... and fuk, McGuinty wasn't much taller than the doc. Heard a whistle off over the settlement.

Turned.

Frowned at a point of darkness against the pale gray.

Watched it grow.

Realized what it had to be about the same time he realized his scanner wasn't working. At all.

"Incoming!"

Torin started up the stairs three at a time. "Sergeant Jiir!"

"Gunny?"

"Get Dr. Sloan off the roof!"

McGuinty heard Stone yell. Took a moment to save the final bit of code. Looked up. Saw the flier, three-dimensional against a two-dimensional sky. Had to be an optical illusion that it was heading right for him. He snapped the major's slate onto his vest and yanked off his own, fumbling the amplifier into place.

Sergeant Jiir wasted a second responding to Stone's cry.

Where the hell had that flier come from, and why weren't their *serley* scanners working?

And what the fuk was taking McGuinty so Goddamned long? The flier was going to lock targeting coordinates in a second, and then they were all screwed.

The private was standing close to the access hatch,
right beside the doctor. Good, two *vertak*, one stone—
he could deal with them both at the same time. Jiir
started to run. "McGuinty!"

He didn't look up from the slate. "It's too close,
Sergeant, I need more time to lock!"

Then Dr. Sloan stepped sideways, putting her noncombatant chip between McGuinty and the flier, effec-
tively keeping the flyer from targeting McGuinty.

Smart move, Doc! Jiir thought. *Save the guy most
likely to save the whole platoon!*

The flier launched all four missiles.

The sergeant realized the doctor's forehead was bare
at about the same time.

McGuinty saw blue. Bright blue.
Sound and fury.
Pain.
Hurt to breathe. Hurt to open his eyes.
He did both anyway.

"Gunny?"
"Not now, McGuinty, I'm a little busy."
Halfway up to the access hatch, jammed sideway in
the narrow stairs, Torin ignored all the shouting . . .
"Dr. Sloan is down! I repeat Dr. Sloan is down!"
"So are the fukking scanners!"
"It hurts! It hurts!"
"Sergeant! She's bleeding!"
. . . and concentrated on clamping her left hand over
the bleeder in McGuinty's neck. Looked like a piece of
shrapnel had . . .

Not shrapnel. Bone. And a bit of bright blue fabric.
Looked like a piece of Dr. Sloan had skipped off the

top of his vest and ripped a hole about a centimeter down from his jaw. The high collar of the bodyliner had probably saved his life by snagging the rough edge of the bone and changing the angle of entry.

A nick in a major blood vessel was one thing. A severed vessel—something a bit more fatal.

She snapped his sealant free and held the tube between her teeth as she grabbed her canteen and thumbed the lid off. A splash on his neck. She had to see what she was doing. Canteen balanced on his . . . lap was close enough, given the way they were jammed in. Knife out of her boot. Slice carefully away from her fingers, keeping the vein clamped, opening things up enough to make sure the sealant hit the hole in the vein.

Start spraying even before she had her left hand away.

Pack the wound with sealant.

Wait.

Finally breathe.

"Gunny?"

"What is it, McGuinty?"

"I think the doctor exploded." He frowned, his eyes rolled up, and his head lolled against Torin's stomach, temple hard up against Private Oshyo's cylinder.

"Gunny!" Sounded like Sergeant Annatahwee was right behind her on the stairs, but Torin couldn't turn. Not far enough. Not and be able to use her spine again later. "Are you hurt?"

Good question. She'd been almost all the way to the access hatch when all hell had broken loose on the roof. McGuinty had landed more or less in her arms a heartbeat later and she'd barely managed to stop them from slamming all the way down to the second floor. Fortunately, he was a skinny little shit. "I'm all right." Where *all right* could be defined as none of the parts that currently hurt, hurt too much to ignore. "Get your hands under McGuinty's shoulders here, lift him over me, and pass him back. I can't move until he's clear."

"Given where your knee is, Gunny, I'm not sure we can clear him until you move."

Oh. That was *her* knee. In combats, they all looked the same. "Try." Because moving it—moving her right leg—didn't seem to be an option.

The sergeant's arms came in to Torin's left. As she lifted, Torin got her one arm under McGuinty and helped.

"Fuk, that's a lot of blood."

"It's his on me, not all his on him," Torin grunted. As his torso moved past her ear, and the pressure holding her in place changed, she amended her *all right* to *mostly all right*.

"Yours?"

"Dr. Sloan's."

"Fuk."

"Yeah." Gravity would have taken her the rest of the way down the stairs if not for the sergeant's hip against her back. Reaching up, she straightened her leg, sucked air through her teeth and got herself turned around. McGuinty had just reached the second floor, held by Ayumi and Lirit while Piroj frantically patted him down looking for more injuries. "He's got a bleeder in his neck. It's sealed, but be careful. Get him to the infirmary—Piroj, careful means you need to stop groping him and let Ayumi and Lirit carry him. They're the same height. When you get there," she continued as Piroj reluctantly backed away. "Tell . . ." It took her a second to pull the name out of memory. ". . . Flint, he's now the medic."

Flint had aced the first aid course. In about ten seconds he was going to regret that.

"Gunnery Sergeant Kerr!" Major Svensson's voice on the command channel cut through the chatter. He

didn't sound good, but he sounded focused. *"What the hell is going on up there?"*

"Flier took a shot at the roof, blew McGuinty back through the hatch and delayed me on the stairs, probably killed Dr. Sloan." Given the bits that came through the roof with McGuinty, the odds were stronger than *probably*, but Torin wasn't willing to commit without proof. "I'm on my way up now."

"Keep me informed." He didn't ask if she was all right; if she wasn't, he expected her to tell him.

"Yes, sir."

About to stand, she noticed a familiar chip on the stairs; she'd probably dropped it when she'd caught McGuinty. She'd likely never know why the aliens who made up the chip had decided to leave Dr. Sloan, and she honestly didn't care. They'd left and, as a direct result of that leaving, the doctor was dead.

"Piroj!"

"Gunny?" He moved out around Sergeant Annatahwee.

Torin looked down at the piece of alien ship—no, the collection of aliens—rippling across the palm of her hand and remembered. They'd been in Big Yellow's copy of the hydroponics garden on Paradise Station . . .

"Heer, don't eat that. It's not a real gitern, it's part of the ship."

The engineer looked sheepishly down at the fruit in his hand. "Ship's partly organic, Staff."

A quick glance at Werst showed the other Krai staring challengingly back at her. His jaw might have been moving. Nothing she could do about it now, and besides, if it came down to a one on one, Big Yellow against a Krai digestive tract, smart money would be on the colon.

Neither Heer nor Werst had suffered any ill effects.

She tossed the chip to Piroj, who caught it one-handed. "Eat that."

"Yes, Gunnery Sergeant."

She was standing before he swallowed. The stairs were clean. Most of the blood had been on McGuinty. The roof . . .

It had started snowing again. Big, thick flakes drifted slowly down to spatter the red with white.

The bulk of Dr. Sloan's body lay on the far side of the hatch from where the spray pattern suggested she'd been standing. The missile had hit the center of her chest, four inches of jacket and her sternum offering enough resistance for it to blow. They could tank a brain and a spinal cord if the med-evac arrived in time, but everything above and most of what was between the impact and the heavier bone of the pelvis had been destroyed.

"Eat with a spoon," Piroj muttered.

A typically Krai diagnosis but inarguable.

From the sound of it—and, about to emerge, Torin had been close enough to hear it clearly—the doctor been hit by a training missile. Intended to be all light and noise but with more than enough explosive charge to kill after being embedded in a soft target. Looked like the other two thunder sticks had missed Marines, limiting their damage.

The actual explosive warhead had hit the northeast corner of the anchor, clipping it off, and most of the shrapnel had been blocked by the building.

Most.

Sergeant Jiir knelt by a prone figure, another Marine kneeling beside him.

Torin flipped up her slate. *Izebela Vega: muscle damage right thigh, right buttock. Thigh bone nicked. No major blood vessels breached.* Nothing vital hit, thanks to the vest. That was Carson beside Jiir, then, because both Stone and Jonin were unmistakable. One team accounted for.

From the exchange of fire with the Marines on the

second floor, the drones were taking advantage of the disruption caused by the flier.

"Do not break cover, people!" Torin snapped into her PCU. "You're helping no one up here if you get killed, and you do *not* want to cause me that much paperwork! I'll check with Jiir," she added to Annatahwee. "Make sure no one else got hit."

Her combats had already tightened around her left knee, offering support to the swelling joint.

Jiir looked up as she limped over. The front of his uniform and his lower nose ridges had been splattered with blood. He followed her gaze and shook his head. "Not mine. Not Vega's either. Dr. Sloan's."

Torin glanced back toward the spatter pattern staining the snow. "McGuinty looks worse. The doc got around."

"So it seems."

"Vega?"

"Stable. I've almost finished field sealing. They can strip her down and do a better job when we get her downstairs."

Vega moaned.

"It's okay," Carson murmured, brushing snow off the other Marine's face, drawing red lines on pale skin with bloody fingers.

"And the scanners?" Torin asked.

"*Serley* things just stopped working," the sergeant told her, sliding the sealant tube back into his vest. "It's how the flier got so close."

Although her PCU was obviously working, everything else was out. The distant horizon was just that, distant. "Couldn't have been a pulse, or no one inside would have been affected."

"You think it's more of the maj . . . of the alien's reprogramming?"

"Might be." But she wasn't sure she'd put money on it.

Jiir rolled back up onto his feet and stood. "Carson, Jonin, get her inside."

As the di'Taykan hurried across the roof, Carson picked Vega's weapon up out of the snow and slung it across her back. "Dr. Sloan's dead," she said. "We're so screwed. Who's going to fix us now?"

"We'll fix each other, Private Carson. Just like we would have had to do had Dr. Sloan not been with us." The sergeant's smile held very little humor. "That's what training on Crucible's all about. Flint the medic now?" he asked Torin as Carson and Jonin carefully hoisted their moaning teammate.

"He had the best scores," Torin answered absently. Something Jiir had said . . .

Training on Crucible. Scenarios.

The scenario they'd been scheduled to run had included surviving the final four days scanner free. It involved a captured weapon the Corps had reverse engineered that wiped out specific tech and left the recruits dependent on their unaugmented senses alone. It was a valuable lesson to learn, and Torin had been looking forward to it.

Except . . .

If the weapon had been a part of the final four days of the scenario significantly farther to the west, how had it gotten here? It hadn't been carried by a drone. It needed too large and heavy a power source. But if it was here, and it certainly seemed to be, it needed to have been carried on something that wouldn't mind the weight.

"Jiir, what does Crucible mount heavy equipment on?"

He shrugged. "Tanks usually. They're the easiest to RC."

"Shit. Marines off the roof, now!" She began hobbling for the hatch. "Marines on the second floor, drop the shelter halves over the windows! Move! Move! Move!"

"*Gunny!*" Major Svensson, wondering what the hell was going on.

"Good odds there's a tank out there, sir. With the scanners down, we're blind and we have nothing to stop it with."

"*So all we can do is give it no specific targets like Marines or windows.*"

"Yes, sir."

"*Get in here, Gunny.*"

"Working on it, sir!"

To give them credit, the Marines on the roof were *moving*. Torin's bad leg brought her last to the access, a position she'd have taken anyway. Stone was the only other Marine on the roof.

"What about Dr. Sloan's remains, Gunny?"

She glanced over at the boots. They still looked great, but she'd never find out what catalog they came from now. "We'll bag it later," she snapped shoving him toward the stairs. "For now, it's best left up here in the cold. Move!"

His head and shoulders were exposed above the edge of the roof, and she was covered only to the knee when she heard the distinctive whistle of an approaching 125mm HE round. Grabbing the shelter cloth-wrapped cover, she dragged it free of the new snow and let herself fall, twisting onto her back and pulling it over the open hatch just as the first shell exploded.

Stone's body cushioned her fall.

"You okay?" she asked rolling off him into the slush that covered the second floor at the bottom of the stairs.

He gasped out, "Fuk you're heavy!" and, reassured, Torin accepted Sergeant Annatahwee's hand up, taking all her weight on her right leg. Jiir slipped past them and adjusted the hatch.

"The tank had to have been aiming at a Marine on the roof. There are no Marines on the roof now, so it has to acquire another target before it fires again. Dr.

Sloan's body may be enough of an anomaly—I have no idea how sensitive its targeting programs are . . ." Unfastening her vest, she shot a question at the sergeants—who shook their heads. ". . . no one does, apparently, so we've got to bag the body, but we can't do it in uniform."

"You can't do it, Gunny." Annatahwee caught Torin's hand, stopping her from removing the vest. "Not with that leg. You take your combats off, I'm betting it won't hold you."

Torin was betting it would. "The tank might be able to read the bag as well as the doctor's body. I can't order a Marine to go to the roof to be targeted."

"I can. Annatahwee, it's your go."

"Yes, sir."

"Gunny, you certain that whatever knocked out the scanners didn't knock out the camouflage function in the shelter halves as well?"

"Unfortunately, sir, with our scanners down, there's only one way to find out." Jiir was disappearing under his load of Annatahwee's gear. Torin took her weapon from him, and he nodded his thanks. "Marines, pull back from the west wall! Get another wall between you and those windows!"

"A di'Taykan could get undressed faster," Jiir muttered.

"Thank you, Sergeant Obvious." Annatahwee stepped out of her boots up onto the first step, avoiding the slush on the floor. She refused Torin's bag, having snapped her own off her vest. "What should I say?"

Good question. "Major Svensson, did Dr. Sloan ever express any religious beliefs."

"None that I recall, Gunny."

"Rest in peace it is, then." The sergeant nodded and raced up the stairs. A shoulder under the makeshift hatch, and she rolled out onto the roof, sliding the hatch back into place as one/one and the three remaining members of one/two came out of the west rooms.

"Uh, Gunnery Sergeant Kerr, you're dripping."

"Not a problem, Kichar," she said without turning. "As long as I'm not dripping any precious bodily fluids."

"It looks like slush."

"Then let's not worry about it." Combats were entirely waterproof, but Torin could feel a cold wet spot where some slush had soaked into the collar of her bodyliner. She missed the timer on her scanner; subjective time was just too damned slow. Depending on how far out the tank had stopped, the snow might be slowing the targeting computer, but there wasn't much wind and it wouldn't slow it for long. She wanted to tell Annatahwee to hustle, but she knew the sergeant was moving as fast as Humanly possible.

Maybe she *should* have sent a di'Taykan.

Sergeant Annatahwee and the next round landed simultaneously.

Torin grabbed the front of her bodyliner as the sergeant slid past, a spray of snow drifting down with her, blown in by the blast.

"I don't know why we even have those stairs," Annatahwee muttered, as Kichar raced by and adjusted the cover. "No one seems to be using them." Twisting within the fabric, she got her feet under her and stood, holding out a familiar metal cylinder as Torin released her. "Will you . . . ?"

"They might as well stay together." Torin slipped the doctor into her vest next to Oshyo. "What . . ." She cut the question off as Annatahwee held out McGuinty's cracked slate and the crushed amplifier. There were plenty of slates, McGuinty could use, but the amplifier, that was another matter. "Well, that's annoying."

Sakur made a choking noise.

Torin turned toward him, lifting an enquiring brow. "Problem, Private?"

He opened his mouth, but a tank round hitting the west wall drowned him out. When the noise died, and Torin was clearly still waiting, he shook his head, the ends of his hair swinging in a choppy counterpoint under the edge of his helmet. "No problem, Gunnery Sergeant."

"Good." She touched her PCU. "Listen up, people. The tank's to the west—everything's coming in on the same trajectory and not hitting a window, so the shelter halves are working. West windows stay covered. Clear the windows on the other three walls; we need to know what the drones are doing."

"Drones are making a move on the door, Gunny!"

They were efficient little bastards, she'd give them that. "All right, you lot." Her gesture took in both displaced teams. "Get in there and help."

"Gunnery Sergeant Kerr?"

"Kichar."

Another round hit the west wall. And another six seconds after that.

"It's trying to blow through," Torin said in response to Kichar's expression. "Don't worry, this thing was built to be dropped in from orbit. That tank's carrying nothing that can hurt it. What did you want, Private?"

"Want?" Her eyes widened. "Right." She nodded toward the closest door, the door to the fake medical facility. "These are all made of the parts that seal the windows. Why don't we crush more of them?"

"Because we don't want to leave the drones too much cover . . ." Torin waited out another round. ". . . close to the air lock. They're not programmed to pick the pieces up and use them as shielding, but we still don't want to provide . . ."

The distinct sound of a grenade cut her off.

"Whoever threw that better have taken out more than one drone," she yelled at the doorless entrance to the south room.

"Six, Gunny!"

"Four, you dipshit!"

"Those other two are fukking limping!"

"Four's good, six is better. Now, shut up and get your attention back on those drones!"

"Yes, Gunnery Sergeant!"

Unison. Torin smiled, handed Annatahwee her weapon, and then turned her attention back to Kichar as the sergeant trotted off to check on the drone's attack. "Don't you have somewhere you have to be, Private?"

High cheekbones flushed. "Yes, Gunnery Ser . . ."

The new round sounded different. Torin had half a heartbeat to identify the sound before the roar made it obvious.

"Fuk! Incendiary!"

"But the shelter halves are fireproof!"

"Fire resistant, Kichar." Torin splashed through the slush and laid her hand on the door in the inner west wall. "Damned little is fire*proof* given enough accelerant." The metal didn't feel hot but that was hardly surprising. As she'd just told Kichar, the anchor had been designed for an atmospheric entry and these doors were made from part of the outer shell. Only one way to find out if their camouflage had been breached.

"One, soft target impact. Two, soft target impact." Standing to one side, she opened the door.

Three.

Hanging inside the north window was a sheet of flame. Over the smoke and the stink of burning shelter half, Torin could smell the distinctive odor of acetate. Not good.

Four.

The burning fabric dropped to the floor and went out, smoking heavily.

Five.

It was still snowing, the flakes blown back by the heat of the flames roaring on the side of the building.

Six.

Torin slammed the door and dove to the left, one arm wrapped around Kichar, taking the younger Marine to the floor with her as an explosion blew the door off its hinges, slamming it across the hall, followed by a spray of shrapnel that ricocheted around the second-floor landing sounding like a swarm of angry wasps. Large, angry wasps. Very large.

"Why are the fukking tanks loaded with nothing but live rounds?" she snarled as the last few pieces rang against the floor. Rolling clear of Kichar, she tried for her feet, bit back an oath, and found a shoulder shoved up under her arm, heaving her back to the vertical. "Thank you. Now move, we haven't much time."

"Gunny?"

"We're fine. Six-second reload!" Torin snapped, and Sergeant Annatahwee's head disappeared back into the south room. She gave Kichar a shove toward that same door, told her to join her team, and headed for the stairs. The round that came through the window while she was halfway to the first floor was a thunder stick.

Okay, not only live rounds. Sometimes, it was important to be lucky.

"...and now it's lobbing everything it fires through that window. As long as we pay attention to the count and stay out of the second-floor hallway when it's likely to be buzzing with the nasty shit, we should be fine. Fortunately, it doesn't have an angle straight through from the window to the door without moving a few degrees south."

Used to the rhythm now, Torin cradled her helmet against her side and braced for the next impact.

Nothing.

"Maybe it's moving," Major Svensson said dryly. "Stop giving it ideas, Gunny."

"Sorry, sir."

They could joke because she'd said it, not him. She could see that knowledge in his eyes. Along with something else.

"Painkiller wearing off, sir?"

"I'm . . ."

She raised an eyebrow and stopped the next word cold.

". . . ready for another," he amended.

As he swallowed, she stretched her bad leg out and crouched on the other to examine the stump. It looked good—given that it was the brutally hacked-at remains of an arm—but there was a shadow she wasn't happy to see. When she stretched out a fingertip toward it, it stretched out to meet her and an instant later, she had another piece of Big Yellow, twice the size of the chip rolling around her palm. It had extruded out of the major's arm and through the sealant too fast for her to see it move. Or maybe in pieces to small for her to see it move although that wasn't much more reassuring.

"Is that what I think it is, Gunny?" All things considered, the major sounded remarkably unconcerned. It could be training, not allowing those under his command to see him flustered. It could be the painkillers. It was probably a bit of both.

"Yes, sir."

"Seems to like you."

"Yes, sir." Likely because of the same brain scan that allowed her to remember the escape pod.

"What exactly are you planning on doing with it?"

Closing her fingers around it, she felt it moving within the confines of her hand, not trying to escape, just feeling for the edges of its space. She wanted to throw it aside and wipe the feeling off her hand. She hung on. "I plan on feeding it to Private Piroj, sir."

"That seems a bit harsh, Gunny."

Torin shone the light a little more fully on his face. He looked serious.

"Why don't you put it in the body bag with the rest?"

"Sir, opening the body bag may result in the *rest* escaping."

"Except that precedent suggests it'll leap right into your hand. It's an unknown life-form, Gunny. Something brand new in known space."

"Yes, sir. And it's responsible for two deaths and several injuries and the amputation of your arm."

"And it's our prisoner."

He could have made it an order. A lot of other officers would have, even though, technically, given the amount of painkillers he was on, he wasn't in command.

Torin opened her hand and stared down at the alien. Collection of aliens. Life-form. For all she knew it was staring back. It hadn't exactly surrendered, but the major was right, it was their prisoner, and Marines did not eat their prisoners. Not even the Krai, who'd previously had a long tradition of doing just that.

Shuffling awkwardly back, she turned, snagged the body bag with her free hand and dragged it closer. "Sir, you may want to . . ."

He snorted. "Not the first time I've lost an arm, Gunny."

It was surprising tricky unsealing the bag; she'd never done it before. It wasn't exactly a surprise to see a large lump of alien waiting at the sticky end of the major's arm. It rose up and touched her hand. The smaller piece flowed into the larger, then the larger settled back inside the bag.

She'd seen how fast it could move. If it wanted to be gone, she wouldn't have seen it leave. It might have been afraid she could fry it before it could get clear, not knowing the charge wouldn't go off if the bag was unsealed, but Torin didn't think so. Although it was always dangerous to layer known behaviors onto an unknown species, it seemed to be cooperating.

Thumb on the seal, she paused, leaned a little closer. "If you can hear me, we'll see what we can do about getting you a voice as soon as we've finished passing your little test. Until then . . ."

It almost looked as if it waved as she resealed the body bag. But the shadows were tricky, and it could have just been an effect of the light.

FIFTEEN

"My blood?" McGuinty asked, fingers just above the screen of his broken slate. The stains were a dark and ugly red in the light from his cuff.

"Probably not," Torin told him. "Probably Dr. Sloan's."

"She, uh . . ." He blinked rapidly, ignoring the tears that ran down his cheeks. "The doc, she thought she was saving me, you know?"

"She did save you. But you've saved us all a few times; you were due."

"She died for me."

"Technically, she died to give the platoon a fighting chance, so you can spread the guilt around."

"I don't . . ."

Torin waited. They needed McGuinty up and functional. Without him, they had nothing to fight that tank unless they scampered out to the other crashed flier in their bodyliners and carried back the unfired missiles.

When he looked up at her, only his eyes moving because of the sealed hole in his neck, his face was bleak. "How do you stand it, Gunny?"

"By remembering it's not about you." Turning so her bad leg could stretch out along the length of his bedroll, she squatted beside him and touched the back of his hand, skin to skin as though he were di'Taykan. "It's about Dr. Sloan—her choice, her sacrifice, her death. Then you try living up to her example."

"How?"

"Well, to start with . . ." She settled back, weight on her heel, knuckles of her left hand against the floor for balance. ". . . can you fix the amplifier?"

Disbelief replaced bleakness. He flicked a tiny piece of circuit board off his stomach and onto the floor. "It's not broken, it's been destroyed. With time and parts, I might be able to fix my slate—but not the amp."

"And you'd need the amplifier to actually send the jamming signal?"

"Yes, Gunnery Sergeant."

"Then forget your slate for now. Keep working on getting a signal through my implant up to the ObSats."

"The major's slate took some damage." Setting his own slate aside, he took up the major's and scraped a bit of dried blood off the casing.

"Is it functional?"

"Well, yeah, but I can't guarantee that none of the data's been corrupted."

"Only two guarantees in the Corps, McGuinty. First in, last out, and no one gets left behind. There is a third, lesser-known guarantee," she added as McGuinty's brows began to draw down, "but it involves the Navy and a lot of lubricant, and it's need to know, so I can't tell it to you until you get that first hook."

He stared at her for a long moment, his disbelief shifting parameters, then he snorted. Then he smiled. His lips were gray and it wasn't much of a smile, but he had a hole in his neck big enough to shove her thumb into and a certain amount of soft tissue damage, so she'd take it.

"You comfortable?"

His upper body had been propped up at about thirty-five degrees on packs padded with bedrolls. "I can't move my head."

"Can you see the screen on the slate?"

"Well, yeah, but . . ."

"Then you don't need to move your head." This time, she wrapped her hand around his forearm—reassurance with a bit of distance. "Just get us an uplink before that tank starts firing again."

"Maybe it's out of ammo."

"These things have next to no weight restrictions, Private, so I very much doubt that. It's all up to you."

"But no pressure."

"You're a Marine, can't see why there would be." She gripped his arm a little tighter, then reached for his canteen, dropping an analgesic and multivitamin from her vest into the water where they dissolved almost instantly. The Corps' first CMO had hated taking pills. "You need to replace the fluids you lost," she told him, handing it back. "Drink this."

"Hurts to swallow."

"Tough."

McGuinty took a small mouthful and made a face, even though both additions were tasteless.

"Get it all down you," she said as she stood.

"Gunny?" He stopped her before she could walk away. "Is this what it's like all the time?"

Being covered in someone else's blood trying to jury-rig a solution before artillery blows us to hell? The silent corollary was almost louder than the actual question.

Torin raised an eyebrow and snorted. "Of course not. Sometimes it gets exciting."

"All right, if McGuinty was your recruit most likely to hack the system, who was most likely to crack the casing and hot-wire a tunepod into the shower system?"

Jiir snorted. "I remember hearing about that. That was one of your platoon?"

"Ingrid de Buda, she's teaching now at MidCore Station."

"Well, with this lot, I'd say your best bet is probably Iful if you want something creative."

"I want the remains of that desk cannibalized to give that alien a voice. Pull the transducers—audio out and in—and the speakers and come up with a way for it to interface. It doesn't have to sound good; it just has to be audible."

"Yeah, that's creative." Nose ridges slowly opened and closed. "You want to talk to it?"

"I want some answers from it."

"You think it'll talk to you?"

She shrugged. It seemed to like her, but she wasn't about to mention that.

Jiir stared up at her for a long moment, then he nodded. Torin had no idea what he was nodding about, nor did she particularly want to know. "You think it speaks Federate?"

"It seems to program in Federate, so I assume it's got the verbal part worked out."

"Gunnery Sergeant Kerr!" Bynum, calling her from his position by the major. He'd taken over *observing the alien* duties while, a couple of meters away, Stevens held the light so Flint could remove the shrapnel from Vega's ass.

Torin gave him a "one minute" sign and turned back to Jiir. "The alien's already proved it's more familiar with our tech than the major was; just give it something it can work with. Zero broadcast capabilities."

"I'll get Iful on it." The sergeant sounded doubtful, but Torin didn't care. She'd seen what Big Yellow could do if bits of it had something to say, they'd talk. As Jiir called Iful and told him to get his butt to the office, she crossed to where Bynum was shifting his weight from foot to foot, eyes never leaving the major's face.

The last lot of painkillers had knocked Major Svensson cold although according to his med-alert his vitals were steady. Stress levels were reading high, but Torin felt that could probably be explained by having just had his arm hacked off. "What's the problem?"

Bynum pointed.

There were two gray tear tracks running in narrow lines from the inside corner of the major's eyes down toward the corners of his mouth, the path ignoring the effects of gravity on a liquid. "Well, that's . . . interesting." Grabbing Bynum's good arm, Torin grunted, "Stand still," as she lowered herself down. Reaching out, she lightly touched the major's cheek at the end of the nearer line. The line closed the small distance between them, thickened as the last of it pulled free of the tear duct, and then wrapped a spiral around her finger. A moment later, the second line joined it— merged into it. There was no discernible weight, but it felt warm against her skin.

While she was down there, thighs straining, bad leg stretched out to the side to get her in close enough, she checked the stump. What she saw didn't exactly surprise her. It looked like the alien—aliens—had been waiting for her. Or waiting for the bit of itself attached to her finger. As she stretched out her hand, the semipermeable seal blushed momentarily gray, a ghost of movement slid across her fingers, and suddenly, there was alien puddled in her palm. Enough alien that she could feel the press of its weight at the end of her arm. The weight had a finality about it that suggested there'd be no more.

Major Svensson had been abandoned.

Torin trusted her instincts but had no intention of announcing *that* without a full body scan in support.

"Up," she said.

"Uh, Gunny, when you reached for the stump, how did you know what you had with you wasn't going to jump back in?" Bynum asked as he hauled her back to the vertical.

"Why would it go out the eyes and back in the arm?"

"Why do the Krai eat their grannies?"

Making assumptions about alien motivations would, in some parts of known space, end with dessert, and the odds were about even where the cherry would be placed. Torin knew that, but she also felt she knew Big Yellow, at least as much as anyone did, and this particular bit of it seemed to like her, for lack of a better word. She bent at the waist to open the body bag—they were just going to have to cope with her ass in the air, there were only so many one-legged squats she felt like performing.

This new bit flowed into the main bulk as eagerly as the last bit had.

"Still working on getting you a voice," she told it as she closed it in. It seemed resigned, but that might have been lack of sleep talking. Another night with less than three hours, and she was going to have to take one of the stims she carried. She was definitely starting to miss the days when she could stay up a tenday on coffee and adrenaline.

"Gunnery Sergeant Kerr!"

Ayumi. And quite possibly the di'Taykan reaction to her ass in the air. She sighed and straightened and, by the time she turned, realized Ayumi's call had nothing to do with her. Staff Sergeant Beyhn had arced up off his bedroll until only his shoulders and heels were touching.

"Shit."

She didn't have his stats in her slate.

And the only person on Crucible who had the slightest idea of what was happening to him had caught a missile with her sternum.

Up close, his eyes were so pale all the light receptors had to be closed, tendons were standing out on his throat, and a fine sheen of sweat made his skin glimmer. His breathing was ragged and desperate sounding, not so much like he was trying to force air past a constriction but like he was breathing too quickly and too shallowly for his system to deal with it.

"It looks like a seizure."

Suddenly he collapsed, his whole body going limp.

Almost his whole body.

Impressive. And more than she really wanted to know about her former DI.

"Flint!" She held out her hand, and he put Doctor Sloan's slate into it. Fortunately, the doctor had left it in the infirmary when she'd taken that last airing on the roof. Or not so fortunately—symbols and numbers filled the first screen. The second was mostly fluctuating bar graphs. "Can you read this?"

"No." He pointed at a section of bars consistently spiking into the orange. "But that can't be good."

Keening, Beyhn drummed his heels against the floor. He reached out wildly. Ayumi grabbed his flailing hand and hung on.

"Gunny, you have to do something!"

She could see that. "Sedatives?"

Flint shook his head. "I'm afraid I'll kill him if I give him any more, but I think this means he's dying anyway. Dr. Sloan would have known."

Torin had a sudden vivid memory of boots and blood and snow. "Not really relevant, Marine."

"Yes, Gunnery Sergeant!" Then his shoulders sagged. "It's just the staff sergeant seems so desperate."

He did at that. Painfully desperate. "Ayumi." The di'Taykan looked up, green hair whipping around her head so quickly Torin could have sworn she heard it cut through the air. "Let go of his hand for a second."

"Gunny . . ."

"Give me a *one Ventris Station* and then you can hold him again."

"But . . ."

"Do it!"

The bars spiked past the danger zone and the value

of at least half the numbers jumped. She could see when Ayumi let go, she could see when, almost sobbing, she took hold of the staff sergeant's hand again, and she had a feeling, given the condition of Beyhn's body that she knew what had to be done. "Flint, take his other hand."

The effect of her last command still lingering, Flint dropped instantly and wrapped both of his hands around the fingers Beyhn had twisted in his bedroll.

"Ayumi, give me another *one Ventris station.*"

The same spikes as before.

"Let him go, Flint." As the new medic stood, Torin handed back the doctor's slate and touched her PCU. "Jonin."

"Yes, Gunnery Sergeant!"

"Meet me in the kitchen."

"What hasn't Staff Sergeant Beyhn had since this started?"

"Sex." The longer he was on the first floor of the anchor, the faster Jonin's hair moved.

"Sex," Torin repeated. No surprise it was the first thing Jonin had thought of. It was the first thing a di'Taykan usually thought of. "You told me that when a change comes on you, your closest *thytrin* help you through the process. I think I know what kind of help it is. I think someone needs to have sex with him."

Jonin's eyes darkened, paled, and darkened again. "Gunnery Sergeant, Staff Sergeant Beyhn is qui."

"I know. That's why we're in the kitchen, so we can talk about this in private." It wasn't like she could order one of the platoon's fourteen surviving di'Taykan to have sex with the staff sergeant for medicinal reasons—this went above and beyond knowing what her Marines were capable of. The kitchen also had the added benefit of being as far from the staff sergeant as it was possible to get and still be on the first floor. "Physical intimacy . . ." She paused, aware she sounded like a bad STD vid, and started again. "Sex is important to your species. The staff sergeant has an erection we could use to punch through that tank, and Ayumi's touch is the only thing keeping his numbers on the chart. He's not reacting to anyone but another Taykan. We have to try something, or he's going to stroke out."

"And die?"

"Without an immediate med-evac, probably."

"What you say makes sense," Jonin admitted reluctantly. "It is very likely true he must have sex or die."

Torin frowned, studying the private's face. "Which you knew," she said slowly. "Long before I brought it up."

"We *suspected* it, Gunnery Sergeant. We didn't *know*."

"Did you tell your sergeant what you suspected? Did you tell Dr. Sloan? Do we have to have the *this is a Marine Corps problem* discussion again, because if we do, I'm going to have it with my boot up your ass."

"There was no point saying anything. Staff Sergeant Beyhn is qui. We cannot have sex with him."

Torin sighed and only barely resisted the urge to slam her forehead into the counter a couple of times just so the growing pain behind her eyes made sense. "I know di'Taykan who didn't care if their partners were mammals, so you're going to have to explain the problem to me. Why can't you have sex with him? Don't the parts fit?" The look he shot her wavered just one side of insubordination. In the interests of getting through an uncomfortable conversation as quickly as possible, she decided to give him the benefit of the doubt. "Okay, the parts fit. What's the problem?"

"He is qui, we are not. Therefore, we cannot have sex with him. We must protect him and nurture him but can-

not treat him as if he is other than qui. We do not want
him to die, but . . ."

"But?"

Jonin's eyes went dark, light, dark again. "But he is
qui."

"Are there laws against it? Will it damage either the
staff sergeant or whoever is with him?"

"No."

"No to what question, Private?"

"No to all three questions, Gunnery Sergeant. But he
is qui."

The content of the Corps xenocultural courses definitely needed to be expanded. Torin decided to stick
with what she knew. "He's a Marine. You're all
Marines. Marines can have consensual sex with other
Marines."

"If that's true, Gunnery Sergeant Kerr, if we are all,
first, Marines, then why are you speaking to me as
though I lead the di'Taykan of the platoon? If you do
not truly believe it, why should we?"

She really wanted to smack that smug, superior,
upper class look off his face. Mostly because he was
right. Staff Sergeant Beyhn's condition had pushed her
right into the same species-specific way of looking at
things that she'd warned Jonin about. The staff sergeant
was either a Marine or qui'Taykan. He couldn't be both
and survive. "Thank you, Private." And she meant it.
"That will be all."

"Yes, Gunnery Sergeant." He paused at the door.
"Gunnery Sergeant?"

"Yes, Jonin."

"Staff Sergeant Beyhn is qui."

"I think we've covered that."

"The qui are breeders."

She'd called on Hisht to hack off Major Svensson's
arm rather than asking for volunteers because his skills

made him the best Marine for the job. In this particular instance, there were a number of Marines who could help the staff sergeant although it was weird to think of sex based solely on gender.

"But Staff Sergeant Beyhn is qui!"

"I'm going to shoot the next Marine who says that." She almost meant it, too. "Look, we have a Marine with a medical condition—you six are the only Marines in the platoon qualified to help. I'm asking for a volunteer to do what's necessary to keep the staff sergeant alive."

The presence of the six female di'Taykan around his bedroll had stopped the staff sergeant's numbers from spiking, but they were still climbing steadily, and some had already crossed into the red. Masayo seemed to be praying—no big surprise—but the others looked like they were considering the possibility and given where their eyes were tracking, the staff sergeant seemed to be making a case for their participation all on his own. The di'Taykan were, if nothing else, predictable in their response to a . . .

Challenge.

She had a sudden memory of Haysole surrounded by Silsviss.

"You know, it just occurred to me. No di'Taykan has ever had sex with a qui'Taykan before—you guys can't have a lot of new frontiers left."

Six pairs of eyes lightened speculatively.

"Well, there's the H'san," Lirit murmured, sketching something—Torin neither knew nor wanted to know what—in the air.

"Prize money for that keeps going up," Kirassai agreed.

But the taboo seemed to be holding, and the staff sergeant was running out of time. His numbers were . . .

Numbers.

When a new species was introduced to the Corps, the brass made sure there were minimum numbers in every single category, enough to create a support system and allow functioning under new and occasionally terrifying conditions. Torin had hoped to send the other five Marines back to their positions, but that no longer seemed possible.

She sighed, hoping she sounded like she was tired of the whole situation—not exactly a stretch. "Fine, since nothing seems to be shooting at us right now, why don't you all pick up the staff sergeant's bedroll and carry him carefully into the kitchen, close the doors, and make up your minds there."

"He is our DI," Lirit said thoughtfully. "That's got to be as close as a *thytrin* bond."

"We'd be saving his life." Ayumi's hair had begun to move at the same speed as the staff sergeant's.

"Or you could just stand around and talk about it about it," Torin snorted.

Kaimi glanced around at the other five, picked up a signal invisible to a non di'Taykan, and nodded. "Let's go."

"Keep an eye on his stats," Torin warned them, handing Ononan Dr. Sloan's slate. "And keep the noise down," she added as, three to a side, they picked up the bedroll and headed for the kitchen. "There are Marines in this room trying to convalesce."

"Gunny?"

She turned to see Flint nod down at Major Svensson. Since he didn't seem panicked, she assumed the major had woken up. When she got closer and saw the sliver of pale gray between his lashes, she realized this was, indeed, the case. The question became: How long had he been awake?

"Don't think I've ever heard of anyone having to talk a di'Taykan *into* having sex before, Gunny. This'll be one for the record books."

That long.

Although his skin didn't have a lot more color in it than his eyes, he managed most of a grin as he added. "There'll probably be another Bronze Cluster in it for you."

"Yes, sir." She paused just long enough to make her point and added. "Need your painkillers adjusted, sir?"

He laughed then, a harsh dry sound in the back of his throat.

Suggesting Flint go check on Vega, Torin eased herself down to the floor beside the major, popped the lid, and handed him his canteen. An arm behind his shoulders lifted him enough to drink. When he passed the canteen back, she lowered him gently back to the bedroll.

"I won't break if you drop me, Gunny."

"I'd rather not prove that wrong, sir."

"How's the leg?"

She glared down the length of her stiffened combats toward her boot. "Awkward. Annoying. Pretty much as expected, sir." Turning slightly, she nodded toward the stump of his arm—the sealant had shown no gray since the last of the aliens had been removed. "It seems as though you're free of alien life-forms."

"Glad to hear it. So . . ." He settled his shoulders against the padding and wrestled his focus onto her face. ". . . bring me up to speed, Gunnery Sergeant."

No point in mentioning that his speed was barely above a full stop. "Yes, sir. Private McGuinty is recreating the uplink used to control the drones . . ."

Major Svensson rolled his head left until he could see McGuinty tucked into a far corner of the common room working in a circle of light.

". . . Iful is further cannibalizing the desk to give the Big Yellow aliens a voice. The tank has stopped firing at us, which is good news, but now we don't have a location for it, which is bad. It did some damage to the second floor but nothing too serious, and no one was hit. One/one and one/two have been moved back to the west wall but we're staying off the roof for the time being. All tech except for the PCUs is still off-line. The situation with the rest of the drones has not changed. And six Marines are using sex to stabilize Staff Sergeant Beyhn."

Pale brows rose. "So, basically, another glorious day in the Corps?"

"Yes, sir."

"And the aliens are . . . ?"

"Still in the body bag with your severed arm, sir."

They turned together to look. The lump of the arm was obvious, the aliens not so much.

The major took a moment to breathe—in, out, in again—before saying, "That's a little gruesome, Gunny."

"It doesn't seem to be bothering them, sir. Also the Krai have offered to eat your arm should the need arise, but the need would have to be dire and I'm not sure we want to encourage that kind of behavior."

"I'm damned sure we don't," he muttered, eyes closing again.

"Yes, sir."

"What the hell . . . ?" Back against the wall under the window, Stone frowned at the rounds smacking into the upper third of the back wall of the anchor's fake barracks. They made ugly holes and an uglier sound and no sense at all.

"Why are we taking fire?" Carson whined, cradling her KC-7 against her chest. "It's not like they can hit us, it's just annoying."

"What do you think, Jonin?" The di'Taykan had been quiet since coming back from talking with the gunny, and Stone was starting to get a bit concerned in an *I hope I don't have to smack him upside the head again* kind of way.

Jonin pulled off his helmet, his hair spreading out in a cobalt-blue aurora. "I think the same thing you do. They're trying to keep our heads down."

Carson snorted. "Working."

"If they're trying to keep our heads down, you *se ckenen ton ivernin*, there's something they don't want us to see."

"Hey!" She jabbed him with an elbow. "If you're going to insult me, do it in Federate."

Eyes light, Jonin smiled. "Fine, you're . . ."

"Play nice, kids." Stone figured if he had to, he'd just knock their heads together and, without the buffer of Vega between them, their stubborn skulls connecting would make a very satisfying sound. He yawned against the back of his hand. "Should we tell the sergeant?"

All three of them leaned out enough to get a look at Sergeant Jiir at the other end of the room.

"Is he doing what I think he's doing?" Stone asked.

Jonin shrugged one shoulder. "You think he's taking off his combats, so he can look out the window without being shot?"

"Yeah, pretty much."

"I don't think it'll help. The drones aren't actually aiming. He's just as likely to take a stray round if he strips naked."

"And thank you for that image."

"Well, I think he's fukking nuts," Carson snorted, settling back against the wall.

It was darker outside than Jiir'd expected. Sunset came early in this hemisphere at this time of the year, and a gentle curtain of soft white snow helped reduce the visibility. Fifty meters, tops, and he doubted a Human or di'Taykan could see even that far. Krai vision had evolved to deal with shifting patterns.

He spotted movement between the buildings. Drones from the west and east, moving in on the south.

"Fukking *ablin gon savit, serley chirka*!" A round

scored the edge of his jaw. The angle too shallow for penetration, it skittered along the heavy bone and continued over his shoulder. Slammed around, he dropped to the floor and scrambled for his sealant, still swearing in all three languages.

"Sergeant!"

Palssan's voice. Probably Palssan trying to move his head.

"Don't get your fingers near his mouth!"

One of the Humans. Probably Leford. Same fireteam.

He shoved Palssan away and, as the sealant hit the wound, numbing it, he blinked himself back to a more immediate awareness of his surroundings. There were still rounds hitting the upper third of the back wall, and all eight Marines in the room seemed to be staring at him.

"What?" he demanded.

"You were hit, Sergeant Jiir!"

"Well, that explains why my *serley* jaw fukking hurts," he snapped, shrugging his combats up over his shoulders and reaching for his vest. "I'm heading downstairs to talk to the Gunny. Stone, you're in charge. Jonin, get your *serley* helmet on!"

". . . and maybe half the drones that were attacking the east and west walls are changing positions, moving south."

Leaning against the wall by the air lock, Torin pushed a hand back through sweaty hair. Assuming their programming didn't include doing dumb ass things for the hell of it, there could be only one reason the drones would be shifting their numbers. "Any sign of the tank?"

Jiir snorted; he'd clearly been thinking the same thing. "Not yet, Gunny, but it's nearly dark and starting to snow again. The tank'll be at the door before we can see it."

"Odds are good that's where it's heading," Annatah-wee muttered. "Two, maybe three shots on that door, and we're wide open. How do you figure it knows?"

"Knows where the door is?" Torin shrugged. "Maybe the drones told it. You guys said they had basic self-programming. Maybe it got enough intell off its targeting scans to identify the building. Doesn't matter."

"So we're screwed."

Torin ignored Annatahwee's matter-of-fact observation—accurate though it may have been. "It shows up before McGuinty's fixed that uplink, we ignore the drones—unless the little fukkers have figured out how to fly, they can't get to us—and throw everything we have left at that tank to buy him more time. It'll be close enough the 9s can do damage and a few well-placed grenades could throw the targeting off."

Both sergeants stared at her, their expressions close to identical in the dim light.

"Okay," she admitted, "they'd have to be *very* well-placed grenades."

"If it's aiming at the door, it won't be aiming at the roof," Jiir pointed out. "And because it has the tech blocker mounted, it won't be carrying a top gun."

"Good. We'll put weapons on the roof the moment it's up close and personal."

"Not what I meant." He leaned in, dropping his voice slightly. "We do what we did to salvage the flier. I climb down a rope in my bodyliner with all the grenades we have left."

"While the drones are firing randomly to keep our heads down?" Torin nodded toward the gouge along his jaw. "How's that been working out for you so far? And you even think about throwing me some 'good of the many outweighs the needs of the one' bullshit, and I'll flatten you."

"Gunny . . ."

"Yeah, okay, fine. It's a plan. It's not a good plan, but

it's a plan. Hold it in reserve." She yawned and pushed off the wall. "You two make sure the 9s are ready to move to the roof the instant they hear the word. I'll check on McGuinty."

Annatahwee jerked her head toward the north end of the anchor and kitchen. "What about the recruits in with Staff Sergeant Beyhn?"

"Go tell them they've got ninety seconds to finish up, then they're to move the staff sergeant back to the infirmary and check with you for duty stations."

"Why me?"

Torin grinned. "You brought it up, Sergeant."

"Why ninety seconds?" Jiir wondered as Annatahwee rolled her eyes and headed down the hall.

"It's SOP for di'Taykan in the field."

"Leave it to the di'Taykan to have standard operating procedures for sex."

"Are you kidding?" Torin snorted. "They have combat positions. Get a couple of teams building a barricade out of the packs—half circle from there . . ." She pointed. ". . . to here. If we don't stop the tank in time, we may be able to bottleneck the drones and hold them a little longer."

"Soon, Gunny," McGuinty grunted without looking up from the screen.

Torin translated that as *sooner if you'll go away and stop interrupting*. Bad leg out behind her, she bent and picked up his canteen. Still mostly full. "I told you to drink this."

"I was working." His skin had picked up a greenish tint, and he wasn't so much blinking as maintaining a constant up-and-down motion of his eyelids.

"I don't give a H'san's ass what you were doing." Her tone snapped his gaze up off the screen. "If I tell you to do something, you do it. Is that clear?"

"Yes, Gunnery Sergeant!"

"So drink the damned water."

"Yes, Gunnery Sergeant!"

She watched him take three small swallows, then turned as the door in the far end of the common room opened and the di'Taykan emerged, the six of them once again carrying the sergeant's bedroll. "Keep drinking," she snapped, and started across the room.

They were setting the bedroll back in its previous position when she reached them. As an observation that the staff sergeant seemed limp would no doubt be taken entirely the wrong way, she merely bent and checked his pulse.

"He's asleep?"

"Well, there were six of us, Gunny," Ayumi pointed out.

"And he's old," Lirit added.

"He's asleep," Flint agreed, standing at the end of the bedroll and poking a finger at the doctor's slate. "His temperature's low, but all his other stats are back to normal."

"So it wor . . ."

"Gunny! Tank's approaching the open area to the south!"

"Roger, Sergeant. Get lights and weapons on the roof! You six, duty stations! Move! And put your Goddamned helmets on!" she added as all six took a look at the packs stacked waist high between the common room and the hall and pounded back the way they'd come, heading for the stairs. "Should fukking record that and just loop it through their heads," she muttered, grabbing the bedroll by Beyhn's head. "Flint, help me carry him back into the kitchen."

It was the farthest point from the door. And the tank. She should have had him left there.

"Yes, Gunnery Sergeant. Your leg . . ."

"Not the time to get on me about lifting with my

back, Flint. Stevens, Bynum, throw your good arms
under Vega and get her in there, too."

"Gunny, we can . . ."

"You can go down fighting if the drones get that far.
Until then, move!"

Bonninski squinted through her sights, the bulk of the
tank just visible between the buildings. They had maybe
ten minutes before it maneuvered itself around to get a
clear shot. "Sergeant, without the scanners, how are we
supposed to hit anything crippling?"

"We're taking out the targeting array."

"Sergeant, we can't see the targeting array!"

"This is where you prove you were paying attention
to the lectures on artillery specs, Bonninski. You see the
tank?"

She blinked a large snowflake off her lashes. "Yes,
Sergeant."

"Well, you should know *serley* well where the targeting array is without having to see it, shouldn't you?
Ready 9s! Fire!"

The major safely stowed in the kitchen, Torin and
Flint headed for McGuinty.

His eyes were closed, one hand lying palm up at his
side, the other still clutching the major's slate.

Flint dropped and pushed two fingers carefully
against the skin at the edge of the seal on his throat.
"He's under, Gunny."

"I can see that." She kicked the canteen. Still mostly
full. If they survived this, she was going to have words
with Private McGuinty.

"Gunny!"

She turned to see Iful gracefully leap the waist high
barricade of stacked packs.

"I think I've got something that'll work. For the

aliens," he added when she stared at him a moment too long.

"Sevens, don't waste ammo on drones you can't see!" Annatahwee's voice cracked out over the Group Channel. *"If they get into the anchor, we'll need every round."*

Taking the cobbled-together voice box from Iful, Torin tossed him her slate and snapped, "Record this!" as she bent to open the body bag. The seal had barely cracked when the aliens surged out and then back again through the larger opening, like fluid under pressure. Setting the bits of electrical flotsam down, she snatched her hand back as they engulfed it.

Not the time to wonder if they could hear her. "Tell us how to turn the drones off!"

"That's a speaker," Iful whispered as the gray blob re-arranged itself.

"Still. Collecting. Data."

The voice reminded Torin of an ancient midi file at one of the precontact museums. Then, almost too fast to see, the bag held a small jumble of assorted electronics, a severed arm, and . . .

"What is that, Gunny?"

"It's exactly what it looks like," Torin snarled. The aliens had re-formed themselves into a skeletal hand and a set of truncated lower arm bones. *Aliens? What aliens?* it was saying. *Nothing in here but some polyhydroxide alcoholydes used for medical purposes. No idea how we got out of the arm.* Okay, maybe she was reading a bit much into it, but they were clearly not planning on saying anything else. She resealed the bag with a vicious emphasis she wished she could use on the alien. "Grab the major's slate and see if you can figure out how far McGuinty got on that uplink while Flint and I drag his ass out of here."

*   *   *

"We do what Gunnery Sergeant Kerr did!"

Sakur turned to stare at Kichar, a little startled by the sudden outburst. "We what?"

"She used the tank to stop the tank! The second night by the lake," Kichar added when Sakur and Hisht stared at her blankly. "She had it shoot through the ice so it sank!"

"Solid ground out there, genius," Sakur snorted, hair flicking toward the window. "Not ice."

"So we change the specifics!" Her eyes were gleaming. "Hisht, your people use nets, right?"

"Yes, but . . ."

"We weight the corners of a shelter half, you throw it like a net over the tank, the camo in the half scrambles the tank's internal sensors, an HE missile goes off in the tube. Bang. No more tank."

The 9s took another shot, their combined firepower having no effect at all.

"That might just work," Sakur admitted.

Kichar rolled her eyes. "Thanks for sounding so surprised! Get a half from the east windows. Stay low, don't get shot. Hisht, come on, we'll tell the sergeant."

"What do you plan to weight the half with?" Torin asked.

"Boots," Jiir told her. *"Hisht's and Piroj's."*

The liners would keep their feet warm, and they'd be happier without the boots. Given the situation, they might be the only happy Marines in the area. Well, them and Staff Sergeant Beyhn.

"That's a pretty big distance to cover horizontally."

"We use the wind, Gunny, it's what we do. And we're stronger than we look."

She couldn't do it, but since she wasn't doing it, that didn't matter. "You have a go. Good luck. And Kichar?"

"Yes, Gunnery Sergeant?"

"Good idea."

"Thank you, Gunnery Sergeant!"

"Gunny?" Iful appeared suddenly at her left shoulder. "I think McGuinty was done. Looks like he was running a final diagnostic."

"And?"

"It's not one hundred percent, there's still corrupted files in the program, but if I'm reading this right, it should run. We just need to work out how to execute. Maybe if I turn the slate off and . . ."

Torin grabbed his wrist before he could follow through. "Do we know when McGuinty saved last?"

Iful's eyes paled. "No, Gunny."

"Don't close anything. Don't turn anything off. Just find the program."

"Tank will be in position to fire on the door in less than ten seconds."

"That's not really helping, Kichar."

She flushed. "Sorry, Sergeant."

"7s! Covering fire! Keep their heads down! Hisht! Go!"

Wearing only his bodyliner, Hisht surged up onto his feet a little west of the tank, the angle allowing for the wind. There were a lot of rounds in the air and while ninety percent of the firing was at the drones, ten percent wasn't, and a few of the rounds buzzed by uncomfortably close. He thought about home, wondered for a moment why he'd ever left it, gratefully stretched out his toes, and imagined throwing his *jerkeen's* heavy hunting net over a passing flock of *vertak*.

The shelter half opened up, then the weighted corners began to drop as Hisht toppled forward off the edge of the roof. No branches to grab, nothing but a straight drop . . .

Then the rope around his waist jerked him back.

By the time he untangled himself from Sakur's grip

and smacked the di'Taykan's hands away from his crotch, the shelter half had landed, covering about two thirds of the tank.

"I don't know, Gunny . . ."

He could hear Sergeant Annatahwee talking.

". . . between the snow and the dark and the camo function, it's damned hard to see. We may have enough coverage or . . ."

The explosion was everything the vids said a tank exploding at close range should be. Only louder. Ears ringing, Hisht shoved Sakur off him and crawled to the edge of the roof.

The top third of the tank had split open like a fungus throwing spores.

The bottom third, damaged servos howling loud enough to be heard even by the half deafened, continued grinding toward the double doors.

"Oh, fuk." He felt Sakur's hand close over his shoulder. "It's going to crash straight through the door. You think it's got enough left?"

Hisht pointed toward the drones massed in and between the buildings. "They think so."

Plastic casing of the major's slate creaking in her grip, Torin would have rather charged through the air lock and tossed a bag of grenades under the tank than allow an alien program to bounce into orbit by way of her skull. Unfortunately, it wasn't an either/or scenario.

She took a deep breath, tapped transmit into her implant with the tip of her tongue, and started the program.

"Number three squad, down to the barricade. Everyone else—stop as many drones as you can before they get to the building."

An uncomfortable vibration in her teeth, a buzz in her jaw, told Torin the interface was working. She almost thought she could feel bits of the code going by, but that was ludicrous. All she could feel was . . .

Pain.

The buzz had become a buzz saw.

Since she hadn't noticed the major screaming at any time in the last five days, it had to be the corrupted files. Corrupted files fukking hurt. Who knew?

It took her a moment to realize that the shriek of metal separating and the crash of the air lock doors slamming back into the anchor was not actually happening inside her head.

Although, at the moment, putting her head under the tank seemed like a wonderful idea.

The sound of KC-7s firing at close quarters got her attention. When had she fallen to her knees? Both knees. And, holy fukking hell, that hurt!

And then it didn't because there was only enough wetware space available to handle the pain in her jaw.

"*Ablin gon savit*, Gunny! Your face!"

Heat. Burning.

"Iful! Turn it off!"

Torin curled her body around the slate. They'd have to go through her to get it. She'd see this out.

She noticed the quiet first. Well, the relative quiet— there were boots and voices and the slamming about of metal and plastic. Probably the drones being mistreated. She tried to say something about misuse of Corps property, but her mouth didn't seem to work. It didn't seem to hurt either, so she wasn't exactly complaining.

At some point during the upload, she'd fallen onto her side. Her face was in a puddle. Not slush. Too warm to be slush.

Oh.

Blood.

There seemed to be a lot of it pouring out of her mouth.

"Gunny? Gunny, can you hear me? Fuk! How do I seal this without blocking her throat?"

She wondered who Flint was asking, Dr. Sloan being dead and all and the rest of the platoon having no more idea than a litter of kittens. She liked kittens. Well, she liked cats, but there needed to be kittens first.

Then it wasn't so quiet; something roared past the anchor and someone yelled it was more fliers.

"Whoever just ID'd that as a flier is redoing their vehicle recognition course!" Annatahwee bellowed close by.

VTA, Torin thought and let go.

"We will not allow Big Yellow to win by changing our lives to suit its invasion!"

"One escape pod," Torin snorted at the *Promise*'s main vid screen. "Hardly an invasion."

Arm thrown over her waist, Craig gave her a quick squeeze and said, "Shut up."

On the screen, the Confederation Premier, a Dornagain female currently named Listens and Considers, unfolded to her full height and stared gravely at Presit, her golden fur almost red under the studio lighting. "While we do not at this point know if Big Yellow was working alone or as part of a planned act of aggression by the Others . . ."

"Not very aggressive," Craig muttered.

Torin snorted. "Maybe not where you were."

". . . we will continue as we have. We will be vigilant, but we will take up our lives again."

"Off!"

The screen went dark before Presit could ask her next question.

"I was watching that!" Torin protested.

Craig stopped her before she could get an elbow back into a sensitive spot. "You've seen it before."

"Yeah, but I still had tank head."

"The posturing was the fun part. From here on, it devolves into politics. Presit's in fine form, and at least twice it looks like she's about to bite the premier on the ankle."

"Seriously?"

"Seriously."

Settling back against Craig's chest, Torin snickered. "I remember that, but I thought it was the tank talking."

"Yeah, well, you were lucky you missed the live action version."

Not a lot of people would consider having the lower half of their face rebuilt as lucky, but Torin agreed with him. By the time she came out of the tank—its surface scribbled over by every surviving member of Platoon 71 before they were posted away from Ventris Station— the hysteria had essentially played itself out.

Not to say there hadn't been a few loose ends to tie up.

"Do you realize, Gunnery Sergeant Kerr, the scope of the diplomatic incident you could have created between the Taykan home world and the Corps? At the time of the incident, Staff Sergeant Beyhn was qui."

Hands tucked behind her back, Torin's right index finger twitched. "Yes, sir. So I was told."

The colonel standing to the right of High Tekamal Louden's desk frowned, searching for insubordination, but Torin's delivery had been letter perfect.

"Fortunately," the Commandant of the Corps continued, "qui'Allak Beyhn spoke for you. He said that as he was a Marine at the time of the incident that made it a Marine problem not a Taykan concern, and it therefore required a Marine solution." She paused, waiting.

"Yes, sir."

"Do you usually consider sex to be a Marine Corps solution, Gunnery Sergeant?"

"That would depend on the problem, sir."

The colonel sputtered but remained essentially silent.

"The six Marines who were part of your solution are refusing to say which of them administered the lifesaving action, as it were. You seem to have had an influence on them."

"Thank you, sir."

The colonel sputtered a bit more, but the high tekamal said only, "I'm recommending you never be allowed near a recruit platoon again."

Gunnery sergeants did not smile at the Commandant of the Corps, but, at this point, Torin thought she could probably get away with allowing honest feelings to show in her voice. "*Thank* you, sir."

"You are indeed carrying the same protein marker as Civilian Salvage Operator Craig Ryder and the reporter Presit a Tur durValintrisy."

Torin bit back a weary, *no shit*.

Nose ridges flaring, the major/doctor stopped by the edge of the examination table and leaned in close. "I saw your interrogation of the alien. *Still. Collecting. Data.* What do you think that means, Gunnery Sergeant."

"No idea, sir. You need to ask the alien."

His voice dropped, and he leaned closer still. "Can't. It's gone. Every piece of it the Corps had in custody, including the bit you cleverly trapped in the body bag. Officially, they've left known space to rejoin Big Yellow. Unofficially, though?" He tapped his skull. "I'm scanning my brain at frequent intervals."

Torin bit down on her brand-new tongue.

From her position on one of the upper galleries, Torin braced her forearms on the railing and studied the Humans, di'Taykan, and occasional Krai filling the public terminal from bulkhead to bulkhead. They were so young. She didn't think she'd ever really noticed that before.

"We have to stop meeting like this, Gunnery Sergeant. People will start to talk."

She straightened, turned, came to attention, and snapped off a perfect salute.

"Knock it the hell off, Gunny."

Her new mouth felt stiff when she smiled. "Glad to see you up and around again, Major."

"I've been up for a while." As she rested her weight back on the railing, he took up an identical position beside her. "Arms take less time to regrow. I wouldn't have been tanked at all except . . ." They watched a group of di'Taykan surging close then apart, looking like some kind of multicolored undersea creature from above. Eventually, he said, "Apparently, there've been no lasting effects. Psych just cleared me for light duties."

"Light?"

"Nothing sensitive."

"Nothing sensitive about combat, sir."

"That's what I told them, Gunny. They weren't amused."

"Psych's a tough room, sir."

He stared at his left wrist, the skin pale at the edge of his cuff. "I hear Intell's been all over you."

"They've been . . . thorough. There was a rumor going around that they wanted the H'san to come in and lift the memories right out of my head." She felt the original half of her lip curl. "Commandant shot them down."

"Why do you figure, Gunny?"

"I suspect there may be things in my head she doesn't want the Elder Races to know, sir."

"Major, do you ever wonder if the Elder Races are screwing us over?"

"It's interesting to note that not one of the diplomatic

attempts to negotiate an end to this war have ever included a member of the three races actually fighting this war. Since hostilities started before we got involved, all we have is the Elder Races' word for it that they don't know why the Others *are fighting."*

He switched his gaze to his right wrist and made a nonspecific noise.

Torin rubbed the inert trim along the edge of her desk and waited for the call to go through. He'd already have been contacted, of course, but this was still something she had to do.

The desk chimed. The man on the center screen, frowning up at her in some confusion, looked tired.

"Dr. John Sloan?" When he nodded, she took a deep breath and rolled both hands into fists down on her lap where he couldn't see them. "My name is Gunnery Sergeant Torin Kerr; I was with your wife on Crucible . . ."

Her new implant had the same old codes.
I've docked. Section 12, slip 9.
Craig Ryder made it back to Ventris as soon as the Corps allowed.

The bunk on the *Promise* wasn't really big enough for both of them for any length of time, not if they weren't actively using it, but they'd stayed there to watch the recording of the premier's speech, and it didn't seem like they were going to move any time soon.

Torin suspected they were stuck together, but she was comfortable so she didn't mention it.

"So, you'll be rejoining Sh'quo Company." Craig's not-a-question was warm against the top of her head.

"The premier said we were going to take up our lives again. That's where my life is."

He shifted just enough to prove her suspicions, then

pulled her in closer still. "You know, your life could be ..."

Time passed.

She was tempted to ask *Could be what?* just to hear what he'd actually say, but looking around the cramped, worn cabin she realized that maybe it could.

Just not quite yet.

Tanya Huff's
New *Confederation* Novel

VALOR'S TRIAL

Torin Kerr's Continuing Adventures.
Read on for a preview.

Now Available
in hardcover from DAW Books

"GUNNERY SERGEANT KERR! Good to have you back!"

"Good to be back, Sergeant Hollice." Torin thumbprinted the release that would send her gear straight to her quarters and fell into step beside the sergeant as they crossed the shuttle bay. "And congratulations on the promotion." Adrian Hollice had been in her squad when she was a sergeant and then, when she made staff sergeant, her platoon. She'd fast-tracked him onto his SLC and had been pleased to see her decision justified when Command had given him his third hook. Not that she needed reassurance that she'd been right—these days, she needed reassurance that Command didn't have its head so far up its collective ass it was cutting off all oxygen to its collective brain. "The squad have any trouble getting used to it?"

"Not after Ressk and Mashona knocked a couple of heads together. They said I'd been leading them around by the *diran avirrk* for months anyway, I might as well get paid for it."

Torin grinned. The Corps tried to keep combat units together when it could. Familiar faces strengthened both stability and loyalty under adverse conditions, and Marines had their own ways of working through the disruptions promotions brought.

"The captain was a little afraid they were going to send you to Recar'ta HQ," Hollice told her as they stepped onto the lower beltway.

"So was I." She'd asked to be returned to Sh'quo Company. They were short NCOs and, as she'd pointed out, she'd be wasted in a staff position. Although the Corps reserved the right to send her wherever the hell it pleased, both points were inarguable and she'd gone home. It hadn't hurt that the Commandant of the Corps had agreed with her—although *wasted in a staff position* had not been the phrase used.

Given the hour, the lower beltway was nearly deserted.

"They've started sweeping our Division," Hollice said as they rode toward the heart of the station. "Started at 1 Recar'ta, of course, so the war could bloody well be over before they get to us. Scuttlebutt says they haven't found anything."

He tugged at his collar tabs and Torin hid a smile at the tell. In a poker game, he'd have been bluffing. In a conversation, he was trying to draw her out. This was why he'd come to meet her; she'd been with the recon team on Big Yellow—the alien spaceship that turned out to be the actual alien, or aliens, the terminology remained uncertain—she'd initiated the investigation into why no one remembered Big Yellow's missing escape pod, and had actually spoken to a collective of the alien on Crucible. Granted, melting her jaw had meant she'd been tanked during the initial *There are aliens among us!* hysteria and she'd missed the development of the search protocols, but she was the closest thing to an authority in the Sector.

"You think they will, Gunny?" Hollice prodded. "Find anything, I mean?"

"Find bits of a shape-shifting, organic plastic alien that boots through our security protocols like cheddar through a H'san?" Torin asked him blandly. "One that can separate into microscopic pieces to avoid detection and then recombine itself back to sentience when the danger has passed? I very much doubt it." Search protocols be damned. "Not unless it wants to be found."

"Great."

She had to admire the dryness of his delivery. He'd deserved that promotion. "Not really."

"What does it want?"

"It told me it was collecting data."

"Studying us?"

"So it seems."

"Why?"

"No idea. We may never know." Little pieces of plastic were ubiquitous throughout Confederation space. The alien could be a part of any of them. It could *be* any of them. It could mimic other materials, and while the parts they'd most recently been in contact with had been gray, Big Yellow proved rather conclusively that didn't have to be the case. The handrail on the beltway could be recording data for the alien—as the alien—while she passed. Torin, who by both circumstances and disposition was more paranoid than most, had made a conscious decision not to think about that.

"It could make us all forget it was ever here," Hollice pointed out, his voice fraying a bit around the edges.

"Not all of us, Hollice."

He turned, stared at her for a moment, and smiled. "That's right. It can't mess with your head."

"Took a look inside and was scared off. If it wants to get to Sh'quo Company, it'll have to get through me." Which was both the truth and complete bullshit since she had no more way of stopping the alien, singly or collectively, than she had of convincing the Navy that a straight line was the shortest distance between two points. But it was bullshit Hollice needed to hear and bullshit he needed to repeat to his squad. Or maybe it was the part of the statement that was the truth he needed to repeat. Whatever worked.

The shortage of NCOs meant that Torin had only to put in a request to the station Sysop to have her old quarters reassigned. The recon mission to Big Yellow had been a temporary posting but the promotion before traveling to Ventris to brief Command on the Silsviss had destroyed the certainty of a round trip ticket—integrating an aggressive reptilian species into the Corps would take decades and she'd essentially been responsible for their willingness to join. That made her, if not an expert on the species, someone whose opinion Command intended to exploit. Fortunately, new information from the Marines stationed at the Embassy on Silsviss had pushed her experience from the center of the target. Some of those Marines were trained xenopsychologists rather than noncoms with good instincts and a willingness to kick ass when required and, more importantly, none of them had been expected to kill a senior officer.

Torin suspected a few people were concerned because they still weren't sure if she'd have gone through with it had General Morris' sacrifice actually been necessary. She supposed it didn't help that when asked directly she'd said, *As it* wasn't *necessary, I guess we'll never know.*

Which was the absolute truth; it wasn't something anyone could know until it happened—no matter what they believed themselves capable of.

When she dialed the door open, her quarters looked just like she remembered them, right down to the Silsviss skull hanging on the wall over her entertainment unit. Weird, since when she'd left for Ventris, she'd put everything she wasn't taking with her in station storage.

"Messages?" she asked as the door slid shut behind her.

She'd verbalized so the station did the same. "One message to Gunnery Sergeant Kerr from Staff Sergeant Greg Reghubir. As follows:

"Welcome back, Gunny. We figured the last thing you'd need to do was sort your crap out so we did it for you. Lance Corporal Ressk says you need stronger encryptions on your storage unit." Greg sounded matter-of-fact but Torin would have bet hard currency that he'd changed his own unit's setting immediately after he saw what Ressk could do with an eight-digit code. "Twenty-thirty tonight in the SRM; don't be late or we'll start without you."

Torin patted the skull fondly as she passed it on her way to the shower. It was good to be home.

"There's been a lot of action out on the edge of the Sector. Long-range sensors have picked up Susumi portals here, here, and here." Captain Rose touched three points on the star field currently mapped out on the briefing room's HMU and frowned at the resulting red lights. "Navy swears they're not responsible."

Second Lieutenant Jarret's lavender eyes darkened as light receptors opened to give him a better look at the map. "Civilians, sir?"

The captain sighed. "It's always possible some dumb-ass corporation or university has decided to scout the perimeter—those types always think they're invincible until they find out they aren't and we have to pull their butts out of the fire—but I don't honestly think so. We usually get some kind of a head's up just so we're available to pull those butts out of the fire and, so far, no one's admitting they've gone visiting."

"What about independents, sir?" Second Lieutenant Heerik was brand new, on her first posting with none of her enthusiasms blunted, and more than one of Sh'quo Company's officers and NCOs bent over their slates and hid a smile.

"What kind of independents did you have in mind, Lieutenant?"

"Well, maybe Civilian Salvage Officers." Her nostril ridges flared. "It was a CSO who found Big Yellow."

And Torin felt the attention of the room shift to her.

"Gunnery Sergeant Kerr?"

Torin had served with the captain long enough to know he was amused her *relationship*, or whatever the hell it was she had, had made it into a briefing—although the odds were good no one else could see it. "CSO Craig Ryder found Big Yellow because of a small error in his Susumi calculations." She waited out the murmur of reaction. Small errors in Susumi calculations were usually fatal errors. "Spaced as they are . . ." She nodded toward the map. ". . . these portals are clearly deliberate. Salvage operators follow rather than lead, and there's nothing happening out there. No debris, no reason for them to be deliberately jumping that way."

"Unless there's something happening out there," Lieutenant Jarret said thoughtfully.

"Unless," Captain Rose agreed. "Which is why the Navy has sent the *Hardyr* out to have a look around. Captain Treis came out of Susumi space here . . ." Another touch on the star map illuminated a fourth portal, this one green. ". . . and is proceeding with due caution to this system . . ." One last touch. ". . . here." The system was equal distance from all three red portals.

"How long is due caution expected to take, sir?" Lieutenant Joriyl wondered.

"You'll likely be headed Coreward before it happens, Lieutenant."

Her pale orange eyes darkened as she smiled. "And not a moment too soon, sir."

Lieutenant di'Pin Joriyl was the senior platoon officer. With her heading into Ventris on course that meant . . .

Torin blinked as she realized that meant Second

Lieutenant di'Ka Jarret would be senior. The voice of reason and experience for Second Lieutenant Heerik and an even greener twoie to be named later. It hadn't been quite a year since a very green Lieutenant Jarret had been tossed into a stew of giant lizards and diplomacy gone bugfuk and, suddenly, Torin felt old. Life was moving just a little too fast of late.

"Captain Treis will keep Recar'ta Station informed, Recar'ta will keep Battalion informed, and if we're really lucky Battalion will let us know what the hell is going on before they ship us out to deal with it. Platoons are nearly at full strength for the first time in a long time, so let's make sure everyone's geared up and ready to go." The star field flicked off. Captain Rose swept his gaze around the room and then nodded, once. "Details have been downloaded to your slates, now get out there and get ready to save the galaxy's ass yet again. Gunnery Sergeant Kerr, remain behind."

"Yes, sir." Torin stood as the officers and NCOs made their way out of the small briefing room, Jarret throwing her a distinct *we'll get together later* before turning his attention back to Heerik, who continued talking about the best responses to possible foothold situations, unaware of expressions passing nearly a meter over her head. Torin had been Jarret's staff sergeant for that giant lizard bugfuck diplomacy trip and she'd been impressed by the way the young officer had handled himself—both independently and under her guidance. If he stayed beyond his first contract, he'd be a credit to the Corps and she'd be happy to serve under him again.

When the room emptied, she followed Captain Rose and First Sergeant Siaosi Tutone through the door to the captain's office.

"Opinion, Gunny?" he asked, dropping into the chair behind his desk. Captain Rose's voice had always seemed about three sizes too big for his body but here, in the relative privacy of his office, he sounded tired. No, weary. Tired of all the crap that came from being a fair distance down the military food chain.

Or maybe Torin was reading too much into it.

"I think three Susumi points definitely indicates the Others are interested in something in that end of the Sector," she told him. "I think the lack of any significant attempt to hide their presence means they're coming through in force. I think the Navy should have sent more ships because if the Others get that force on the ground, we're looking at Battalion moving the whole Ground Combat Team out in response. And I think that the music selection in the Senior Ranks Mess changed for the worse while I was gone."

"That would be my selection," the first sergeant pointed out. His voice was as deep as the captain's, although less incongruous, rumbling up as it did from the depth of an enormous barrel chest. Torin was tall but Tutone topped her by a head and a half—taller even than most di'Taykan—and proportionately broad. His hands were enormous and muscle strained against the confines of his Class C's.

"Good choice, First. It's past time I broadened my musical tastes," Torin added, although she wasn't sure whether she was aiming for more or less sincerity.

Tutone grinned, teeth flashing white against the rich mahogany of his skin.

Captain Rose leaned back in his chair and smiled as well. "Welcome home, Gunny. It's good to have you back."

"Thank you, sir."

"Recar'ta Station agrees with you, by the way. When the orders come down, they'll come down for the entire GCT. That's why you're here, specifically here with Sh'quo Company when we don't generally rate a gunny. Aman's short and she's not reupping. Unless we deploy in the next tenday, that'll leave Jura's platoon with a shiny new second lieutenant and Heerik, who's almost as shiny, with a green staff sergeant. We'll move the new staff sergeant in under Jarret, since he's got a whole year of experience ..." Pale eyes rolled although for the most part he kept the sarcasm from his vice. "... but that's going to leave the company scrambling for experience among the officers and senior NCOs. We need you to be a kind of utility player, coming in off the bench where needed both at the platoon level and keeping the company connected."

"Off the bench is a sports metaphor," Tutone offered. "Baseball."

His tone was dry enough that Torin couldn't quite tell if he was being helpful or facetious, so she settled for a neutral, "Thank you, First Sergeant." The league on Paradise had teams on all three major continents and the year she left to join the Corps, New Alland—a minor continent or large island depending on who was speaking—had petitioned to have their teams recognized as well. According to the news download in the most recent packet from her younger brother, they still hadn't managed it.

"Until we ship out," Captain Rose continued, "you'll base at a desk by First Sergeant Tutone's, your primary duty to liaise with the rest of the GCT as we attempt to get ready for whatever's coming down the fukking pike. Eventually, I expect you'll be in the first sergeant's desk."

New gunnery sergeants were expected to indicate which way they intended their careers to go—to the combat position of first sergeant or to the staff position of master sergeant. After the incident on Crucible where both the system and the officer in charge had been taken over by unknown alien forces and Torin had led the training platoon of one-thirty recruits while they fought both the system and the aliens to a standstill, Command had made it quite clear which choice they'd prefer Torin to make. Fortunately, it was the choice she wanted to make. Tutone's desk had been her goal since she'd received her corporal's hooks.

"I wasn't planning on going anywhere, sir."

For an instant, Torin thought the first sergeant had been reading her mind and then she realized he'd been responding to the captain's statement.

"Glad to hear that. First, I was just starting to get used to you. So, Gunny, is it true what Command says, that there's nothing we can do about the microscopic bits of a big yellow alien scattered throughout known space?"

"That's the gist of it, sir."

"Since the search teams haven't found anything, any chance they've buggered off back where they came from?"

"The bit I spoke to told me they didn't have enough information, sir. I expect they're still collecting data."

"Why can't the search teams find them, then?" Before she could answer, Tutone raised a massive hand. "Never mind. The answer is probably that they can't find their anus with both hands and a map so . . ." He waved off the end of the sentence.

"Any chance that when they spoke to you, they were messing with your head?" the captain wondered.

Given that some of them had just emerged from Major Svensson's head, Torin sure as hell hoped not. "I don't think so, sir."

Captain Rose sat and stared up at the ceiling for a moment. Specifically stared, at the ring of gray plastic around the recessed light over his desk. Tutone followed the captain's gaze but Torin refused to look. "It's like discovering the enemy is an inanimate object," he muttered, dropping his gaze. "Any inanimate object." Then he shook his head and double tapped his desk, blows ringing against the plastic. "All right. Let's get going on a job we can do."

Both NCOs recognized the dismissal, coming to attention and snapping out a "Sir!" in unison.

Rolling his eyes, the captain stroked one hand down the edge of the lower, right side screen. "I'm sending your first problem out to your desk, Gunny. And I know you've got things to deal with, First Sergeant, so let's have a little less smartass spit and polish and little more work out of both of you. Gunny?"

Torin paused at the door. "Sir?"

"Can we be expecting General Morris to drop by any time soon?"

General Morris had become Torin's personal pain in the brass. He'd sent the platoon out to Silsviss, he'd sent her out to Big Yellow, and he'd been contaminated by the alien. Torin had a feeling he blamed her for the latter. After all, if she hadn't blown the whistle, he'd never have known. Or, specifically, no one would ever have known it about him. Given their history, the thought of him showing up once again at the Four Two made her feel a little chilled. Their time spent together never ended well.

"I sincerely hope not, sir."

"Glad to hear it."

In the outer office, Torin settled in behind her desk—easy enough to identify as it was the one the first sergeant hadn't settled his bulk behind—and opened the file the captain had sent.

"New desk, new job, eh, Gunny?"

She looked up to find the first sergeant watching her. "Same old war, First. Same old war."

He smiled and nodded but she had a suspicion that he didn't entirely agree with her. She had no problem with that. There were days when she didn't entirely agree with it herself.

"Do you ever get the feeling that there are things the Elder Races aren't telling us?"

"It is worth noting, Gunny, that none of the diplomatic missions sent to the Others *have ever included a member of the species doing the actual fighting."*

Granted, it had turned out not to have been the Elder Races messing with the memories of those who knew about Big Yellow but Big Yellow itself and, while that was moderately less distressing than the alternative—always better to be screwed over by an unknown factor than an ally—that didn't actually address either question. Were there things the Elder Races weren't telling the Humans, di'Taykans, or Krai who fought their war? And why hadn't one of the three Youngest ever been invited to join the missions sent out to try and end the war? Over a century of attempted diplomacy had resulted in a few thousand dead diplomats so why hadn't Parliament tried every possible option?

And, most importantly, had she been discussing the Elder Races with Major Svensson or with the alien living in his brain? If the former, was there discontent growing within the Corps? If the later, did the aliens know something the Youngest didn't?

Too many questions.

Torin wanted to go back to the days when the only question she ever asked was, *What do I have to do to get my people out of here alive?* Unfortunately, once the round was out of the barrel there was no stuffing it back in.

Tanya Huff

The Confederation Novels

"As a heroine, Kerr shines. She is cut from the same mold
as Ellen Ripley of the *Aliens* films. Like her heroine,
Huff delivers the goods." —*SF Weekly*

A CONFEDERATION OF VALOR
Omnibus Edition
(Valor's Choice, The Better Part of Valor)
978-0-7564-0399-7

THE HEART OF VALOR
978-0-7564-0481-9

and now in hardcover:
VALOR'S TRIAL
978-0-7564-0479-6

To Order Call: 1-800-788-6262
www.dawbooks.com

DAW 73

Tanya Huff

Tony Foster—familiar to Tanya Huff fans from her *Blood* series—has relocated to Vancouver with Henry Fitzroy, vampire son of Henry VIII. Tony landed a job as a production assistant at CB Productions, ironically working on a syndicated TV series, "Darkest Night," about a vampire detective. Tony was pretty content with his new life—until wizards, demons, and haunted houses became more than just episodes on his TV series...

"An exciting, creepy adventure"—*Booklist*

SMOKE AND SHADOWS
0-7564-0263-8 $6.99

SMOKE AND MIRRORS
0-7564-0348-0 $7.99

SMOKE AND ASHES
0-7564-0415-4 $7.99

To Order Call: 1-800-788-6262
www.dawbooks.com

Tanya Huff

The Finest in Fantasy

To Order Call: 1-800-788-6262
www.dawbooks.com

DAW 21

CJ Cherryh

Classic Novels in Omnibus Editions

THE DREAMING TREE
Contains the complete duology *The Dreamstone* and *The Tree of Swords and Jewels*.   0-88677-782-8

THE FADED SUN TRILOGY
Contains the complete novels *Kesrith*, *Shon'jir*, and *Kutath*.   0-88677-836-0

THE MORGAINE SAGA
Contains the complete novels *Gate of Ivrel*, *Well of Shiuan*, and *Fires of Azeroth*.   0-88677-877-8

THE CHANUR SAGA
Contains the complete novels *The Pride of Chanur*, *Chanur's Venture* and *The Kif Strike Back*.   0-88677-930-8

ALTERNATE REALITIES
Contains the complete novels *Port Eterntiy*, *Voyager in Night*, and *Wave Without a Shore*   0-88677-946-4

AT THE EDGE OF SPACE
Contains the complete novels *Brothers of Earth* and *Hunter of Worlds*.   0-7564-0160-7

THE DEEP BEYOND
Contains the complete novels *Serpent's Reach* and *Cuckoo's Egg*.   0-7564-0311-1

To Order Call: 1-800-788-6262
www.dawbooks.com

DAW 9

RM Meluch

The Tour of the Merrimack

"An action-packed space opera. For readers who like romps through outer space, lots of battles with gooey horrific insects, and character sexplotation, *The Myriad* delivers.."   —*SciFi.com*

"Like *The Myriad*, this one is grand space opera. You will enjoy it."   —*Analog*

"This is grand old-fashioned space opera, so toss your disbelief out the nearest airlock and dive in."
    —*Publishers Weekly* (Starred Review)

THE MYRIAD   0-7564-0320-06

WOLF STAR   0-7564-0324-3

and now in hardcover:
THE SAGITTARIUS COMMAND
0-7564-0457-4

To Order Call: 1-800-788-6262
www.dawbooks.com

DAW 48